The Gossip Garden Mysteries

By L.R. Haines

Dedicated to my Mother

Table of Contents

Killer Bees

Sometimes I wonder if I could have changed anything, I mean if I'd done things differently. If I'd been a better friend... Maybe if I'd altered the waggle dance, warned them of the danger...but how could I have known the venom would kill? I still cry when I think about that day.

I had cleaned all morning as usual and planned to take Boris, my six-year-old Terrier-mix, to Lily Park in the afternoon, as I often do. Being a stay-at-home mom, and now an empty nester whose husband has his own dental practice, most of my time centers on my home.

When my husband, Barry and I moved into the Brookstone neighborhood in our small mid-western town of Aster Heights eighteen years ago, my neighbors became my daytime companions and social colony. And aside from Barry and Boris; my closest friends.

It was a sunny June day, and right after lunch, the scream of sirens broke through the silence of our picture-perfect subdivision. My first thought flew to my elderly next-door neighbor Erle. I rushed to the window, just in time to catch the flashing lights soaring down our street, passing Erle's house. An uneasy feeling spread through me, as I wondered which neighbor was in trouble.

I hooked the leash to Boris, and we ran out the door in time to see the last police car turn right onto Marigold Drive. We hurried down the sidewalk after it, my uneasiness growing as we passed each grandiose home matching in style, with their impeccably manicured lawns and gas-guzzling SUVs in the driveway.

Our fast jaunt slowed to a quick walk as we turned the corner. From there I could see several police cars and a firetruck occupied the driveway and street in front of the house of my good friend, Hazel.

Neighbors and spectators had gathered in her yard and nearby, probably in anticipation, excited and possibly craving a morsel of scuttlebutt they could later share. My heart pounded hard against my chest as I edged my way through the crowd.

Hazel lived alone. A retired bookkeeper and health food nut, who played pickleball four times a week, and although ten years older than me, was in far better shape.

She'd been the first person to welcome us, when Barry and I moved into the neighborhood. Hazel showed up at our door with a smile on her face and a plate of cookies in hand.

I'd been anxious about meeting my new neighbors. Afraid they wouldn't like or accept me. Moving to a new neighborhood took me back to my childhood and the many moves. I felt like the 'new kid at school' again. The outsider. Ignored. Left out. Yet Hazel always included me. She'd even picked me to be her Euchre partner. Our friendship continued to flourish over time.

As my thoughts flittered through the lights and commotion around me, I silently prayed nothing had happened to Hazel.

I searched the crowd for a familiar face. My neighbor and friend Crissa, who lived directly across the street from Hazel, stood looking over the confusion and disorder, her teenage daughter next to her. I made my way toward them, trying to catch her attention.

"What's going on?" I asked.

"I haven't heard anything, but I assume it's Hazel." Crissa pushed her short brown hair from her face and hollered over the noise.

Hazel's front door opened, and two paramedics brought out a stretcher with a body shrouded under a sheet. I couldn't see a face, but I knew it must be Hazel. *Who else could it be?* They placed her in the coroner's van and slowly drove away.

I gripped Boris' leash even tighter. A lump swelled up in my throat. *Hazel. No, no Hazel.* Tears welled up in my eyes, and afraid to let others see me cry, I quickly wiped them away.

By now the swarm of spectators had grown. I spotted Maribelle, another neighbor and friend among them. She eyed me with an anxious look. Her husband Ray had wrapped his arm tightly around her waist, as if to protect her. Their teenage son and daughter stood with them, taking in the scene with interest.

A few minutes later, the coroner's van and fire truck drove away, leaving behind two police cars and a few policemen.

Dazed and trembling, I wrapped the leash around my hand several more times, then unwrapped it. What had happened to Hazel? An accident? Heart attack? Whatever it was, it must have happened last night after I spoke with her, or early this morning. I shuddered at the memory.

Our conversation the night before hadn't ended well. Now, I couldn't take it back, couldn't make up for it.

Hazel had called me, anxious, and worried. The incident played over in my mind.

"I think the neighbors are upset with me. Have you heard from anyone? Has Maribelle said anything to you?"

Hazel was direct like that. She always came right to the point.

Taken by surprise, I wasn't sure how to answer. I didn't want to hurt her feelings. "Uh...umm..." The lie stuck halfway down my throat. "No."

If Hazel noticed my hesitation, she ignored it.

"Well...I posted something online. Not Facebook. Another site. I kinda said I'd seen my neighbors supplying alcohol to teenagers, and I didn't think it was right." She paused for a moment. "Anyway, today I got a message from Maribelle. She's furious with me. Says I should talk to her before I bash her on social media. Told me to 'mind my own business.'"

"Um...yeah...I saw the post," I confessed.

"So? Was I wrong?" Her voice grew higher. "I never mentioned any names. It could have been anyone." Hazel waited for validation.

Maribelle had called me. An angry bee looking for a target. She'd informed me that Sondra and Crissa were both mad too. From the sound of it, the whole darn gossip garden was full of angry bees. Hazel had made the unforgiveable error of criticizing the queen.

"Um. Well...I think..." I tried to word my reply carefully. "Some people don't like to be told what to do. Especially when it comes to their kids." After an uncomfortable pause, I said. "You can't make them stop. I think they feel it's better to have the kids drink at home. That way they can keep an eye on them."

I could see both sides. If Maribelle and Crissa thought the kids were going to drink anyway, it would be better if they were at home, where they could monitor them.

"You mean, you think it's okay then?" Hazel's voice waned. "These kids were drunk Delila! They were barely able to walk. What if it happened to your kid? What if they were supplying your son with alcohol?" She paused to let it sink in. "I saw two of the kids come out of their house drunk last week and get in a car and take off. What if they were killed? Or killed someone else?"

She was right of course. Still, I wasn't about to get dragged into the middle of their riff.

"I'm just saying that if they want to do it, they're going to. People have different points of view." I didn't want to get involved in her battle. And I certainly didn't want to stir up the bee's nest.

We ended the uncomfortable conversation in a polite yet abrupt manner. Why couldn't she just let things go, try to fit in? I think she'd guessed that I'd betrayed her. But what could I do? I certainly didn't want the swarm coming after me.

While the memory circled around in my head, I wanted to go back. A do over of our conversation. *Why hadn't I been more sympathetic to her feelings?*

A police officer approached one of the people in the crowd. He had a notepad and pen in his hand, asking questions then moving on to the next person.

Should I say something? After all, I may have been the last person to speak with Hazel alive.

But what could I say? That I had let my friend down? If I explained the situation, I'd have to betray the others.

I let my nerves get the better of me and decided to take Boris home instead. Before I could leave, Hazel's next-door neighbor pointed at me, and the police officer headed in my direction. I waited for him.

He wrote down my name and address, then asked. "You were a good friend of hers?"

Shame and remorse started to surface. Her friend, yes. Good friend? Maybe. I hadn't stuck up for her when I should have. Hadn't listened to her when she really needed me. Now it seemed I never would. A gnawing ache arose in my stomach.

"Well, yes," I said hesitantly. "I talked to her last night. What happened, Officer?"

"We don't know yet, ma'am. What time did you speak with her?" He looked at me over the top of his glasses.

"About eight o'clock I guess." I pulled my phone out, blinked hard to clear my eyes, then scrolled through the calls. "She called at 8:10 actually."

"Can you tell me about your conversation? Was she worried about anything?" he asked.

In the corner of my eye, I saw Maribelle staring at me, her arms crossed over her chest. "No."

"Did she say she had been threatened or anything like that?"

"No. She sounded perfectly normal," I assured him. Why would he ask me that? "Officer, can you tell me what happened? Please?"

"I'm sorry for your loss, ma'am." He turned and moved on.

We buried Hazel the following week. A few of the neighbors attended, but not as many as I expected. Maribelle, Crissa and Sondra were all absent, and although they didn't know her as well as I did, I thought they might have at least made the effort to attend her funeral.

Hazel's sister flew in from Georgia to make the arrangements. After the service, with nothing more she could do, she flew back home that same evening.

The next day, Boris and I walked to Lily Park, a garden-like area with a large grassy field and a pavilion, in the center of our neighborhood, where flowers as well as gossip, were pollinated regularly.

Surrounded by the sweet scent of the lilies, fresh-cut grass, and curiosity, neighbors looked forward to hearing the neighborhood buzz. When none was available, it sometimes appeared anyway.

By the time Boris and I arrived, Maribelle, Sondra, and Crissa were already there, busily discussing recent events.

Maribelle relaxed on the top of a picnic table, her face to the sun, copper-colored hair wafting in the breeze. "I heard the police think it was foul play."

I sat at a table across from Maribelle, listening, but reluctant to say much. Boris lay on the cool cement floor of the large, timber-frame pavilion.

Crissa sat on the seat next to Maribelle. "What do they think happened?"

"I don't know," Maribelle admitted, "but I think someone broke into her house. Probably a home invasion gone bad." She said it flippantly. As if Hazel were someone we didn't know. A Jane Doe in another city.

"Does anyone know how she died?" Sondra tilted her long blonde hair back and leaned against one of the pavilion's wooden support posts.

I hadn't said much up until now, but I did have some inside information. I don't know why I told them. I guess I just wanted to feel a part of the circle.

"She was bashed in the head with a cast iron frying pan."

They all turned and stared at me.

"Barry has a friend on the police force." I explained.

"So, it was a burglary?" Sondra shook her head in disbelief. "Well, that does it, I'm getting more security cameras!" Then as an afterthought she added, "Poor thing."

"They don't think anything was taken, so they don't really know if it was a burglary that went wrong, or if..." I paused and bit my lip, "or if it was something else."

"What, like murder? Like *pre*-meditated murder? Who would kill Hazel?" Crissa didn't even try to suppress a smirk. "I mean, she *could* be a bit of pain at times."

"Yeah, she was such a stickler about everything!" Sondra nodded in agreement.

"God, she could drive me crazy." Crissa raised her eyebrows, looked at Maribelle, and smiled.

"I guess we don't have to worry about her saying stupid shit on social media anymore!" Maribelle looked at the ground, then turned her head back toward Crissa, and grinned.

They all giggled like high school girls with a secret joke.

I felt my face turn hot and flush. Why would they talk about Hazel that way? She wasn't perfect, but to make fun of her when she'd just died. Who were these people? I gripped the seat of the picnic table.

"And how about the time she accused Mitzi of cheating at cards?" Crissa joked. "Remember that? Mitzi was so mad she threw the cards all over the table and stormed out."

They laughed even louder this time.

It was true. Hazel had accused Mitzi of cheating at one of our Euchre Club games. Hazel and I were partners, and at the time I suspected Hazel was right, but I hadn't said anything. I hadn't backed her up.

I started to say something in Hazel's defense, but some teenagers drove up on motorbikes. They turned off the engines and two boys got off their bikes and came over to the table.

"Hey mom, the guys want to come over tonight. Can you pick up some food and stuff?" Maribelle's son, Asher, a good six feet, hovered over his mother. Crissa's son, Jeremy, stood next to him.

"Who? How many?" Maribelle asked.

"Ah, most of the team." Asher and Jeremy looked at one another and laughed as if they shared some inside joke. They were both on the high school football team, and always together, like inseparable twins.

"Ok." Maribelle sighed, turned her head toward us and rolled her eyes.

More teenagers arrived on motorbikes, revving their engines loudly. I decided to leave, grateful that my own son was grown and in college.

I waved to the others, then let Boris lead me away. As we walked home, it occurred to me that no one seemed upset that Hazel was dead. That she had been murdered. I felt puzzled. Were they really that insensitive?

That night, Barry and I sat down to watch the 11 o'clock news. Barry turned the volume up for the story about two recent home invasions in Rhododendron Hills, the wealthiest neighborhood in Aster Heights.

"The suspect, now called the 'curio bandit', is thought to have broken into at least three other homes recently and appears to take unusual or token items. The thief's favorites include older objects, such as family heirlooms or small antiques. In the most recent break-in, a home security camera caught this photo of the thief." The photo showed a person wearing a light-gray hoodie, and sweatpants.

"Could be anybody," Barry said, "whoever it is, they know how to avoid showing their face."

"The police have not commented on whether they think these break-ins are related to the murder that took place in the Brookstone Neighborhood a little over a week ago." The news anchor stood in front of the Rhododendron Hills sign. "For now, they are suggesting people keep their doors locked and eyes open."

"Why would someone risk going to prison over something worth so little?"

"Probably gets some kind of thrill out of it." Barry answered, then turned his attention back to the television and sports updates.

Had the curio bandit broken into Hazel's home to steal some little trinket? Had she surprised him, and he grabbed a frying pan and hit her with it? Whoever he or she was, and whatever the reason, the crook was still free. Still breaking into people's homes. And Hazel's killer still on the loose too.

We were all on high alert now, worried any one of our houses could be next. Barry organized a neighborhood watch. He held a meeting, ordered signs for our houses, and created a group text for the entire neighborhood. Everyone settled back into their normal routines.

I couldn't stop thinking about Hazel and her killer. The police weren't sure if anything had been taken from her house. Hazel lived alone, and her sister hadn't visited her in a few years, so she couldn't answer that question for the police.

Our last conversation kept replaying in my mind. Why hadn't I been nicer? More understanding? She'd been upset. Worried. Not that someone was going to kill her, but that one of the teens would get hurt. Or hurt somebody else. She cared about others. And I let her down.

For several days, I brooded over the loss of my friend. To help take my mind off my loss, I took an online cellphone photography class. I would document everything around me in photos. I could start a photo journal and track my life in pictures.

After completing my first online class, I decided to check my facebook page. I'd posted some pictures of Hazel and me. Had a couple of likes, and one care, but not as many responses as I'd expected to see. I scrolled down my news feed, until I came to some pictures Maribelle had posted. Photos of Crissa, Sondra, and Maribelle, along with two other neighbors having lunch at the Fab Fountain Inn. One of the nicer restaurants in town. They were laughing, toasting their good time, and clearly enjoying themselves.

Deep within me I felt a sting of envy. I'd been invited to all the neighborhood block gatherings, but somehow never included in the private parties. I felt left out. We'd been talking in the park together just before their luncheon, yet they hadn't invited me. I looked at the photos again.

I wanted to pick up the phone and call Hazel to ask if she wanted to go shopping. But she wasn't there. She'd never be there for me again. Someone had brutally killed her and left her lying on the floor.

I scrolled down a little further. Nothing interesting caught my eye.

As I started to close my laptop, a new friend request popped up inviting me to accept or delete it. I checked the picture and name. *Hazel!*

Hazel? How could it be? Her account must have been hacked. Someone stole her photo and name and created a fake account. It had happened to me once. But this was different. Was Hazel reaching out to me from the dead? Or was this just a coincidence? I quickly closed my laptop.

Boris had come in and sat down beside me. Now he nuzzled my leg. I patted him on the head, then wrapped my arms around his neck.

A couple of weeks had gone by since Hazel's death, and the police didn't appear to have any new leads. I talked to Hazel's sister on the phone. She told me she was planning on putting the house up for sale soon, she thought the police had pretty much finished with it. We worried that Hazel's killer might never be caught.

The news from the night before had brought even more disturbing information. The anchorwoman had reported, "The curio bandit has struck again." They showed surveillance video of the thief inside the home.

"The burglar broke into a couple's home and stole a treasured vase from their kitchen table while they slept." The video then switched to the homeowner.

A female about thirty-five years old spoke into the microphone. "We woke up in the morning and at first, we didn't notice the vase missing. But then my husband asked me what I'd done with the flowers he'd brought me. We looked around and couldn't find the vase and flowers anywhere."

"The couple then scrolled through the video footage from their surveillance camera from the night before. They were terrified when they saw someone in a gray hoodie sneak through their home." The reporter then spoke with the woman's husband.

"When she first saw the video, she thought it was me in a gray hoodie. But then the video showed the guy hovering over us, where we'd fallen asleep on the sofa. The crazy thing is our dog was sleeping on the floor next to us and he never woke up either."

The reporter then went on to say that the police chief was hopeful that with stepped up patrol cars and the large presence of cameras in homes now, the perpetrator would be caught soon.

I couldn't shake the creepy feeling the curio thief had snuck into Hazel's home and been surprised by her. I pictured Hazel approaching the person, lecturing him on the risk of stealing. But the police still hadn't found anything missing.

I'd read an article about an elderly couple, whose house had been broken into, where the police thought nothing had been taken. Later the couple's children went through the home and discovered their parents' expensive coin collection had been stolen.

The next day, as Boris and I walked past Hazel's house I began to think. The police had been over everything, yet they didn't know her the way I did. How would they know if something was missing? But I would know. If I could get in there, look it over, I might find a clue, something to tie the thief to the crime. Something that would help convict her killer!

My mind was made up, I had to check. I'd be able to tell if something had been stolen. I'd need to do something soon, because once they got rid of all Hazel's things, there would be no way to find out if something had been taken.

The police still had the house sealed off, so I'd need a story. I concocted a plan in case I got caught. I'd say I was looking for something I'd loaned Hazel. That I needed to get it back and didn't think the police would mind. My story was lame, and I knew it. It would be a big risk. But I owed it to Hazel.

Certain Barry would disapprove, I decided to investigate the crime scene when he wasn't home. His dental office stayed open late every Wednesday, so it seemed like the perfect time. With him at work, I wouldn't have to explain myself. That evening, just as the sky started to darken, I grabbed my flashlight and cellphone, and snuck out.

Police tape covered Hazel's front door. I looked across the street at Crissa's house, to make sure no one saw me, then slipped around to the rear. Tape covered the back door as well, so I carefully pulled it off on one side. The door was locked, but I knew where Hazel kept a spare key.

Inside I looked around. Shadows draped the walls. I'd been in this kitchen so many times. My flashlight scanned the chalk outline of her body, and I shivered. Poor Hazel, she didn't deserve this.

Carefully, I stepped around the outline and went into the living room. Family photographs were arranged haphazardly on the bookshelf. I stopped to look at a large picture of her son. The last one taken of him before he died. I blinked back a tear.

Back in the kitchen, I shined the light around the counters and cupboards. Hazel prided herself on her cleanliness. It wasn't that she kept everything perfect, she didn't mind things being out of place. It was that she liked things to be clean. I looked at the stove, searching for the frying pan. It wasn't there of course. Probably at the police station as evidence. With my cell phone camera set to night-mode, I took several snapshots.

Hazel's spices lined the counter next to the stove. They were in perfect order, with all the labels facing outward. Hazel loved to cook, and I thought she must have been planning to make something special the next day.

I'm not sure why, but I walked over to the wastebasket and peaked in. It was empty. I shined my light around it. Behind the basket I noticed a toothpick and something shiny. I reached down for the silver gum wrapper. Hazel never chewed gum. At least, I'd never seen her chew gum. I took another picture. But when I stood back up, I bumped my head hard on a cupboard.

"Ouch!" My hand quickly covered my mouth. I shined my light around again and this time it fell on the kitchen table. There was the candy dish I'd given Hazel for Christmas two years ago. I picked up the empty dish and remembered how excited she was when she opened it. I felt deflated. There would be no more holidays together, no more cookouts, no discussions of our dreams and hopes for the future.

A noise came from behind me, and I swung around to locate the source. The bowl slipped from my hand and smashed on the floor. The sound was deafening. Slivers of glass scattered across the surface. I stood frozen for a moment, straining my ears.

I didn't know what to do. Was someone outside the back door waiting for me? Had they heard the crash of glass breaking on the floor? How could I clean up the mess? I decided there was no time to do anything. I needed to leave and fast! I listened again. After what seemed an eternity, I tiptoed to the back door.

Outside I peeked around to see if anyone was lurking about. It had turned dark by this time. I fixed the crime tape back over the door as best I could, shined the flashlight on the ground and stepped off the porch. It was then that I noticed it. The slight imprint left in the grass. Too large for a bicycle. It had to have come from a motorbike. A sinking feeling came over me.

A few days after my escapade at Hazel's house, our entire neighborhood prepared for the annual community garage sale. The proceeds always went to improvements to our park. I gathered some items earmarked for the occasion and piled them into the car.

The other ladies were already there setting up. The husbands, Ray, and Craig, who Hazel and I had secretly referred to as the 'drones', were moving tables and putting up signs. Sondra and Maribelle were placing price tags on items. I plopped my stuff down on a picnic table.

"Oh, not there. Put them on that table." Maribelle pointed to a table toward the back. "Crissa will process them."

Slightly annoyed, I picked up the box and took it to Crissa. I smiled and set it down. How was it that Maribelle was always in charge?

"Thanks." Crissa said, not bothering to look up.

Mitzi, card cheater, and our most flamboyant neighbor plopped a box down next to me. "Hi Delila!" She turned and smiled.

My eyes fell on her brightly colored top. One thing about Mitzi, she was easy to spot in a crowd. She always wore the brightest colored clothing. Today was no exception, her chartreuse blouse practically glowed. I hadn't meant for it to happen, but my eyes darted to the top of her head. Down the center of her thick black hair ran a white streak about three inches wide.

"Yes," she smirked, "I'm letting my hair grow out. Next time you see me I might be all white. Or gray." Then she pulled out a large ceramic horse and held it out in front of her. Crissa looked up with interest.

"I made this in a ceramics class years ago." She smiled at the horse. "I bet its worth at least $75." Next, she took out a mask that looked like a cross between a clown and a vampire. "Um. Should be able to get at least $45 for this."

She must be joking! Who would want that thing? I nearly laughed.

My heart went out to Crissa at that point, who would need to keep a straight face as she placed price stickers on each bizarre item she found in Mitzi's box. To my surprise, Crissa seemed impressed.

"Ah, these are great Mitzi! Thank you." Crissa picked up a glass paperweight with a quarter inside it and smiled.

I walked back to the parking lot to get more items from my car. The teenagers Jeremy and Asher drove up in their pick-up truck and parked next to me. The boys jumped out, a handful of balloons in tow, and raced toward the pavilion.

The truck was an older model, dark blue, Ford pickup in great condition. I thought it belonged to Asher, but I was never quite sure. Hazel had noticed first. She'd asked me one day which boy owned the truck. "I don't know." I laughed. "One drives it one day and the other one the next. Maybe they both own it!"

I pulled a large box out of the back seat of my car. As I struggled to get by the truck, it struck me that the front quarter panel looked as if it had recently been repainted. I took a closer look.

I've always been one for noticing details. It's as if my eyes narrow in on little things like that. The paint was just a slightly different shade on that corner. Kids! I shook my head and lugged the box to the far picnic table for Crissa.

Sondra's husband showed up around 9am, carrying a twelve pack of beer, and an open bottle in his hand.

"Hi Leo." I smiled to greet him.

"Hey Delila, what's up?"

He didn't wait for a reply but beelined it past me toward the drinking buddies, the smell of beer trailing behind him.

We ladies busied ourselves with unloading and tagging things as they were brought in. Then we circled around the sale items, arranging, and rearranging them to our satisfaction. I positioned something one way, then someone would fly over and reposition it. Finally, I gave up and just stood back and watched.

"Asher!" Maribelle called. "Go get me more change." She handed the teen several twenty-dollar bills. "I need mostly fives and singles." The two boys laughed and raced to the truck.

I watched them take off and thought about how they'd already managed to mess up their vehicle. I tried to think back on how long they'd had the truck. Probably about a month before Hazel was killed. I didn't recall seeing it much before that.

It occurred to me, that now I thought in terms of before and after Hazel died. Her death was like a landmark in my mind. I used it to find my way around recent events.

Ray was straightening items on one of the tables. I watched him for a minute and marveled at how carefully he refolded clothes and straightened each of the items. I laughed to myself and thought about how Barry's table would look. A moment later, Crissa's husband, Craig, went over to talk to Ray.

Craig was the opposite of neat. He dropped something on the ground and didn't even bother to pick it up. Then the two of them went over to help unload another car of goodies. What a difference between these two men, I thought. Ray the neat freak and Craig the mess maker.

I zigzagged through the tables and early shoppers, until I finally got to Maribelle. "Looks like we got a lot of great stuff this year. Better than last year I think."

"Yeah, we should do well." Then she raced after a customer, as if she didn't want to speak with me.

I stood there alone, feeling a little foolish, and perhaps if truth be told, a little hurt. I wanted to fit in with these ladies. Be real friends. Yet so often they didn't include me in their inner circle. Was it because of our age difference? I was about ten years older, and my son grown, already in college, perhaps they felt we had little in common.

Aside from my new cell phone photography, I lacked hobbies. A stay-at-home mom without a child to fuss over, I had more time available than I cared to admit. Finally, I put a smile back on my face and headed for my car.

That night, I tossed and turned and couldn't sleep. Next to me, Barry's snoring resonated throughout the room. But he wasn't rumbling solo. Boris played backup vocalist, their splutters in perfect harmony.

I quietly rolled out of bed, staggered to the kitchen, and poured a glass of water, then plodded back down the hall to my office. I opened my laptop to scroll through our local online newspaper, searching for articles about Hazel's murder.

'Hazel had been a beloved member of the community. She'd volunteered at several local charities as well as the library.' Her picture, taken several years back, popped up with the article. Nostalgia hit me like a rock. I sat there for a minute and let the tears roll down my cheek.

The next article was from before Hazel's death. She'd been in a car accident. A classic hit and run that happened about a month before she died. I'd forgotten all about it. She was driving home from the grocery store when someone tried to pass her. They cut over too soon, enough to nip the front of her car. Hazel's Buick went off the road and came to a halt in front of a tree. Although shaken up, she wasn't hurt. Hazel couldn't give a description of the vehicle to the police, and they never caught the offender.

I scanned through more articles until I came to the most recent one.

> Last week, 63-year-old Hazel Walters was found murdered in her home on Marigold Drive in Aster Heights. Details surrounding the death remain cloudy. The police have offered few details in the case. One neighbor said they heard a gunshot, however; police said no gun was involved. The homicide has shaken this close-knit community. The police have no suspects in custody. Anyone with information is urged to contact the Aster Heights Police Department.

Then I pulled up her obituary and read it for the third time.

> Walters, Hazel age 63 of Aster Heights. Preceded in death by her loving husband (and best friend) Marley Walters, and son Lee Walters. Hazel volunteered at several organizations including the local library and MADD (Mothers Against Drunk Driving), where she was an active member. A memorial service will be held this Friday at Grace Funeral Home.

I closed my laptop and quietly glided back to bed.

The following Saturday afternoon, Barry walked into the kitchen, his nose tilted upward sniffing the air. "Umm, what do I smell?"

"I'm made mini tarts for the party tonight." I finished placing the pastries on my favorite serving platter.

Barry looked over my shoulder. "You've certainly out done yourself! They look delicious."

"I've got smoked salmon pate, artichoke dip and chips, brie, and a variety of cheese and crackers, some shrimp cocktail, and mini tarts." I added, patting myself on the back for the beautiful array of appetizers.

"What? Why so much? Just to go to a neighborhood party?"

It was the first time we'd ever been invited to a party at Maribelle's house. I wanted to make a good impression. But now that Barry brought it up, I wondered if I'd gone a little overboard on the 'bring a dish to pass' plan.

"Can you grab two bottles of wine from the cellar?" I asked Barry. "One white and one red. Get the good ones, none of that cheap stuff."

"Is that a new outfit?" Barry asked as we gathered up all the goodies and stuffed them in the car. "Are we going to have any money left in the bank account after going to this party?" He teased.

"A little." I smirked.

Maribelle's formidable house was packed with people, many of them neighbors. After setting our goodies out on the food tables, we began to make our way through the crowd.

Barry stopped to talk to a group of husbands who were deep in a conversation about sports. I pressed my way into the swarm of ladies that surrounded Maribelle. They were discussing kids.

The dining room and kitchen were crowded with party goers, and I began to feel claustrophobic. No longer having teenagers at home, I grew bored with the conversation. I felt out of place and longed for Hazel.

I began to look around. I'd been inside Maribelle's house once before, but only for a few minutes. I wandered into the living room and marveled at her elegant taste in decorating.

Interesting artwork hung on the walls, and I zoomed in for a closer look. Mitzi stepped up next to me. "Most of these are done by Ray and Asher. Impressive, aren't they?"

"Oh, they are." I smiled.

"I think Asher may be even more talented than his father." Mitzi stood there for a moment, then turned and walked away.

I meandered down the hallway, where numerous pictures of the kids hung, including a large photo of Asher in his football uniform.

Ray's office was the first room I came to. I peeked in. It was an office anyone would love, with its contemporary furniture and decor. Ray was a graphic artist and worked from home, so it made sense that he'd have an office like this. I admit I was a bit envious.

I skimmed his bookshelves and was impressed with the neatness, how everything seemed to be perfectly in place. I began to feel a little uncomfortable and worried someone might see me. Might think I was snooping. I scurried back to the dining room where Maribelle and the other ladies stood nibbling on snacks and tipping wine glasses. Their discussion hadn't changed much, they were still talking about kids.

Through the sliding glass doors, I could see a dozen or more teens playing in and around the swimming pool. I watched as some of them sucked on beer bottles. To the side of the pool a beer pong game was taking place, with boys at one end and girls at the other. They were clearly enjoying themselves, laughing, tossing ping pong balls, and downing glasses of beer. Some were looking quite tipsy. I was starting to see Hazel's point.

The noise level had grown considerably as people tried to talk over one another. I turned my attention back to the ladies.

"Oh yeah," Maribelle's voice rang out. "Asher got calls from three colleges in the top ten. We're just waiting to see who gives him the best offer."

"Jeremy got an offer from State already." A satisfied smile crossed Crissa's face as she shared her excitement.

"That's great!" Everyone nodded and agreed.

Ray left the group of husbands and walked through the glass doors to the pool. I watched him talking to some of the teens. He checked the cooler of beer, then disappeared around a corner.

Sondra stood next to me, and I watched her eyes as she glanced in the direction of our husbands. I saw Leo sway; beer bottle gripped tightly in his hand. He leaned into Barry, who caught him and straightened him back up.

Then Sondra turned back to the group. "Hey, what about the fall party? We need to start planning it, don't we?"

"Yes, but we need more volunteers. We still need someone to take over the kid games and prizes and decorations." Maribelle said.

"I'll do it" I offered.

There was a slight pause as everyone turned to Maribelle. "No," She shook her head. "You don't have any kids at home. Crissa, how about if you oversee the games and decorations?"

Stunned, I stood in a fog for a moment. Maribelle's words stung. Apparently, one had to have kids still living at home to be a part of this clique.

The room felt stuffy. I looked around for a less congested area. I needed some air. Outside I found a table by the pool and sat down. I took a deep breath and thought about Hazel. I thought about our shopping sprees, pedicures, and the times we just sat down over tea and played a game or worked on a jigsaw puzzle. She was so easy to talk to. I missed her terribly. I looked through the glass doors at Maribelle. She could never be as good as Hazel. None of them could.

A woman I didn't know, sat down beside me. I couldn't help but notice the low-cut top with large ruffles and skin-tight pants. She was probably in her late forties and attractive but pushing her youth.

"That's my son over there." She pointed to a young man playing the pong game next to a young girl in a bikini.

I nodded graciously. There was a slight slur in her words, she had clearly had several drinks already.

"These kids are over at my house almost every week." She took another long swallow of beer. "I let them drink at my house too." She confided. "I'm a single mom, so it's nice to have them around. My ex used to get upset about it."

"Um-hmm." I acknowledged.

As I watched the kids, I wondered how many of them would become alcoholics. If this was where it started.

"Yeah. They like to hang out with me. Oooh, look at that young, oooh!" She took another swig of beer and pointed with her pinky at one of the young men. "Wow, what a bod!"

I forced a faint smile.

Ray filled up the cooler with more beer. He talked to one of the teenage girls, then watched as she walked away with one of the boys. A moment later, he noticed us, grabbed a couple of beers, and walked over to our table.

"Would you ladies like another drink? Beer or wine? There's still plenty of food inside too." He grinned and held out the beer for us.

Although she still had half of a beer, the woman accepted another. “Ah, you are a great host, Ray!”

I shook my head. “I’m good, thank you.”

“Ok, but don’t say I didn’t offer.” He smiled at me, and a few minutes later, returned to the house.

“I think the kids are spending the night.” I heard her say. “I always have them stay the night at my house too.”

“Um, good idea.” I wondered why a woman in her forties would want to hang out with a bunch of teen-age kids. Particularly the boys. Was she a child predator? Did she…? I shuddered to think about it. I wondered if I had anything in common with anyone here. I’d always thought these parties were fun, that I’d somehow been missing out. Now I just wanted to go home.

I waved to Barry who had stepped out of the sliding glass door onto the patio and appeared to be looking for me.

“Ah, here you are…” he said, then turned and smiled at the woman.

I introduced the two of them, then turned to Barry with *the look*.

“Are you ready to leave?” He asked. I love Barry.

Two days after the party, I received a call from the police. I felt nervous. Had they found the broken bowl or my fingerprints at Hazel’s house? I had my explanation ready. I was frequently at her house, so of course my prints would be all over. After all, we were good friends. Other than Barry, no one had heard our last conversation.

They offered to come to my house, but I preferred to go to the station. All I needed was for my neighbors to see me talking to the law. I made an appointment for that afternoon.

At 3pm sharp, I walked into the police department. My heart pounded hard against my chest as I entered. Once inside a receptionist ushered me to a desk where one of the officers sat. It was the first time in my life I'd been inside a police station.

"Hi. I'm Officer Jayco." He waved his hand for me to have a seat and studied me carefully.

"Have you found out anything about Hazel's death? Do you think it was that thief? The one who keeps stealing odd things?" The questions leapt from my mouth. I think he could tell I was nervous.

He gave me a quick smile. "We're working on it. I'm wondering if you might help us out with a few things." He looked through some notes in a file on his desk. I guessed they were the notes taken the day they found Hazel's body. "You and Mrs. Walters were good friends. Is that correct?"

"Yes."

"And you were most likely the last one to speak with her." He said it with little expression.

I wasn't sure if it was a question or statement. "Except for the killer." I offered.

"Yes. Of course." He smiled again. "Can you tell me about your conversation that night?"

"Well," I began, and my voice started to crack. "We talked about some of our friends, and I guess, some neighborhood stuff."

"She was pretty involved with Mothers Against Drunk Driving, wasn't she?"

I nodded. "Yes. Hazel's son was killed by a drunk driver just before his high school graduation. That was about 15 years ago, but she still felt very strongly about it." Tears formed in my eyes. Suddenly I knew her killer had to be found.

He made a note in the file, then leaned back in his chair. "Mrs. Clark, do you know anyone who owns a 9mm handgun?"

All the way home I kept thinking about the handgun. Why was Officer Jayco asking about a gun? Hazel was hit over the head with a frying pan for crying out loud. Did I know anyone? Yes, of course I did. Barry had a 9mm. But I knew Barry hadn't done it.

Leo had an entire arsenal in his basement. He collected guns and ammo. He most likely had a 9mm too.

I finally brought it up at dinner. I'm sure Barry knew I was upset about something. I told him about my meeting with Officer Jayco, and the question regarding the 9mm. He looked up at me and grinned.

"You don't have to worry. I haven't been shooting it off anywhere."

"But I can't understand. Why are they asking about a gun when Hazel was killed with a frying pan?" I protested.

"I don't know." He admitted. "But they must have a reason."

After dinner, I took Boris for a walk to clear my head. As we passed Hazel's house, I decided to get a better look at the back yard. I wanted to see things in the daylight. I didn't care if anyone saw me. I was determined to have another look.

The ground revealed two tire tracks, not one. They were faint. I was certain they were marks from the boy's motorbikes. I took out my cellphone, squatted down and got some good shots.

My handiwork with the tape remained intact. Apparently, no one had seen that it had been removed and put back. And evidently the police had not returned either. I looked closely at the back door for signs of forced entry but saw none. I felt like an amateur detective. The front door hadn't looked forced either. So, what had happened that night?

Boris and I found the path behind Hazel's house and cut through a break in the thick bushes. After we'd walked a block or so on the path, we came upon an opening that led to the park. The pavilion was at the opposite end, and I noticed some teenagers sitting on the picnic tables. I stopped for a moment to let Boris sniff, and so I could watch the kids.

I squinted to see better. Jeremy and Asher were talking with two girls. Boris wandered to the edge of the park, and I followed, keeping an eye on the teens. I couldn't shake the feeling that these boys knew something. They'd clearly been at Hazel's home, at her back door, not front. Had they spoken with her just before she died? Did they know something about Hazel's murder?

The girls stood up and waved back toward the boys as they walked toward their car. I tugged at Boris' leash and headed straight for the boys, totally unsure of what I would say. I was determined to find my friend's killer, even if it meant a confrontation.

"Hi." I tried to sound cheerful.

They acknowledged me with uninterested looks.

If I were ever to learn what happened, I'd have to question them. Maribelle and Crissa would be upset. But I no longer cared. Hazel deserved justice. The truth needed to come out. Anyway, if they weren't guilty, it shouldn't matter.

"It's a nice night out, isn't it?"

The boys looked at one another and grunted a "yeah." They started to leave. I had to say something right away.

"It looks like you had some work done on your truck." I began. "I noticed the paint was slightly different on the front quarter panel."

Asher scowled. "So?"

The boys trudged over to where their motorbikes leaned against the pavilion support posts. I had to think quickly. "I was wondering," I spurted out. "Were you over at Hazel's just before she died."

They turned and looked at me.

"I'm only asking because I noticed tire tracks from motorbikes like yours behind Hazel's house. I thought maybe you'd seen something?"

Asher spit out a piece of gum not far from my foot. Then both boys got on their bikes and revved their motors. They took off spinning tires and grass.

I wondered if they'd tell Maribelle. Well, so be it.

Barry was relaxing in the living room, watching a ball game when Boris and I returned home. I was still irritated with Asher for his disrespectful behavior. Barry listened patiently as I explained what had happened. I felt bad that I pulled him away from his game, but I confessed everything, including my excursion to Hazel's house.

"So, you accused the boys of...?" Barry began.

"No, I didn't accuse them." I cut in. "I just told them I'd seen tire tracks from motorbikes like theirs at her house and asked about them. And I mentioned the paint on the truck."

He let out a large sigh. "Well," he didn't argue with me, but asked the tough question. "Do you think one of them killed Hazel?"

I'd known Asher and Jeremy since they were little children. Watched them ride their bicycles with training wheels, rollerblades, and play ball at the park. I couldn't fathom the idea that someone so young could commit such a horrendous crime. I looked down at my hands. "I don't know."

I wondered if I should tell Maribelle. Afterall, if my son behaved that way, I'd want to know. But I knew Maribelle. She wouldn't appreciate me confronting her son. Wouldn't like it if I said anything negative against him. If she weren't my friend, I thought, I'd surely tell her. And yet, she *wasn't* my friend. She was, however, the queen bee, and like it or not, I had to respect that fact.

Barry watched the rest of the game and I attempted to read my book. Then I got up and started cleaning. My habit when under stress. I cleaned out the refrigerator and one of my cupboards. Finally, eleven o'clock news time. I sat down with Barry, so we could watch it together.

Boris heard something first and let out a little bark. He ran to the back of the house. Then both Barry and I heard a noise on the patio. We have a walkout basement and fenced-in backyard. I wondered if we'd forgotten to shut the gate. Maybe a dog or raccoon had wandered in.

For a moment Barry and I stared at each other, then he went downstairs to the sliding glass patio door with me close behind. He flipped on the porch light and peered outside. I peered out a window into the darkness.

We saw it at the same time. The shadow of a person, dressed in dark clothing, crouched over. The patio culprit suddenly stood up. I think he saw us because he turned and ran away from the house. Barry jerked the door open and yelled, "Hey!" He ran outside in his stocking feet, stopping just shy of the open gate.

"I didn't see which way he went," Barry told me when he came back inside, slightly out of breath from the chase.

"What was he doing out there?" I wondered, "Could you tell who it was?"

"No, he was too far away. Plus, he had a good head start on me. He knocked over that pot of flowers. That must be what we heard. I think it was a man, but I can't really be sure."

"Do you think it was that bizarre thief who keeps stealing weird things?" I whispered.

"I don't know. But one thing's for sure, whoever did this, left on foot, they didn't drive off in a car."

Barry locked both doors, then pulled out his gun. That night the gun stayed next to our bed.

*T*he next morning after Barry left for work, I decided to clean up the patio. I also wanted to look for evidence left behind by our intruder, or to see if some small thing had been taken. Instead, what I found terrified me.

A drawing of a rat with an X through it, sprayed in black paint on our cement patio. And the message written next to it, equally horrifying. It read, "Dead rats can't talk."

I stood for a moment, not knowing what to do. Who would do something like this? Why? I grabbed my phone and took a picture. My hands shook as I sent the text to Barry. Then I called him. He'd probably just walked into the office. I hoped he wasn't with a patient yet.

"Barry, I'm scared." My voice was shaky.

"I'll call Jim."

Barry's friend, Jim, worked for the Aster Heights police force. The two had met when Jim had come in for an emergency toothache. Over the years the two formed a friendship.

"I don't know Barry. Are you sure that's a good idea? What if someone tries to kill me because I've told the police?"

"Someone is just trying to scare you." He assured me.

"They're doing a good job of it!" My voice started to crack.

"Look, I really think we need to call the police. If whoever is doing this knows the police are involved, they're more likely to be afraid to do anything." Barry rationalized.

I thought about it for a minute, then finally agreed. Fifteen minutes later I received a call from Jim and within an hour, I had a knock on my front door.

Officer Jim Higgins stood about six foot two inches. Standing on our porch, I thought he looked especially attractive, as well as official, in his uniform. I invited him in, then took him to the patio and pointed to where the criminal's artwork marred the concrete.

I watched Jim take pictures and wondered how much I should share with him regarding what I'd found at Hazel's. I didn't want to say anything about the tire marks or Asher's reaction to my comments. After all, he was just a kid. Maribelle's kid. She would be furious if she knew I'd told the police. No telling what venom she'd release in the gossip garden.

My mind then raced to the thief who'd been seen on video breaking into houses. I shuddered at the thought of someone watching me sleep all the while trying to decide on some little thing to steal. Had the thief tried to get into our house? Did he think we were asleep? Did he care? Was it the danger of getting caught, the rush, that he craved? Yet, I hadn't found anything missing, and this was a threat. Someone sending me a message. Had the thief seen me at Hazel's? Could that have been who I heard?

"Do you think it was the thief who's been stealing odd items from people's houses? The curio thief or whatever they call him?" I asked.

"It's hard to say. He hasn't done anything like this before, but you never know." Jim edged his way toward the door.

Something had been bothering me for some time and I hoped Jim could clear it up for me. "Jim, I've been wondering. How did the police know to go to Hazel's house that morning? I mean when they found her?"

Jim gave me an 'I'm sorry' smile and said, "I'm really not supposed to discuss the case." He seemed genuinely disappointed and started to open the door to leave. Then he turned and quietly said, "Someone tipped us off. We had a call that morning from someone saying they'd heard a gunshot the night before. They suggested we check on her. Didn't give a name."

I thanked Jim for coming and invited him to dinner. It had been Barry's idea. Jim was single and a home cooked dinner always appealed to him. It took a bit of convincing, but he finally agreed.

After Jim left, I sat and contemplated the circumstances surrounding Hazel's death. I wrote down all the facts I knew and all the little details that haunted me. Then I started to clean. My therapy, my meditation. I zoned out and let thoughts come to me.

Once I had dusted the entire house, I went back to the kitchen and even though it didn't need it, I began to clean it again. I put the finishing touches on the stove, and that's when it came to me. Details.

With unanswered questions and no proof, I felt like I was letting my old friend down. But time was running out. How long before the killer would strike again? How long before the leads would all go cold, and Hazel's killer would go free?

I went down into our basement and pulled out some photos not yet placed in albums. I yearned for my old friend as I flipped through them. Pictures of Hazel and me on girls-night-out. Hazel and me on our trip up north. Barry, Hazel, and me at a picnic. Tears rolled down my cheeks as I browsed through them. Then I came to a picture of Hazel and stopped. Taken about two weeks before she died the photo got me thinking. I blinked hard and wiped the droplets from my eyes. I carefully pulled the photo from the stack and carried it upstairs.

On my computer I made some notes and put together a timeline of recent events related to Hazel. I scanned through the news articles again. I skimmed the pictures on my phone until I came to some that Hazel had sent me. To confirm my suspicions, I made several phone calls and made notes. Then I printed off my proof, placed all the pages and pictures in a folder and set it neatly on my desk.

Boris watched me with interest as I put dinner together. Eggplant Parmesan, an antipasto salad, and garlic bread. Anxious with anticipation, I worked out my plan as I prepared the meal.

Jim arrived at 6pm sharp, beating Barry by only a few minutes. Both were hungry and ready for dinner.

"We had a rather interesting day at the office today." Barry said as he took a piece of garlic bread. Barry often had fun stories from the office to share. Jim and I both stopped eating for a moment to listen.

"Ok, I'll bite. What happened?" Jim asked.

Barry gave Jim a sideways grin. "Well," he paused for effect. "We had an elderly patient who needed to have a couple of extractions. He asked to be sedated, so we sedated him. The procedure went well--" He paused to take a bite of bread, chewed, swallowed, and continued. "That is until he woke up. Then he started yelling that he couldn't see. Of course, my assistant was worried and pulled me in to help calm him. He just kept yelling, 'I can't see'!" Barry took a drink and went on, "Well there's no reason for him not to be able to see from this procedure. So, the assistant, still trying to calm him down says 'I put your glasses on, so you'd be able to see when you woke up. You should be able to see.' She was worried. Then he yells 'I don't wear glasses!'"

At this we all laughed, and Barry added, "Apparently, the glasses belonged to the patient before him."

Jim finished his second helping of eggplant then leaned back in his chair. "I've got some news for you too."

"Oh? Let's hear it!" Barry said.

"We've caught the curio thief." He didn't try to hide his satisfaction of being able to share the good news.

"Is that right? Ah, that is great news!" Barry gave Jim a congratulatory smile, then turned to me, "Delila will feel safer tonight, knowing that. Won't you?"

"Yes." I agreed.

"The best part," Jim leaned forward, excited by his own story. "He got pulled over for not having tags on his car. The officer who pulled him over happened to notice a strange looking tea pot in the back seat. The description fit the last item that was stolen by the 'curio thief', so he brought him in for questioning. That's how he got caught."

We all laughed. It felt good to finally enjoy some good news.

"Do you think he killed Hazel?" Barry asked.

"We're checking his fingerprints against what we've found at her house to see if they match up. We hope to have an answer soon."

"I'm afraid all we have for desert is cookies." I said, setting the bowl of peanut butter cookies on the table. "I've got some news I'd like to share too. And Jim, I'd like to ask a favor."

I'd contacted my neighbors before dinner and asked them to meet me at the park at 7:30pm. Maribelle started to put up a fuss, but I insisted she'd want to hear what I had to say. The rest of the neighbors agreed more readily, especially after I told them I had news about Hazel's killer.

For a second, I thought about bringing cookies or brownies, but then remembered the seriousness of this meeting. It wasn't to discuss any of our annual events or some special party. No, I needed to expose Hazel's killer and hoped for a confession.

At 6:50pm Boris and I sat down at a picnic table. I held my folder tightly to my chest and rehearsed my speech. I'd gone over it all afternoon and I'm sure Boris was sick of hearing it. I should be ready. But as I waited for the participants to arrive, I worried what would happen if the truth didn't come out. My heart began to pound rapidly, and droplets of perspiration formed on my forehead.

Crissa, Jeremy, and Craig were the first to arrive. Sondra and Leo showed up next. They all eyed me with suspicion, and no one said anything as we waited for the others. Tension clung to us like winter coats, and even the niceties normally spoken were minimal. Maribelle and Ray came late and Asher a few minutes later.

I looked at each face. I'd once thought of them as friends. Now I saw they were just people that I thought I knew. My real friend was gone, and I'd never have her back.

They all stood looking at me, silently demanding a reason for the intrusion into their day.

I stood up to face them. "First, let me tell you that the police have the curio thief in custody." I waited a moment and let them process the information. "But that's not why I asked you here tonight." Frowns and curiosity covered their faces.

"I asked you here to discuss who killed Hazel." I studied each face and incredulous look carefully.

"Ok so tell us," Maribelle folded her arms over her chest, impatient for an answer. "Who killed her?"

"I'm not sure if you know, but Hazel's son, her only child, was killed by a drunk driver." I spoke slowly and looked from Asher to Jeremy. "I know she sometimes went a little overboard with it, but that's why she felt so strongly about young people drinking alcohol." The boys looked uncomfortable and stared down at the ground. "And she was afraid..." I paused for a long moment, waiting for Asher to look up at me.

"She was afraid when you ran her off the road and nearly killed her, that the next person might not be so lucky." I stared at Asher. The surprise was obvious. He opened his mouth to deny any wrongdoing, but quickly closed it. "She knew it was you, didn't she?"

Asher looked at his father, then his mother. "No... how do you... why do you think it was me?"

"That's a very serious accusation." Ray's voice sounded low and stern.

"How dare you!" Maribelle shouted, "How dare you accuse my son of trying to kill someone!" The blood rushed to her face as she hurled her rage toward me.

I didn't allow her outburst to stop me. "I did some digging and created a timeline of events related to Hazel's death." I set the folder on the table and pulled out the timeline for everyone to look at, along with articles from the paper. "You can see that this is when Hazel was run off the road."

Necks stretched out and around one another as they tried to view the papers.

"So. That doesn't tell us anything new." Maribelle, still fuming, folded her arms.

"I called around to the body shops in town asking about a dark blue Ford pickup truck until I found someone who had repaired a front quarter panel. The truck came in the day after Hazel was run off the road, by a young man in a big hurry to get it fixed. Needed it done ASAP. His description of the young man matches Asher."

"That doesn't prove anything." Ray stepped closer as if to intimidate me.

I pulled out another picture from my folder. "Hazel sent me this photo of her car after the accident. You can see that whoever hit her had a dark blue vehicle, the same color as Asher's." They moved closer, then crowded in around the photos.

"It still doesn't prove anything." Ray said, although he sounded less confident.

"She probably asked you boys to come over for a talk, didn't she?" I let my eyes meet Jeremy's and then Asher's. "That's why I saw tire tracks left by your motorbikes at Hazel's back door." I pulled out the photo of the tire marks.

Jeremy looked at Asher. "We didn't hurt her. I swear, we didn't touch her!"

"We did go over to her house," Asher admitted. "She knew it was us who ran her off the road. She asked if we'd been drinking." Clearly shaken by his own story, the boy cleared his throat, then continued. "She wanted us to tell our parents. She said it was a serious crime and we could go to jail. Hit and run."

"But... she said she wouldn't tell the police if we quit drinking, and our parents stopped giving teenagers alcohol." Jeremy added.

"Alright boys, you don't need to say anything more." Ray's tone was like that of a lawyer, authoritative and demanding.

"So, you promised to be good, and she just let you leave? Just like that? Took you at your word?" I kept at them.

"Yes. Well, she wanted our parents to agree too." Asher looked at his parents and then at the ground.

I scanned the faces. "Boys," I looked at Asher and Jeremy. "I'd like to speak with your parents alone." The boys seemed uncertain, but their parents nodded for them to leave. "Oh, one more thing."

The boys stopped and looked at me.

"The mural on my deck, was that your artistic hand Asher?"

His eyes grew large and frightened. He looked at his father, who shook his head, then back at me. "Ah..." His guilt was obvious, yet he couldn't say anything. His father waved him off and the boys sprinted for home.

I turned back to Ray. "So, you knew the boys had run Hazel off the road? And what did you do? You didn't go to the police. Instead, you went to see her yourself." I hoped my stare would get him to say something, but he just stared back. I went on. "But you didn't go alone. You took your buddies with you."

Leo and Craig looked over at Ray.

I turned to Craig. "I believe the police will find a toothpick in Hazel's house," I pointed to the photo of the gum wrapper, a toothpick next to it, "with your DNA. I've noticed you like to chew on toothpicks and then drop them. I think you dropped one at Hazel's house the night she died. You left a gum wrapper as well."

Stunned, Craig drew back. "I... you think I killed Hazel?" He shook his head. "I didn't kill her!"

"But you were there when she was killed, weren't you?" I felt angry. They'd murdered Hazel. They needed to admit it. I couldn't let them get away with it.

"Craig, you don't have to say anything." Ray's lawyer voice spoke up again.

I turned and looked at Leo. "And Leo, why did you shoot off a gun? The police already found the bullet lodged in her wall. They can match it up to your gun."

All three women turned and stared at Leo, who stood sheepishly not knowing what to say. He lost his balance for a second, then steadied himself with the help of Sondra's shoulder.

"Someone reported the gunshot to the police," I looked at Crissa. "That's how they knew to look for a bullet." I explained.

Crissa glared at me. Clearly surprised that I knew she'd made the call.

"I just wanted to scare her. I wasn't plannin' on shootin' her." Leo held tightly to the bottle of beer in his hand. His words slurred with alcohol.

"Shut up Leo." Ray warned. But he was too late.

"I was jist gonna shoot the gun off so she would realize she couldn't threaten us. Nobody wanted her to get hurt. It was her own fault, she--" The words tumbled from Leo's drunken lips.

"Leo, you idiot, shut up!" Ray shouted.

"Hey, it was an accident." Leo continued. He looked at Ray and then at Sondra. "It was an accident."

"What happened?" Crissa surprised me by demanding an explanation.

Craig and Leo both looked at Ray. We all turned and looked at him.

"Ray?" Maribelle asked quietly. But Ray remained silent.

"Were you afraid Asher would lose his scholarship? Maybe not even get accepted into a good school." I challenged. "Afraid he could lose his license or even go to jail for a hit and run. And it would be your fault. You let him drink before he left that day."

"We just wanted to talk to her." Craig spoke up. "She was talking about turning the boys in. We wanted to make sure she understood. Make sure she knew that it would ruin their lives. I mean they're only kids."

"We were jist tryin' to protect 'em." Leo swayed and grabbed Sondra's shoulder once again.

"What happened Ray? I know you were in Hazel's kitchen." I pulled out a picture of Hazel in her kitchen. "Notice the spices? This is how they normally looked. But you lined them all up perfectly, with their labels neatly facing outward. Hazel never did that. She was clean, but not OCD." I paused to give everyone time to think about it. "You are OCD though, aren't you? So, you were standing next to the stove. You grabbed the pan and hit her, didn't you?"

"That's pretty circumstantial evidence." Ray looked smug.

Maribelle was in shock. Accustomed to being in control of every situation, she found herself powerless to do or even say anything. She looked at him with fear and love. "Ray?"

"Ray, I think you need to tell the whole story." I could only hope he would admit to killing Hazel. "Craig and Leo witnessed everything. That makes them accessories."

Unwilling to confess, Ray turned to Maribelle. "Let's go home babe. We heard what she has to say, now let's leave." It was then that he noticed Barry and Jim standing behind them.

Jim wasn't in uniform, so he pulled out his badge. "I'm officer Higgins, and I'm placing you under arrest for the Murder of Hazel Walters. You have the right to remain silent..."

Barry stood next to the grill, flipping burgers, while Jim and I sipped iced tea on the deck.

"So, can you tell me anything about the case?" I asked, forgoing all subtlety.

"I can't tell you everything of course, but I can tell you that both Craig and Leo have confessed to their part in the killing. The lawyers worked out a plea deal with the Prosecutor, they won't do that much jail time since they testified against Ray. Ray had no choice but to admit he was the one who hit her after they confessed. Judge gave him 20 years."

"It's so sad that Hazel had to die. Honestly, she just didn't want the kids drinking and driving. I doubt if she'd have turned them in either. Is anything going to happen to the boys?"

"No. That was part of the deal, Ray agreed to plead guilty if they didn't bring any charges against the boys. And you said you weren't pressing charges."

"That's good, I do feel bad for those boys." Barry said as he sat a tray of burgers on the table next to us. "Hopefully, they learned a lesson from all of this."

"I don't know how they couldn't." I said and put a hamburger and bun on my plate. "I mean after everything that they've gone through."

"Looks like Ray's wife sold the house?" Jim shook the mustard bottle and squeezed some on his hamburger.

"Yes. She moved shortly after that day at the park, and I saw the realtor putting a sold sign up yesterday."

"No more teen drinking parties?" Jim asked.

"Nope. At least not around here." I took another bite of potato salad.

Once we finished our meal, Boris and I took a walk to Lily Park.

The neighborhood had changed. Sondra, Crissa, and Maribelle took flight; moved their nests far away where no one would know them, where they could make a fresh start. And in their place new people moved in.

Boris and I reached the park and walked directly to a young tree, planted in memory of Hazel. She had loved trees, and I knew she would have been pleased.

I heard the buzzing of voices and looked over at the picnic tables. Several people were gathered, chattering amongst themselves. I smiled at the tree as I reached out and gently touched one of the branches, then Boris and I walked over to join our new neighbors.

Mosquito Bites

***B*reaking News Alert.** The television banner flashed across the screen. Several police officers waded through marshy ground, police lights flashing in the background. I turned up the volume. "An unidentified man was found in Tupelo Park around 8pm this evening. A jogger, out for run, found the man face down in the marsh. Police are on the scene now."

Barry and I looked at one another. Tupelo Park was about four miles from our house, on the outskirts of town. Hiking the trails was a Sunday evening ritual with us, and the highlight of our terrier, Boris' week. Tonight was no exception. We'd headed for the park directly after dinner.

"We might have walked right by him." I traced the details of our walk. All along the path, past the lake and through our normal trail. Had we walked right past this man's body?

"We would have seen him." Barry brushed it off as if I were making something out of nothing. "If he'd been there when we were, we'd have seen him. Boris would have for sure. It must have happened after we left."

It was true, we would have seen him. Still the thought of being so close to where someone died only a short time before was a little unsettling. "Do you think we should notify the police? I mean we were there just an hour before the jogger found him."

"No. What would you tell them? That we were in the park but didn't see anything? The guy probably just had a heart attack." And with a sharp glance my way, he dismissed the conversation.

Barry might be right, but his tone irritated me. We'd argued lately, which was unusual for us. We went to bed without further discussion, yet I couldn't sleep. For several nights I'd had a difficult time sleeping. Was it the *secret*? The first real secret I'd kept from my husband. I tried to push it away. Think about something else. But after an hour of restlessness, I gave up.

I laid there in the darkness, wrestling with recent events in my mind. I thought about the dead man in the park and shivered. I wondered who he was, and what had happened to him. I rolled over and thought about Barry. How distant he felt to me lately. We'd always gotten along so well. A disagreement here and there, an argument maybe. But nothing that lasted more than a day or so. How had we come to this bump in our relationship? I ran through my memory. It had begun the night of the Euchre Club party, nearly a month ago.

It was our turn to host the games, and we set up the card tables in our walkout basement. I found lots of great card decorations to set around to add to our fun. Barry laid out the snacks and drinks on the bar so that people could help themselves throughout the evening.

At first everything was going fine. Everyone seemed to get along and appeared to be enjoying the evening. Lively chatter filled the room as the games began. A nervous hostess, I scanned the tables and faces, just to make sure.

Satisfied that all was well, I relaxed and began to enjoy the evening myself. Barry and I were up against Mitzi and Ned in the first game. I was glad we played couples Euchre. Cards, and Euchre in particular, were one of mine and Barry's favorite activities.

We loved the strategies and challenges. When we played together it was as if we were locked in an intimate mind set. A telepathic understanding of sorts. We didn't use signals or anything that would be considered unfair or unethical, but we did seem to have an intuitive understanding of what cards to play for each other.

Mitzi, along with her new partner and fifth husband, Ned, were the first couple we played. Ned wasn't as good a card player as his wife. I expected him to be better at it, being a CPA and good with numbers. I wondered if that disappointed her. He wiped a few small beads of sweat from his balding head.

"Pretty blouse Mitzi." I noted.

She beamed at the compliment. Mitzi loved to dress in bright colors that seemed to draw people to her. Her clothing, like her personality sparkled brightly.

At the table next to us, our neighbors Rudy and Nia were teamed against Chuck and Kitty. I could hear Chuck talking about his latest venture, a new Multi-Level-Marketing business selling vitamins and shakes. I overheard most of Chuck's sales spiel, which I was all too familiar with. One thing about Chuck, he loved to talk about himself or whatever new thing he was trying to sell. In fact, that was about all he ever seemed to want to talk about. Nice guy, but boring. I thought Kitty must be a saint to live with him.

Rudy too, seemed to be in an animated mood that night. He leaned his thick body back in the chair and clutched his cards tightly against his chest. The smirk on his face led me to believe he had a good hand. "Come on," he motioned impatiently, "play."

I turned my attention back to my own table. Barry was looking at me over his glasses and I realized it was my turn. I looked at the score cards. We were down by a few points. I had the type of hand that could go either way, depending on how I played it. I didn't make the best choice and they took the point.

It was Mitzi's deal. She studied me carefully, a teasing smile on her face. As much as I liked Mitzi and admired her gregarious nature, I scrutinized her card playing closely. Ever since my friend Hazel had called her out for cheating two years ago, I watched with wary eyes. I must admit I don't know what I would do if I caught her at it.

I heard laughter coming from the table on the other side of me. I turned to see Aleena laughing at something her boyfriend Dean was saying. She looked so happy. Aleena and her daughter moved into the neighborhood the year before, shortly after her divorce was final. It wasn't long after that she'd met Dean on GreatDates.com, a popular dating site, and become totally infatuated with him. Dean was a looker, no doubt about that. And at 48, Aleena too, was attractive. They made a nice-looking couple.

"He's perfect!" She'd confided in me. "He's smart and kind, and he treats me like a princess." A few weeks later, Dean had moved in with her.

I watched as they flirted with one another and felt nostalgic for those early days when Barry and I shared secret passionate smiles and light touches. I admit I was slightly jealous of that new love, those dreamy looks they gave one another. That unchartered relationship where each day brought new exploration and pleasure.

As I eavesdropped on the couple, Dean began to cough. It was a dry cough that seemed to go on for longer than it should. Aleena pulled an inhaler from her purse and rushed to give it to him. She rubbed his back tenderly.

"Sorry, just my asthma." He said, as if embarrassed, and a few moments later went back to his card playing.

My interest quickly returned to my own game, where Barry and I weren't doing too well.

"That's a game," Ned said jovially, and we all stood up for a break.

We headed to the bar for a drink. That's when Rudy, in a loud gruff voice bellowed out, "Dammit Chuck! Are you going to play cards or try to sell me crap I don't want?" The room suddenly grew quiet. We all held our breath waiting for the answer.

"I'm sorry Rudy," Chuck stammered like a schoolboy who'd just been chastised by the class bully. "I thought... well never mind." His face turned red as he realized the whole room was listening. He played his cards.

"Euchre!" Rudy roared and flung his cards down on the table. His boisterous laugh was a little too loud.

Barry poured me a glass of iced tea, and we waited at the bar for the rest of the teams to finish their games. I marked the sheet that showed Mitzi and Ned as the winners. Rudy came up behind me and put his hand on my shoulder.

"Mark us down as the winners, will you darling?" Rudy purred at me. I could smell the alcohol and felt his breath on my neck.

I gracefully pulled away and marked the score sheet. "You seem extra cheery tonight," I remarked.

"Oh, I am darling. Things are really turning around for me." Rudy was eager to share that he had just switched his 401K over to Aleena's boyfriend, Dean's investment firm, and that Dean was his new financial advisor. His enthusiasm spilled all over, along with his drink. I grabbed a paper napkin and began wiping it up.

"I'll be able to retire at the end of the year." Rudy said proudly. We all congratulated him on his good news.

I looked at Barry and thought about when he might retire. It would be so great to do some of the things we'd always dreamed about.

That's what I wanted. For Barry to be able to retire so he and I could begin really enjoying life. Traveling to exciting new places. Visiting our son in Colorado. Spending endless evenings just being together without the stress of his work.

It never occurred to me then that things would go in such an extreme direction. That this evening could find us entangled in a plot that would see one of us killed, and the rest of us terrified. Instead, I became a blind participant, waiting my turn to have the idealism sucked out of me, and the reality of making poor decisions come swooping down on me, just as they had on the dead man in Tupelo Park.

We switched teams and the good-looking couple, Dean and Aleena, took seats at our table. I asked Dean about his company. I was intrigued by his knowledge of the finance world, something I knew nothing about. Barry had always taken care of our finances and investments. It was a territory I'd never entered. Nor had I been interested before. But Dean had a way of making the world of bonds and the stock market sound exciting, where before it had always seemed so complicated, and inaccessible.

"I'd be happy to take a look at what you've got and see if I can do better." Dean offered.

I was still thinking about what Dean had said, when the evening games were over, and our guests had all gone. Barry and I were cleaning up when I broached the subject of our finances. "Maybe we should switch to Dean's investment company." I suggested. "I'd love it if you could retire sooner."

"I already have a financial advisor." Barry's voice was flat and uninterested.

"Well, does it really make a big difference who you go with?" I asked innocently. "I mean they all do the same thing, right?"

"They all invest your money if that's what you're asking. But they are not all the same."

I may have missed Barry's cue that he didn't want to discuss it any further. I pressed on. "I'm sure Dean is good though. He seems to know what he's talking about. And if Dean helped Rudy so that he can--"

"I'm not switching." His voice grew stern.

"I just think it's nice to help friends and neighbors. And it wouldn't hurt just to see what he could do for us." I persisted.

"Drop it, Delila."

"Why? Why do you make all the decisions when it comes to money?" I raised my voice. After all it was my life and my future too.

"I said I'm not changing financial advisors and that's final." Barry stormed upstairs, leaving me to finish cleaning up.

It must have been about a week later, after Barry had finished breakfast and gone on to work, I contemplated my little secret. I'd never done anything like this before. I felt energized and excited for the first time in a long time.

Boris lay on his bed. He looked tired, but I hooked up his leash anyway. "Get up, buddy. Time for your morning walk." He didn't move. I tugged. "Come on. Wake up sleepyhead!" I pulled it again. Finally, he stretched his legs, and we headed out the door.

Every morning Boris and I walked to the park in our neighborhood. The sign at the entrance read, 'Lily Park,' because of all the lilies that were planted there. But secretly I referred to it as 'The Gossip Garden.'

Mitzi and Nia were sitting at a picnic table talking when I arrived. Mitzi's little red poodle darted around the park with Nia's new dachshund puppy trying hard to keep up. Boris had no interest in playing with the other dogs. He roamed over to sniff some flowers instead.

"I really like you with red hair." I told Mitzi. At one time, her hair had been black. She'd started to let it go white, then decided it made her look like a skunk and dyed it red. The auburn color really was her best look.

"Thank you, Delila. I like it too." Mitzi seemed genuinely pleased with the compliment. "Nia and I were just talking about poor Aleena."

I looked from one to the other to see who wanted to spill the rumor first. It was Nia who spoke up.

"Poor Aleena is broke. She's behind in her bills and doesn't have a cent in the bank." Nia unloaded the news in one rapid info dump.

"Maxed out on her credit cards too." Mitzi added.

The shock must have shown on my face because Nia lightly touched my arm. "I know dear. That's what we thought too."

Aleena had made out well from her divorce. The house she owned free and clear, and she'd also received a large cash settlement. Six months and she'd lost it all? Wow. How had that happened? I didn't think she was a big spender. But she did have a teenage daughter getting ready for college. Still, she said her ex-husband was paying for everything for the girl.

They gave me a couple of minutes to digest the rumor before going on to the next piece of news.

"And did you hear, Tilly's sister died." Nia spoke in her softest voice.

Tilly and Jack lived two doors down from Aleena. They grew an impressive garden in their backyard, and frequently bestowed bags of veggies on us. Boris loved Tilly, probably because she was always standing by with a treat for him.

It wasn't only the veggies and dog treats that endeared Tilly to our family; she was always doing nice things for us. Once when Barry and I went on a week-long vacation, Tilly and Jack took care of Boris for us. While we were gone, she made him a beautiful dog quilt, and even embroidered his name on it.

"Poor Tilly!" I didn't try to hide the shock I felt. I'd met her sister once when she had visited, a nice, younger version of Tilly.

"Suicide." Mitzi added.

After the Euchre party, Barry and I did not discuss our finances again, but it frequently played on my mind. For the first few years we were married, I worked in an office, while Barry built up his dental practice. His business took off so well that when our son was born, we agreed that I would stay home and raise him.

I never regretted being a stay-at-home mom, however there were times when I resented not having my own money. Barry was generous and never said anything about me spending money on household expenses. Yet, I sometimes felt almost guilty about not contributing financially. And when I wanted anything, I felt like I had to ask for it. Had to get approval or even permission.

When our son entered high school, I took on a part-time job. I didn't make much, but I loved the feeling of independence and began saving up. Unfortunately, the company closed, and once again I had to rely on Barry for whatever material things I wanted. It didn't bother me too much at the time, but recently I had begun to itch for self-sufficiency once more.

I was thinking about Barry and our finances when I heard a knock at the door.

"Hi Kitty," I grinned. "Nice to see you."

"Hi Delila," she said in her usual soft-spoken voice. "Do you have a minute?"

"Sure. Come on in." I offered.

Kitty followed me inside, but she didn't budge from the foyer. "I really can't stay Delila. I just came to tell you that Chuck and I are dropping out of Euchre Club."

"Oh Kitty, why? We love having you guys in the group!" I felt anxious. We had exactly six couples and couldn't afford to lose players. It had taken so long to get the club back up and running, I certainly didn't want to start over.

"Well," Kitty looked at the floor. "Chuck says he doesn't want to do it anymore."

"Was it because of Rudy?" I asked.

"No. Although Rudy is mean to him sometimes."

Clearly, she was hiding the real reason. I waited for her to explain.

"It's Dean. Chuck went to see him about opening a retirement account." She took a quick breath then continued. "And Delila, you know we don't have a lot. We invested it all in Chuck's previous business. And you know what happened with that. Anyway, so we don't have a lot."

I nodded. I did have to give him credit for trying. Chuck had started at least four businesses since I'd known him.

"So, Dean told him to just put his money in a CD at the bank. That we don't have enough to even bother with." Kitty sighed. "Chuck felt like Dean was laughing at him. He was so embarrassed. Now he doesn't want to be around him." She stopped for a moment, and I could see the frustration building up in her. "Delila, it really bites. I mean, would it kill Dean to let Chuck invest just a little? He really hurt him."

"Oh Kitty, I'm so sorry." What else could I say? I made a mental note to order more vitamins from Chuck.

Several days had gone by since I'd heard about Tilly's sister committing suicide. I'd sent a card and flowers, and I knew I could do nothing to ease the pain, but I wanted to see her anyway. I packaged up some homemade chocolate chip-macadamia nut cookies, leashed up Boris and headed down the street.

Boris stopped to sniff something just as we neared Aleena's house. That's when I saw Rudy's vehicle pull up in front. I watched him get out, slam his car door, and march up the porch steps. He banged loudly. Boris continued to sniff, while I stood back, hidden by the bushes.

Aleena answered the door. She looked surprised.

"Where's Dean?" Rudy demanded.

Dean appeared behind Aleena within a moment. "Hey Rudy, how's—"

"Where's my money?" Rudy shouted. "I want it. Now!" His voice boomed through the quiet neighborhood.

"Ok, ok. Calm down Rudy. Why don't you come on in and—"

"I'm not here on a social call, I want my money and I want it now. All of it!"

No one had seen me, and I didn't want to cause any embarrassment, so I waited at the edge of the sidewalk, with Boris, concealed by the shrubs.

"Look, Rudy, you know I don't have that kind of cash laying around the house. I'll have to sell your shares and send you a check. That's the way it's done. You'll get your money, don't worry." Dean's voice sounded calm, reassuring.

But Rudy wasn't having any part of it. "I better have it, and soon! If not, you'll pay! I'll kill you- I swear I will!" He shook his fist in Dean's face. I'd never seen Rudy so worked up; he looked as if he might burst. He stormed back to his car and drove off, screeching the tires.

Aleena and Dean quickly retreated and shut the door. I pressed against the bushes and held the leash tight, feeling my heart racing. I waited a moment longer, then passed their house at a quick pace.

By the time I reached Tilly's house I still felt a little jittery. I took a deep breath and tried to calm myself. Tilly answered the door and looked pleased to see us.

"Wait just a minute," she said and disappeared back into the house. A moment later she returned with a treat for Boris.

"Thank you," I said and handed her the package of cookies. "And these are for you!"

She gingerly took the goodies. "I'm sorry I haven't thanked you for the card and flowers, Delila. I've been so busy going through my sister's things. I still have a hard time believing she's gone." Tears began to roll down her face.

My eyes welled up in response to her pain. I reached out and touched her arm.

She pulled away. "It's just not right. She had so much to live for. Just a couple of months ago she was happy and carefree. Why would she do it?"

I shook my head, and we stood silent for a moment absorbing the sadness.

"She didn't even leave a note. At least not that I've found." Tilly confided.

Tilly's husband Jack came to the door and took his wife's arm. "Are you ready?"

"We have to go pick up another load of her things. Everything needs to be out of the apartment by the end of the week or we pay another month's rent." Tilly said. "Thank you, Delila."

The following day, I was feeling anxious about life. Like I often did, I began to clean my already clean house, hoping to clear my anxiety.

Thoughts had begun to run through my mind that made me wonder about my friends and neighbors. Why had Dean been so mean to Chuck? And why had Rudy demanded his money back from Dean? As I pondered these questions my cell phone buzzed.

"Hello Delila." It was Tilly. "I wondered if you'd like to go through some of my sister's things, see if there is anything you want. I think you are about the same size, some of these clothes might fit you. Whatever you don't want, I'm going to donate."

I could hear the sadness in her voice. I imagined her tear-stained face as she held each article in her hand and considered giving away the last connections to her sister. Tilly was a home body, with few friends. I suspected she wanted someone to be with her. Jack was great, but he was a man. I promised I'd be over in a half hour to help her sort through the items.

Boris pushed through the screen door, as excited to see Tilly as she was to see him. Dozens of boxes stood piled in the hallway. I could see how overwhelmed she must feel. What to do with all this stuff. She led me to the guest room. "Let's start here."

Tilly wanted to talk about her sister. To share her worries. It helped her put things into perspective. Helped her work through her grief.

"She'd been seeing someone, and she was so happy." Tilly reminisced. "She'd met her Adonis, her prince charming. Then he dumped her. Just like that. He broke her heart, Delila."

"Did you ever meet him?" I asked.

"Nope, never did. He didn't even come to her funeral." Tilly sighed.

"Heartless jerk." I offered.

We continued to sift through her sister's belongings. Tilly's much younger sister had never married. Tilly said her sister was a saver, rarely spent anything on herself, and looking through her things, I could see she hadn't exaggerated.

Methodically, Tilly looked at each piece of clothing, meticulously checked the pockets, then folded them carefully.

The linen and dishes were in good condition, but inexpensive. Same with her jewelry. "Is there anything you want Delila?" I felt she wanted to spread pieces of her sister around so she wouldn't be easily forgotten. As if the items gave significance and value to her sister.

Unfortunately, there was really nothing I wanted, so I selected a token vase.

"She didn't have much in the way of personal items." Tilly explained. "Her car was over ten years old. Her clothes she sometimes bought second hand. She rarely took vacations." Tilly waited to catch my eye. "But she once told me she'd saved up over a million dollars."

I'm sure the shock showed on my face.

"Yep." She nodded calmly. "I haven't found it." Tilly continued. "Yet." She added.

A couple of days after I'd helped Tilly sort her sister's things, I decided to join the gym. I'd been feeling daring, almost antsy for trying new things. I needed exercise and something to do.

It was my first day of working out, and I was exhausted. Feeling I deserved a treat for all my hard work, I decided to stop in at the little coffee shop not far from our subdivision. I love their double chocolate latte, and decided I deserved it after an hour of working out.

As I was waiting for my sugar fix, I noticed Aleena and Tilly sitting at a table in the far corner. I thought about yelling "hi," but I could see they were deep in a serious conversation. It's a small shop and I overheard their voices but couldn't make out what they were saying. Aleena looked clearly upset. Were they arguing?

I got my latte to go and headed home. I thought it interesting that Tilly and Aleena were having coffee together. I'd never known them to be friends particularly. Oh well, it was none of my business.

As I drove down my street I was nearly run over by Rudy. His car sped around a corner and nearly hit me head-on. He was out of control.

We all were, we just didn't know it yet.

I awoke tired, the night before still haunting me. I'd stayed up for hours brooding over every detail of the last few weeks. Those thoughts co-mingled with our walk in the park and hearing the news report about the dead man found in Tupelo Park.

Barry escaped to work, leaving me to mull over my guilt. I wanted to confront him, to argue, tell him how I felt. How, as a partner, I wanted to be included in financial decisions. But it wouldn't be good. Besides, Barry didn't like to fight before work.

I poured another cup of coffee and stared into space. My phone startled me, its blaring ringtone against the dead silence of the morning.

"Delila, turn on the news!" Mitzi sounded excited.

"What? The news, why?" I asked.

"Just turn on channel 4." She insisted.

"Ok, I'm turning it on now." I aimed the clicker at the television and hit the on button.

The banner that flashed across the screen read "Man found in Tupelo Park identified as Tobin Sullivan..." The picture on the screen, however, showed someone else. Someone we all knew.

"Dean!" I gasped.

"Yes! Isn't that crazy? He's been lying to us all along!"

"Oh." I managed. Inside me, fear stirred.

The news reporter's voice rumbled through to my consciousness. "Police continue to investigate the unusual circumstances surrounding the death. It appears that Mr. Sullivan died after having been heavily sprayed with a toxic chemical used in insect repellent."

I shook my head in disbelief. Insect repellent? Had the park sprayed for mosquitoes that night? Wouldn't they have told us if they were planning on spraying toxic chemicals?

So many thoughts flashed back and forth through my mind. Dean! Dead. I stumbled through my own feelings and fears. Someone I knew and liked had died, and yet he was someone I really didn't know. I felt confused, not sure if I should feel sad at the loss, or angry at having been conned.

Did Aleena know? Or had she been duped too?

"Mitzi, does Aleena know? Have you spoken with her?"

"You didn't hear?" Mitzi asked. "They broke up two days ago."

News travels fast to a dentist office. Barry had seen Dean's picture on the television screen at work along with his real name.

"What a shock." Barry's voice was excited. "Rudy needs to get in touch with the brokerage house immediately. I never trusted that guy. Rudy should be worried. He invested his entire retirement with him. Have you talked to Nia today?"

I blinked. Was I shaking? I wasn't sure. "No." My voice sounded strange even to me. "I haven't talked to her. I'll give her a call in a bit."

Barry looked at me with questioning eyes. "Delila?" He knew me too well.

It was time to confess. Come clean about my financial infidelity. After so many years together, I knew it was best to get it out in the open. The guilt had been building up for some time. I'd wanted financial independence. Now I longed for a different kind of freedom. Truth. Honesty. To break free from my lies.

"I invested with Dean too." I said quietly.

"How much?" He asked.

"My entire 401k plan, plus a little of what I had saved up." I confessed. I searched his face for a reaction, backlash.

My emotions were all over. In my frustration, I wanted to shout at him that it was his fault. If he'd only included me in our financial decisions, in our future, we could have talked about it. I wouldn't have run off and secretly invested with Dean.

But I knew, deep down, that it was my fault too. That I should have tried harder. I should have consulted him before making a rash decision. Up until the night of the Euchre party, I'd never had an interest in our finances. I'd always let Barry handle it because I trusted him, and it was easy for me. I never had to worry about it.

"Did he give you any paperwork?" Barry asked.

I nodded.

"Tomorrow morning you need to contact the company." He took out his wallet, pulled out a card and handed it to me. "Our lawyer. You might need to contact him too."

I didn't want to check the paperwork in front of Barry, so the next morning I waited until he'd left for the office before, I pulled out the folder Dean had given me. At the time I'd been impressed with my dossier, my portfolio. I felt powerful, in charge of my own future. Now, those same documents looked vague. There was no address for the company, only the corporate name and Dean's phone number and a bunch of numbers.

"Damn!" I threw the papers down on the table. "That creep!" I covered my mouth and screamed. I was angry. The fear of losing my entire retirement savings, although not all that large, sucked. The idea that I might have been tricked was humiliating. I had to get my money back!

I searched the internet for the company name and was relieved to find that this financial investment firm did indeed exist. I called the number listed.

"What did you say your advisor's name was?" The voice on the other end asked.

"Dean Hartman," I said. "Or Tobin Sullivan."

"I'm sorry, I don't show any advisor with either of those names."

"Can you look up my account by my name?" I gave her every piece of information I could think of.

"I'm sorry mam'. Perhaps it was a different company. We show no account for you."

Heartbroken, I began to cry. Now what? What had that jerk done with my money? I thought about Rudy. He'd invested his entire retirement as well. He and Nia were planning on living on it for the rest of their lives. It wasn't like he could go back and start his career all over. Would he have to work the rest of his life? At least I had Barry. Thank God for Barry!

There was only one thing I could think of to do. I put on my sunglasses and headed to Aleena's house. She must know something!

Full of rage, I wanted to bang on her front door. Why had she brought that schmuck into our lives anyway? How long had she known about him? I took a deep breath and pushed my anger aside for the moment. Afterall, I told myself, Aleena may not have had any knowledge about his lies and deceit. Or maybe she found out and that's why she kicked him out. In any case, if I wanted to learn more about what happened to my retirement fund, I needed her help. I pressed hard on the doorbell.

It was a minute before Aleena answered the door. "Hi Delila." She peeked her head around the door. "I'm really not feeling up to talking to anyone right now." Her face showed signs of extended crying. Her eyes were puffy and red.

At one point, I had wondered if she was part of the scam. But judging by her unkempt appearance, I quickly threw out any such idea.

"Aleena, I'm sorry to bother you. I know you've been through a difficult time, but I need to speak with you. It's really important."

She stood there looking at me, not saying a word. I took it as an invitation to continue. Although I really hadn't prepared to interrogate her, questions ran rampant in my head.

"Aleena, remember that day when I met with Dean, here in his office?"

She nodded.

"Well, I invested my entire retirement plan with him. This morning, I tried contacting the company and they'd never heard of him."

"His name wasn't Dean--" Her voice quivered.

Annoyed, I cut in. "I know. I checked both names. He never worked there under either name. I need to find out what he did with my money." I gave her a moment to process. "Aleena, is there anything you can tell me about him? What do you know about his family? Do you know how to contact them? Or where he worked?" Panic ripped through me once again. Was I really going to lose my retirement, my savings?

"I don't Delila. That's the crazy thing. I never even thought to ask him much about himself. Besides, everything he said was a lie anyway. He told me he'd spent 20 years in the Airforce. Showed me medals, all kinds of things. All lies. I checked. He was never in the Airforce or any other part of the military." She looked deflated.

I began to soften as I realized she too had been deceived. "He might have left something behind that will give me a clue. May I come in and look through his office?"

"There's really nothing there. He cleared out most of his stuff when we broke up."

I hadn't thought of that. "May I look anyway? Just in case?"

She held open the door that had been a barrier between us and I stepped in. We walked slowly down the hall to the room that had been his office.

"Do you know where he kept the money when he lived here? I mean, did he have a safe or a file cabinet that he locked up?" I asked.

"I don't know. Honestly, he was super secretive about stuff like that. He never let me in here. Not even to clean. Said it was business and proprietary."

The desk was still there, and the room looked pretty much the same as it had when I met with him. I realized everything in this office must belong to Aleena. I opened each drawer and looked under the desk and all around the floor. I searched the wastebasket.

Aleena stood watching me. Her eyes darted around nervously. "I um, I cleaned up after he moved out. I'm sorry Delila."

For a moment I felt irritated with her, then realized I'd have done the same. I began to scan the bookshelves. I noticed the books too, must belong to Aleena. Romance novels mostly. I continued to look anyway. I was feeling desperate.

Then I saw it. Sitting on top of some novels, a slip of paper folded in half.

I examined the paper, just an offer for a credit card. Junk mail really. But the name and the address were for Alec Sullivan. Dean's real name was Sullivan. Was Alec another alias?

Aleena looked at me with questioning eyes.

"It's nothing really. Just an old credit card application. But I might be able to get some information from it. Would you mind if I keep it?"

Aleena agreed and I left wondering how this credit card application would help me get my money back.

At home I took out our attorney's card. I spoke with him briefly and gave him a summary of what had happened. He promised to 'look into' it for me.

Barry also suggested I contact Officer Jim Higgins, a friend of his who'd been of help to us before. I thought the police probably had more information and may even be able to help me. Plus, I might need to file a report. I dialed Jim's number.

Jim said he could meet me later in the afternoon. In the meantime, I took Boris for a walk, hoping the gossip garden might provide some useful information.

From a distance, I spotted what looked like a large flower, but it turned out to be someone in bright green capris and a red, orange, and yellow flowered top. Mitzi. Her little poodle ran to greet Boris, who promptly tried to avoid her.

"Oh Delila. Hi!" She greeted me warmly. She seemed famished for camaraderie, as if she hadn't seen anyone all morning. "Can you believe all this stuff about Dean?" She dove right in.

I cautioned myself not to let too much slip out. No need for the gossip channel to broadcast news of my financial blunders. "Hi Mitzi."

"I'm not sure if you heard, but apparently, there has been a rash of women duped by Dean." Mitzi's words landed on me with annoyance.

I had been one of those women, I thought. He'd charmed me with his light, easy talk. I never even felt him sucking the money out of me.

"He was an attractive man, and so charming. I can see why they fell for him." Mitzi zoomed in on the details. "He used several different names and stories. Poor Aleena."

He deceived me, deceived Rudy. Was it what they called a Ponzi scheme? Or had he just pocketed our money and taken off? My own thoughts had interrupted Mitzi's message. Now I scrambled to understand what she was talking about. I had been so wrapped up in thinking about my situation, I didn't realize there might be more to the story.

"Wait, what?" I asked.

Mitzi nodded solemnly. "Aleena was so easily taken in, so vulnerable. And he was so attentive and charming. No wonder she fell for him. Too bad it was all a big put on."

"Umm. You said there were others? What do you mean?" I asked.

"Oh yes. Apparently, Aleena wasn't the first one he charmed out of her money." Mitzi volunteered. "At least that's what the police think."

Officer Jim Higgins arrived at 3:00pm promptly. He was wearing his uniform and looked quite official. I thought my neighbors would see the patrol car parked in my driveway and wonder why the police were at my house. I wondered if some crazy story might get circulated through the rumor ring. I chuckled to myself, well, let it.

I offered Jim a seat at the table, poured him and I each an Arnold Palmer, his favorite tea and lemonade drink, then sat down with him. He asked how I'd met "Mr. Sullivan."

Then I went into a long story, probably giving him more details than he needed or desired. But I wanted to make sure he had enough information. I told him how Aleena had met Dean on the dating site. How Rudy had invested his retirement income with him, and that I had too.

"Do you think there is any way I can get my money back?" I asked hopefully.

He didn't sound especially optimistic on this matter, but he did try and give me some hope. "Of course, we'll do everything we can, but you should contact your attorney. There may be several people trying to get their money back. We've had a few reports. Apparently, he's been conning women for some time," he told me.

"Jim," There was one more thing I wanted to know. "Did the park spray him with something? I mean we walk

Boris in that park all the time. Is it safe? I didn't think they could do that."

"It wasn't the park that sprayed him. You should be careful walking there, however. Until we find out what happened exactly."

He left me with assurance that he would fill out a report and do his best to help me. What else could he say or do? Somehow, I didn't feel as comforted as I had hoped I would.

It wasn't until after Jim had left and I cleaned the kitchen and fixed dinner that I remembered the credit card application I'd found at Aleena's. I pulled the address up on the map on my phone. It was about a 30-minute drive. Barry would be home soon, so no time today. I promised myself I'd drive over there in the morning.

I spent the first part of the morning avoiding my planned investigation. I looked at the map on my phone once again. Slowly I closed the front door, got into my car, and headed for the address on the application, with no idea what to expect or what I might find.

I had 30 minutes to think about what I would say to whoever I found at the address, but I didn't spend the time as wisely as I should have. I pulled up to the curb and checked the number on the house. It matched the paper.

It was an older home, in an older part of town. The houses were decent, but not nearly as nice as our neighborhood. I sat in my car and looked at the house. It was a two-story wood frame, probably built in the 60's. The big front porch looked like it could use some paint. I located my courage and walked up the sidewalk.

My knock sounded louder than I had intended. A woman I guessed to be around thirty something, answered the door, securing a toddler on her hip. From her rumpled clothes and hair, I gathered I'd caught her in the middle of her morning cleaning routine. She looked at me with suspicious eyes, as if I might be selling magazines.

I felt jittery and anxious. I reminded myself that I was there because I'd lost my retirement, and I wanted it back. "Good morning," I said in my most upbeat voice. "I'm looking for Alec Sullivan."

She studied me for a minute before replying. "Why?"

I had my plan. "I have something of his and want to return it." It was just the credit card application of course, but it was something. Not a complete lie.

She looked around me, probably thinking that whatever I had for him was in the car. "He's away on a business trip. He won't be back for a few days."

So, she thought he'd be back in a few days. Apparently, she hadn't seen the news. Hadn't heard that the man she thought she knew was dead. That possibly the father of her child was someone else altogether. I didn't want to be the one to rock her world, but she needed to know.

The little boy wrapped his arms around her neck and nestled his head against hers. What a jerk, I thought. How could he do this to her? To them.

I contemplated telling her that her husband was a con artist, a common criminal, not the loving man she thought he was. But how could I? It would shatter her world. Her life as she knew it would be over. I couldn't. At least not now.

"You can give it to me." She said smiling.

"I'd rather give it directly to him. I'd also like to talk with him first." I wasn't handing anything over without getting some information.

"Who are you anyway? How do you know Alec?" Irritation or perhaps fear, began to seep into her voice. "Alec is at an insurance convention."

I pulled a small notepad from my purse. "Look, let me give you my name and phone number. Have Alec call me when you talk to him. Or you can call me." Pushing the notepad against my purse, I jotted down my information.

She snatched the paper from my hand and quickly closed the door, leaving me alone on the porch.

The drive home gave me a chance to think about the conversation I'd just had with this woman. I felt sorry for her. I wondered if they were married. Could someone get married using an assumed name? Well, she had my number. When he didn't call, and didn't return, then perhaps she would call me.

I pulled into our neighborhood. As I drove by, I saw Nia sitting alone at a picnic table in Lily Park. I parked my car and got out. Nia's petite little body looked so small and fragile, the opposite of Rudy. I imagined her listening to him yelling about his money. I half expected to find her crying.

"Hi Nia." I sat down across from her.

"Hi Delila." She put on an obligatory smile but didn't bother to disguise her sadness.

We sat there without saying anything for a few long moments. Finally, Nia spoke up. "You probably heard already that Rudy lost his retirement."

"I wasn't sure Nia. I'm so sorry." I hadn't told anyone other than Barry and Jim about my own loss. Aleena knew, of course, but other than those three, no one else knew. I wanted to console her. "I did too." I said quietly.

Now she looked at me. "Oh Delila. I had no idea that anyone else had invested with Dean. Did Barry invest his entire retirement?"

I felt annoyed that she thought I wouldn't have any money of my own. "No. Barry didn't invest anything with him. Just me. I had a small fund from where I used to work." Suddenly, I began to worry who Nia might tell. I hadn't done anything wrong, but I didn't want everyone to know my personal business either. "Nia, I'd rather it didn't get around, if you know what I mean."

Nia gave a caring nod. "Of course." After a moment she said, "you know, he bled poor Aleena too. He asked her to lend him a ton of money. Drained her savings account. He also racked up a fortune on her credit cards."

I was stupefied. Here I had been so wrapped up in my own loss, it didn't even occur to me that Dean was the reason Aleena had shot through all her money. That he'd stolen from her too.

A car horn blared in the street, and I turned to see Chuck driving by. Nia waved.

"Chuck got a new car?" I asked incredulously.

"Yep, yesterday." Nia confirmed.

I wondered how Chuck had gone from flat broke to the owner of a brand-new car, almost overnight. Surely, he hadn't sold that much in the past week. "Wow." I managed to say.

Nia grinned at me. "Marvelous, isn't it?"

I arrived home and found Boris waiting at the door for me. He looked miffed, having been left behind for a few hours. I ruffled his head. "I'm sorry ole boy."

I'd missed lunch, and my stomach growled to remind me. I grabbed a cookie to hold me over and picked up the leash.

Having just been at the park, I decided to walk Boris over to Tilly's. I wanted to check in on her anyway. The temperature had risen considerably so I grabbed my visor before we headed out into the bright sunshine.

As we passed Aleena's house, I noticed the grass had not been mowed and the shrubs were looking scruffy. Her curtains were closed too. So much had changed in just a few weeks. Everything about her life had been turned upside down. I felt torn. Maybe I should be checking on Aleena too. Later, I told myself and kept walking.

Tilly opened the door, a blank look on her face as if she didn't fully recognize us at first. She looked tired, and the creases between her eyebrows seemed to have deepened. She invited us in and as always went to get Boris a treat. I could smell something delicious baking in the oven.

The stacks of boxes in the hallway had shrunk. "You must be making some progress." I said lightly, pointing to the pile.

She nodded. "Yes, we took a bunch of things to the Salvation Army."

Tilly led us to the living room, where we sat for a moment in awkward silence. I wasn't sure what to say. I wanted to know if she'd found her sister's pot of gold yet but couldn't just come right out and ask. Did her sister really have a big stash of money?

"What did your sister do?" I asked. "I mean her job."

"She worked at Sunray Trust Bank. The one in Cortland, not the branch here. She lived in Cortland you know. She was the vault clerk. She was so proud of her job."

The oven timer went off and Tilly hurried off to the kitchen.

While I waited, I tried to imagine her sister's life. Going to the bank every morning. Counting thousands of dollars all day long, and then coming home to her little apartment. Saving every penny. For what? Her retirement? Perhaps she loved the money for itself, not for what it could buy. Some people simply liked to hoard and count their money. Yes, I could picture her life. And even though

Cortland was only an hour drive from her sister, she must have been rather lonely.

Tilly reappeared holding a bag with something that smelled scrumptious. "Zucchini bread," she said handing me a piece.

That night I lay in bed with thoughts of Dean buzzing all around me. I pulled the covers up over my head but couldn't get him out of my mind.

I tossed and turned as I thought about him, convincing Aleena to give him all her money. And his "so called" wife and child, leaving them alone and probably broke too. And Rudy. And me. What had he done with all the money? Had he put it in a bank account somewhere? Would the police be able to find it?

As the possibilities flew through my head, I also thought of Barry. I could tell he was still upset with me for not confiding in him. But why should he be so upset when he wouldn't even discuss our finances?

And just as I started to fall asleep, Dean landed in my thoughts once again. I began thinking about the day I signed over my retirement. We were in his office, and he was grinning, I was grinning.

"Delila, you're making a smart move."

"Thanks Dean. I'm excited to watch this account grow." Intoxicated with my newfound independence, I wanted to celebrate.

As I signed the last piece of paper, Dean began to gasp for breath. Another asthma attack. He took out his inhaler and breathed in. A minute later, the attack subsided.

"Have you always had asthma?" I asked. The surprise on my face must have shown because he quickly tried to defuse my fears.

"Yes, since I was a kid. My parents had to move us to Arizona, it was so bad. Don't worry, I'm fine. Doctor Hurbis keeps me supplied with these babies." He held up his inhaler.

Those words came back to me now. That was it! Dr. Hurbis. In the morning I'd call and make an appointment with her. Maybe she could shed some light on things! And with that I fell sound asleep.

The next morning, after Barry left for work, I picked up the phone and made an appointment with Dr. Hurbis.

"Can you squeeze me in today? I promise I won't take long," I assured the receptionist. "I just really need to see her as soon as possible." I made it sound urgent, while at the same time not giving away my real reason for needing the appointment. The receptionist said the doctor could see me around noon.

Dr. Jane Hurbis and I had gone to school together. In high school we'd been good friends, however we'd gone to different colleges and life took us down separate paths. We remained friends, and occasionally met socially. But Jane was so busy, it was difficult to see her without an appointment in the office. I didn't want to overstep, but she might know something that could help.

We sat across from one another and had our usual conversation, Jane caught me up on her life, her kids. I knew we only had about ten minutes so, when it was my turn, I assured her we were all fine, then quickly dove into the story about Dean.

"Oh Delila, that's terrible!"

I nodded. "You know Jane, he was a patient of yours."

She looked directly at me. "Tobin Sullivan?" She asked. "It's been all over the news how he cheated women out of their money. I still can't believe it."

"Jane, can you tell me anything about him? He lied about so many things. He told us his name was Dean."

"I wish I could Delila. You know HIPPA prevents me from saying anything."

"I don't need his medical information. Maybe an address or something."

"Have you talked to his wife? Elsa Sullivan. She lives just down the street from me."

I know I was staring. Jane lived in Rhododendron Hills, the most prestigious neighborhood in town. That must mean he had another wife. Was that even possible? How many did he have?

As soon as I got home, I looked up Elsa Sullivan's address on the internet. I made up my mind to pay her a visit right after lunch, and after I took Boris for a quick walk.

There are a couple of up-scale neighborhoods in Aster Heights, Rhododendron Hills being by far the most affluent. I stopped at the gatehouse and told the gatekeeper I had an appointment with Mrs. Sullivan. I suppose because I dropped her name, he let me in. I drove through the gates into the posh streets, where houses were known as estates, and situated on one-acre perfectly manicured sites. No expense was spared in the building of these mansions. Was this where my money had gone?

Flowering shrubs and plants lined the long driveway, all the way up to the Sullivan's residence. I parked my car near the front of the house. I couldn't call it a house really. It was a palace. Apparently, this wife got the better end of the deal, I thought. Or had the house belonged to her to begin with, and she had been conned by Dean too?

I walked up to the front entrance. Once again, I found myself on unsure footing. What would I say to Elsa Sullivan? Suddenly I felt intimidated by the situation. But I had to try and get my money back, and this woman might just know where it was. I decided the truth would be my best option. I rang the doorbell.

It was a long minute before a uniformed woman answered. "May I help you?"

"I'm looking for Elsa Sullivan." I suddenly felt warm and nervous. "My name is Delila Clarke." I added.

"Do you have an appointment?" She screened me with her stern look.

"I'm sorry, I don't. I knew Mr. Sullivan." I hoped the little reference might get me past the doorkeeper.

"One moment." She closed the door.

I stood on the porch feeling out of place and anxious for what felt like an eternity. Finally, the maid returned to the door and ushered me into the great hallway. "Mrs. Sullivan will be with you in a moment."

A massive stairway loomed just beyond the hall. I'd been in beautiful homes before, but this was by far one of the most grandiose I'd ever seen. I tried to imagine what this 'Mrs. Sullivan' would be like.

I was admiring the large paintings and museum like artwork when I heard heals clicking on the Italian tile. I knew it was her making an entrance. I summed her up as I'm sure she was assessing me. Mid-fifties and confident. My guess was that she'd always lived a life of privilege. It seemed quite natural on her.

"I'm Elsa Sullivan, what can I do for you?" She did not extend a hand or much of a smile.

"Thank you for seeing me." I said in my most courteous voice, hoping to win her over. "I was a friend of De..., Tobin's."

She raised her eyebrows. "What is it you want Ms. Clarke?"

"Mrs. Sullivan, I'm not quite sure how to say this, I know this is not a good time and I'm sorry for your loss." I said, hoping all my pent-up nervousness wasn't showing. "I invested my entire retirement and some of my savings with Mr. Sullivan. Since that time, I've been unable to locate exactly where it went. I was hoping you could help me."

Elsa Sullivan looked me up and down. "Tobin never discussed his work with me." What little smile she'd had, now completely disappeared. Her blunt tone sounded dismissive.

"I understand, but I thought perhaps you could tell me where his office was or anything about the company he worked for—."

"Again, I don't know anything about his work. I'm sorry Ms. Clarke, I can't help you. Now if you'll excuse me, I have arrangements to make." She turned abruptly and walked away.

As I drove home, I wondered who could be married to someone and not know anything about their work? Clearly, she was lying to me. But why?

Nor did she seem to be especially sad that he was gone. I'd have been crying my eyes out if anything happened to Barry. I know not all married couples are close, but still, I would have thought she'd at least have been a little upset. Had she known about his other women?

I realized she hadn't asked me how I'd met Tobin, or anything about myself either. She must have wondered though. Or had others come to her with the same request? He'd taken Rudy's money and who knows how many others.

At home, Boris greeted me with a wagging tail, as if I'd been gone for weeks. I sat down on the couch and scratched him between the ears. I felt like such a loser. I'd lost my entire retirement and most of my savings. I'd probably never get it back. I betrayed my husband, my best friend. I'd trusted a con artist. How could I be so blind? So stupid? I wrapped my arms around Boris and let the tears roll.

Boris licked my face and seemed so worried that after a few minutes, I managed to stop crying. Why had Dean done this to us? How could he be so heartless? He'd hurt Aleena the most. Not only financially, but emotionally too. Well, I wouldn't give up. I wiped my tears, opened the back door and let Boris out.

I checked the time and saw that it was already four o'clock. Barry would be home around six, and probably hadn't had much of a lunch, so he'd be hungry. I looked through the fridge and cupboards for something to fix for dinner. Nothing sounded good. I decided on Chinese take-out. Barry and I still hadn't talked about things yet. In fact, we hadn't talked much at all since my confession. Maybe changing our usual dinner plans would help ease the tension.

As I thought about what to order, my cell phone started to buzz. The word 'Restricted' came up on the screen. Meaning it was someone I didn't know who preferred not to announce themselves. "Hello," I said cautiously.

"Hello, Ms. Clarke?" A male voice I didn't recognize, asked.

"Yes, who is this please?"

"This is Alec Sullivan. You asked me to call you?"

Stunned, I managed to squeak out a "Yes." How could it be? Had the woman with the baby found someone to pretend to be him, just to find out what I had? Or had I messed up and gotten the wrong person altogether?

"You told my wife you have something of mine? What is it? You've really got me curious."

"I...yes, I do." I admitted.

"Well, can we meet somewhere, and you can give it to me? I could come to your house."

I had to think. I certainly didn't want him coming here. Should I meet him at his house? That felt a little creepy. I could meet him at the Gossip Garden. But that would be too close to home. Tupelo Park then? No, too desolate. I also didn't have a lot of time.

"Can you meet me at The China House restaurant on Main St.? Say a little after five?" I asked. That way I could pick up dinner and meet him. It was a public place, so I'd feel safe. And it wasn't super crowded on a weeknight before six. He agreed.

I arrived early and placed my order to-go, requesting they wait until around 5:30 to have it ready. I chose a table where I could easily see the door and everyone who entered. I checked my purse; the credit card application was still there. The dim light of the restaurant had a calming effect on me.

A couple came in and the owner seated them. Then a man entered and looked around. From his profile I thought I must be seeing things. I stared at him. It couldn't be. Dean?

Unbelievable. Dean was dead, and yet this man looked just like him. I stood and waved him over to my table. As he came a little closer, I could see it wasn't really Dean. Yet, from a distance and in the dark lighting, I thought I'd seen a ghost. "Alec? I'm Delila Clarke."

We sat down and suddenly I wasn't sure where to start. "Are you," I began, "are you related to Tobin Sullivan?"

He seemed to withdraw slightly and put up his guard. "Why?"

"I knew him. We were friends." I couldn't stop staring. "At least, I thought we were friends. He was dating a friend of mine. Are you, his brother?"

"Do you have something of mine?"

"I do, but I was hoping to get some information. You see I knew him as Dean. He said he was a financial advisor."

"Ha! Sounds like my brother. Ms. Clarke, I'm sorry, but my brother was a con man." He softened his tone. "He's hurt a lot of people over the years. I'm sorry if he did anything to hurt you."

"Well, he invested my entire retirement plan. I can't, however, find where he invested it." I hoped maybe this brother could help shed some light on where the money had gone.

He gave me a look of pity before replying. "Ms. Clarke, my brother wasn't a financial advisor. He was just a con." He seemed genuinely sorry for me. "Have you asked his wife?"

"Yes. She wasn't any help." I pulled the application from my purse. "This is all I have for you. I found it at my friend's house after Dean, er Tobin, moved out. I was just trying to find out more about him. I'm sorry to drag you down here for nothing."

He took the paper from me and shook his head. "He must have stolen this from me and planned to take out another credit card in my name." We sat silently for a few minutes, the smell of Chinese food hanging in the air around us. "You know, I did care for my brother, even if he was a con." He looked at the paper. "And a thief."

"Do they know any more about his death? Was it an accident?" I asked.

"I don't think so. I don't think the police have found whatever he was sprayed with, and he wouldn't have sprayed himself. Tobin never used those kinds of pesticides because of his asthma."

I watched him leave the restaurant and thought how difficult it must have been having someone like Dean for a brother. I wished I'd asked him if his brother had always been like that. Then I realized I was right back to square one. Nowhere. I still had no idea where my money had gone. But I did think more about what had happened to Dean. There must have been plenty of people who wanted him dead.

A bag of hot Chinese food was plopped down in front of me. I took the food and headed home. Barry and I had enjoyed many dinners at The China House over the years. Maybe the Moo Shu Chicken, fried rice, and chopsticks would help ease the strain between us.

The dinner started ok. It felt like we'd broken off a few pieces of the iceberg that had grown between us. However, when we'd nearly finished the meal, Barry cleared his throat and looked down at his plate.

"I spoke with our accountant this morning. I told her about your retirement account." He paused to consider how he would phrase what he wanted to tell me. "She says we have sixty days from the time you withdrew the money to roll it into another retirement account, or pay a ten percent penalty on the money, plus the tax."

My appetite vanished. I set my chopsticks down. "I'm sorry. I never would have done it if I'd known—"

He put his hand up to stop me from saying more. "I know. I know. I'm just letting you know what she said."

The following morning after Barry left for work, I sat down and figured out how much that ten percent penalty would be. Plus, the additional tax. It would wipe out everything I had left in my account, and we might have to take some out of our joint savings to cover the rest.

My phone rang and pulled me out of my own head. It was our attorney. Unfortunately, he didn't have good news to offer either. "I'm sorry Delila. It's a homicide investigation now. Apparently, there is a long list of people this guy conned. And he doesn't seem to have any assets."

After we'd hung up, my thoughts lingered on the words 'homicide investigation'. I guess I had suspected all along that there was something wrong about his death. I knew he'd been sprayed with a strong insect repellant. Someone must have known about his asthma and that a spray like that could kill him. But who would do it?

There were plenty of people who might want him dead, he'd cheated so many. But why kill him? Why not expose him and send him to prison? Force him to give the money back.

He doesn't seem to have any assets. The words hummed through my mind as I finished vacuuming. How could he not have assets when he'd taken Aleena's, Rudy's, and my money? And who knew how many others? What had he done with it? Not even a bank account? And where had he gone after he left Aleena's? Back to his wife? I felt frustrated with so many questions and so few answers.

As I finished cleaning the kitchen, I noticed my gym card, stuck on the refridgerator with a magnet. I hadn't used it in several days. Maybe the gym was what I needed. Later, I told myself.

I called Jim and asked if he could join Barry and me for dinner. It had been Barry's idea to invite him; to learn if there were any updates in the case. Jim, being single, always enjoyed a home cooked meal. He agreed to come around seven.

Boris needed a walk, and so did I. The losses were wearing on me. The loss of my retirement. The loss of Barry's trust. The loss of my own naive trust in others. I kissed Boris on the head and hooked up his leash. He wagged his tail. At least he still loved me.

As we walked along the sidewalk, the sun made me squint and wish I'd remembered my sunglasses. We headed for the Gossip Garden. I hoped someone might be there. Someone with new information, good news. But when we arrived, we found the park empty. I sat alone at the picnic table, and let Boris enjoy all his favorite smells.

Meditation can be good for the soul. I let my mind be silent for several minutes. When my brain could no longer be silent, I let my thoughts run free. They kept running over my meeting with Dean. The day I'd turned over my account. I closed my eyes and tried to picture his office, the way it was that day. I saw the pictures on his desk. One of him and Aleena, another of him at a younger age. His key ring with lots of keys. A small black leather appointment book.

Then my thoughts drifted to Aleena. I'd been angry with her for bringing Dean into our lives. In some ways, I'd blamed her for my problems. Now I thought maybe she'd been hurt more than any of us. It wasn't her fault a con man had infiltrated her life. Had stolen not only her money, but her heart. I still had my home, financial security, and my precious Barry. I had been so caught up in my own problems, why hadn't I thought about what Aleena was going through?

The scene at her house played over in my mind. Had I been heartless when I spoke with her? I'd been blunt. Had I made her feel like it was her fault? I couldn't remember my exact words, but I knew they weren't kind.

"Come on Boris." I tugged at his leash. Reluctantly, he pulled himself away from the flowers.

I dropped him off at home before heading to the coffee shop to pick up some scones and two double lattes. Aleena's favorite.

My car rolled up to the curb in front of her house. The yard, still un-mowed, had numerous new dandelions growing. The curtains were drawn, and the house looked dark. I rang the bell and waited. I rang it again. I thought the bell might not be working, so I banged on the door.

A haggard-looking Aleena answered. She seemed to lack energy to even open the door.

"Hi Aleena. I've got coffee and scones!" I held up the bag.

"Sorry, I don't feel like talking to anyone." She started to close the door.

"Aleena, please let me come in."

"Look, I know I screwed up and ruined everything. I didn't mean to hurt anyone. I had no idea he was a con man. Please go away."

"That's not why I came. I just want to make sure you're ok." I didn't know how I could make her understand that I wanted to help her.

"Ok. You've done your civic duty; you can go now." Again, she tried to close the door, but I pressed against it with my elbow -to prevent her from shutting me out.

"At least take the coffee and scones." I pleaded. "Along with my apology for having been so insensitive last time I was here."

She opened the door, sighed, and motioned for me to come in.

"Sorry, I'm not dressed yet." She pulled her robe tighter as we sat down at the kitchen table.

"That's ok. I should have called first. But I was afraid you'd tell me not to come." I opened the bag, pulled out a coffee and handed it to her.

"That's exactly what I would have said." She took a sip of coffee.

"You've been through so much. I'm sorry I haven't been a better friend to you during this time."

"Thank you." Aleena said softly. "I'm sorry Dean stole your money. I had no idea he was running a Ponzi scam."

"I know." I pushed a scone in her direction.

"When I met him, I thought he was the greatest guy I'd ever met. He was kind and funny. And so darned good looking!" She reminisced. "He took me to the big city, to fancy restaurants and nightclubs." She took a sip of coffee, then continued. "We even took a weekend trip to Toronto to see a play. He was so charming." She was quiet for a minute. "He told me stories about when he was in the air force. I guess he must have made them up. He was a good liar." She looked up at me. "Did you know he had a wife the whole time he was living with me?"

"I heard." I wasn't ready to share everything I knew with her yet.

"He told me he wanted to marry me. Even bought me an engagement ring." She seemed to think about this for a moment. "I wonder if he used my money to buy it?"

"Do you still have it?" I asked.

"No, I gave it back to him when we broke up. I was stupid. I drained my bank account to invest with him too. All the money I got from my divorce. Now I don't know how I'm going to pay my bills. I need to find a job."

"I'm still hoping we can get our money back. If we can find where it went. I'm sure he didn't spend it all in that short of a time."

Suddenly I had an idea. "Come with me to the gym tomorrow. You can come as my guest. They have job openings. If you like it, you could apply there."

Aleena shook her head. "No. I'm not ready for that yet." She picked up her cup and dumped the rest of her coffee in the sink. "I'm really tired." She yawned.

I took my cue. "Ok, but if you change your mind, call me."

Jim arrived on time as usual. Barry was in the back, getting the grill ready, and I was putting the finishing touches on the salad. He looked so different without his uniform. Relaxed and casual. And he was attractive and young. I'd thought about asking if he wanted to bring a date. But I'd been preoccupied thinking about the case.

"Barry's at the grill," I said, and led him to the patio. "Can I get you something to drink?" I felt excited. There were so many questions I wanted to ask him. But I'd wait. After all I didn't want to overwhelm him. It wouldn't be fair to blast him with a barrage of inquiries the minute he walked in the door.

It was a beautiful evening. We sat at the patio table- as the sun set in the background.

Barry kept us amused with stories from his week at work. One of his patients, a middle-aged woman, was in severe pain from a toothache. Unfortunately, she was terrified of the dentist.

"Everyone in the office tried to calm and reassure her. The woman literally had tears running down her face," he told us. "She wailed so loudly, we thought she was going to upset the other patients. She insisted her husband be by her side so she could hold his hand. Made him pull a chair up right next to her. The husband sat so close there was no room for my assistant." Barry looked animated as he spoke. "Then, when I leaned in to look at the tooth, her husband stood to look too, and knocked right into my head." He rubbed his head to show us where he was hit. We all laughed.

As dinner came to an end, I brought out the key lime pie I'd made earlier in the day, along with the whipped cream. "Pie anyone?" I watched Jim's eyes light up.

"So, Jim," Barry began. "Delila spoke with our lawyer, and he says Dean's...I mean Tobin Sullivan's death is now considered a homicide."

Jim nodded his head and pressed on the tip of the whipped cream can, swirling the cream in a large pile on top of his pie.

"The lawyer told me that the guy was a con man and ran a Ponzi scheme, but that the police hadn't found any assets the guy owned." I added.

Jim nodded again. "That's what I heard too. I'm not really on the case. I passed your statement on to them, but that's all I could do really." He took a large bite of pie.

"So, he didn't have any bank accounts or anything?" I asked.

Jim swallowed, "well, like I said, I'm not working this case, so I don't really know all the details. But I don't think they've found anything."

"Delila spoke to his wife. She lives in Rhododendron Hills." Barry offered.

"The house is huge. And she has a lot of money. Have they talked to her? Do you think she has the money he took?" I was hopeful.

"I really don't know, but I think the house belongs to her, and that she has her own accounts. But really, I don't know." Jim shoveled another bite of pie into his mouth. "This pie is really good."

The following morning, I finished clearing the breakfast dishes, sat down, and stared out the kitchen window. Pesky little questions fluttered around in my head. Where had Dean gone after he moved out of Aleena's house? Someone must have told her about him... Who? But mostly, where had he stashed all the money?

Boris walked over and sat down next to me. He placed his paw on my knee and raised his eyebrows.

I grinned. He was the only one who could pull me out of the rut I was falling into. "Ok, ok. Let's go for a walk." I hooked up his leash and knew the walk would do us both good.

As we approached the park, I saw a bright pink hat and a little red poodle.

"Hi Delila," Mitzi smiled when she saw me, and her poodle ran over to greet Boris.

"Hi Mitzi. How are things with you?" I reached down and unhooked Boris's leash. When they were young, the two dogs loved to run around the park and chase one another. But now, they seemed content to peruse the park for the variety of interesting smells it offered. They touched noses, then Boris meandered over to sniff a large rock.

Mitzi lifted the flap of her hat to get a better look at me. "I'm great, thank you for asking. I heard you joined the gym?"

"Yeah. But I haven't been going. I tried to get Aleena to go with me."

"Aww. Aleena's been having a hard time. I've tried to get her out too. She feels so bad about everything that happened."

We both sat down at the picnic table under the shade of the pavilion. Mitzi took the large hat off and set it down. After a moment of silence, I asked the question that had been pestering me for so long.

"Mitzi, I was thinking, I mean, I was wondering, where do you think Dean went when he moved out of Aleena's house?"

"Oh, I know exactly where he went. Ned and I saw him with his rich wife at a fundraising dinner about a week after he and Aleena split up." Mitzi took her sunglasses off and set them down on the table next to her hat, then continued her story. "You can imagine how surprised Ned and I were! But we never gave on."

"Really? How do you know the woman was his wife?"

"It turns out, Ned's sister, Lena, is best friends with the woman." Mitzi explained. "I don't think he was happy going back to her, however."

Mitzi had a grin on her face I'd seen many times. The one she wore when she was about to share something. The grin that said, 'this is pure gossip'. I leaned in.

"At the fundraiser, he wore a forced smile, and it looked like he was just pacifying the woman. More like an escort, if you know what I mean. She's not as pretty as Aleena you know. Plus, Lena told me his wife wasn't sure she wanted to take him back. I guess she knew about the affair."

In the corner of my eye, I spotted Boris start to dig a hole. "Hey. Boris. Stop it!" I yelled to him, then turned back to Mitzi, "Wow. Do you think his wife has the money? I mean, maybe he left it at her house."

"I don't think so. She told Lena that the police searched her place."

"Did they find anything?"

"She didn't say, but I don't think so. That lady is a smart cookie. If she'd found Dean's stash, she'd have put it somewhere safe." Mitzi glanced in the direction of the dogs.

"That would be a lot of money to hide." I wanted to continue with the conversation. I wasn't worried about the dogs. "He must have had at least a couple of million, maybe twice that."

Mitzi nodded. "Yeah, that's a lot of cash. It would be hard to hide that much."

"If it were all in $100 bills, a million dollars would fit into a normal size carryon suitcase."

Mitzi's eyes grew wide.

"I googled it." I explained.

She threw her head back and we both laughed. "Of course. So, we're thinking there were between one and four carryon suitcases full of $100 bills."

"Right." I agreed. We sat in silence, visions of cash in suitcases filling our thoughts.

"I suppose he could have hidden it in the walls." Mitzi suggested. "But that would mean construction, and the staff might have noticed that."

"And I can't imagine Dean digging a hole big enough to put all those suitcases in the back yard." I grinned.

"Well, if he put it in a bank account, the authorities would know about it. So, what did he do with it?" Mitzi pondered.

"And does his wife know?" I added, still deep in thought. I hadn't noticed Boris come up next to me but felt his cold nose against my leg. "So, you don't think they were in on it together? Dean and the wife?" Thoughts began to form in my mind. Maybe Mitzi could find out more from Ned's sister.

"Ah!" Mitzi yelled. "Look at the sky! I think we better get going."

I looked up to see the dark clouds racing toward us.

Boris and I returned home just as giant drops began to fall from the sky. "Wow! That was a close one!" I panted. We had run half of the way home. I wasn't used to cardio exercise, and now I could feel my heart pounding hard.

I gave Boris his cookie and looked at the clock. It was almost noon. I fixed myself a sandwich and sat down to eat my lunch. My mind began to wander as I thought about Mitzi's revelation. Dean's wife had known about Aleena. She must have been upset with him, but he convinced her to take him back. Maybe he offered to share the money with her. But then again, he may have been conning her too. In that case, it was unlikely that he would share the money or leave it where she could find it. That meant it could be anywhere.

The realization that the money may never be recovered frightened me. As if getting back the money were the only way to get my own life back and restore my marriage. I wanted Barry to look at me the way he did before. To feel the warmth of his affection, not mistrust and suspicion.

I knew what I had to do. Slowly, I walked into my bedroom. I pulled down the lock box from the top of my closet and set it on the bed. The key turned easily, and the box popped open.

Inside were some pieces of jewelry I'd inherited as well as a few thousand dollars. I could deposit the cash in our account to cover the taxes. I looked at the jewelry. I'd planned on giving it to a future daughter-in-law, or perhaps a granddaughter someday. Now I contemplated selling it to cover our losses.

It wasn't necessary. Barry and I had the money in our joint savings account. But guilt pushed me toward making a sacrifice. I pulled the pearl necklace from the box and wondered what it was worth. Then I picked up my grandmother's garnet ring. I locked the box back up and placed it back on the shelf.

There. I thought I could make things up to Barry by selling some of my most precious jewelry. But I also needed to help Aleena now. Afterall, I had added to her suffering. I picked up the phone and dialed her number.

Much to my surprise, Aleena agreed to go to the gym. "I'm not going to be there very long," I'd assured her. "I have to get back in time to cook dinner."

An hour later we were making our rounds on all the equipment. By the time we finished, both Aleena and I felt a little better.

On the way home she confided, "I'm so glad you invited me. I really needed to get out of the depression den I've been in for the past couple of weeks."

"I'm glad you came too," I admitted. "I needed the motivation!"

"You know, when I first found out about Dean...well, I didn't believe it. And then I started thinking about all the times he had to go to meetings and out-of-town conferences. Then I thought about him borrowing money for this reason or that. And wanting me to invest with his company."

I made the turn into our neighborhood. "So, how did you find out about him?" I asked. We pulled into her driveway. I listened with interest as Aleena filled me in on who had sounded the alarm and her final days with Dean.

I took out some veggies and began chopping. The workout had energized me and making something special for Barry's dinner seemed like a good way to begin trying to regain his trust. Barry loves lasagna, but it must be put together in a special way and with a variety of vegetables. It takes a lot of effort to do it his way, and it would be worth the time if it helped us connect. I learned long ago that relationships are made up of a lot of little things. Spoken words are fine when there are plenty of 'little things' to support them.

By the time he got home, the aroma of the hot pasta had filled the house. Barry was drawn into the kitchen, nose first. He made a special point of sniffing the air and smiled. "Smells great! When do we eat?"

Based on the size of his second helping, I could tell he had enjoyed the lasagna. I hoped his favorite meal would mend the awkwardness in our communication. And we did enjoy small talk throughout dinner. But after he finished eating, Barry went directly to his study. I finished cleaning up the kitchen then sat down and started looking through the photos on my cell phone.

The last pictures I'd taken were at the euchre party. Mitzi and Ned, their arms wrapped around each other, forehead to forehead, as if about to kiss. Chuck, big smile, his arm proudly around Kitty's waist. Rudy sitting at the table, his cards held tight against his chest with one hand, and a thumbs up with the other. Nia bent down next to him. Both smiling at the camera. And Aleena and Dean standing next to one another at the bar, grinning and holding up their drinks. We were all so happy that night.

It irritated me to think that the entire time he had been playing us. All of us. Was it that he was so clever? Or were we just so naïve and trusting? I pushed the thought aside. No point in going over and over it. I wanted to know where the money was. And who killed him.

I studied the picture intently. I enlarged the photo to have a closer look at Dean. His face. His body. His shoes. I looked at the two of them together.

I thought about the massive house in Rhododendron Hills. That incredible staircase. The Italian tile and enormous paintings on the walls. The maids. The woman in designer clothes.

What had Mitzi said? He wore a forced smile, and it looked like he was just pacifying the woman. In that case, she probably wasn't in on it with him. She might even be another victim herself. Besides, the police had searched the house without finding anything.

I heard Barry turn on the television in the living room and joined him to watch the late news. I curled up on the couch, while he sat comfortably in his chair. We listened to the usual car accident and a burglary in a subdivision across town. The weather report showed mostly sunny days for the coming week. But then a small segment on Dean's murder case brought both of us to full attention.

"Police are still investigating the murder of Tobin Sullivan, the man found dead in Tupelo Park." The reporter stood with the area of Tupelo Park where Dean had been murdered. "His body had been heavily sprayed with diethyltoluamide, also known as DEET, often found in mosquito repellent. Mr. Sullivan was asthmatic and suffered a fatal attack from the heavy concentration of chemicals. Police have also learned that Mr. Sullivan had been involved in a Ponzi scheme and had conned dozens of people out of their retirement and savings accounts. It is unknown if he was working with others, however police believe he worked alone. So far none of the stolen money has been recovered. Police are still putting together the pieces and are looking for any help from the community. If you have any information regarding the case or Mr. Sullivan, who sometimes went by other names, please contact your local police. Channel seven, action news. Back to you."

So that was it, nothing new really. We finished watching the sports, then went in to get ready for bed.

"Is that your grandmother's jewelry on the dresser?" Barry asked.

I explained my plan to sell the jewelry and pay the taxes we owed, but he shook his head.

"No Delila. We have enough to cover the taxes without you selling your family heirlooms. Someday we may have grandchildren, and you'll want to pass them on. You need to put those away."

"Ok." I was grateful that he understood. "But I am going to put this cash in the bank to cover some of the expense." I returned the jewelry to the box, leaving the cash on the dresser. I locked the box and set it back on the shelf. I stood there in the closet and closed my eyes. I squeezed the key in my hand.

Barry was so good to me. I should have known he'd never let me sell them. Relief. I could feel the little points of the key pressed into my skin. I opened my eyes and studied it. It wasn't a normal sized key, but smaller. Something stirred in the back of my mind. Where had a seen a key like this before?

"Are you coming to bed?" Barry called.

I turned off the light and slipped in next to him.

*I*n the morning, after Barry had gone, I waited impatiently for the bank to open. And although it only takes ten minutes to get there, I was in the car and on my way at a quarter to nine.

I waited in my car for the Sunray Trust employee to unlock the doors. A few customers had gathered in front, ready to enter as soon as the doors opened. I joined the others, anxious to make my deposit.

"Good morning Mrs. Clarke, how are you?" The teller greeted me with a smile.

I always liked that about our bank. All the tellers knew me by name, and greeted me warmly, like we were old friends. I guessed they were encouraged to do so by management, but it still felt sincere.

The teller processed my deposit and chatted on about her sick father who had just moved in with her, and her not so understanding husband. She handed me the receipt and I wished her good luck in dealing with her family.

Back in my car, I looked over my receipt. My little deposit might not cover all the additional taxes, but it would cover some.

Through the bank's large glass windows, I could see my teller, busy cleaning up the lobby area. It was interesting, I thought, how people could share so much personal information with a stranger. Well, I suppose I wasn't really a *complete* stranger. After all, she'd seen me enough times. And she must know something about my finances. But still. I wondered how much I shared with others. With people I barely knew.

For whatever reason, that teller struck me with a thought. Someone else may have shared their life with a stranger. And it may have had fatal consequences. I toyed with the idea for several minutes, turned it over and over in my mind. Was it possible? There was only one way to find out. I started the engine and pulled out of the parking lot.

Boris stood looking out the window when the car pulled into the driveway. My inquiries would have to wait until after his walk.

Mitzi and Nia were deep in conversation when we arrived at the park and didn't hear us approach.

"Hi ladies, mind if I join you?"

"Of course not," Nia said, but looked at Mitzi, as if for reassurance.

"Actually, we were talking about...the case." Mitzi leaned in closer and lowered her voice. "I was telling Nia, - that Ned's sister, Lena, told me the police believe Dean's wife has some of the money."

"Really?" It was difficult to contain my excitement. "So, we might recover some of our money after all?"

"Isn't that great?" Nia folded her hands as if in prayer. "I can't wait to tell Rudy."

"But how do they know? I mean I thought they searched her house and didn't find anything." I blurted out.

"That's true," Mitzi said. "But I guess when they questioned the servants, they found out she had recently bought a bunch of expensive paintings. Like a million dollars' worth of paintings. Of course, she's got a lawyer, so we'll see what happens." Mitzi turned to Nia. "I wouldn't get Rudy too excited about it yet, Nia, just in case."

As soon as we got home from the park, I rang my attorney. Maybe, just maybe, there was a chance to recover some of my lost retirement. Yet, even as I left a message with his secretary, I knew the chances were slim. Dean had stolen millions, yet it sounded as if only a million dollars in artwork had been discovered. I wondered where I was on the list to get some of the recovered money. Where were Rudy and Aleena on the list? And who else was on that list?

Several million dollars unaccounted for. Had Dean's wife found that money as well? I pictured her in my mind. Mrs. Tobin Sullivan, in her massive house wearing her high-fashion clothing, draped in diamonds and rubies, living her posh lifestyle. I thought about her finding the money and deciding to buy expensive paintings to hide from the police. All the while knowing that the money had been stolen. That it belonged to people like me and Rudy, who had saved it up for years, for our retirement.

It must have crossed her mind. All the people who'd been hurt. People like Rudy who might never get to retire now and may have to work the rest of his life. And Aleena, who would need to pull herself from the deep depression she'd fallen into and go back to work. And all because they trusted in someone. The wrong someone.

I couldn't help but wonder if Mrs. Sullivan had ever worked. Had she ever known what it was like to depend on a job to survive? Had she ever lost everything with no place to turn? Why hadn't she turned the money in to the police? What role had she played in this game of hide and seek?

Then my mind drifted back to the bank teller. How she had unwittingly told me so much about herself. I realized how easy it was to learn people's secrets. Like Ned's sister sharing Mrs. Sullivan's business with Mitzi. Not knowing that Mitzi's friends were involved in the case.

Could I learn more if I got the right people to talk? Would they tell me, a stranger, things they wouldn't say to the police? Or would the police even think to ask? Maybe. It was worth a try. I pulled up the map and directions on my phone and headed for the door. It would take a few hours, but my had-to-know adrenalin had already kicked in.

Driving back home gave me plenty of time to think about all I'd learned from my excursion. Dean was a con man no doubt, and easily tricked people into seeing him in the role he needed them to. We believed him because we wanted to. Were we greedy? Or did he just make it possible for us to believe in our fantasies?

Aleena had visions of Mister Right. He was the prince charming in her own personal fairytale. For Rudy, Dean was the financial whiz who could make his retirement goals happen overnight. And for me, he was an independence maker. Yes, he fed our fantasies, but then he stole our money, and our future with it.

I stopped at a red light, mechanically pressed the brake pedal. The surroundings were familiar, but I barely noticed. I was still deep in thought.

When we learned that we'd been cheated, we reacted. With anger. I've heard that depression is anger turned inside out. They go hand in hand. We'd all waffled between the two, anger and depression. We looked to blame. Blame Dean for lying and stealing. Blame Aleena for bringing him into our lives. Blame the world for allowing it all to happen.

The light changed to green, and the car began to move again. I pictured Aleena, innocent and vulnerable, the day she learned about Dean. Her whole life shattered, financially as well as emotionally. Aleena, sweet and trusting.

Then it hit me. Aleena! Suddenly I accelerated. There was no time to waste. I pushed on the pedal. My destination only minutes away, the car sped forward, seconds beating in my chest.

I pulled up in front of the house and put the car into park. I pressed hard on the bell, and then pressed a second time.

"What..." Aleena opened the door, and I bolted in past her and quickly closed the door. I pulled out my phone and texted Jim.

"Aleena, you could be in danger. I don't have time to explain. I want you to lock all the doors and wait until my friend Jim, who is a police officer, gets here." I took a long breath. "Don't open the door for anyone except Jim! You might not be safe. Honestly, wait for him. He'll be in uniform." I gave her a short description of Jim before walking back out of the front door. I waited to make sure she'd locked it after me.

Then I walked to Tilly's house. Before I went up the steps to her front door, I messaged Jim again. I explained as much as I could in a text and hoped he could get there quickly enough. Taking a deep breath, I walked up the three steps to Tilly's porch and rang her bell.

A minute went by before Tilly answered. "Hello Delila." She seemed genuinely surprised to see me. "How nice of you to stop by." She looked around. "No Boris today?"

"No, not today."

"Well, come in." Tilly opened the door for me to enter.

I hesitated. Should I go in? I glanced down the street toward Aleena's house. Tiny beads of sweat formed along my hairline. Beyond Tilly, I could see her husband Jack watching us. I forced a smile.

"Well...come in." Tilly said again.

We sat looking at one another, me in a chair, and Tilly on the sofa. For some reason I found it difficult to speak. I didn't know where to start.

"Is everything ok Delila?" She asked. "You don't look well. Let me get you something to drink. Water or tea?"

"No, no. I'm fine. Tilly," I began. "I went to the bank this afternoon." I watched her face. "The Sunray Trust Bank... in Cortland." I looked around nervously for Jack.

Tilly raised her eyebrows. "Why?"

"Well, I wondered. I remembered you saying your sister had been seeing someone who broke her heart. And that she worked at the Sunray Trust in Cortland. And that you couldn't find what happened to all her money..."

She was silent, waiting for me to continue. Her eyes were intense, piercing.

"So, then I thought...well... maybe she had been a victim of Dean too." I swallowed hard.

"What are you saying Delila?" I heard the chill in Tilly's voice. "You think my sister was seeing Dean?"

"Yes. I know she was. I drove out to Cortland today. To the Sunray Bank, where your sister worked. I showed them a picture of Dean."

Jack stood just outside the room, peering in on us. Listening.

"But you knew that, didn't you?" I continued. "You warned Aleena. That day in the coffee shop. You told her how your sister had been swindled by him. But she didn't want to believe you. Then you showed her the pictures of the two of them. The ones you found on your sister's phone."

Tilly stiffened. Her eyes grew wider. Still, she said nothing.

"When you found out that Dean had been the one who broke your sister's heart, drove her to suicide, stole all her money, and that he was doing the same to Aleena, you must have been livid. I know, I would have been."

Jack came into the room. "I think you'd better go now." His voice was stern. Commanding.

I looked at Tilly. "Tell me," I said quietly. "Tell me the truth. That's when you decided to confront him, isn't it? When you realized Aleena might end up just like your sister."

A tear trickled down Tilly's face, and she wiped it away.

"He was a monster. A blood sucking parasite, preying on innocent women. My sister worked her whole life, saved every penny. She went without so that she could enjoy a wonderful retirement. She'll never have that now. He cut her life short. He as much as killed her himself!" She covered her face with her hands and wept.

After a few moments, I said, "tell me what happened that night Tilly. In the park. How did you get him to meet you there?"

Tilly wiped her face with her hands. "I had his phone number from Aleena. I lied to him. Said he'd left something behind at Aleena's, and she wanted me to give it to him."

"Tilly, stop. Don't say anything more." Jack cut in.

"Jack, I have to tell her. I can't keep it in anymore. I didn't mean for it to happen, but I'm not sorry. He can't hurt any other innocent women now." She looked at Jack. "I am sorry for all that I've put you through, Jack."

Jack sat down next to her and put his arm around her.

Tilly turned back to me. "He agreed to meet me there, that night in Tupelo Park. At first, I was just going to talk to him. Try and get my sister's money back, and Aleena's too. But I kept thinking about how he'd hurt my sister. How he'd sucked the money out of her, then dumped her. I kept thinking how devastated she was, picturing her killing herself that day. I couldn't stand it. I'd thought about it before; when I first found out it was him. How he was like a mosquito sucking everyone's blood." She stopped to wipe her eyes with a tissue. "We argued."

She leaned her head against Jack. He took her hand in his. After a moment she sat upright again and continued her story. "I asked him what he'd done with the money, but he wouldn't tell me. He said my sister gave it to him. All of it, so it was his. When I told him she'd killed herself, he just looked at me and said, 'So? What do you want me to do about it?' I didn't mean to kill him. I didn't know he was asthmatic. I was just so angry. I thought I'd just show him what happens to parasites. That's when I sprayed him. I just kept spraying him." She looked down at her hands.

"He started coughing and choking. He fell to the ground. I just stood there watching him. He couldn't breathe. I didn't know what to do." She closed her eyes. "I should have called an ambulance, I suppose. But honestly, I didn't want to. He'd made my sister suffer. He'd made Aleena suffer. I thought he should suffer too. Then, I was scared. I ran. Left him there, choking. I didn't know he would die."

None of us said anything for a long time. We didn't look at one another. Poor Tilly. So, it was an accident really. I wondered if the police would charge her with murder. If a jury would convict her, put her in prison for the rest of her life. She had killed him after all. And she had intended to hurt him.

My phone was nestled in my hand. I could see that Jim had returned my message.

A few minutes went by, allowing us time to digest the situation. Finally, I broke the silence. "Tilly, would you be willing to tell the police what you just told me? It wasn't intentional. You didn't mean to kill him. You need to tell them." I waited a moment before going on. "I have a friend who is a police officer. He's at Aleena's house right now. Would it be ok if I asked him to come over?"

I placed a final large shrimp on the skewer next to the green pepper and set it on the plate with the others.

"Wow, they look beautiful Delila!" Barry slid an arm around my waist, snuggled up to me and kissed my neck. Then he asked, "What time did you say Jim and Aleena were coming?"

Barry and I have always enjoyed entertaining. It's something we like to do together. Planning the menu, and bouncing ideas off each other, trying to come up with just the right food and drinks.

For this occasion, we had decided on beef, chicken, shrimp, and scallop shish kabobs. We were both excited.

"They'll be here in about a half hour." I smiled, enjoying the moment. I returned his kiss, then took the plate of skewers and put them in the refrigerator. "Is the grill ready? Don't you need to hook up that new propane tank?"

"Yeah." Barry grinned.

I heard the doorbell and quickly wiped my hands.

Chuck stood on the porch smiling, his new car still running in the driveway.

"Delila how are you?" he asked, a broad smile plastered across his face.

"I'm fine, how are you?" I asked as I opened the door a little further.

"Great! What do you think of my new car?" His happy salesman face still in place. "I just wanted to let you know I'm working for BMW of Aster Heights now. They let me drive this beauty, and I can tell you, it's the best car I've ever driven. Pure luxury! Now, if you're thinking about getting a new car, let me know, OK? I'll get you a great deal." Chuck shoved a business card at me.

"Ok, thanks Chuck." I took the card. He flashed his salesman smile at me, but it was the grin in his eye that said he was truly happy.

"I'm still selling the vitamins and other stuff too, so if you need more, just say the word." He chuckled then turned and headed for the shining new BMW.

A few minutes later Jim and Aleena drove up. Aleena wore a new sundress that looked incredible on her. They linked arms as they waltzed up the sidewalk. Jim too looked great, and I guessed it might be the I'm-proud-to-be-with-this-beautiful-woman smile he was wearing.

Everyone relaxed around the pool with drinks, and although the food and barbeque grill were ready, we were in no rush to start cooking. Jim and Aleena pulled their chairs next to one another, and I felt like a successful matchmaker.

"I started teaching classes at the gym this week," Aleena said, "and I love it!" She looked from me to Jim. She went on to tell us about her Zumba class and encouraged me to join.

Barry finally began grilling and I looked at Jim. I felt I'd waited long enough, and it was fair to start asking him all the questions that had been building up for the past several days.

"Have they charged Tilly?"

"Yeah. They charged her with manslaughter. She's lucky. But she will probably still do some jail time." Jim said.

"I really wish she hadn't killed him." Aleena spoke very softly. "I mean, he deserved to be in prison for what he did, but not dead." We were all silent waiting for her to continue. "Besides, now we may never find the money. Delila and Rudy may never get their retirement money back. Me either."

"Well actually," Jim began. "We may not recover all of it. He spent some, as did his wife. But Delila gave us a great lead. She figured out where a lot of the money was stashed."

They all looked at me.

"It was there? How much did they find?" I heard the squeak in my voice. It was all I could do to contain my excitement.

"I think there was around two and a half million. Maybe more."

"Woo!" Barry exclaimed. "Looks like you might get to retire after all Delila!"

We all laughed.

"Yeah, along with what his wife had stashed in those paintings. Is she going to be charged for that?" I asked.

"No." Jim shook his head. "In fact, I'm not sure that money will ever be recovered. There may be no way to prove where she got the money to buy that artwork."

"But we know..." Aleena stared at him.

"There's no evidence." Jim said. "Without proof, it doesn't matter if she took the money or not."

"So where was the rest of the money?" Barry asked, pulling a skewer of shish kabobs from the grill.

Jim motioned for me to tell my story.

I looked at Aleena. "You remember how Dean always had that big wad of keys? I never really thought about them much, but I kept looking at a picture of him and remembering his keys. They weren't like normal house keys. They were smaller, squattier keys. While I was unlocking my own safe box, I was reminded of his keys. Then when I was at the bank, I asked to see their safety deposit keys. I thought he probably felt that would be the safest place to keep his money. If he left it at your house or his wife's house, someone might find it. But no one could get into a safety deposit box without his permission." I gave Jim my most-grateful look. "Or a court order."

"I'm impressed Delila." Barry spoke up.

"You should be too!" Jim grinned. "She even figured out which bank to check first. How did you know?" He asked.

"I realized Dean must have met Tilly's sister as a customer of the Cortland Sunray Trust Bank. So, I figured he couldn't use a regular bank account, or his wife could gain access to it. But he might have had a safety deposit box there." I felt proud that I had figured it out.

"Yeah, well it was more than one box. It was several." Jim added.

"How much of the money he stole was recovered?" Aleena asked.

"I don't know for sure. At least half of it, maybe more. We still have ladies coming in that say he conned them too." Jim took Aleena's hand.

"Does that mean Delila and I might not get our money back?" Disappointment cracked through Aleena's voice.

Jim shrugged his shoulders. "It's hard to say. I guess it's up to the court to decide."

"I'm sorry, Delila."

"Oh Aleena, it's not your fault! Anyway, I'm fortunate that I have Barry. And, I have some good news." I said, hoping to brighten things up. "I'm going to start a new retirement fund. I got a job!"

Jim and Aleena both looked at me in surprise.

"I'm going to be working part-time at the church. As a bookkeeper."

"That's wonderful Delila!" Aleena seemed as excited as I was with the news.

Barry carried the platter of shish kabob's over to the patio table. "Come on over and get a plate."

We sat down around the food and began to fill our plates. Barry sat next to me. Under the table, where no one else could see, he took my hand and squeezed it gently. I blushed.

"So, Jim..." I asked. "Do you play Euchre by any chance?"

Praying Mantis

Mrs. Waverly had been dead for nearly six months by the time I started doing the bookkeeping for the church. The backlog looked like a train wreck. Receipts were stacked in piles all over the desk, in the drawers, and on top of the credenza.

Situated near the front of the building, our church office was a large enough room. However, the bookshelves, filing cabinets, our two desks and all the other furniture and clutter, made the room feel much smaller.

I'd spent the better part of the first two weeks organizing and learning about some issues that seemed to arise. Among the most serious problems were a water shut off notice, and past due utility bills with late fees. And on top of all that, documents were missing and there were some unusual transactions.

My husband Barry's accountant had trained me to do the bookkeeping for his office so I could fill in whenever she took a vacation or was sick. That's how I knew what to look for, and what the rules were when it came to basic accounting: what could or couldn't be done; what was legal and what wasn't.

When I discovered that cash from the donation baskets was being tossed into a drawer and used for petty cash instead of being deposited into the bank, I knew we were in trouble. By law, all cash received must go directly into the bank before it can be dispersed. The IRS is funny that way.

The church, however, didn't take that step. When someone needed to get reimbursed for an expense, they simply dropped a receipt on the desk and took the cash from the drawer. And no one was keeping track. If Mrs. Waverly had a system for handling reimbursements, it disappeared when she passed.

Two months into the job, I had finally started to catch up. I was proud of myself for being so annal in my work, patted myself on the back. I printed off a report and checked over the columns to make sure nothing had been missed.

Something brushed against my foot. I glanced down and saw a dustmop running along the floor, I looked up the mop handle to the young man at the other end. Apparently, I'd been so engrossed in the numbers, I hadn't noticed Kai come in.

"Good morning, Miss Delila." He looked up at me with a grin that said 'gotcha' then slowly pushed the duster around the room in a swishing motion.

"Good morning, Kai," I replied, taking a moment to acknowledge him.

Kai flashed a large toothy smile at me. At 22 years old, he'd already had a difficult life. When Reverend Olin Hudson and his wife met him, Kai was living in a homeless shelter. He suffered from depression and hoped to find solace in God. He'd come to the church looking for refuge.

Everyone at church had heard his story. His parents had both died by the time he was 19, and he found himself with no place to go. He'd started medical school but had to drop out to support himself.

Mrs. Hudson, the reverend's wife, had taken pity on the young man and convinced the reverend to help him out until he could get back on his feet. The young man was allowed to stay in the small apartment behind the church.

He agreed to clean the building in exchange for his room and board. In addition, the Reverend had insisted on paying him a small salary. The congregation also took up a collection to raise money for Kai's tuition and expenses, so he could return to medical school.

Kai continued to push the mop around the room, taking longer than needed.

A few minutes later Anie, the office manager, and wannabe boss, arrived. She performed mostly secretarial tasks but behaved as if she was responsible for everything and everyone who entered the office. Something I didn't appreciate, since I was nearly twenty years her senior and reported directly to the reverend.

"Good morning." Anie said to me in her patronizing voice. She sat down at her desk and turned on her computer.

"Good morning," I said, trying to match her mock cheerfulness with my own phony politeness before returning my attention to my work.

Our desks were on opposite sides of the room and faced one another, fortunately with plenty of space between them. I could feel Anie peer at me making mental notes of everything I did. I guessed she was fishing for something to report back to Reverend Olin.

Anie turned a disapproving eye toward Kai. "What are you doing Kai? You don't need to dust in here." Her voice sounded harsh and louder than necessary.

He turned from the bookshelf, gave me a goofy look, and winked, completely ignoring the reprimand. Then he turned to his challenger and said, "Why Miss Anie, it's my job."

"You don't have to dust in here. You can dust the classrooms and sanctuary." She insisted.

"I'm almost finished." Kai said in a pleasant voice and turned back to the bookshelf in defiance.

Anie glared at the back of Kai's head, her cheeks red hot with anger. "You're only supposed to do the floors and trash in here. Now go!"

Her eyes darted toward me. I tried to keep my own expression blank, and with some difficulty suppressed the smile that was forming at the corners of my mouth. Secretly I was cheering for Kai, but I gave Anie a small head shrug to say, 'I have no idea why he acts that way', then quickly looked at the computer screen.

Kai finished cleaning the bookshelf as slowly as he'd done everything else then headed for the door. "You ladies have a nice day," he said and walked out with a satisfied smirk.

After Kai had gone, Anie turned her gaze to me. "Do you have those financial reports ready yet? Jannie wants to pick them up this morning. There's a board meeting this afternoon."

Jannie the church treasurer, and the person in charge of all the church's finances, had her own private CPA practice. I suspected she had taken on the position of church treasurer to drum up business for her firm. It was she who'd failed to pay the bills after Mrs. Waverly died. She'd promised the reverend she'd straighten up all the loose ends. I was still looking for any signs she'd done anything at all. It appeared she wanted the title, but not the job.

"I'm almost finished." I clenched my teeth but tried to keep as polite a tone as possible. Still being new to the job, I didn't want to make enemies.

"Oh, and I need to get reimbursed for the supplies I purchased last night." She walked over to my desk and tossed some receipts down.

I pulled out a paper and handed it to her. "Could you fill this out please?"

"What's this?" She grabbed the paper from me and looked at it.

"It's the new reimbursement form. I created it so we can keep track of purchases. The reverend approved it yesterday." I said quickly, hoping to stop her from going off on me.

In a huff, she scowled, scooped up the receipts and went back to her desk.

As I scanned the printed reports once more, trying to understand why the numbers didn't seem right, I heard shuffling feet and wheezy breathing. An elderly woman stopped at the doorway.

Lulu Jackson lived a block from the church and at 93, still made a point of walking over to visit at least once a day.

"Why," she took a heavy breath. "Good morning, ladies."

"Good morning." I smiled, grateful for the interruption.

"Good morning, Lulu!" Anie's exaggerated smile and nauseatingly sweet voice didn't fool me. Lulu was one of the church's largest donors.

Lulu hobbled up to my desk and plunked down an oversized purse. She pulled out her checkbook.

"I need six tickets to the fundraiser this Friday night." She waited patiently, expectantly, for her kudos.

"Ok," I said, giving her the attention she craved. "Let me guess. You're taking Mitzi and Ned, Lena and her husband, Lydia and yourself?" Lulu had three children. Her girls, Lena and Lydia, and her son Ned, who was married to my good friend Mitzi.

"That's right!" She was clearly excited. "How much dear?" She began to stoop over and write out her check.

"Oh here, sit down." I got up and pulled my chair around the desk for her. "Tickets are $50 each, so $300."

Lulu began to write out her check. Anie watched us. She liked to monitor me, hoping to catch me doing something wrong. I suspected I'd get a lecture later, probably because I allowed someone to sit at my desk where we kept the accounting. As if we had to worry about Lulu. I pulled six tickets from the stack and set them next to her.

"I'm really looking forward to this dinner. Lydia says it's a wild game dinner?"

I explained that we had moose and mountain goat from one of our patron's hunting expedition last month, and whitefish and steelhead from another, who was an avid fisherman. And buffalo meat from a member with a stake in a buffalo farm.

"Oh, I can't wait!" Lulu handed me her completed check. "It sounds so lovely."

Anie popped up from her chair and walked by us on her way to the printer. "I love your shoes Lulu," she said. "Are they new?"

I looked down at Lulu's shoes. Of course, the shoes weren't new, just Anie's way of butting into the conversation. And in my opinion, an obvious attempt to get on Lulu's good side.

"Oh no, no. But they are my most comfortable pair!" Lulu laughed, a sweet, low sound. She picked up the tickets and placed them in her purse. Then she pulled out a bag of hard candy. An inexpensive brand of red and white pinwheels. "I brought you ladies some candy for the office too."

"Ohh, yumm! Peppermints are my favorite!" Anie squealed in exaggerated glee. "Lulu you are so sweet!"

I maintained the smile on my face, even though I felt annoyed by Anie's insincere performance.

"Well, I'd better let you ladies get back to work." Lulu closed her purse and slowly stood to leave.

"There you are mother!" I heard Lena's deep voice even before I saw her. "I've been looking all over for you. Lydia said you'd probably be here." Lena had a small sturdy body. She hurried to her mother and clutched her arm. "I wanted to take you shopping. Come on, let's leave these ladies alone." And Lena escorted her mother out.

Once they'd gone, I added in Lulu's check, then went back to reviewing the statements. The church, it seemed, was in trouble financially. I hoped the Wild Game Fundraiser Dinner on Friday would be a success.

The numbers in the reports were correct, but something didn't seem right. I ran a report from the previous year, and another from the year before. Careful not to let Anie see me, I checked the profit and loss statements against the current one. I'd heard membership was up, so why was the church bringing in less money than previous years?

When I arrived home that afternoon, Boris, my faithful terrier, greeted me as he normally did, prancing in circles, tail wagging and tongue hanging out of his mouth. I reached down and patted him on the head. Even though I only worked 20 hours a week, Boris didn't like it when I was gone.

"Ok, ok. I'll take you for a walk, just give me a minute."

The church's financial problems continued to plague me as I reached for the leash. I'd checked everything over and the numbers didn't lie. The church didn't have enough money to cover the existing bills. Had I missed something? I didn't think so.

How had Mrs. Waverly managed things? I'd mentioned my concerns when I handed the reports to the treasurer, Jannie. I tried to read the look on her face. Did she believe me? Was she already aware of an issue? Did she know why we were short?

Boris licked my hand, his tongue wet and impatient. "Ok, ok." I hooked up the leash and we started our walk, my mind still on the church's difficulties. Jannie hadn't seemed concerned. That seemed strange to me. Either she knew something that I didn't, or she just didn't care.

Fortunately, ticket sales to the fundraising dinner were doing well, and that would help keep us afloat for a short time anyway. Deacon Curry had pledged a large donation, and I wondered how long it might be before that money came in.

We walked along the sidewalk, past the rows of designer houses to our community park. Lily Park, or the Gossip Garden, as I referred to it. It was where neighbors congregated for social pleasure that usually resulted in neighborhood tell-all's, and where I got all my best news, and how I kept up on the lives of my friends and neighbors.

Boris tugged at the leash to get closer to the little red poodle sniffing at the flowerbed. The two dogs glanced at them.

"Hello Delila!" Mitzi's cheery voice welcomed me with enthusiasm usually reserved for when she wanted something. She was wearing one of her signature hot pink and lime green blouses. An outlandishly bright colored top that looked so good on her, but that no one else could ever pull off.

Aside from a couple of children playing at the other end of the park, we were alone. A light breeze swirled around in the air and felt refreshing against the humid day.

I unhooked Boris' leash then slid onto the seat across the picnic table from my friend, Mitzi, who had an uncanny knack for knowing everything that went on in our neighborhood, and in our church. We made small talk as we always did, a necessary precursor to the daily scuttlebutt.

Mitzi gave me what I knew to be her most virtuous look, when she finally brought up the topic she really wanted to discuss. "Lena is concerned about Lulu."

"What do you mean? Why?" I asked.

"Well, she thinks Lulu is starting to lose it." Mitzi seemed to be carefully choosing her words. "You know, she's getting forgetful, confused."

I hadn't noticed Lulu being even slightly confused or forgetful. "She seems fine to me." I ventured.

"Oh well, I don't think it's anything serious. But I guess she couldn't find her purse the other day. They searched the whole house. Finally found it in the bathroom."

It didn't seem like a big deal to me. "What does Lydia think? She lives with Lulu. She sees her every day."

"Oh, Lydia isn't sure." Mitzi seemed to be building her case. "I've noticed she's not as sharp as she used to be too. She got really confused the other day when I took her shopping."

"Hmm." I wondered where all this was going.

"I think they are both worried that someone is going to take advantage of her. You know she's always talking about her will." Mitzi looked at my face carefully. "They think she might do something crazy like leave all her money to the church."

I imagined the three women and Ned all discussing Lulu's intentions. I'd heard about the will game before. Lulu was a sweet old gal, but she did love to see her kids jump hoops to win her affection and good standing in the inheritance competition. Now it seemed she was throwing the church into the ring too.

Obviously, I was being pumped for information. Even if I had known, it would have been unethical to tell. "I'm sorry Mitzi, I honestly don't know."

"Ah," Mitzi gave a little nod. She was willing to let it go for now, but I knew her intention was for me to tell her if I found out anything.

"Mitzi," I waited for her attention to shift to a new topic. "What can you tell me about Mrs. Waverly?"

My friend barely blinked before answering. "Well, she was a nice old lady. A widow, no children. And she took care of books at the church before you." Mitzi stood up to leave, "You should ask Lulu if you want to know more about her. They were best friends you know."

On Thursday before the big fundraising dinner, several people gathered to help set-up. The kitchen and fellowship room were next to one another with a large access window between them, ideal for passing food and dishes from one room to the other.

Kai was pulling out the large aluminum serving stations when I arrived. I quickly went over to help him steer them into place. We positioned the cafeteria style units in front of the large kitchen window, then set up long eight-foot tables on either side of them.

Next, we began to pull out the large round tables and set them up. Each table could seat eight people.

Some of the other volunteers had come into the makeshift dining room and were helping as well. They hauled out stacks of chairs and placed them around the tables. Laughter and noisy clamor echoed though the large room.

This event would need to bring in enough money to pay a few overdue bills. I was the only one who knew that little detail, yet these volunteers had come out to help, spending their precious free time, for the church. They pulled me in with their enthusiasm and I suddenly felt a part of their circle. A sense of belonging I had not felt in a long time.

The Reverend arrived, dressed in jeans and a polo shirt. Accustomed to having attention, he quickly made his presence known. He stood inside the doorway, raised his arms in the air, and cleared his throat loudly. He waited until he had our attention. He wore his silly smile, the one where he contorted his face like a child trying to be funny.

"I want to thank you all for coming. You're doing a fantastic job. Give yourselves an applause." He clapped his hands. "We're going to have so many people here tomorrow for this dinner. In fact, I think we're going to have more than we've ever had before. And it's going to be the best dinner we've ever put on."

When he finished, he walked over to a group of volunteers and began speaking with them. I watched him mechanically smile and nod, then move on to the next person.

Deacon Curry scurried into the room a few minutes later, looking as if he was late. His triangular shaped face was flush, and his glasses had slid down his nose. He had an intellectual look about him. He was also friendly and charismatic, which made him highly popular among his fellow church members. People listened and nearly always agreed with him. I watched as he pushed the glasses up and searched the room. Once his eyes landed on Reverend Olin, he strode over to greet him.

Kai and I finished setting up the last of the round tables near the main door. "I'm glad you're here."

"Thank you, Kai. I'm glad you're here too--"

"Delila, there you are!"

I turned to see a white-haired woman wobbling toward me, a bag in one hand, cane in the other.

"Hello, Lulu--" I started to walk toward her, however, Deacon Curry and Reverend Olin swooned in. The Deacon took her hand and led her away, to a table and chair where she could sit down.

"My dear Lulu," I heard the reverend's voice. "It's wonderful to see you." He sounded as if it had been months since he'd seen her, yet I knew he'd spoken with earlier.

"I brought cookies for the volunteers." Lulu handed him the bag.

"God bless you, dear." He patted her hand. "You are so thoughtful!"

I watched the minister and deacon hover and fuss around the elderly woman. It was obvious that Lulu basked in their attentiveness, as if queen for just a few minutes.

"They appear to care for her." Kai whispered in a low voice, with an edge of sarcasm in his tone.

"She loves all the attention." I pointed out.

"Most lonely old people do." Kai seemed to size me up. He must have decided I was trustworthy because he added, "The other old lady did."

"You mean Mrs. Waverly?"

Kai nodded. "Sure. She loved it."

"You don't think they truly care about her?" I asked.

"It's all about the money." His cynicism had intensified. "They don't care about anyone. If they act kind and pious, they can get more money. They use people, then throw them away." Kai was clearly agitated.

I wasn't sure if he was talking about them using Lulu, Mrs. Waverly, or himself. But he obviously didn't trust either the deacon or Reverend Olin.

"The church does need money to operate." I said to justify their excessive devotion.

"Yeah, sure." He wasn't having it. "Then why don't the church have any?"

It was a good question. Did Mrs. Waverly have a lot of money? Had she left money to the church? I hadn't seen any evidence of it in the books. It was common for people to bequeath money to their place of worship, so it would have made sense. If she hadn't left it to the church, who had inherited it?

The deacon set the cookies out on the table and invited the volunteers to come and get some. Again, he looked around the room. This time, his gaze fell on Kai and me, and he appeared to be studying us. I felt uncomfortable.

Kai was staring back at the deacon. Then he turned to me. "I should go now. Thank you for helping me." He flashed his quirky little smile then walked away.

After he'd gone, I stood for a moment lost in thought about our conversation. How did Kai know the church had no money?

Friday morning, I arrived at the office early. I wanted to look over the accounts one more time to make sure I hadn't missed anything. Still worried about the lack of church funds, I carefully double checked all the deposit slips. Then I went over the paid invoices.

Anie the coldhearted, showed up an hour later, and with as little energy as she could muster, wished me a "good morning."

She barely looked at me. The corners of her mouth were turned up, suggesting she had a secret that pleased her. I watched her settle into her chair and turn on her computer, trying to gauge her mood. Then I saw a sly glance my way. What was she up to?

Anie was not an especially pretty woman, not ugly, but not good-looking either. Maybe it was just my opinion of her that made me think her face was too large. Too hard. Too Callous.

I looked back at the reports, trying to spot any errors. Had I missed a deposit slip?

I heard men's voices coming down the hall and looked up to see the reverend, followed by Deacon Curry enter the room. The deacon closed the door as the reverend walked up to my desk.

"Good morning, Delila," the reverend said quietly. "I trust you are well this morning?"

I nodded. It wasn't like the reverend to visit me in the office, and he was devoid of his usual perfunctory smile. He was clearly on a serious mission.

"Good morning, Reverend. Good morning, Deacon Curry." I pasted on a hasty smile for them.

"Delila, I understand there have been some problems with our accounts. We are short on funds, is that right?"

"Yes. But hopefully tonight's fundraiser will bring in—"

"Of course. But I'm trying to figure out how we got this low in the first place. I've looked over the reports and it just doesn't seem right. Do you think we might be missing a deposit?"

"Actually, I've double checked everything and as far as I can tell, everything is here and accurate."

"Umm." His voice was still soft and low. "I was looking back through our reports and the deposits seem to be smaller than they were last year at this time. Do you have any idea why that is happening?" He stepped a little closer toward my desk and leaned in, clasped the edge of the desk with his hands. Pushed his face a little too close to mine.

I leaned back in my chair and took a quick breath.

He held his eyes firmly on mine. "I'm not suggesting you had anything to do with it; I'm just trying to figure out why our accounts seem to be dropping when our membership has gone up. It seems like we should have more money in our account, not less."

The room was silent except for the three sets of accusing eyes.

"Honestly Reverend, I don't know. I've gone over these accounts several times." I could feel my cheeks turn hot.

"Yes, but it looks like we are missing funds."

What was he implying? That I had taken money from the church? I'd put in at least ten hours a week without pay since I started cleaning up the mess. Setting the books straight. Playing catch-up on bills. Putting things right. I paid my tithing every month and made additional donations too. How could he—how could any of them—think I was stealing from the church? Or did they think I didn't know how to do the job? Did they think I was incapable of doing the work?

"Ok, I'd like you to go over them again." He placated me with his calm voice.

I sat there not knowing what to say next. My thoughts stuck in a roundabout, not knowing where to get off. I knew that no matter which direction I took, there wasn't enough money in the accounts, and someone had to take the blame. Apparently, I was the designated scapegoat.

A light knock on the door broke up the silence, and Kai entered. "Excuse me. I need to get the trash." He walked over to the wastebasket and began fiddling with it.

Grateful for the distraction, I took a deep breath. Standing behind the reverend and Deacon Curry, Kai gave me a quick wink.

The reverend stepped away from my desk. "Let me know if you find something." He turned and walked out the door.

Deacon Curry gave me a solemn, almost pitying look, then quickly followed the reverend. I looked over at Anie, whose eyes quickly darted from me to her computer. She swallowed her smirk, but not before I saw it. The cat caught with a bird in her mouth.

I looked back at the accounts but could no longer focus my attention on the numbers. Instead, I felt devoid of feelings. Empty. Deflated. I'd given so much to this job. Worked so hard to make things better for the church. I'd helped with decorating, baked cookies for the bible study groups, stayed after every Sunday to help clean after the service. Not to mention, I'd frequently put up with Anie's bad moods and snarly comments.

Should I quit? I'd made a lot of new friends and enjoyed being around them. I was part of the flock. I liked working here. I liked the work itself. I cringed. What if they thought I was a thief or equally as bad, saw me as incompetent?

Awww! I closed my eyes and screamed. A silent scream. Yes. I should quit. I didn't deserve to be talked to like that. Yet, if I quit now, surely it would make me look guilty.

No, I couldn't leave. I'd have to figure out what happened. Get to the bottom of why we didn't have as much in the accounts as we should. Help the church get back on its feet. I decided to look at the numbers again.

Most of the donations came in the form of monthly tithing, sometimes as a direct withdraw from members bank accounts and deposited into the church account. Other patrons mailed in checks every month. Many still put their money in the baskets that were passed around every week. Some paid both their monthly tithing and put money in the basket.

It wasn't unusual for people to drop money off at my desk either. I'd come in to find envelopes addressed to the church, cash or check inside. Or someone would stop by to donate. Our members were generous.

And we had a new method of donating. People could text a donation from their phone. It was easy. They simply entered their credit card information into a phone app and pressed the button.

So, with all that money coming in from all these sources, where was it going? I pulled out the previous year's reports. It looked like our expenses were only slightly higher than last year.

Monthly bank tithing was higher now. Cash donations were lower. But that made sense as more people were using automatic payments and phone apps. Deposits were made twice a week and consisted of both checks and cash, that came from mail and the Sunday baskets.

All mail was opened by Anie, who gave me any checks. The Sunday baskets were picked up by both Anie and the deacon and brought directly into the office and locked in the room. Monday mornings, I counted the money and completed the deposit slips.

Anie stood up, looked over at me, then locked her desk drawer. Did she think I was going to steal from her? Her high heels echoed down the hall. Nevertheless, I felt immediate relief with her out of the room. It was an uncomfortable feeling, working in an office with someone who was constantly watching me, judging me.

Kai came over and stood next to me. In a low quiet voice, he said, "I seen her going through your desk last week."

"Who Anie?"

He nodded.

There wasn't anything for her to find, so I shrugged it off. "Thanks for the warning."

"I know you didn't take the money." He added with another of his famous winks.

"Really? How do you know?"

A sly grin spread across his face. "I know where the money went."

"Where? Who took it?" I asked. "And how do you know?"

He didn't answer but kept looking at me as if wondering if I could be trusted. "I could tell you lots of things. I know things." He was teasing me now. "People don't see me because I don't matter to them." He paused to let that sink in. "But I see them." He laughed. "I'm smart you know. But they still treat me like I don't know anything."

I knew Kai was smart. Afterall, the church was paying for his tuition and living expenses for medical school. Sometimes I wondered how he had time to study. He was always doing things around the church. First person to volunteer for anything.

Footsteps outside the door caused us both to stop talking. Kai quickly turned to leave, intentionally brushing up against Anie on his way out. She in turn, made an indignant huff.

Anie plopped down in her seat and dropped the mail on her desk and began opening it. I glanced over, hoping to see her pull out checks.

We sat not speaking. Anie purposely not looking at me. Had she said something to the reverend? Had she found something in my desk? What had she been searching for? Was she stealing money from the collection baskets? I thought about Kai and what he'd seen. Had he seen her take money?

The silence broke with the dramatic entrance of Lydia, Lulu's youngest daughter and leader of the church choir. That was the thing about Lydia. She was a performer. And, like an actress in old silent films, she used exaggerated hand gestures to communicate.

"Oh, hello Delila. I'm so glad you're here. I need some petty cash to buy goodies for choir practice. We're completely out of bottled water and I want them to have a treat tomorrow too, -you know, something special to look forward to." She put her hand to her heart and continued. "I've been trying to decide what sweets would be best. I might get cookies, or I thought about fruit."

That was the other thing about Lydia. She was like a faucet that was difficult to turn off. I glanced at Anie. I could tell by her smirk that she was enjoying the scene.

"Fruit might be a better option, healthier I think." She decided.

"I'm sorry Lydia," I cut in. "We don't have anything in petty cash right now. Did you speak with Reverend Olin? We are a little low on funds."

"Are you saying there's no money for water for the choir?" She emphasized the word water, as if I were withholding the most basic and necessary of human needs.

I looked at my purse, tempted to pull out a $20 bill and hand it to her. But then I remembered that Kai had insinuated someone was stealing from the church. I also remembered that Lydia was one of several people who had a key to this office. A key to this desk.

"I'm sorry Lydia. Maybe after the fundraiser tonight. Let's see what that brings in, ok?"

My friend and Lydia's sister-in-law, Mitzi, had warned me that Lydia had no sense about money. She was good at spending it, no concept of how to bring it in. She'd lived with her mother for most of her life, except for the short time she she'd been married. The marriage lasted only three months, and broke up mainly because of Lydia's lack of responsibility, and expensive expectations.

"They're going to need water before Sunday. You can't ask them to sing without water." Lydia threw her head upward and made a tisking sound with her mouth, her signature expression, to let me know she wasn't happy with me.

I gave her my 'there's nothing I can do' look.

Lydia wasn't giving up easily. "You know Delila, we have one of the best choirs the church has ever had. We've added membership because people wanted to be part of our choir. If we want them to stay, we have to treat them right."

Normally I might have grinned at the melodrama, but today I felt irritated. It wasn't my fault we had no money. I hated being the bearer of bad news. The messenger who everyone wanted to shoot.

"Sorry."

Lydia rolled her eyes, "We had plenty of money six months ago!" She turned, and made a dramatic exit, glancing at Anie as she left.

By noon, a full-blown headache had lodged itself in the back of my head, right at the neckline. I looked at the numbers on the screen and at the reports in front of me. I'd gone over them so many times I thought I might start seeing double. I filed the papers away and closed my computer.

"What? You're not leaving, are you? Reverend Olin told you to find out why we don't have any money." Anie scowled.

I didn't care what she thought. It was none of her business anyway. I'd already put in 30+ hours of my 20-hour work week. I had a right to go home. Besides, I wanted to get rid of the headache before dinner.

"I did. The numbers haven't changed. There is nothing more I can do. Not that it's any of your business," I added. I wasn't normally so blunt, but I'd had enough. I knew she'd run straight to the reverend and tell him, but I didn't care.

I drove home still fuming from the morning's events, and my headache pounding even louder. I no longer cared about going to the dinner. Maybe I should just skip the event. But I knew that wouldn't happen. Barry had been looking forward to it for weeks. And we had invited Jim and Aleena to join us.

It was a celebration of Jim's promotion in the police department. He'd been made detective and received an award for saving a choking baby. We were proud of our good friend. The timing of the Wild Game Dinner seemed like a perfect way to show him. So, I'd purchased four tickets and invited them to join us.

Boris was happy to see me as always, but disappointed when I turned him loose in the backyard rather than taking him on his normal afternoon walk.

Our plan was for Barry to leave work early, so he'd be home around 5pm. And Jim and Aleena would meet us at our house around 5:30.

I started to clean. The kitchen, dining room, living room, bathrooms, bedroom. I cleaned all afternoon. It wasn't that my house needed extra cleaning. It was my OCD kicking in. Finally, around 4pm I thought about getting dressed.

I pulled out a green dress and tried it on. Too casual. I tried on my little black dress. Too formal. Blue dress. Yuck. I pulled out some black slacks and put them on then tried on several blouses. Nothing seemed like a good fit for the evening. I settled on slacks and a blouse. Afterall, it was just a stupid church dinner.

The four of us rode together to the Church, chatting merrily as we went. My headache had started to fade, and I was feeling better in the company of friends. Safe and more relaxed.

"We had a pretty exciting day today." Barry looked at Jim and Aleena in the rearview mirror.

He immediately had our undivided attention. We all waited in anticipation of a Barry story. We loved to hear about the crazy things that went on in a dental office. And Barry could tell them so well.

"This afternoon a fellow came in for a dental cleaning. A middle-aged fellow. He was new, first time in our office. They got him all set up in the chair." He paused to make a turn, then continued.

"The assistant came to me and said the hygienist didn't want to work on this guy. So, I immediately thought maybe this guy was making derogatory remarks or something, but she assured me it was nothing like that." Barry glanced at Jim and Aleena in the mirror again. "I couldn't imagine what the problem was. I wondered if his breath was so bad- she couldn't stand it, even with her mask on." He paused with a chuckle, "That happens more than you think. But the assistant said no, it wasn't that either. She had her hand over her mouth and was trying not to laugh.

'He's got bugs coming out of his beard!' she said. There are bugs living in his beard!"

"Oh Barry! And you're telling us this just as we are on our way to dinner?" I admonished. "What happened?"

"I suggested she cover the beard with the dental bib and use an extra if necessary. What else could we do?"

We all laughed, and for the first time that day, I didn't think about work.

A long line of hungry customers twisted from the sidewalk outside the church, in through the door and to the tables where the board treasurer, Jannie, and another volunteer were selling tickets.

The four of us sailed by the line and past the ticket table since our tickets had been purchased in advance. I was thrilled to see the big turnout. Hopefully, this would keep the church going for a few more weeks.

We took our trays and carefully selected from the array of delicacies. I tried the two types of fish, while I noticed both Jim and Barry piled on the moose, goat, and buffalo meat.

The room was noisy with the large crowd of people talking and trays clanking. We had to hunt for a table. We finally found one with four empty seats.

A family of four sat across from us, and I recognized them from church. We said hello and introduced ourselves then went back to our own conversations.

"We are really proud of you Jim," Barry was saying. "Congratulations on making detective!"

The looks between Jim and Aleena didn't go unnoticed by me. It was obvious that they were crazy about each other.

"I'm proud of you too Jim!" Aleena rubbed his arm.

"Thank you. And thank you for dinner!" Jim took another bite of the buffalo. "This buffalo is delicious!"

I had just put a fork full of whitefish in my mouth when I felt someone tap me on the shoulder. "Delila. Can I see you for a moment?"

It was one of the volunteers from the kitchen. A young woman, probably not more than 18 years old, who had helped us set up for the event. I couldn't imagine why she needed to see me. No doubt there was a problem. Had they run out of food? Did a volunteer quit in the middle of cooking? I followed her through the door of the kitchen.

"What's going on?" I asked when we were away from the earshot of the crowd.

She kept walking. I followed. She led us through the back door of the kitchen into a back hallway of the church. We walked to the end of the hall, where she stopped. On one side, a door to the back parking lot, and the other side of the hall, a closet. Her face looked pale and drawn. She still didn't say anything. Slowly she turned the handle of the closet door, opened it, and pointed.

I saw a pile of laundry on the floor. Kitchen towels, tablecloths and rags heaped up, a large mess. I smelled the strong odor of vinegar and saw pieces of glass and pickles all over. I looked up and saw two giant gallon jars of pickles still on the shelf. Had she brought me back here to clean up this mess?

"What should we do?" The girl whispered.

"Clean it up." I said with irritation. Was she expecting me to clean it up?

"You don't think we should call for help?"

I looked again at the mess on the floor, this time more carefully. I stepped in closer and saw that underneath all the pickles, glass, and linens, was a body. A person who was not moving. I leaned in closer. There was blood on some of the material. I shook the body lightly. Nothing. I uncovered the face slowly, so as not to get blood or pickle juice on myself.

"Ouu!" I covered my mouth to muffle my scream. "Kai!" I said, feeling light-headed. I shook him again to see if I could rouse him. The pickles and fish combination had begun to make me nauseous. "Kai, Kai!" But there was no movement from him.

The paramedics arrived and officially pronounced Kai dead, although Jim had already confirmed my fears long before they arrived.

It wasn't long before a tv anchorman showed up along with his cameraman. A good night for them.

Jim sealed off the closet and the police took pictures and treated it as a crime scene. When I asked him about it, he told me it was procedure. Until they knew how Kai died, they needed to take every precaution. It may have been an accident, but they couldn't be sure. The autopsy should provide more information.

Reverend Olin, Deacon Curry, Jim, and I watched as the last of the police officers finished up.

The reverend stretched his neck toward the closet then looked at Jim. "It looks like the poor fellow was trying to reach for a pickle jar and it fell on him, knocking him to the floor. He must have hit his head hard in the fall." He put a finger to his lips as if in deep thought. "And he must have grabbed at the shelves to catch himself, pulling the linens down instead. Dreadful accident."

My eyes filled with tears. I rubbed them and imagined the scene.

Deacon Curry nodded. "Yes, that must be what happened. Poor kid."

"Yes... yes. An accident. Terrible, sad, accident." Reverend Olin repeated.

Barry and Aleena had stood at the other end of the hallway patiently waiting for all the excitement to subside. Finally, around 10pm we were able to leave the church, Jim and I taking our cold, half-eaten meals with us.

Later, after Jim and Aleena had gone home, Barry and I watched the scene play out again on the late-night news and caught a glimpse of Jim. The anchorman spoke to the girl who'd found the body. She no longer looked pale or timid as she gave them her account of finding the body. Apparently, television had cured her of her earlier panic. As for me, I had stayed clear of the cameras.

It had been a long day, and I was exhausted. But sleep didn't come easy for me that night. I rolled from one side to the other. Still keyed up from the day's emotional events, I thought about Kai and how he'd tried to break the tension between the reverend and myself. Kai said he knew what happened to the money. Did he mean someone had stolen it? That was what I thought he was implying at the time. It would remain a secret now. Forever.

Kai. Funny. Hardworking. He'd had a great future ahead of him. He might have been a doctor or surgeon. How tragic! I shoved my face into my pillow and cried silently. I didn't want to wake Barry. Didn't want him to know how upset I felt.

I rolled over again. Barry moved closer and nestled up next to me. The tension in my body began to release. I felt protected. Safe. Loved. Finally, my mind quieted and welcomed sleep took over.

Fundraiser dinners were nearly always on a Friday. This gave us Saturday morning to count the money and make a deposit. I felt it best to have three people count. More accountability that way. I'd asked Anie since she was the self-proclaimed 'office queen,' and Jannie, church treasurer,

CPA and 'financial overseer,' to count with me. We met in the office at 9am.

Each of us took a turn counting the piles of money. While Jannie counted, I took the first ticket on the remaining roll of tickets. I liked to save the first ticket and the last ticket of an event. That way I could tell how many tickets we had sold altogether. This time, I'd also written down the first number of the tickets sold at the door.

As Anie took her turn counting the money, I figured out how many tickets we sold that night. Based on my calculations, we should have taken in $2800.

"$2500!" Anie called out proudly.

It was the same number I had arrived at.

"Yep. That's what I had too." Jannie agreed.

"Did we lose any tickets," I asked Jannie. "I mean did any get thrown out or destroyed or anything like that?" That would explain the difference.

"Nope. Why?" Her answer, accompanied by a look of suspicion.

Tread carefully, I told myself. "Just making sure." I didn't want to alarm anyone. Didn't want to set off the sirens. So, we were $300 short. I started to say something, then decided against it.

I should tell someone. But who? Who could I trust?

Jannie offered to drop off the deposit at the bank and I headed home, still pondering the missing tickets and money. Had 12 people been given free tickets? Or had Jannie's helper been so bad at giving out change that she made $300 worth of mistakes? Not likely. The girl worked at Jannie's accounting firm. She couldn't have made that many mistakes!

That afternoon I discussed it with Barry. I told him everything. I knew there was nothing he could do, but he usually gave me good solid advice.

"I don't know if I should tell the reverend or not. He already thinks I'm stealing money from the church."

"I doubt he really thinks that, Delila. He is probably just frustrated that there isn't enough money to cover expenses. Unfortunately, you are sitting in the hot seat." Barry, pragmatic as always, patted my shoulder. "I wouldn't worry too much. You're probably feeling especially sensitive right now. After all that happened last night."

The image of Kai lying on the closet floor covered in tablecloths, broken glass, and pickles, once again played out in my mind. I tried to blink away the tears. "Poor Kai!"

Barry put his arms around me and held me close for several minutes, and I allowed the tears to fall shamelessly. Finally, I pulled myself away and looked at him.

"Do you think it happened the way the reverend said? Do you think Kai was trying to reach for some pickles and fell? I mean, they are huge and super heavy jars, but could that actually kill him?" I'd taken the reverend's statement as the only possibility up to this point. But now the logic of the situation seemed questionable.

"I don't know." Barry admitted. "It is strange. But what alternative is there?"

Sunday morning arrived. I dreaded going to church for the first time since I'd started working there a little over two months ago. Yet, I needed to go. I needed to be around the people who shared Kai's loss with me. Barry and I were both up and around in time for the early service. We sat in our usual spot in one of the center pews.

The reverend, dressed in his flowing black robe, appeared at the entrance of the sanctuary. He held his bible in his hand and wore a serious look on his face. We all stood in his honor. He walked slowly and ceremoniously up the aisle, as if royalty, appointed by God, to his place in front of the room. Dramatic organ music accompanied him.

He stood erect, regal, behind the podium and looked out over the parishioners, allowing his eyes to fall on us. The organ music stopped, and the room became silent.

"It's a sad day." He began. "Yes, a sad day for our congregation. God has called upon one of our own. Many of you knew Kai, the young man who spent so much time here at the church. A medical student who planned on becoming a doctor. Many of us helped him with his endeavor. We supported him, gave him shelter and food. We even helped with his tuition."

There were nods among the worshippers as they thought of all the times, they'd put money in the basket or wrote checks for Kai.

"And now, we must ask for your help again. You see, young Kai had no family. An only child, he'd lost his parents before we even knew him. We became his family. Now we need to lay him to rest."

I hadn't thought about who would bury Kai, or who would pay his funeral expenses. As upset as I was with the reverend, I felt pleased that he had stepped in for Kai.

"Let us remember, it is the people who tithe every paycheck, the parishioners who give more than they planned, that receive their reward in heaven." He took a brief pause then continued.

"It is not how long we have lived, but how generous our stewardship. It is not how much wealth we accumulate over our lifetime, but how we use that wealth to support our families, our community, our church..."

As the sermon continued, I found myself trying to decide how much money to donate to Kai's funeral while missing some of the finer points of the oration. I was pulled back in by a change in the reverend's voice and demeanor.

He leaned in and cradled the podium; began to speak to the audience as if they were good friends and family gathered for a special event. He was comfortable on stage. Enjoying himself.

"You know," The reverend tilted his head and smiled his goofy smile. "We have a couple that come every week. They're good people. They pay their tithing every month." He swung one arm out toward the people as he spoke. "One day they came to me and said they wanted to do more. So, I said to them, you know, I think people would enjoy having a garden area behind the church. Somewhere they could go and just relax. You know lots of flowers and a bench. Well, that couple donated the money, and we now have a beautiful area in back of the church. You've seen it. The Raymond and Shelly Smith Garden. If it weren't for Ray and Shelly, we wouldn't have that gorgeous garden..."

He shifted his position, still clutching the podium. His voice became a little louder and his face more serious. "We want our church to look nice. We want to help those in need. There's only one way to make that happen. We each need to do our part. We must give a little more, volunteer when we can. Together we can do it. We can do incredible things. Let us pray."

After the service I wrote out a generous check for Kai.

Monday morning, I arrived at work around nine am, my usual time. Anie was already sitting at her desk typing. Her failure to give me more than a glance and her half-hearted, "good morning," told me I was still not popular.

I unlocked my desk and found an envelope full of checks written out for Kai's burial. They added up to $5,950. Then I counted another $150 in cash.

"I counted $6,100," Anie said.

I hadn't realized she'd been watching me count. And she had obviously gotten into my desk and counted the money before I did. I chose to ignore these thoughts.

"Yes, that's what I got too."

"The reverend wants you to contact the funeral home and make the arrangements for Kai's burial." She added.

"Me?"

The disgusted, irritated look on her face said, "Yes you! Who else?"

I spent the next couple of hours calling funeral homes and getting prices on funerals. By midafternoon I had compiled several options and took them to Reverend Olin.

The most basic option was $8,000 total and the prices went up from there. The reverend chose the basic option.

"So, we still need $1900 for burial?" He asked.

Obviously, Anie had already informed him of how much we'd taken in. I nodded.

"Ok, call the University and tell them what happened. See if we can get some of the tuition money refunded to help pay for the funeral."

I went back to my office and immediately called the University. I was transferred from one department to another until I finally found someone who could help.

"Just a minute, I'll check into it. How did you spell his name?"

I spelled his name slowly and carefully.

After a few minutes she came back on the phone. "I'm sorry, we don't have anyone by that name in any of our records. Could he be listed under a different name?"

"I don't think so," I replied. "Did you check the medical school?"

"Yes, he's not listed anywhere. We've never had a student here by that name. Do you have his social security number?"

Because we'd paid him a stipend for cleaning the church and provided him with a small apartment behind the church, we did have his number on file. I pulled it up on the computer and gave it to her.

"I'm sorry, we don't have this number in our system either. Another school perhaps?"

There were no other schools within 30 miles of us, and Kai didn't have a car. I considered other possibilities. Could he have been taking online classes? How would I ever find that out? He didn't have any friends I could ask. I could search his apartment. Maybe I'd find something on his laptop.

Anie made it her business to know everything that was going on in the church, and especially in our office. She'd overheard my phone calls, and while it bugged me that she listened in on everything, it did save me the trouble of having to explain the situation to her.

"I think I need to go through Kai's apartment and look for his laptop." I said to her. "I want to see if I can find where he was enrolled in school. Maybe it was online or something."

"Yeah right." She gave a light, sarcastic snort. "Can't get in."

"What do you mean? Why?"

Miss know-it-all raised her eyebrows and grinned, "Police taped it off this morning. They're not letting anyone in."

When I arrived home that afternoon, I called Jim. I wanted to know what was going on. Why had they taped off Kai's apartment? Had they learned something more?

"I wish there was more I could tell you, Delila." Jim said. "We are treating Kai's death as 'suspicious,' so we don't want any evidence being tampered with if possible."

"Oh," I said politely. I didn't want to say anything, but I thought it was a little late for closing it off now. Anyone could have gotten in there over the weekend. "How long will it take to get the autopsy back?"

"Well, we have the preliminary results back now. It'll take a couple of weeks for the final autopsy to be completed."

"Really? What did they find?" My heart raced.

"They'll be releasing a statement on the news in a couple of hours. Let's just say we're going to investigate what happened to your friend." Jim hesitated. "Delila, what can you tell me about this young man? How well did you know him? Are you available to talk now? I can be there in 20 minutes."

After we hung up, I thought about his question. How well did I know Kai? I thought I knew him. Smiling, cheerful. Always helping at the church. A bright, young medical student, working his way through school. But was he a medical student? If he was, where was he going to school? He was a good, church going, God loving, boy. Why would he lie?

Jim arrived in uniform. A plate of cookies and a cold Arnold Palmer (his favorite lemonade and iced tea drink) awaited him on the coffee table.

He asked again. "So, Delila, tell me what you know about this man."

I told him what I knew about Kai. About him having lost his parents and the reverend taking him in. The church paying for his schooling and food and letting him stay in the apartment behind the church. What a well-mannered boy he was, always helpful.

Then I told him about the university not having him on record as ever having attended. "Maybe he was taking classes online?" I posed the question to Jim. "His apartment was already sealed off, so I couldn't look on his laptop to find out. Could you check that out for us? If we can cancel his classes, we might get some money back and use it toward his burial expenses."

"We have people checking his laptop now. I'll let you know if we find something." Jim promised.

He thanked me for the cookies and drink, then left the house. I hadn't learned anything from him. I knew his job prevented him from telling me more, but it was frustrating. After all, I'd found Kai's body. And I was probably one of his closest friends. If you could call me that. What were we though, really? ...Co-workers? ...Acquaintances?

One thing I had learned. The police were investigating Kai's death seriously. That must mean it might not have been an accident. I could barely wait for the six o'clock news to hear more.

"**P**olice are investigating the death of 22-year-old Kai Williams, found Friday evening at the Church in the Flowers, where he worked." The anchorman stood in the parking lot, the church in the background. "The young man was found dead in a closet, Friday evening, where he appeared to be getting supplies for the fundraising dinner the church was putting on at the time."

"Police are not sure if this was an accident or a homicide. The preliminary autopsy showed the young man died of a blow to the head. What's not clear is what caused the blow."

The anchorman gripped the microphone and pulled it closer to his mouth. "The young man himself appears to be a mystery as well." A picture of Kai's face appeared on the screen. "He appears to have no family or close friends, and it is unclear where he lived prior to coming to Aster Heights. A background check did not shed any light on his past either. The young man had been taken in by the church a year ago and has been living in an apartment belonging to the church ever since." The screen flashed back to the news anchor. "The young man claimed to be a medical student; however, no evidence has been found to support that story. The homeless shelter where he had been living prior to being taken in by the church also had no information on him. Apparently, he just showed up one day needing a place to stay. Police are asking for anyone with information to please contact the department."

Barry and I sat speechless for a minute. Like many of the church members, we'd heard the story of how Kai had lost his mother to cancer and his father had died many years before that. He'd arrived at the church looking for help and the reverend's wife took pity on him and convinced the reverend to let him stay in the apartment. No one thought to question him beyond that. He slid in without anyone noticing and quickly became a fixture of the church.

The members all chipped in to help him. He was a symbol of our generosity. Our Christian values. Our morality. We clothed him. Gave him shelter. Even paid for his education. But none of us ever really tried to know him.

The fundraiser had brought in enough to keep us running for another month, so the reverend stopped asking me about the finances. He'd moved on to other concerns. Mainly, how to pay for Kai's funeral expenses.

After the news report, donations for Kai's burial had dried up. It seemed no one wanted to pay for the 'mystery man,' the homeless person, to be laid to rest. Even the reverend's attempts to cajole some of the wealthier members led nowhere. A few more donations came through, but we were still $1100 short.

We did, however, receive a large donation to upgrade the fellowship room. Along with a new sign that read "donated by George and Carrie Graham". Apparently doing God's work was more popular when it came with a sign and lots of recognition.

It was Barry who came through in the end. One of his long-time customers ran the largest funeral home in town. When Barry asked him if he could help, he reduced the price to the exact amount we had raised.

Kai was buried a few days later with the reverend presiding. There was a surprisingly large turnout. I wondered if it was because the reverend was officiating or because people were curious about the mystery man.

Over the next few weeks things began to settle down and went back to a more normal situation. Cash donations remained lower than expected, yet membership picked up some. The publicity hadn't hurt us at all.

Funds were dwindling again, and although we had enough for now, it was just a matter of time before we'd run low again.

I considered asking the deacon for a small donation. Afterall, he was a wealthy man and could well afford it. He'd already promised a big donation, just hadn't said when that would happen.

Yet, I couldn't bring myself to do it. I liked to imagine myself soliciting money for the church and getting our largest donation because of me. But it didn't happen. I never asked.

I'd need to run a report again the following week for the treasurer to take to the board meeting. Haunted by the reverend's reaction to the last report, dread pounced in and took over my emotions. I played the horrible scene once more in my mind.

The reverend's angry face leaning in toward me. Accusing. Kai coming in to break the tension. Kai telling me that he knew what happened to the money.

He knew. Something had 'happened' to the money. It must have been there, but someone had taken it. Was it him? Had Kai stolen the money and felt guilty when he heard me being accused?

If so, where was the money now? In fact, since Kai hadn't been in school, what had he done with all the tuition money the church had given him? And the money for books and clothes?

Had the police found money in Kai's room? Were they holding on to it in case a relative of his showed up? I made a point to remember to ask Jim. I continued to ponder Kai's relationship with the church's money. It finally occurred to me that if Kai had been the one taking money from the church, we wouldn't be having a problem any longer. Yet, we were.

Anie stood up and pulled a new Kate Spade purse from her desk drawer. She started to walk out the door, then almost as an after-thought turned to me. "I've got an appointment this morning if anyone should ask. I'll be back this afternoon."

"Ok." I nodded. Moments later I leaned back in my chair and relaxed. A wave of contentment surged through me.

In fact, I was so comfortable I didn't hear anyone in the hallway.

"Good morning, Delila!" Lulu stopped inside the doorway to catch her breath.

"Good morning, Lulu!" I jumped up and pulled an extra chair to the front of my desk for her to sit down.

After a minute more of heavy breathing, Lulu flashed her heart melting smile at me. The kind you can only get from toddlers and the very elderly. In toddlers, it's the pure innocence and joy of them experiencing everything for the first time. In the elderly it's the wisdom that goes beyond knowledge to awareness and total acceptance.

"How are you darling? What a sad time for the church, what with losing the boy. You were fond of him, weren't you? So tragic." Lulu patted my arm.

It surprised me that she knew Kai and I had been friends.

"It's hard to lose people," Lulu continued. "It was hard for me when I lost dear Mrs. Waverly."

I'd forgotten that I'd wanted to ask her about Mrs. Waverly. A perfect window of opportunity for me.

"You and she were good friends, weren't you?" I prompted.

"Best friends."

"She had this job before me, didn't she?"

"Yes, she did. That's how we met. Such a dear sweet woman." Lulu smiled at the memory.

"I wish I'd known her." I considered how I could ask these personal questions without sounding like I was interrogating her.

"Oh, you'd have loved her. Everyone did. She was especially close to Deacon Curry and the reverend. They were always doing nice things for her. You see she didn't have any family left, poor dear."

"I heard she was pretty wealthy." I decided to push my luck and bluntly go where it was none of my business. "Pardon me for saying so, but I would have thought she'd have left her money to the church."

Lulu's eyes smiled brightly. "No, she didn't leave it to the church. She left it to the one person she truly loved."

Who was she referring to? Herself? I'd already gone this far so I decided to pry further with the other question I so wanted answered.

"Lulu," I said in my softest voice. "How did Mrs. Waverly die?"

She looked at me in surprise. "You mean you don't know? Why, she just collapsed right there in that chair you're sitting in. They said it was a heart attack, but I always wondered."

I started to ask what she wondered. Why did she think it might not have been a heart attack? But before I could say anything I saw a small creature dart into the room.

It was fast and I couldn't tell what it was. Within a minute, the reverend raced in, an animal carrier in hand, and quickly closed the door behind him. He looked frantic. His wild facial expression and disheveled appearance startled me.

I'm not sure he noticed us at first, he was so intently set in his pursuit. He chased the poor animal into a corner where it arched its back and hissed. Once he had it trapped, his expression turned to one of glee.

When he finally looked our way, his demeanor changed slightly. He must have seen the shock in our faces. "Oh, sorry ladies." In his attempt to apologize, he added, "Kai's cat."

Lulu and I remained silent.

"I was going to take it out to the country and let it go. It's quite wild."

I looked at the frightened animal once again, and realized it was just a kitten. Was he really planning on dumping it in the country? The area was plagued with coyotes. The kitten looked so small; I wondered if it could survive on its own.

The local animal shelter would be better, yet the tiny creature might remain in a cage for months, or even years, hoping for adoption. I read an article on how over-crowded the shelter had become now that it was a 'no kill' shelter. I stood up and went over to get a better look. The reverend stepped back.

The grey fluff ball began to relax slightly. "It's ok. It's ok, I'm not going to hurt you." I used my most soothing tone. But the kitten, still terrified, hissed once more.

The reverend lurched toward it again. Excitement, and perhaps a little fear took over and I yelled out in a slightly louder than normal voice, "It's ok reverend! I'll get it. I'll take care of it."

The reverend backed down and pushed the crate toward me. "Ok, fine. You take care of it!" He turned and with a bit of a huff, he shut the door behind him.

I set the crate down with the door open. "It's ok, little one. It's ok, you'll be fine." I used my body to block the kitten from escaping and pushed it toward the crate. Somewhat reluctantly, it entered the cage and I quickly shut the door.

Lulu watched, with amusement. "You have a way with animals."

"I don't know about that." I said and peaked in at the fluff ball. "It's a cute little thing."

"The reverend doesn't like animals." Lulu said matter-of-factly.

"He doesn't?" I was surprised.

"No. His wife told me she once asked for a dog. He told her the only animals allowed in his house, were the ones on the supper table."

I left work early, taking the kitten with me. Boris, excited by the crate and newcomer, wouldn't leave it alone. I put the kitten, crate and all in the laundry room and shut the door.

An hour later, after a rapid trip to the store, I placed a box of kitty litter and dish of food and water on the laundry room floor. I opened the door to the crate, but she didn't come out.

I guessed she was about three months old. Maybe older, but not much. Alone. Homeless. No one to care for her or about her. Perhaps like Kai himself. She'd found shelter at the church, but danger too.

Boris scratched at the door. "Go away Boris."

I looked at the frightened kitten and the image of Kai popped up in my mind. Holding her tenderly. She was probably the only family he had and the only one who genuinely cared about him. Suddenly I felt ashamed. Why hadn't I tried to get to know him better?

More scratching, this time louder, more intense. "Boris, stop it! You're going to ruin the door!" I left the kitten and went in to spend time with my own jealous fur baby.

"Come on Boris, let's go for a walk."

I hooked up his leash. We were almost out the door when my phone's loud ring tone brought us back inside.

"Hello Jim!"

"Hi Delila. I told you I'd let you know if we found anything on Kai's laptop. Unfortunately, there was no evidence of him being enrolled in classes. I'm sorry. I know the church was hoping to recover some of the money they gave him."

"Hmm." I was disappointed but not surprised by the news. "Jim, did you find any money? I mean, the church had given him all that money for tuition, books and even extra for lunch money. Did you find any of that? Did he have a bank account?"

"Well, I can't really tell you much. But I don't think there was anything of significance."

I knew he wasn't allowed to share that kind of information.

"Have you determined how he died?"

"Well, I can tell you it was a blunt force hit to the back of his head. The information was released to the press about an hour ago. We don't believe it was an accident. The cuts he sustained from the pickle jar were post-mortem. That's not what killed him."

It took me a minute to digest what he was saying. "So...Kai was murdered?" How could that be? Who would want to kill him? I immediately thought about the missing money. I started to say something.

"Well, I've got to go Delila, I just wanted to let you know."

"Thank you, Jim--" I started.

"Talk to you later." And Jim hung up.

I wanted to say something about the missing money. To tell Jim what Kai had said. It might have something to do with his death. I couldn't be sure, but the police should have that information. I decided to tell him the next time we spoke.

Boris tugged at the leash, and we headed out the door for our walk. We found Mitzi at the park. Her little poodle began to run circles around Boris. We unleashed our fur-babies and sat down at the picnic table.

"It's terrible about Kai, isn't it?" Mitzi began. "I mean I still can't believe someone died in our church. And during a fundraiser at that!" she shook her head as if in disbelief.

"Yes," I agreed.

"I'd have thought it would hurt our church having something like that happen," Mitzi continued. "But I heard our membership has actually gone up since it happened."

It was true. The publicity had helped rather than hurt our popularity in the community.

"For some strange reason people are attracted to that kind of thing." Mitzi continued.

I wondered if I should share the new information I'd just learned from Jim. It would be made public in a couple of hours anyway. And if he could share it with me, I saw no reason why I couldn't share it with Mitzi. Afterall, if you want to collect on scuttlebutt, you sometimes needed to divulge a little gossip too.

Convinced I was doing the right thing, I shared what I had learned from Jim.

"Wow." Mitzi considered it for a moment. "Well, I bet that will bring in more members too."

I was a bit incensed that she wasn't more concerned. "Mitzi, Kai may have been murdered!"

"I get that. But, I mean, he was kind of a twit. Always talking about how he was a medical student. Getting us to pay for everything for him. And I heard he may not even have enrolled in any classes! You've got to admit Delila, he kind of did a con job on us."

"He didn't deserve to get murdered! Anyway, who would want to kill Kai?" My voice rose to a high pitch, a reflection of the irritation I felt.

"Calm down Delila. I'm just saying he wasn't a saint, ok? He lied about a lot of things. He was always sneaking around, listening in on people. Spying on people."

The defensive hairs on the back of my neck stood up, "what makes you say that? He was just doing his job. And that may have put him in a position to hear or see things. It doesn't mean he was spying on people."

"Ok, ok." Mitzi bit her bottom lip and shot her 'whatever' look at me. She looked at her watch. "Oh, I better get going. Ned will be home soon."

I watched her walk down the street and wondered if my response had been too strong. Might I have learned more from her if I'd just listened instead of reacting?

Barry looked at me with one raised eyebrow. He wondered what my plans were for the kitten.

"Honestly, I thought we could keep it until we found a good home for it. The poor thing has been through so much." I held the kitten tight against my chest to protect it from Boris, whose front paws were on my hips as he tried to reach and sniff the newcomer.

None too pleased with the idea, Barry had his own solution. "What about the shelter? Can't they find it a home?"

"The shelters are overrun with kittens. Some of them never find homes and are stuck in a little cage for the rest of their life." I nestled my nose into the fur. Boris growled.

"What about Boris? I don't think he wants you to keep it."

"Nonsense. Boris just wants to play with little Jewel." I looked down at Boris. "But you have to learn how to play nice with her. You can't be rough."

"So, you've already named it?" Barry chose not to respond any further. He shook his head and went to the den.

The next morning at work, under Anie's ever watchful eye, I sat down at my desk and began to straighten things around. That's when I first saw it, lodged in the corner of the drawer, under several other papers. How long had it been there?

I pulled it out and read it. What did it mean? Who sent it? I couldn't be sure. It didn't make sense. A note with neat and delicate handwriting. The words sounded gentle, playful, and teasing. Printed on church stationery, it must have been written here. Why hadn't I seen it before? I started to read it again.

I want you to know—

"Do you have the monthly report ready?" Anie shot me a smug look.

"Don't worry, I'll have it ready when Jannie gets here." I fired back.

I waited until I was sure she wasn't looking, then quickly folded the paper back up and stuck it in my purse. I could look at it again a little later.

"Do the numbers look better this month? Our membership has really increased!"

After the news of a possible homicide, the church, found it's pews full of even more worshipers.

"Hmm. Somewhat." I printed off the report.

I worried that once again we might not have enough to pay all the bills, and I'd be facing another uncomfortable visit from the reverend.

There had been a slight uptick in spending over the past two weeks, and I attributed it to people thinking that with all the new membership, there would also be an abundance of new spendable cash.

The reverend had ordered several new shirts and a new robe. He'd also gotten himself a new office chair, complaining that the old one hurt his back. And since the deacon spent so much time with him, he ordered him a new chair as well.

"I hope there's enough for the reverend's new podium." Anie shot me a questioning glance.

The reverend had decided he needed a new podium. There was really nothing wrong with the old one, but he wanted something more elaborate. He wanted people to feel the 'wow' effect when they entered. To be moved, mesmerized, by the sheer beauty of our gathering place.

I shrugged my shoulders.

"We need it really," Anie continued. "We want to continue to grow our church, so we need different types of members. And if we want to attract upper-class donors, we need to have a phenomenal church. Wealthy people never go to a poor looking church."

I supposed she was right about that. Nevertheless, I wondered what that had to do with worshiping God.

"The reverend has big plans to make this church great. He's thinking of adding on a whole new sanctuary or maybe building a new church. With so many new members, we need a larger sanctuary." Anie's daydream continued.

"Umm." I admit I'd been excited about all the new members and the possibility of an addition or even a new church. Yet today I found my interest in the topic waned. I really wanted to make my escape. To get home and re-read the note.

"I heard the deacon is going to make a large donation toward the new addition or building." Anie went on, as if talking to herself.

"That would be nice." I glanced down at my purse and thought about the mysterious document well tucked away.

"Delila," Lena waltzed into the office, all smiles. "Ready for lunch?"

I'd nearly forgotten that Lulu's eldest daughter had asked me to lunch. I loved that about my job. People were always wanting to have coffee or lunch. It made me feel a part of something bigger than myself. A sense of belonging I'd not experienced before.

"Hi Lena. Yes, of course." I put my computer on sleep mode and slid my purse onto my shoulder. "Ready."

Anie gave us a sideways glance, probably perturbed at not having been invited.

At the restaurant, Lena was talkative. She told me about her mother's health ailments, her sister's preoccupation with the choir, Ned's super busy schedule, and the trip Mitzi was planning.

I tried to recall what was in the note. You mean so much to me. You have no idea how you've changed my life...

"So, what do you think? Do you want to join us?" Lena was saying.

"Well, I—"

"It's going to be incredible! Mitzi says it will have to be next month though because there's nothing available until then. I'm so excited! I've never been on a girl's weekend before."

"I'll have to check with Barry. Let me know when you have a date. Wait, where did you say you were going?"

"Well, we want to stay at the Roquer Hotel." She sighed. "We can get the spa treatments, rent bikes, maybe hike some trails, they have a gorgeous pool, and some of the cutest little shops!" Lena grew more and more excited. "And I've heard the food is incredible!"

"It does sound wonderful!" I agreed. "Yes, count me in!" It would be my first 'girl's weekend' too.

On the way back to the office I felt completely energized. There would be eight ladies from the church going. I'd share a room with Lena. A rush of joy shot through me. I was a member of this lovely group of ladies. One of them.

Back in the office, I held my head a little higher. Let Anie criticize me. Let Jannie wonder if I was capable. I had friends, so who cared what they thought!

Jannie looked over the report. "Are you sure this is all the cash we took in?" The deep lines between her eyebrows grew deeper. "With all the new members, seems like we should have more."

"That's what I thought too." I pulled out the deposit slips in case she wanted to look at them.

Jannie began to pour through the slips. She pulled my adding machine toward her.

The reverend walked in, followed by the deacon. "Good news ladies!" Giddy with excitement, he continued, "We are starting a new project. The committee has agreed that we need a new sanctuary and given approval to begin. It will be called 'The Great Sanctuary'. We are going to ask parishioners to contribute toward a new sanctuary that will be incredible. I've got an architect working on it as we speak."

He turned to the deacon and put his hand on the deacon's shoulder as if congratulating him. "And Deacon Curry is going to be the first donor!"

The deacon nodded and smiled, "that's right. I'll bring you a check for $1,000 later this week."

"Thank you!" I blurted out.

"That's wonderful!" Jannie said and put the deposit slips back in the folder.

"Fantastic!" Anie chortled. She wore the look of a schoolgirl crush.

"Yes," The reverend agreed. "God Bless You!" His grin stretched wide across his face.

The reverend's good mood was to be celebrated. No one wanted to bring him down from the clouds today. But secretly I thought, the $1000 the deacon promised, probably wouldn't even cover the architect's fee for the drawings.

Once I'd settled in at home and taken care of my daily responsibilities, I allowed myself the luxury of a little time to myself. I sat down on the sofa and unfolded the note.

> *I want you to know how much you mean to me. It brings me such comfort knowing you are near. I can't imagine my life without you. I am so thankful to have met you. You make me feel special when I am with you. You have no idea how you've changed my life. I love you my friend and I don't know what I'd do without you.*

We don't always realize the impact we have on other people's lives. I certainly never knew how much I meant to Kai. I let a tear roll down my face and tried to read it again through blurred eyes. I wished I could have told him how much he'd meant to me too.

Little Jewel ran across the room and landed at my feet. I picked her up and hugged her.

"Oh Kai," I whispered. "What happened to you?"

Excited by Mitzi's latest email, advising us on what clothing to bring for our girl's 'getaway' put me in an especially good mood. She suggested swimming suits for the pool, and a nice outfit for a fancy dinner. Comfortable shoes and clothing for the museums and lounging clothes. It was so like

Mitzi to have everything spelled out, down to the clothing and shoes we should bring.

It also pleased me to learn that neither Anie, nor Lena's sister, Lydia would be coming. Lydia had to stay home and take care of Lulu. And Anie was not part of this clique, it seemed.

"Good morning, Delila."

Still planning what to pack, I barely heard the reverend and deacon come into the room. "Oh, good morning, Reverend. Good morning, Deacon."

Anie jumped up from her desk and rushed over. "Good morning! I have something for you." She held out a plastic container. "I baked you some brownies."

"Why thank you Anie," The reverend turned around to face Anie. "That was very kind of you."

She handed the container to the deacon. "I didn't put nuts in them. Just in case you don't like nuts." Her lashes fluttered, as she smiled up at him.

"Thank you, Anie, I'm sure they will be delicious!" The reverend turned back to me. "Delila, the architect is coming in a few moments." He handed me an invoice that he'd held in his hand. "I need a check made out to him."

I looked at the invoice. The total price: $14,000, with $2,000 due now. I swallowed the urge to shout at him. We only had $1768.26 in the account. I'd have to pull some out of the little savings we had. And there were other bills due as well.

"Ok," I squeaked. "I'll take it out of our savings account." I hoped the deacon would realize we needed his check asap. "I'll have to hold off paying the water bill again though."

"What do you mean?" The reverend demanded. "We should have plenty of money in our account! What is going on here?"

"We've been spending a lot lately." I stammered. "The new furniture. Supplies have increased. The building is open longer and that adds to our costs." I was grasping to give him a reason. Any reason.

"Reverend," The deacon intervened. "Don't worry about it. I'll bring a check tomorrow and I'll double what I was going to give." He turned to me. "Will that cover the architect's check for today, Delila?"

"Yes. Thank you, Deacon!" I hoped the deacon knew how relieved I felt. How grateful for his help.

The reverend tipped his chin and raised his eyebrows at me. "The check?"

That afternoon dragged on. I decided to get the mail just as an excuse to get up and move around. When I returned, Anie was on the phone. I didn't mean to eavesdrop, but I couldn't help overhearing her side of the conversation.

"I agree. And she dresses like a...a hussy!" She laughed, then lowered her voice and turned away when she saw me. "I can't believe she wore that purple flowered dress Sunday."

I set the mail on her desk. She cast a sideways glance that said 'keep away' so I walked to the other side of the room, trying not to seem like I was listening. Of course, she had to know I was.

"She's not a good Christian either. Up until she married him, she rarely came to church. In fact, I don't think she ever went to church. Even now, she skips service at least once a month."

I kept my back to her so she couldn't see me cringe. I knew who she was talking about. Why say such mean things? Why the need to show her in a bad light? It irritated me. I knew she didn't like Mitzi. It seemed she wanted others to dislike her as well.

"Ah, umm." I spun around, cleared my throat loudly, and marched to my desk.

Even if some of what she was saying was true. It still bothered me. But then, hadn't I done the same thing? Hadn't I said something negative about someone I didn't like to make them look bad?

Anie looked over at me, then spoke into the phone, "I've got to go now. I'll call you later."

Her words about Mitzi's status as a Christian especially hit a nerve. Lately I'd heard a lot about who was a good Christian and who wasn't...who made the cut. I wondered where I stood. Before taking the job at the church, I admit, I didn't show up as often. Now I suspected there had been plenty of talk about me too.

Who should get to decide who's a good Christian and who's a bad one? Apparently, certain church members thought it was their duty to make these decisions.

And how did all that work anyway? Did you get turned down at the pearly gates for not having shown up at Church every week? Would St. Peter say "Oh I'm sorry ma'am; you did a lot of good for the world, helped numerous people and were a generally good person. But we're not going to let you in because we see here, you missed going to church three times last year. You're not a good Christian!" Somehow, I didn't think that was how it would go.

"Are there any more checks today, Anie?" I'd already seen an envelope from Mitzi and Ned, and I guessed it was a welcomed donation.

The following morning, I stared at the overflowing recycle basket and the garbage cans that needed to be emptied as well. Since Kai's death a few weeks ago, we had no one to clean the church. It was obvious Anie wasn't going to empty them. I didn't mind doing my own, and the community baskets, but I wasn't about to do hers.

I bagged up the paper in the recycle basket, and started out the door, almost bumping into the deacon as I did.

"Oh, I'm sorry," He said, "Here let me get that." He gently took the bag of recycles from my hand. "I've brought you a check."

"Thank you, Deacon!" I took the check from his hand and smiled in appreciation.

"You're welcome!" He turned to leave, but Anie popped up out of her seat, and he stopped.

"Deacon! Did you like the brownies?"

I wondered about the look on her face, all smiles and honey eyed. I tried to guess what the look meant.

"Oh yes, thank you Anie. They were delicious!" He grinned and turned to leave. "You ladies have a lovely day."

Grateful for the deacon's donation, I wanted it in the bank as quickly as possible. I made out the deposit slip then looked at the check. Odd. No, I must be imagining it. It was a coincidence. I stared at the check a moment longer, before realizing Anie was watching me. I finished the deposit and walked over to the copy machine. I kept my back to Anie, so she couldn't see me, and as I made a copy of the deposit slip, I also made a copy of the check.

A few minutes later Anie left the room. She was gone for several minutes, giving me time to place the folded copy in my purse.

"The reverend wants Kai's apartment cleaned out." Anie said as she came back into the office.

I understood Anie to mean she expected me to do it. I doubted the reverend had specifically said he wanted me to do the cleaning out.

"The police are finished with it then?" Initially they had been in and out of the church and Kai's apartment, but over time the dust began to settle. Visits from detectives had stopped, and people now talked about other things.

"Yep."

"Ok." I agreed quickly, I didn't really mind. I wanted to do one last thing for my friend. "I'll start on it tomorrow."

At home that afternoon, I pulled the copy of the check from my purse and studied it. It wasn't the amount that was of interest to me. I stared at the beautiful looping handwriting. It couldn't be.

I bolted to my bedroom and found the note I'd safely stored in my jewelry box. Back in the kitchen, I unfolded it, carefully flattened it, and placed it next to the copy of the check.

As carefully as possible, I compared the letters in the note to those on the check. The same! Kai hadn't written this note to me. The note was written by the deacon!

If Barry guessed that something was bothering me, he never mentioned it. After cleaning the house all afternoon and it looked spotless. I could tell he noticed I'd been at my compulsive cleaning, but he said nothing. He gave me space and time to digest, knowing I'd come to him when I was ready.

Over and over in my head I thought about Kai. The deacon. Anie. The reverend. I was confused. If the deacon had written the note, who was it for? He'd always been kind to me, but...no. No, it wasn't meant for me. I was sure.

This note was intended for someone else. But who? Anie? After all, Kai had seen her in my desk. Maybe she'd been searching for the note. A secret hiding place the two shared before my arrival. But they couldn't be seeing each other. The deacon was married!

How could I find out? Would Mitzi know? Or Lulu?

Early mornings were the best time to arrive at work. No one else in the office and I could ease into my day peacefully. I could also get a lot done without interruption. 7:30am worked good for me. It also meant I could leave earlier and have more time in the afternoon to do what I wanted.

Anie on the other hand, liked to show up around 9am. This worked especially well for me. A lot of people knew about our schedules too, so when they wanted to speak to me without being overheard by Anie, they usually stopped in early.

The morning after I discovered the deacon had written the note, he came in to see me during my 'unfettered hours.'

He handed me a box of fine chocolates. "I wanted to thank you for all you've done for the church Delila. I don't think most people realize how much you do here. I know how important you are, and well...thank you."

They were Godiva chocolates, expensive, delicious. "Why, thank you, deacon!"

He didn't wait around, just smiled, and said, "have a lovely day dear."

Dumfounded, I studied the chocolates. Should I take them home or share them here? I put them in my desk drawer and decided to wait and see how I felt later. Then I emailed Mitzi to see if she could meet for lunch.

I took the key to Kai's apartment and set off to clean it out. I'd decided to donate some of the items to the homeless shelter where he had stayed for a while. Anything else of value could go to the salvation army.

The apartment was small, one bedroom, a kitchenette, tiny living area and a bathroom. Yet, it must have seemed like a mansion to Kai. A refuge, where he was safe and at peace.

The furniture belonged to the church, bed, dresser, sofa, table and two chairs. He didn't have much of his own. I began in the bedroom. Pulling his few clothes that were worth anything from the drawers, I placed them in a box I'd found in the kitchen.

Linens and kitchen towels could stay. Beyond his clothes there was little else. I finished putting things in the boxes and within a short time, I felt satisfied that I'd cleared out everything that needed to go.

I glanced around the room. My eyes fell on the little cat bed in the corner. Jewel's bed. I'd take that home to her. I loaded up everything in my car. I could stop at the shelter and salvation army on the way home and drop stuff off.

As I stuffed the last of the items into the trunk, I noticed a text from Mitzi. She suggested we meet for lunch at The Superb Chef, a favorite restaurant of ours. It was nearly lunch time so rather than text her back, I called to confirm our lunch date.

Thehe Superb Chef is famous for its incredible lunch menu. The building itself is quaint, comfortable, however they could stand an upgrade to the furniture. The staff go above and beyond to give good service, but it is the food that draws most people in.

One of the most popular menu items is their seafood chowder, however I always order their cherry salad. With cashews, dried cherries, shredded chicken, goat cheese and cucumber julienned into tiny slices, it's delicious. And I'm totally hooked on their special dressing.

Mitzi and I sat across from one another, having already ordered. "Ok Delila, what gives?"

"What?"

"Why the need to meet for lunch so suddenly? Something must be up."

I'd planned to start out discussing the girl's getaway and casually lead into the real reason, rather than asking too bluntly. I decided with Mitzi it really didn't matter.

"Are Anie and the deacon having an affair?"

Mitzi laughed. "Oh Delila, the look on your face!" She took a drink of her water then still smiling said, "Honestly, I don't know. Are you asking because he gave her that new Kate Spade purse she loves to fling around?"

"He gave her..." I hadn't known. "The purse must have cost a fortune! How do you know these things anyway?"

"You are so funny!" Mitzi laughed again. "Anie and Lydia are good friends. She told Lydia, who told her mother, who told Lena, who told me."

Now I understood how information was dispensed. So many connections. And now I was getting information from Mitzi. Apparently, secrets were unable to remain secrets for long.

Our lunch was served, and I took that first delicious bite. In that moment, I thought only of the flavors rolling around on my tongue.

"So why do you think they are having an affair?" Mitzi wondered.

"Well," I took a breath. "I found a note in my desk. I know it was written by the deacon because I compared the handwriting to a check, he wrote. Who else could the note be for?" I had just joined the circle of chinwaggers. Throwing seeds in the pot of gossip.

"Humm. What did it say?" Mitzi asked.

I covered my mouth and swallowed before answering. "It seemed like a love letter to me."

When I returned to the office after lunch with Mitzi, I found several checks on my desk. It seemed the reverend's request for funding for the new sanctuary was starting to pay off. A big relief to me.

"Thank you for clearing out Kai's apartment Delila." Anie said.

"He really didn't have that much. It needs to be cleaned and linens washed, but otherwise it's ready to go." I knew the church had found a new caretaker and wanted to let him stay in the apartment.

My plan was to leave early and drop off the items at the homeless shelter and salvation army, but people kept coming in with checks. And talk. When someone comes in to donate, they always want to discuss the project. Leaving early turned into leaving late, once again.

Eager to fix Barry a nice dinner for a change, I rushed into the house, nearly forgetting to grab Jewel's bed from the car. Lately dinners had been something thrown together. Not like before I started working, when I spent time preparing gourmet meals, like pecan chicken or crab stuffed flounder.

I looked around for a place to put the bed. It seemed large for such a tiny kitten. Kai must have thought she'd grow into it. I placed it in a corner for her and waited to see if she'd notice it. If she'd remember her old home. Her old life.

She didn't. She completely ignored the bed and ran to Barry's chair instead. Her claws gripped the material, and she began kneading. The claws dug in deeper then, she pulled them out and pushed them in again. I could see the chair was taking a real beating, fraying as the claws became sharper.

"Jewel, no!" I raced over to stop her, and she ran for the drapes. It was amazing to see her scale them in record time. Was she part squirrel? I wrestled her from the curtains and took her to her bed.

"How about you lay down in your bed." I patted the bed. "Come on." I patted it again. It felt hard. No wonder she didn't want to lay in it. It was lumpy. I patted it again. I began searching for a way inside the bed. I found an opening that had been sewn shut. I raced to the den for a pair of scissors and cut it open.

There it was! Kai had hidden the money in the padding. The money given to him for medical school. I sat down on the floor and began pulling it out. I counted. Three thousand dollars! How had I not noticed the unwieldy bed? The weight of it? I guess with all the other things on my mind, I just hadn't paid attention.

Now new questions formed in my mind. What should I do with the money? Should I report it to the police? Return it to the church? How should something like this be handled? Was there a legal protocol for finding money in a dead person's belongings?

Barry and I sat looking at the money. We had to decide. Should we contact Jim or just give the money back to the church? If we turned it in to the police, it might eventually be returned to the church anyway. But if some long-lost relative appeared, they might get it. And in a way, Kai had stolen that money. He had deceived the members into giving it to him.

After much thought, we decided to give it back to the church. Afterall, it was found on church property and should therefore belong to the church.

"I just wonder what happened to the rest of the money." Barry was still thinking about it after dinner.

"What do you mean?"

"Well, I'm pretty sure he was given more than $3,000 for tuition and books, and some clothes to wear to class."

It was a good question. Kai had some decent clothes, but not much. He didn't have any expensive jewelry either. No car. No bank account. What *had* happened to the rest of the money?

"***T***he report certainly looks better than last month." Jannie's eyes scanned the document for possible mistakes. "Looks like we had a very large donation?"

"It was found in Kai's belongings." I spoke in a low voice and hoped Anie wouldn't hear.

"Well, that's good news!" Jannie blurted out, not taking my hint.

"What's good news?" Anie asked.

I cringed. Why had I thought it could be kept secret? I'd discussed it with the reverend first thing in the morning, then I took a special trip to the bank to deposit it before it disappeared. I entered it into the general fund so it wouldn't go toward the new sanctuary, but instead would be used to catch up on bills.

"What's good news?" Anie asked again.

"Some of the money we gave Kai was found." Jannie's voice cheerful, unusual for her. "I wonder what happened to the rest of it?" She eyed me as if I had the answer.

"Good morning, ladies, how are you this morning?" Lulu's cheerful voice a welcomed interruption.

Almost in unison, we all wished her a good morning. I noticed she had a new cane.

"You have a new cane?" I walked over to admire it. "It's beautiful!" It was unusual, but lovely. A marble ball the size of a large round doorknob or baseball on top of a sleek black stick.

She clutched the top and took a step forward. "Yes. It's an antique. It was a gift."

"I've got to get going. It was nice seeing you, Lulu." Jannie said, and walked out the door, the financial report firm in her hand.

"I'm going to go get the mail. Bye, Lulu." Anie gave a small wave and rushed out to catch up with Jannie.

I pulled the chair over for Lulu, then sat down across from her.

"Those ladies seemed mighty happy this morning." Lulu took a tissue from the box on my desk and wiped her face.

"Yes. We found some of the money that Kai had been given." I wasn't going to share where it was found just yet.

Lulu didn't press me for more information. Instead, she smiled, as if she already knew. "I'm glad the other ladies left. I wanted to talk to you alone. Mitzi told me about your discussion the other day. That you think Anie, and the deacon are having an affair." She paused and looked directly at me.

Embarrassed, I squirmed slightly in my seat and waited for her to continue.

"She told me about the note." Here she took a deep breath. "Dear, that note was not intended for Anie."

How does she know that? I wondered.

"I'm reluctant to mention it, but I really don't want gossip getting out that isn't true."

Ashamed, I looked down at my desk. "I'm sorry, Lulu. Do you know who the note was intended for?"

"Delila." Her tone was soft and gentle, like a mother trying to help her child correct a mistake. She waited a full minute before answering. "I may as well tell you. Mrs. Waverly was in love with the deacon. Even though she was much older than him, she was very much in love. And he...well he seemed in love with her too. He said he loved her as a friend. She thought it was more than that. Maybe she just hoped it was."

Lulu must have seen the shock on my face because she quickly continued. "It wasn't like you think, Delila. It wasn't sexual. But he was so attentive to her needs. He'd bring her lunch and little gifts. Not expensive things, but...you know...thoughtful." Lulu rubbed the top of her cane.

"And he needed a woman who understood him. That woman he's married to...well, she's not much of a wife. Unstable you know. Makes him do his own laundry and dishes."

"Does she work?" I wanted to know.

"Oh yes. She works. But he pays most of the bills." Lulu's voice started to rise; her feathers ruffled.

I wanted to calm her and learn more about this relationship. "So, they were in love, but a different kind of love?"

Lulu nodded her head. She reached over the desk and put her hand on my arm. "Yes. You see, she was lonely. She had no one other than her cat. And the deacon was always there for her. Bringing her lunch. Talking with her. Calling her on the phone. Making her feel young and alive again." Lulu looked deep into my eyes. "You understand, don't you?"

I could imagine it. A lonely woman. Constant attention from a much younger, attractive man. She must have been incredibly happy. But what was the attraction for him?

As if to answer my question, Lulu continued, "And even if there was no physical relationship, that is other than hugging, I think he loved her too. I think in his mind she was like a mother to him. She was stable, made him feel good about himself. Built up his confidence. But--"

Lulu stopped and became thoughtful.

"I always wondered if maybe the inheritance had anything to do with all the attention, he gave her. He knew she had money. I think he knew she'd leave it to him. Or hoped so anyway."

"And she did?"

Lulu clutched the large round ball of her cane and nodded. "All of it."

Lulu and I sat in silence for a moment as I absorbed her story about the deacon inheriting Mrs. Waverly's money. I had heard he had plenty of money himself. I knew he lived a lavish lifestyle. He was generous. A lord of the church. Respected.

Now I was even more curious about the deacon. "I thought he was already a wealthy man?"

Lulu looked up at me with an all-knowing sweet smile. "Yes, that's true. He came from big money. East coast." She took a deep breath. "He once told Ella, that is Mrs. Waverly, that when he was a kid, he had a chauffeur that took him to school. The chauffeur also brought him lunch that the family's cook prepared. He had a maid whose sole job was to clean up after him."

"Wow!" I tried to imagine the deacon as a child. A small boy, wandering about in a huge house with servants all over.

I wanted to ask her more about the deacon, but Lydia came in at that moment, making her usual grand entrance.

"Oh mother, there you are!" Her arms flew up in the air, "I should have known I'd find you here." She glided across the room. "Hello Delila."

Ever since I'd said 'no' to goodies for the choir, Lydia seemed to avoid me. She was polite, but cool. It was frustrating at times to have to be the 'bad guy', but my job was watching the money. Making sure we didn't overdraw our bank account.

"We need to go mother. You've gossiped long enough." Lydia took her mother's arm.

"Nonsense Lydia. We weren't gossiping at all. I was setting Delila straight, so she didn't spread 'misinformation' about the deacon."

My face turned flush. I looked at Lydia and tried to find words to exonerate myself. Behind her in the doorway I saw Anie, her face frozen. She must have just walked up, but it was obvious she'd heard us. I forced a smile.

Lulu stood up slowly and with Lydia's help wobbled out the door. Anie stood aside for them to go then walked to her desk, keeping an eye on me and a frown on her face.

Once they had gone, Anie was silent for about three minutes, her face a mishmash of resentment and frustration.

"What were you saying about the deacon?" Her voice was not loud, but it was firm. "He's a good man. Kind and generous. You really should mind your own business, Delila."

Her anger, in my opinion, was uncalled for. Why was she so defensive when it came to him? Was she in love with him? And how could she not see how he was with Mrs. Waverly. Afterall, it was almost impossible to keep anything from your coworker in this office. Yes, I decided. Anie had known about his relationship with Mrs. Waverly.

I was afraid to say anything at first, thinking it would just give her another reason to go off on a rant.

"Honestly, I don't know why you pick on him!"

She was baiting me now. I'd have to defend myself. "I wasn't picking on him. I was simply curious." I'd need to choose my words carefully. Afterall, the last thing I wanted was for her to tell the deacon that I was gossiping about him! So, I said, "I'd heard he was in love with Mrs. Waverly. And that she'd left him all her money." There I'd gotten her back. My turn to bait her. No woman wanted to hear that the man she was in love with, loved someone else.

"He wasn't in love with her. She was in love with him! He was just kind to her because he felt sorry for her." Anie sounded defensive. Protective. "He was kind to her just like he was to Mildred."

"Mildred?"

She looked slightly embarrassed. As if she'd said something she shouldn't have. "Yes. Mildred Hanks. He did a lot for her, several years back. They were good friends. He was devastated when she died."

I knew not to push her. If I asked pointed questions, she'd clam up. I didn't want that. I gave her space and waited for her to continue.

"Mildred's family were vultures!" Anie explained. "She left all her money to the deacon. She had quite a bit from her previous two husbands, but she didn't have any kids, so it made sense that she'd leave it to him. But her siblings were furious when they found out. Took him to court. The judge made him give the money back." Anie seemed to be recalling the story for herself more than for me. "It was crazy, because Mildred wanted him to have that money!"

"But didn't he have money of his own? I mean, Lulu said he came from a wealthy family."

"He had to spend it on his wife's medical expenses. She has mental issues. It's super expensive to cover those costs." She eyed me suspiciously now.

"Oh," I nodded softly. Another question had been rolling around in my head for a while. "What about the money the church pays him?"

She looked at me with vexation. "It's not that much. Her care is super expensive."

I nodded again.

"He gave half of the money to the church anyway." She said in justification.

"He is generous." I agreed. I wondered just how generous. I spent the next hour looking through accounts trying to find out. If he had made a large donation, it would be somewhere in the records.

As I left work, I remembered I still hadn't dropped off Kai's things at the homeless shelter. I made a detour and headed downtown. The shelter was housed in a newer-looking building in an older section of town.

Inside I met with a staff member who kindly offered to give me a tour. He showed me around the building and explained that they could only take certain 'in-kind' donations because they didn't have space to store much, nor did they have the staff to sort it.

So new tee shirts, sweatpants, sweatshirts, underwear were ok, but nothing used. New twin size sheets were ok too. In the winter, they liked to receive new coats, gloves, hats, and blankets.

"Why only new?" I asked.

"Well for one thing, we worry about things like bed bugs. They can come in on used clothing and linen. We don't have the staff to sort through tons of stuff. So, we encourage people to donate used clothing and bedding to the Salvation Army or Goodwill. Then we give our residents vouchers so they can go get what they need. That way we free up space for more beds."

"That makes sense." I agreed.

He led me up some stairs, down a hall, and pushed open a door so we could peek inside one of the bedrooms. It was long and narrow with a window at the end overlooking the street. I was impressed that small though it was, the room managed to fit four twin size beds, along with a tall locker for each bed, where residents could store a few precious goods safely.

Underneath one bed was a pair of large work boots. A baseball cap hung on the short bed post of another. Other personal items were stored under the beds as well. One of the beds was neatly made. The other three were rumpled, but all the sheets looked clean.

"How many people can stay here at one time?" I asked.

"We only have enough beds for around 75 people. And there is a six to eight week wait to get in."

"That's a long time! Where do they stay in the meantime?" I had noticed a lot of people standing at street corners begging for money recently. Now I wondered where they slept at night.

"Some stay with family or friends, couch surfing for a day or two. We offer lockers in a room downstairs where they can keep their things until they can get in here."

I thought of Kai then. I could picture him lying on one of these beds, dreaming of a better life.

"What if they have no family?" I asked.

"We partner with several churches in the area. They take turns allowing people to sleep inside if they have nowhere else to go."

I thought about our church and wondered why we didn't participate. I decided to bring it up to the reverend.

We had wandered back down to the kitchen. "This is where everyone eats. We offer a continental breakfast, as well as lunch and dinner." He grinned. "Ok, we don't provide the meals. That's a different non-profit organization. But they serve the meals here."

As we came to the end of the tour, he stopped by the front door and thanked me for coming.

"But I do have a few things that I think you can take. I'll just run out to my car and get them." I walked out to my car and returned with a package of white t shirts that had never been opened.

He grinned. "That's funny. We had about 350 of these packages donated a few years back. The same tees."

"This package came from someone who had stayed here at one time. Maybe he got them here. Did you know Kai Williams?"

I watched a wide smile stretch across his face. "Sure, I knew Kai. What a great young man! You know once he got that job, he became a big donor here. So sad though. I mean tragic for him to die so young. Did they ever catch the guy who did it?"

"No," I shook my head, but my mind hung up on his previous remark. "What do you mean by 'big donor'?"

"Oh, he donated several thousand dollars. You see he said the people here were the kindest, most giving, he'd ever known. He made some friends along the way too. And he wanted to pay it forward."

I smiled. "I'm sure he did. You said he made some friends here? I'd love to meet them."

"Well, the only one still here is Dora. Most were volunteers or other residents who've moved on now."

"Could I talk to Dora?" I looked around.

"She only volunteers one day a week. She'll be here tomorrow."

I thanked him, then left. I sat in my car thinking about what I'd just learned about Kai. He'd swindled the church out of the money by claiming to be a medical student. Then he gave the money to the homeless shelter. Like Robin Hood.

The next morning, I decided to broach the subject first with Anie. "You know," I said testing the temperature of the idea. "A lot of churches in the area are partnering with the homeless shelter."

"The reverend will never go for it." Anie glanced over at me. "Your buddy Kai already tried it."

My buddy Kai. Why did she hate him so much? I admit, I was upset when I found out he'd swindled the church members out of all that money, pretending to be a student. I felt a little less upset about it since I'd found out he did it to help the shelter. But what was Anie's beef with him?

"Anie, why did you dislike Kai so much?" Now that we were talking a little, I felt she might open up to me.

"Why?"

She gave me her raised eyebrow and scowl that always irritated me.

"Because he was always snooping around, that's why. Blackmailing people."

"Blackmailing? Who did he blackmail?"

"Well, me for one."

"For what?" I was reminded once again of Kai telling me he'd seen Anie rifling through my desk.

"I'm not going to tell you." She looked indignant. "Why would I tell you?"

Ok, but why bring it up at all? What was Anie hiding?

I was caught up at work so there was really no need to stay later. I'd already worked over my four hours, and Anie still hadn't explained about the blackmail. Besides, I had plans to meet with Dora at the homeless shelter, so I left.

A volunteer directed me toward the lunchroom, where I saw a young woman cleaning up trash left over from lunch. She was small and looked like she could be in her mid-twenties. Head down, she was so absorbed in her work that she didn't notice me come in.

Her curly brown hair was pulled back in a ponytail that did little to contain it. She cleared the tables and shoveled paper glasses and plates into the garbage bag. I noticed a slight limp as she moved to the next table.

"Excuse me," I interrupted.

She turned to look at me, "Oh I'm sorry, I didn't hear anyone come in." She pushed her glasses tighter to her face.

Her smile reminded me of an innocent child. I read her name on the lanyard she wore around her neck.

"Hi Dora. You're just the person I was hoping to see." I gave her my friendliest grin. "My name is Delila, and I was a friend and co-worker of Kai's. Do you have a minute?"

"Well," She hesitated. "I'm supposed to be cleaning up. But I guess I can take a short break. Are you with the police?"

"No, just a co-worker and friend." It seemed she needed reassurance before she would trust me. "I have his kitten now." I pulled out my phone and showed her a picture.

She sat down at a table, and I sat next to her. "You and Kai were good friends?"

"Yeah." A blush crossed her face. "He used to call me 'Dorable.' It was his nickname for me."

I smiled with her, understanding her affection for him. I suspected there had been a romantic aspect to their relationship. At least on her part.

"How did you meet?"

"We met my first night here. He was nice to me." A smile crossed her face at the memory. "My parents died when I was 18." The smile faded as she recalled a dark time. "I lived with my aunt for a while, but then I got in trouble. I was drinking and taking drugs. I went to rehab and after that they brought me here. That's when I met Kai." Her smile returned.

"It sounds like you're doing better now."

"Oh yeah. The people here helped me get a part-time job and get on disability. I live in a group home now, but I like to come back and help."

"Dora, did Kai ever talk to you about the people at work? Or about anybody he didn't like or was afraid of?"

"Well, he did tell me there were some people at the church he didn't trust." She eyed me now with a bit more caution.

"He trusted me. We were friends." I hoped she would believe me. Confide in me. "I have a friend on the police force. I'm trying to help him find out who killed Kai. Is there anything you can think of that might help?"

She sat silent for a moment and looked down at her hands. "I don't know."

I could tell there was something she wasn't sharing. I sensed that she wanted to tell me, but something was holding her back. "Look Dora, you want the police to catch whoever did this to Kai, don't you?"

Dora nodded her head. "Yes."

"If you know something, it might help them. Otherwise, they may never catch Kai's killer."

She looked so young. So innocent. Yet at the same time she had already been through so much.

"Well, I don't know if it means anything..."

On Sunday the reverend gave a sermon on what it means to be a Christian. His words trailed off as my thoughts wandered. To me, it meant to be a good person. To care about others, treat them with respect. To do the right thing even when it's not the easy thing to do. Even if it's not the popular thing to do.

I looked around at the congregation. These people were all good Christians. Yet someone was stealing from the church. Someone here was most likely Kai's killer. One by one I began searching the faces for clues.

Lydia stood with the choir. Leader and guardian. She didn't look at the reverend. Instead, she faced the people, a hollow statue draped in a burgundy robe. A perfect actress in her role.

The deacon sat in the front row, on the opposite side of the pews from Barry and me. For the first time I noticed his wife. She sat next to him in a black dress. I thought about this poor woman who'd never made a splash in the world. Known only as "the wife with mental illness".

As if she heard my thoughts, she turned and looked at me. I quickly averted my gaze, but not before noticing her sullen expression and chalky skin.

When I thought she was no longer looking in my direction, I stole a glance at the deacon. He gave his full attention to the reverend. A smile of support, reassurance. I saw the reverend's gaze fall on him and recognize the endorsement.

Anie sat on the other side of the deacon. She sat up straight in her Sunday dress, chin jutted out. She reminded me of a long ago Puritan. She stole a glance at the deacon, and I caught the look between them.

Lulu and Lena sat behind them, with Mitzi and Ned. Mitzi squirmed in her seat and looked bored. It made me smile.

The reverend wrapped up his speech and the baskets were passed down each row. Barry and I sat near the far edge of the pew. I slid out of my seat and escaped the room.

I hid in a corner near the hallway and waited. They would have to pass this way.

The two churchgoers carried the donation baskets into the hall several feet from where I hid. The deacon's low voice whispered, "thanks Anie. I'll take these to the office and lock the money up."

From my hiding spot I could see them facing one another.

"Ok, thanks Deacon." She lingered for a moment, then returned to the sanctuary.

He turned and looked around. I stepped back a little further. I had a good hiding spot near the restrooms. If caught, it would provide an excuse for me being there. Busy looking at the contents of the basket, the deacon didn't see me. He looked around once more, then plucked some of the bills from the top basket and quickly stuck them in his pocket. A moment later he grabbed a handful more.

After church, Barry and I stopped at our favorite little buffet for brunch. It was crowded and many of the congregation were also there. I nodded as I saw them in line and passed their tables.

I wanted to discuss it with him but didn't want to risk having our conversation overheard. I waited until we were back in the car and headed home.

"What do you think I should do?" I asked. Barry was my rock and my best advisor.

He was thoughtful. "That is a tricky situation. You need to be careful Delila." Ever since Kai's death, Barry had been worried about me working at the church. "Maybe you shouldn't do anything just yet."

"But I saw him take the money! You don't think I should confront him? Or tell the reverend?"

"I don't know. It would be your word against his."

It was true, I had no real proof. Deflated, I put on my walking shoes.

Boris lay on the floor, his face on his paws, his eyes watching me. I hadn't walked him in two days. I think he'd given up on me. I'd been so preoccupied with the job, and that sweet little kitten Jewel, I'd not given him much time. I felt a little guilty.

"Come on Boris." I picked up his leash and walked over to him. He rolled over and wagged his tail a little. "I mean it, let's go."

We headed down the street toward Lily Park. There near the picnic tables, in a bright purple blouse, and lavender flowered capris, Mitzi stood and watched her little poodle sniff the edge of the flower garden.

As we entered the park, I waved and unleashed Boris. The little red poodle ran to me, her tail bobbing with excitement. I reached down and patted the soft tuff on top of her head.

"Look at you, look at those pretty purple bows in your hair! You match your momma!" She stood on her hind legs and put her paws on me. "Ah, look your toenails match too. So pretty!" I rubbed her foot for a moment before she jumped down and ran to Boris.

"Did you enjoy the sermon today?" I teased.

Mitzi gave me that look, shook her head and we both laughed. "I guess I'm just not a church person."

We chatted for a few minutes about our upcoming "girl's getaway" then Mitzi surprised me with some new information.

"Remember you asked me about Anie and the deacon?"

I nodded and leaned a little closer.

"So, I've been watching them, and he does flirt with her. It's subtle, but he does. Anyway, I decided to ask around about it. Suzy Siebel, I don't think you know her, but she used to be best friends with Anie. She told me that Anie is undoubtably in love with the deacon. That she would do anything for him."

When Boris and I returned home from the park, Barry and Jim were loading their golf clubs into Barry's Jeep. I was glad Barry was going out for some fun and exercise. They followed me into the house to get some bottled water for their outing.

I couldn't pass up the opportunity to ask Jim about the case. "Any new developments in Kai's case?"

Jim shrugged. "Not really. We don't have any suspects or motive and still haven't been able to find the weapon."

"You're sure it couldn't have been the pickle jar though, right?"

"No, the shape of the weapon was smaller, and round like a baseball." Jim stopped as if he'd caught himself letting something slip. "It's not public knowledge, so don't say anything to anyone, ok? And keep your eyes open around the church."

"Ok." I promised as Barry handed him a bottle of water and they walked out the door.

The afternoon went by quickly. I cleaned and thought about the deacon and the money. Barry had said to leave it alone. Not to get involved. My word against the deacon's. He was right; it was my word against his.

Then my own words came back to haunt me. "Good Christians do the right thing, even when it's not the easy thing to do. Even if it's not the popular thing to do."

The next morning, I counted the deposit and filled out the deposit slip. I entered the amount and checked our balance. Then I looked at our bills. The reverend had asked people to chip in a little more this week. An extra $5, $10 or $20 to help with our current expenses. I'd seen several $50 bills and even a couple of $100's, when the basket passed by me. But there were no large bills in the deposit. And I knew why.

I would wait until the reverend had time to get settled in. I didn't want to hit him with this bombshell too early.

Anie strolled in around 9am, eyed me suspiciously as usual, then settled into her chair. I feared her reaction if she learned I'd accused the deacon of something as sinister as stealing the church's donation money. And why would he? After all, he had lots of money. He donated lots of money. Why steal it?

At 10 o'clock I thought the reverend would be in his office. It was the time I had decided on. My stomach began to flutter. I felt queasy. Maybe I should wait until 10:15. I looked at the deposit slip again.

When 10:30 rolled around I finally got the courage to walk down the hall to the reverend's office. The deacon didn't usually show up until later in the afternoon. The reverend would be alone.

I knocked lightly at the door so as not to startle him. "Excuse me, Reverend. Can I have a word with you?"

"Of course, come in."

I shut the door behind me and took a seat in front of his desk. I set the deposit slip down in front of him. "This is all we got yesterday." I began.

"Humm. Seems rather smaller than I expected." His brows pressed together firmly in anger or irritation, as he studied the deposit slip, then looked up at me.

"I saw two one-hundred-dollar bills and several fifties in the basket when it passed by me. But there were none in the deposit this morning." I waited for that to sink in for a moment.

"Reverend. There's something I feel I should tell you." I shifted in my chair. He waited without comment. "I was in the hallway, next to the bathroom yesterday, when the deacon and Anie brought the baskets out. After Anie left, I saw the deacon take some of the money from the baskets." I stopped and took a deep breath. "I saw him put it in his pocket."

The reverend grimaced and shook his head. "Now why would he do that? He has plenty of money. He doesn't need to steal."

"I don't know. But that's what I saw."

He leaned back in his chair and scowled. "This is a very serious allegation. You realize that of course?"

"I know. And I would never say it if I hadn't seen it with my own eyes." I was pleading now. I had to make him understand.

"The deacon is one of our most generous donors. He's an upstanding church member." He stopped to think for a moment. "He probably dropped the money in accidentally and was just taking it back out when you saw him."

"But I—"

"I know that's what you think you saw, Delila. Now please go back to your office and finish your work."

I sulked down the hall to my office and plopped down at my desk. Had the deacon put that money in there to impress Anie, then taken it back out later? It was possible. I pouted for a few minutes then went back to work.

After an hour or so, I began to worry. Would the reverend tell the deacon what I said? Would he tell anyone else? Anie already didn't trust me.

What would Lulu think when she heard? And Lena. They already thought I was gossiping about the deacon. Suddenly I wanted to take it all back. Undo what I'd told him. Why hadn't I taken Barry's advice?

But it was too late. The damage was already done. Deflated, I longed to go home. To hide. I couldn't. If I left before noon, Anie would know something was up and would surely pry it from the reverend. Besides, I had a luncheon planned with Lulu and Lena.

I pulled some of the invoices from the stack and began to print checks to pay them. When I came to the credit card statement, I paused. It was our largest expense. We'd always carried a high balance, at least it had always been high since I'd been doing the bookkeeping.

It wasn't my job to worry about those things. That's what Jannie had informed me when I started. She was the accountant and the treasurer. It was her job. If there was anything amiss, I should inform her, and she'd take care of it. My job was to pay the bills and enter the data into Quickbooks, the accounting software we used.

I scanned the credit card statement now. Annoyed that we were spending so much on interest, I wondered if we could somehow lower the bill. I saw several expenses for the new sanctuary.

As my eyes scrolled through the various charges, they fell on one I'd seen every month since I'd arrived, yet I had no idea what it was for. Goodgirlfund.com. I'd never paid much attention to it since Jannie looked over the statements and approved them for payment. But now I was curious.

Anie was busy on the phone, so I walked over to the filing cabinet and looked through some previous statements. It was a reoccurring charge and higher than most of the other charges. Between $500 and $1,000 a month. Could it be a donation to a girl's orphanage or perhaps a scholarship fund of some sort?

I made copies of some of the statements dating back several years, while Anie was still preoccupied on the phone. I carefully folded the copies, then discreetly placed them in my purse.

A few minutes later, Lulu and Lena arrived to take me to lunch. They were cheerful as we left the office, so I knew they had not heard about my tattling on the deacon.

Once we were seated in the restaurant and had ordered our lunch, I broached the subject. If the church did donate to a scholarship or orphanage, these ladies would know.

"Have either of you ever heard of Goodgirlfund or Goodgirlfund.com?"

Both ladies shook their heads.

"No dear. Why do you ask?" Lulu smiled, an innocent glint in her blue eyes.

"Oh, just curious. I heard about it and just wondered what it was." I didn't want to say anything that might send off an alarm. Yet, the fact that the church was making such a sizeable donation to this organization should mean that one of these ladies would have heard of it. I would have to check it out later. Fortunately, our food arrived at that point and the topic was quickly dropped.

I went directly home after lunch and hurried to the computer. I searched Google for goodgirlfund. I was taken to a website that asked me to login or join for free. I didn't join.

At the top of the page, I saw a tab that said 'our girls'. I selected the tab. I nearly choked on my shock. Whatever I expected, it was not this. These certainly were not the kind of girls a church would support!

Stunned, I sat there for several minutes. I couldn't believe my eyes. Had I gotten the wrong site? I pulled the papers from my purse and checked again. The reality of the situation began to sink in. The air grew thin, and I found it hard to breathe. What should I do? Who should I tell?

Anxiety spread throughout my body. This was big. A scandal like this could ruin the church. And whoever was embezzling the money and funneling it to this website could go to prison.

I decided to wait for Barry. My confidant. My advisor. And the wisest person I knew. He would know what to do. I'd have to confess to telling the reverend against his advice. I hoped he'd understand.

As always when I'm nervous, scared or upset, I clean. It is the only way to take my mind off my fears. I usually start with the kitchen, then make my way through the rest of the house.

I glanced over at Jewel, asleep in her little bed. Boris lifted his head. He watched me with knowing eyes. He'd seen it before. But he never made a sound.

Dinner was on the table when Barry arrived home. A chicken Caesar salad and fresh bread rolls. Homemade peanut butter cookies for dessert. Simple and easy, it could wait if he wasn't ready to eat right away.

"Umm, what's this?" He said looking over the meal, "Looks delicious."

I wanted to rush right into the news of my latest discovery but held back to give him time to unwind from his own busy day. When I was younger, I didn't realize how important it was to give him this time to decompress. I waited until after dinner. After the table was cleaned and dishes were done, but before he could start some project that would take his mind far away.

"Barry," I caught him as he headed for the garage. "I need to talk to you. Can you give me a minute?" It may have sounded silly to ask but I needed his full attention.

First, I confessed to not taking his advice. Explained why I had to tell the reverend. He listened without commenting, and I went on to tell him of the reverend's response. "But that's not the only thing I need to tell you."

He stood there looking at me as if I'd said a zombie apocalypse was upon us. I could see him processing the situation in his mind, much the way I had. Our eyes locked in a moment of fear and understanding. I read the concern on his face. "What do I do now?" I whispered.

"Let's call Jim." Barry suggested.

"But if the police get involved, we'll have another big scandal. Just like when Kai died. Reporters all over the place. Oh Barry, I don't want to deal with that again. Do you think the police could keep it out of the news?"

"I don't know." Barry admitted.

"If it gets out, it could close down the church. I mean, no one will want to donate to a church where money is being embezzled." I'd had all day to think about it, but Barry was just now considering the gravity of the situation.

"I'd probably lose my job," I said. What I didn't say was, I'd lose my friends.

"Let's not get too far ahead of ourselves." Barry reached out and rubbed my arm. "Ok, look. You take some time and think about it some more. But a man was murdered in that church. You caught someone stealing money. And now you found that someone within the congregation is using church funds to support pornography." He sighed and patted my shoulder. "I'm going out to the garage for a little bit."

I picked up a peanut butter cookie from the kitchen table, walked into my office, plopped down at my computer, and stared at it. I considered Barry's summary of the issues. Were they all related? Could the deacon have charged the church for an erotic website without anyone realizing it? How had Jannie allowed that?

My phone pulled me from my trance with a loud ring. I didn't recognize the number but answered it anyway.

"Hello?" The voice was soft, hesitant. "Is this Delila?"

"Yes. Dora?"

"Hi Delila. I hope it's ok to call." She took a deep breath. "I thought of something else Kai told me." Her voice was soft and quiet.

I heard voices in the background.

"I don't want to tell you over the phone." She half whispered.

It was nearly 7pm. She'd probably already had her dinner. And it was too late to grab a cup of coffee. "Do you like ice cream?" I asked.

We drove to the north side of town, to a cute little ice cream shop called Big Frosty. I'd brought my son here many times when he was young. The store had aged a bit, not quite as clean and orderly as it had been when it first opened. Yet, it still carried the charm and excitement for both young and old.

A giant fiberglass snowman stood just outside the door holding a sign that said 'welcome.' A bench on the other side of the door looked like a giant ice cream sundae.

Dora's eyes grew large as she perused the many flavors. She smiled with pure delight. It took her a few minutes to choose, but she finally settled on a flavor called moose tracks, while I chose my favorite, salted caramel.

The teenager behind the counter scooped our ice cream then went back to looking at his phone. We sat at a table and chairs shaped like ice cream cones, near the front window. We were lucky to have the place all to ourselves.

I let the sweet cream melt on my tongue and watched Dora smile and do the same.

She looked up at me. "Thank you for bringing me here."

"You're welcome."

"I thought about what you said. About helping catch whoever killed Kai," She took another bite of ice cream. "Kai did tell me something else. Something he saw." She became more serious.

Patiently I waited for her to continue.

She looked up at me as if to make sure I was listening. "He was trimming bushes around the building. He could see into the office."

I nodded.

"He saw someone make some tea for an old lady who worked there."

Mrs. Waverly, I presumed.

"Then he saw them put something in the tea. But the old lady didn't see it. And later that day, the old lady died." Dora took another bite of ice cream.

"He didn't tell the police or anyone?"

"No. He was afraid they wouldn't believe him."

"So, what did he do?"

"He went in later and found something in the wastebasket. He said it was a wrapper from some allergy medicine. An ana, anaimine, or something."

"Antihistamine?" I asked.

"Yeah, he said the old lady seemed ok, so he didn't do anything. But then later she died."

The door of the parlor opened and a woman with two small children paraded up to the counter.

I tried to pump Dora for more information.

"I don't know. I don't remember." She pouted.

Did she know more? I couldn't tell.

The following morning, I still hadn't decided what to do about all the new information I'd found. Had Kai witnessed the murder of Mrs. Waverly? Or had it been a coincidence that she died after having taken some allergy medicine?

Should I tell Jim? What could he do? Exhume the body? Based on what? Even if they found the meds in her, whoever gave it to her could say she asked them to. I didn't even know who that person was. And the only real witness was dead.

Tired from not having slept, I walked over to the Keurig Machine and started to make myself a cup of coffee, then stopped.

Barry hadn't wanted me to come in to work. But I insisted I'd be ok. We'd argued a bit and finally he warned me to be extra careful.

Now I looked at the pods and wondered if they could be tampered with. I decided I could go without another cup of coffee this morning. I was on edge. I closed the door to the office and sat back down.

My mind returned to the goodgirlfund.com situation. Only a few people were allowed to use that credit card. Jannie must know who authorized the charge initially. I composed an email to her.

However, before I could hit the send button, I received a text message from Anie saying she wouldn't be in today. I deleted the email and picked up the phone to call Jannie instead. No one would be in the office to overhear our conversation.

Should I explain why I'd been going over the credit card bill, after she had specifically told me not to? No. I no longer cared. She was the one who needed to explain herself. She'd intimidated me long enough.

"Honestly, I had no idea it was a porn site Delila." Her voice had a high pitch, almost frantic. "The reverend told me it was a donation and to just ignore it."

"Every month? You thought we were making this donation every month?" I wasn't letting her off the hook that easily.

"Well… I asked the deacon. He said the reverend has a right to his discretionary funds. The reverend decides where those funds go." She paused again as she thought about it. "Of course… they shouldn't go there."

"Jannie don't say anything about this to anyone. If you do, it might be perceived that you tipped someone off. And that might implicate you." It was a warning. A threat. I hoped she'd heed my advice.

After I hung up the phone, I sat thinking about the reverend. Did he really think he'd get away with it? I looked around the room. An eerie feeling crept over me. Knowing that Mrs. Waverly was probably sitting at this same desk when she drank tea that caused her to have a heart attack. Had she found the website too? Had she confronted the reverend?

Deep in thought, I almost didn't hear the knock on the door. I looked up and saw Lulu rapping with her cane.

"Oh, come in, come in!" I motioned to her, then sprang up and opened the door.

Lulu sat down in a chair next to my desk. "Good morning, Delila. I wasn't interrupting anything was I?"

"Oh no."

"Good." She glanced toward Anie's desk. "Anie not here today?"

"No. She called off today. I'm not sure why. Just said she wouldn't be in."

"That's odd. She rarely misses work." Lulu set her cane next to her chair and rubbed her hand.

"Your hand hurting this morning?" I tried to make light conversation.

"The ball of this cane is too large for my hand. It hurts when I use it too long."

I looked at the cane. I remembered that it had been a gift. "Lulu, who gave you that cane?"

The board meeting was scheduled for 7pm. Jannie had explained to them that I would be attending with her, to provide additional information on funds.

The meeting room, which sometimes doubled as a classroom, had always been one of my favorite rooms in our church. The outside wall had three large windows and three smaller stained-glass windows that cast beautiful colors around the room. In the center, sat a large rectangular table that seated twelve people comfortably and more if needed. Tonight, the sideboard next to the wall held a plate of chocolate chip cookies, coffee, iced tea, and water.

Jannie and I arrived early and took seats across from the door. A fluttery feeling rose deep in my stomach. Silently, I took a few deep breaths and put on a polite smile.

One by one, board members, the reverend and the deacon entered the room, picked up a cookie, something to drink and sat down. The room was noisy with the exchange of greetings and small talk.

It was the first board meeting I'd ever attended, and I'd assumed it would be very formal, but friendly conversation filled the room. And, for the first time, I was in a setting where the reverend and the deacon were not the leaders. They were here as staff members, just like me. Tonight, we were equals.

The clock showed a little past seven. The chatter continued for another ten minutes, until the last board member arrived and hurried to his seat.

The meeting was called to order by the president who recognized me and thanked me for coming. I wondered how he'd feel after the meeting. If he'd still be thankful that I'd come or wish he'd never laid eyes on me.

An agenda was passed around the room. Jannie and I were first to present, after the minutes from the previous meeting were approved. Jannie handed out a stack of financial papers. We all began to review them.

"The reason I've asked Delila to join us tonight is because she's discovered some places where we might be able to save money." She passed around another single sheet of paper. A copy of our most recent credit card statement.

I took my cue. "When I was going over expenses, I noticed a charge that I was uncertain of. If you look down the list, you'll see a charge for 'goodgirlfund.com'." I took a deep breath and looked at the reverend and the deacon. Neither looked up or changed their expression.

"I wasn't sure what the charge was, so I investigated and learned it is actually a porn site." I let that sink in for a minute before going on. "What's more, we've been paying for this for some time. The church has given thousands of dollars to this site."

Gasps and stern faces reached out to the reverend for answers. What could he say? An uncomfortable silence filled the room for what seemed like several minutes.

I sighed. I'd done everything I could. I'd spent days pouring over the numbers, trying to make sense of the accounts. All the endless hours of worry over how the church would pay the bills. Even putting in my own money to try and help. I looked around the room, knowing that many of these board members had also donated extra to help make ends meet.

The truth was out. There was nothing wrong with my bookkeeping. My numbers were right all along. I could no longer be blamed for problems with the church's finances.

His kingdom crumbling, the reverend looked to me, as if I might save him. I met his eyes with defiance. All the accusations I'd endured. The bullying, treating me as if I were incompetent.

He'd spent thousands of church funds on a porn site. He knew the deacon was stealing. And he was willing to pass me off as an unqualified bookkeeper, their scapegoat. He deserved to be punished.

The board members seemed to consider the situation. Each in their minds examined the news and processed how it would affect the church. How it would affect them personally.

Then as if in disbelief, the board members reached out for an alternative answer. Something or someone else to blame. The idea that their pastor could be at fault was too difficult to accept.

"There must be a mistake." The board president said. "Perhaps we were hacked or something."

The vice president nodded agreement. "The credit card company may have made a mistake. Got it mixed up with someone else's account."

I'd slid onto thin ice. They didn't want to believe the worst. Couldn't handle the notion of a scandal.

My thoughts raced to Lulu and Lena and all the other church members. My friends. They'd opened their purses and poured their hearts into the church. Would they blame me? After all, I was the messenger bringing down their empire.

The flutter in my stomach returned, and my heart began to pound. I feared I might become the target of the whole congregation's fury. Afterall, they believed the reverend to be a pious man, a good man. They might tell themselves he'd just made a small lapse in judgement. They would feel embarrassed, ashamed. Possibly take the allegations as a personal attack on them or the church. I'd be the snitch, the traitor who'd turned on them. I stood to lose the things I'd worked so hard to gain. Acceptance. Friendship. Respect.

Even so, I knew I had to do the right thing. No matter the cost. Finally, my anxiety lifted, I was free of my previous fears. I took another deep breath. I had no idea how the scandal would affect the church, who would believe me and who wouldn't, who would hate me in the end.

"It's no mistake. I checked with the credit card company." I looked directly at the reverend.

The board members eyes all turned on the reverend. They said nothing, but their silence demanded an answer. The reverend's face went pale. He sunk into his chair.

"I didn't...I mean..." The reverend sounded like a man grasping to find a lie. "It wasn't— I didn't know what it was. I was told it was an organization to help young girls." His story sounded unconvincing.

The president spoke first, anger in his tone. "Jannie, you are responsible for checking over these things. It's your job as treasurer. Why didn't you catch this?"

"I... I asked the reverend. He told me it was to help young girls. And...and I asked the deacon. He said they were the reverend's discretionary funds, and the reverend could decide how he wanted to use them. I tried—" She left her sentence unfinished, knowing, no excuse would exonerate her.

Sweat beaded at the reverend's hairline, his face flush with fear.

"I think we can handle this ourselves. It's an inside matter." The vice president of the board looked around at the other members.

"Ok, we'll take it from here. You may go now, Delila." The board president waved his hand, as if shooing me away.

"But—" I began.

"We've got this. You've done enough, Delila." The vice president growled.

I looked at each of the other board members, but they all looked away from me. None would meet my eyes.

It seemed as if I had become the enemy. I'd told the truth. I'd risked coming here tonight with only the facts to protect me. Maybe honesty wasn't enough.

"We'd like to discuss this privately Delila. We are asking you to leave now." The harsh tone in the president's voice lashed out at me. But I didn't budge. I wasn't ready to leave yet. I still had unfinished business.

Defiant, I turned toward the president, "I believe the deacon set him up."

"Delila, we've asked you to leave." The president's deep authoritarian voice resonated across the room.

All eyes turned on me.

"Let her finish." One of the board members suggested.

Another board member nodded. I waited a moment before I continued, then I turned to the deacon.

"Mrs. Waverly figured out that you were using that site. She must have found the charges on the credit card statement, just like I did. And she confronted you." I stared at the deacon in silence for a moment before continuing.

"You killed her and set up the reverend. You needed someone to blame. And the reverend fell into your game easily enough. He was more than willing to look at the site."

"That's outrageous! How dare you slander me! I cared deeply for Mrs. Waverly." The deacon screeched.

"Kai saw you put something in her tea the day she died. He must have confronted you at some point. That's why you killed him." I barely recognized my own strong and determined voice.

"How dare you!" The deacon threatened.

"The police have the murder weapon. You gave Lulu that cane after you killed Kai with it. They matched it up to the gashes in his skull." I kept my eyes fixed on him, trying hard to contain my own anger. He'd preyed on enough victims. He had to be stopped.

"What proof do you have that I killed him with that cane? You can't prove any of this." He looked around the room at the board members in hopes of an ally. No one came to his rescue.

The deacon stood up indignant. He shook his head in disgust and turned to leave. We watched as he walked out the door, the board members eyes wide with concern.

"Maybe we shouldn't let him leave," the board president began.

"It's ok, he won't get far. There are several police waiting outside for him." I said with an air of satisfaction. How lucky I was to have a friend on the police force.

Lily Park looked beautiful, even though the lilies were long gone. Instead of the sweet scent of the flowers, the air was filled with the smell of freshly mowed grass, and burgers cooking on the grill. White tablecloths, decorated with salads, bags of chips, and deserts, covered the picnic tables.

Mitzi and I gave each other a smile of satisfaction as we put the finishing touches on the tables. It was our annual women of the church's picnic, and the ladies would be here anytime. And we were ready for them.

"Thanks for helping us, Dora," I watched as the young woman added silverware to the last of the place settings. "You sit next to me, ok?"

She nodded. Her excitement at being part of a group, of belonging, of feeling wanted, gave her a special glow. She was someone.

Soon the ladies arrived in carloads, and loud chatter overflowed the park. I sat at a table with Liz and Ellie, two of our newest members. We ate and talked and laughed. I looked out over the crowd. A good turnout, I thought. Yet, some faces were missing. Not everyone had accepted my exposure of the reverend and deacon. Some chose to ignore the facts. Saw me as the *Judas*.

I was ok with that. I knew the truth. Kai's killer had been brought to justice. The church would recover.

Eventually, people began to leave and only a few of us were left. Although surprised, I was glad Anie had stayed. Lulu too had remained, explaining that she'd be having dinner with her son and Mitzi. After Lulu, Anie, Dora, Mitzi, and I had cleaned up, we sat down to relax.

"Thanks for inviting me." Anie looked almost embarrassed. "I think I need to explain some things." She looked down at her hands. "You have to understand. I was in love with him. I thought he was, well, generous and kind. He was always giving people gifts."

She looked at each of us in turn. "I knew it was him stealing money from the baskets. Afterall, who else could it have been? I went to the desk to put money back in. To try and make up for some of what he was stealing. Kai saw me and thought I was the one stealing." Anie's eyes went blank. She gazed off at nothing. "Kai blackmailed me, telling me I had to put more money back into the collections. I couldn't explain why I was there. It would have given the deacon away." Anie looked at me now. "You understand? I had to protect him. But when I found out he had killed Mrs. Waverly and Kai..."

"We are so grateful to you for coming forward. For telling the police what you knew." I wondered if she realized just how important her testimony was in getting him arrested and convicted.

She nodded. "I'd seen him that night at the fundraiser, walking down the hall, by the back of the kitchen. He had the cane in his hand. I had no idea he'd killed Kai. Honest."

"It's ok." Mitzi walked up and stood next to Anie. "He's where he should be now."

"And his wife looks so much better. Have you noticed?" I asked.

"I wish she would have come today." Mitzi said. "I invited her. I can't imagine what she must have gone through."

"Well fortunately for her, he plead guilty, and saved her the embarrassment of a trial." I put in.

Anie nodded. "She's moving back to New York where she's from. I've been helping her pack." Her voice had softened even more. "I can't help but think how lucky she is."

We all looked at Anie, waiting for an explanation.

"I think he married her because she was so wealthy. But her money was all wrapped up in a trust. And the trust would revert to her brother if she died, so the only way the deacon could get any of her money was if she remained alive. Otherwise, who knows what might have happened to her." Anie shrugged. "It's too awful to think about."

I'd almost forgotten that Lulu was with us. She'd been especially quiet as we talked. Now she offered her own words of advice. "There was no way of knowing Anie. Don't blame yourself. He was a master of deception. Look how many people he fooled. We all thought because he called himself a 'man of God' that he was good. Pure." Lulu took Anie's hand and patted it. "He was kind, and generous to us. And we thought because he was deacon of our church that he could be trusted." She looked out over the field of green grass. "In the end, he was just a person. Sometimes we put people on a pedestal because of the position they hold. We forget that they are human."

"Yes, that's true. But still... what drives someone to do such things?" I asked. "To steal and kill. In a church no less!"

"Greed, pure and simple." Mitzi answered. She looked at Lulu and smiled. "Are you ready to go?"

Anie too walked toward the parking lot. "Goodbye Ladies," She waved and opened her car door. "Thank you. For everything."

Dora and I finished packing the last of my things in the car. "Do you want to come to church with us next week

Dora?" We climbed into the front seat. "The new reverend is really nice."

"Sure."

"By the way, Jewel and Boris are looking forward to seeing you. You will stay for dinner, won't you?"

Bed Bugs

The wheels of the suitcase rolled across the highly polished marble floor of the iconic Marseille Hotel; the sound lost in the crowded, noisy lobby. I dropped my key card on the large front desk and smiled up at the man in the crisp uniform, behind the counter.

"I'd like to check out, please. Room 301." My voice raised slightly to make sure he could hear me.

The clerk looked nervous. He cleared his throat and forced a smile. "Umm, thank you. I'm afraid there may be a delay in leaving the hotel." He signaled with his head at something over my shoulder. I turned to see the crowd of people and what looked like several police officers in the mix.

"What's going on?"

"Umm." He cleared his throat. "Ah...um...a body was found this morning. The police are investigating. I'm terribly sorry for the inconvenience."

The noise grew louder, the crowd of people trying to talk over one another. Police canvassed the guests, collecting names, contact information and any other details they could squeeze from the patrons.

"Who was it?" I asked the clerk. "I mean, who died?" Could it be someone I knew? Someone from our church? Could it be....? A tinge of panic settled in.

"I'm sorry ma'am, I really don't know."

"Delila!" Candace Barnes, or Candi as everyone called her, slipped up next to me. She tucked a strand of her bobbed hair behind her ear, and tugged at the edge of her low-cut blouse, inching it up a little. "Hey, I need to tell you something." She pulled her mini skirt down a tad.

"What?" I asked, a bit of irritation in my voice. Candi and Sueann, my roommates at the conference, had both ditched me the first night we arrived. I suspected they'd spent a romantic night elsewhere, and with someone other than their spouses. Shocking, to say the least. Afterall, we were at a Christian conference. We were supposed to be here representing our church.

Not that I should have been completely surprised. Afterall, Barry had tried to warn me that this could happen. But I'd assured him that while these things may happen at a dental convention, they certainly wouldn't happen at a religious conference.

Barry, sweet Barry. I desperately wanted to get home to him. I'd left home all smiles. Full of excitement and anticipation. Barry had watched me place my suitcase, and a large bag, next to the door, ready to load in the car.

Up until the moment I left, I'd been high on anticipation of the upcoming event, planning and running around for days to get ready. Did I have everything? Clothes: three pair of slacks, four blouses. Shoes: two pair of heels, two pair of flats and a pair of sneakers, sandals, and slippers, just in case. Make up, curling iron, comb, toothbrush. And my beloved kindle.

Barry didn't try to conceal the smirk on his face. He peaked in the bag. "What's in here?"

"My shoes."

"One, two, three...how many pair are you taking?"

"Five. Well six."

"For two nights?" He gave a soft laugh.

"Yes. I don't know what I might need." I smiled back at him.

He walked over and gave me a big hug. "Well, have fun, honey." He kissed me tenderly, then picked up the suitcase and bag to load into the car. He mimicked an exaggerated weight of the luggage. "Ahh. Oooh," adding sound effects, then tossed them into the back seat.

"Ha, ha." I grinned. "See you in a couple of days."

For the first time in my life, I would travel by myself. How silly. I would venture into the unknown world of independence. That mysterious, exhilarating, scary place.

Barry waved good-bye as he watched me back the car out of the garage. What a fun and exciting adventure I was about to embark on. Or so I thought as I waved back.

Located on the other side of town, it took only 25 minutes to reach the Marseille Resort, nestled on the top of a hill overlooking beautifully landscaped green lawns. Surrounded by an 18-hole golf course, tennis courts, and a premier garden and sculpture park, the historic icon drew people from all over to enjoy its architectural style, elegance, and gracious service.

Built in 1920, the hotel touted one of the most alluring convention centers in the Midwest, ideal for any large convention with its large ballroom, able to seat up to 350 people, and eight breakout rooms.

Finally, the mystery of what the complex looked like on the inside would be revealed to me. News articles and advertisements of the grand old palace enticed guests to experience the splendor for themselves. Major renovations had taken place ten years ago and I'd wanted to visit then. But with no real reason to go, I hadn't. I'd read up on the history, about the various wings that had been added in the late 60's, the artwork, and the incredible food.

That wasn't the only reason for my burning enthusiasm. I'd never attended a conference before. While Barry enjoyed at the very least, one dental symposium per year, there were no forums for a stay-at-home mom. I stayed back to hold the fort down, while he travelled all over to get his CE credits, learn about the latest discoveries in the dental industry and network with others in his field.

He'd return and tell me about golf, interesting people he'd met or new things he'd learned. It was critical for his business and career I knew, but it often left me feeling empty and alone. And yes, just a bit jealous.

Several people from our church were attending the Christian Conference, a two-and-a-half-day event. And, from the time Sueann Price first mentioned it to me, I knew I wanted to go.

"I went last year," she'd said, "it was incredible! The comforters and pillows are all feathers, so soft and clean. You know, I slept so well there, I think they may pump oxygen into the rooms to make you sleep better. And the food! Yumm!" She tilted her head back and rolled her eyes as if she were reliving the experience.

"Is it expensive?"

"Well, that's the best part. Since we go as a group it doesn't cost nearly as much as if you went by yourself. We share rooms and that saves a lot." She took a step forward and leaned in toward my desk. "And The Vestige Seven is playing. They're a gospel band that are fantastic! You should come Delila. You'd really enjoy it!"

The road leading up to The Marseille was long and winding, with a gatekeeper at the entrance who made me give him my name. "Thank you, Ms. Clarke, a valet will park your car when you reach the front entrance. Please enjoy your stay!"

A young man opened my car door, and I slid out, handed him my keys, and pulled the suitcase and bag from the back seat. A bellhop quickly took my luggage and set it on a cart then followed me into the entrance.

The lobby ascended three stories, with a large domed area at the top that allowed light to filter through.

Vast chandeliers hung near the dome to assist with the lighting. I stood momentarily mesmerized by the sheer size and elegance of the room.

Situated in the center of the atrium, a round marble table with the largest, most beautiful bouquet of flowers I'd ever seen. Gerber daisies, lilies, gladiolas, roses, statis, poms, delphiniums, and some flowers whose names escaped me. I walked up to it and lingered for a long moment, enjoying the beauty, and forgetting that the bellhop was waiting for me.

The clerk behind the desk allowed me to check in 20 minutes early. The bellhop took my luggage to the room. "You are in room 221 with Ms. Sueann Price and Ms. Candice Barnes." He handed me a map of the hotel with our room highlighted and a key card. "The reception room for conference guests is just down the hall." He pointed down a hallway. "Please let us know if we can be of any assistance. Enjoy your stay." He said, bestowing a professional smile.

The bellhop placed the luggage inside the room, then stood at the doorway, waiting for his tip. Not sure of the appropriate amount, I hoped I'd given him enough. I closed the door and looked around. The room was large, with two queen size beds, two chairs, a small table, and a sleeper sofa.

Great, I thought. I'll probably get the sleeper sofa. But I really didn't mind. Staying in this legendary hotel made up for any inconvenience with sleeping arrangements.

From the third-floor window of our room, my eyes scoured the gardens below. Pathways twisted through the many shrubs and flowers; the foliage so thick someone might easily get lost in it.

The sound of the door opening startled me, and I turned to see Sueann and Candi entering the room. Sueann gave the bellhop a tip and closed the door. Candi bounced down on one of the beds. "Ah, we're in heaven! Isn't this awesome!" She laughed.

Sueann checked herself in the mirror, turning for a side view, front view and looking over her shoulder at her back side. Then she combed her long wavy hair and checked her makeup.

Candi too examined herself in the mirror, changed her earrings and added foundation, eyeliner, and lipstick. Then she stood back a bit, pulled her shoulders back, plumped up her breasts and twisted her mini skirt.

It reminded me of my teen years. I caught a glance of myself in the mirror. Perhaps I looked a little plain next to them. But I'd chosen the new blouse and pants for a Christian conference, not a New Year's Eve party.

Sueann looked at her watch. "It's nearly 4pm." Both she and Candi headed for the door, they looked back at me. "Are you coming?" Sueann asked.

"Oh, the reception!" I had almost forgotten; a welcome gathering awaited all conference guests. I'd hurried out the door behind them, not knowing what to expect.

That had been the first night. Now the handle of my suitcase gripped tightly in one hand, I simply wanted to get home. The conference was interesting, if not exactly what I'd expected. The noise level in the lobby appeared to have increased, and I could barely hear Candi. She moved a little closer to me and whispered, her voice low so no one could eavesdrop. "I need to tell you—."

The hotel clerk cleared his throat. "Excuse me ladies." He politely waved us aside to allow another woman to check out.

"You don't need to tell me anything. You're a big girl. You can do what you want." I tried to feign indifference.

"Shhh!" She put her finger to her lips and pulled me away from the front desk. "I need to explain something to you."

"What?" My tone sounded harsh. I didn't care.

"Not here." She searched the room. Seeing a more secluded spot, she pulled me along with her.

"Roy showed up and got a room. He didn't want to go to the conference. You know he doesn't like that kind of thing. I sat with Owen at the conference, and at dinner, but then I went back to Roy's room." Candi said. She stretched her eyes open a little wider.

Candi's husband Roy usually sat or slouched through our Sunday services with an extremely bored look.

"Really? Roy's been here the whole time?" I said, a touch of sarcasm in my voice.

She nodded.

"Where is he now?" I looked around the congested lobby.

"He left early this morning. Then I saw the police all over the hotel." Her large brown eyes grew wider as she spoke. "I heard someone died. Have you heard who?"

The chatter in the lobby grew as more people tried to check-out of the hotel.

"No." I looked over her shoulder and tried to determine how many police were in the room. Why so many? If the person died of natural causes, there wouldn't be any need for all the police. Had there been a terrible accident? Or worse, a murder?

A tall man moved through the crowd to the side of the room, followed by a uniformed police officer. Detective Jim Higgins, Barry's good friend, spotted me about the same time as I saw him. He spoke to the other officer then headed toward me.

"Delila, I didn't realize you were at this conference." He flashed a brief smile then turned to Candi.

"Detective Higgins, this is Candi Barnes. She was at the conference too." I made the introduction.

"Hello Detective. Nice to meet you." Candi's voice sounded a little sweeter than normal.

Professional in his business, Jim jotted down our full names in a notebook, and asked, even though he knew, which church we were with. He spoke with us for several minutes and wondered if we'd noticed anything unusual, then led us to the large front door and told us he would contact us later with additional follow-up questions.

I tried to ask him who, how, and when, but of course he couldn't share any details, even with me. "I'm sorry Delila. We're required to notify the next of kin before we can release a name. But I think that will happen soon. Check the news tonight."

The valet parking attendant put my luggage in the trunk and handed me the keys. I gave him his tip then slid into my car and began the not so long drive home. I barely noticed the beautiful bluebird-day as I headed down the road toward home and ruminated over the events of the conference, the pleasant and unpleasant memories, and considered how much I should tell Barry.

That first night, the hotel was crowded with conference goers from various churches, including ours. The reception felt scary. Within five minutes, I'd lost sight of both Sueann and Candi. Like a child lost in a shopping mall, I felt like I was on an island in the middle of a horde of conference goers. I stood alone, embarrassed, and watched as others laughed and talked, in what appeared to be meaningful conversations. I longed for someone to speak to. A friend. Someone who wanted to be with me.

I felt awkward as people pushed past me, so I searched for a less conspicuous place to stand. Refreshments and snacks were set up near the wall in the back of the room and looked like a safe place. I made my way toward the food sanctuary.

Liz and Darren Anderson, regular members of our church, stood near the drink table talking with people I didn't know. Liz wore a tight-fitting black dress that looked nice on her, even though it showed the extra pounds she'd put on over the past year. She made a funny face and laughed loudly at herself. Darren and the other couple laughed with her. A tall and quite attractive woman walked by them, and I watched Darren's eyes follow her, resting on her backside.

Men. I strolled to the drink table and poured myself a glass of Diet Pepsi. I thought Liz and Darren might invite me to join their little group. Darren made a joke and they all laughed again but no one seemed to notice me. Once more, I scoured the sea of conference goers for Sueann and Candi, isolated amid the inner circle of people. I searched desperately for other members of our church, for someone to connect with.

"Delila!" A deep male voice called out.

I spun around to see the gorgeous face of Evan Wellston, my high school boyfriend, and one-time fiancé. Seeing him at that moment felt like winning the lottery, exciting and unexpected. He waved and navigated his way through the crowd toward me.

The last time I'd seen Evan, we were in college. He in New York, me in a small college in Illinois. A classic story really. Two young people, a long-distance relationship, and an inevitable split.

Suddenly aware of my plain outfit and my 50-year-old body, I worried how he might view me. I weighed a few more pounds than I had back then, and like everyone else, had added a couple lines at the corner of my eyes.

Although thrilled to see him, I wondered as usual, how I would answer the age-old question, 'what have you been doing since I last saw you.' It was a frustrating question for me to answer. I had no impressive career to brag about. What had I done for the past 30 years? I'd supported Barry when he started his practice, even working for him from time to time when he needed me. I'd been a good mom and wife. I'd raised a successful and happy son. And I'd done some volunteer work from time to time. And now, a part-time bookkeeper for our church. Did that count?

It didn't matter. I was married, and Evan was just an old friend.

He hadn't changed much. A gray hair or two and like me, and a few wisdom lines. His body no longer the skinny frame of a 20-year-old, but instead a well-built, middle age physique. And looking even better than I remembered.

"Wow, Delila. It must be...well years since I've seen you. You look great!"

The noise level in the room had increased. "Thank you, Evan, so do you!" I gave him a hug, then stepped back a bit to have another check. Without a doubt, he looked droolworthy.

A man with a microphone stood at one end of the room and welcomed everyone. He encouraged us to explore the hotel and gardens and announced that dinner would be served in this room at six o'clock.

"Want to walk in the garden?" Evan asked. "It might be quieter there."

I pulled my sweater on, as Evan led me outside to the park-like maze. We walked for a short distance, found a bench and settled down. The brilliant orange-pink sky trickled through the bushes like a soft serenade. As if no time had elapsed between us, I felt comfortable and safe with Evan. We picked up where we'd left off, the last time we'd been together.

"So, tell me what you've been doing." Evan took in my entire face and body as he spoke. "It's been far too long Dee."

I told him about Barry, and our son, then checked his expression for signs of being offput. But he seemed genuinely interested. "Our son just graduated college." I added. "What about you?"

"I was married." He looked down at the ground. "My wife died last year. Unfortunately, we never had any children."

Evan and I played catch up on each other's lives for a while, then discussed how we had both come to be at the conference. It seemed his sister had convinced him that he needed to get out more and felt he would benefit from the uplifting convention.

Together we laughed and reminisced. The shadow of pink on the horizon and the slight chill in the air provided the only indicators of how much time had passed. Evan looked at his watch. "Ooh. We'd better get going if we want to catch dinner."

Fortunately, we were able to find two seats together at a large circular table in the crowded room. The hotel staff, dressed in nineteen twenties style clothing, served our meals family style, placing large bowls and platters of beautifully decorated foods on the table. I whiffed in the delightful smells.

The man with the microphone returned to the small platform. "Ladies and gentlemen, can I have your attention, please?" Slowly the room's noise quieted to a low murmur. He instructed us to go to the breakout rooms designated for our church after the meal. Then said the dinner prayer.

Sueann sat at a table next to us eating and talking with a man I didn't know. Owen Chapman sat next to Sueann with Candi on his other side, her lowcut blouse showing even more cleavage than when we'd left the room.

Owen, an account manager-salesman for a local security company, and natural ear tickler, appeared to be schmoozing the ladies. It wasn't uncommon for him, even at church functions. I wondered if his wife Ellie ever got jealous. Liz and Darren Anderson also sat at their table.

Evan and I were sandwiched between people I didn't know. From my seat, it was easy to watch Darren's eyes follow Candi and laugh as she put on her sweet, silly girl act. Liz also noticed the wandering eyes of her husband. Then Candi rested her hand lightly on Owen's shoulder and whispered something in his ear. Sueann glared at Candi.

When the meal was over, I saw what appeared to be an argument between Sueann and Candi. I couldn't hear what they were saying, but Sueann looked angry, Candi unconcerned and dismissive.

I said goodnight to Evan and as directed, went to the designated meeting room. Thirty-five people from our church registered for the conference, yet only about half attended the gathering. We listened to our new minister give us a little divine motivational talk, then wish us a goodnight. The room provided drinks and snacks and a comfortable lounge area for people to linger.

Most of the couples left after the minister's short speech, leaving only a handful of us behind. Karly Greene, a thin gangly looking woman sat in one of the comfortable chairs watching people mingle. Aside from the tall cocktail in her hand, she appeared to be alone. I sat down next to her.

"Hi Delila!" She smiled, then looked shyly at the drink in her hand.

I thought maybe she too suffered from social anxiety. I'd been surprised when after her ugly divorce and all the wagging tongues, Karly stayed with the church. Her husband got the house and the kids and even the dog. I decided it must have been especially difficult for her.

As my eyes scanned the room, I noticed neither Candi, Sueann, nor Owen had attended. "Where is everyone?" I wondered.

"They paired off," One of the single men, who sat nearby said. "Got their own private rooms." He grinned.

I glanced at the man then quickly turned back to Karly. We talked for a few minutes, then I told her I needed to get something from my room. The single men were eyeing us up and I didn't want them to get the wrong idea. I wasn't in the market.

"Mind if I come with you?" she asked and popped up from her seat.

She followed me to the room, and I showed her the view from our window. We noticed a woman in the garden below, who looked as if she were searching for something. I strained to get a better look.

"Is that Ellie Chapman, Owen's wife?" Karly asked.

"It does look a little like her." I agreed. "But Ellie couldn't come. She had to grade papers. Mid-terms. But it does look a little like her."

Karly and I continued our conversation, which moved toward Sueann and Candi. I explained my concerns over my roommates who appeared to have vanished.

"Because of what happened to me you mean?" A troubled look crossed her face.

I shook my head. "What do you mean? What happened to you?"

"I thought everyone knew." Karly's eyes dropped to her hands.

The silent room gave her time to pull her thoughts together, time to find a way to share her pain with me.

"Four years ago, I was at a conference. I met a man there, and." She stopped for a moment, choking back the words. "And I had an affair." She looked at me as if waiting to see if I would hate her for the admission. "I thought I was in love with him. So, after the conference we continued the affair, often at my house. And..." She left off the part about her children being home at the time, but I had heard that part.

Her eyes searched mine for my reaction. "I ended up with an STD. My husband found out, and that's how I lost custody of my kids. I lost everything." She looked as if she might cry. "That's how I lost my life."

"I'm so sorry Karly." What more could I say?

The hotel served breakfast in the ballroom, buffet style on tables along the walls, and consisted of enough sweets to delight and scare anyone trying to lose weight. Ample bowls of fruits and fruit salads, toast and waffle makers also stood ready for those trying to avoid the Danish and sweet rolls. Large stainless steel chafing dishes, warmed by cans of sterno, offered scrambled eggs, meats, and fried potatoes. I looked around for a familiar face and place to sit.

Neither Sueann nor Candi had returned to the room the night before. So instead of spending time with girlfriends, like an old-fashioned slumber party as I'd imagined, I found myself all alone in a large room. I'd finally climbed into a bed, deciding that if they did return, one of them could have the sleeper sofa.

"Good morning, Dee."

Evan's voice startled me for a moment. "Oh, good morning, Evan." I said, relieved to find a friendly face, and have someone to sit with.

We made our way around the buffet, filling our plates and grinning at the beautiful array of food. We took the first two empty seats we found. It felt so good to be with Evan again. I'd forgotten how much we enjoyed each other. How special he made me feel.

The keynote speaker gave an uplifting opening talk as we ate, then everyone scurried off to the individual presentation rooms. Ironically, Evan and I had selected the same lectures. So, we spent the day together, even skipping out early on the last two workshops, to walk in the gardens.

Artwork and cast plaques of poetry were interwoven among the beautiful shrubs and flowers in the garden. We stopped to read the lyrical words, then moved on to the next piece. It was well into the afternoon, and we'd gone deep into the garden, when we heard giggling coming from behind a bush.

Evan and I stopped and listened for a moment. I thought I recognized Candi's voice with a man in a romantic and perhaps compromising situation. Evan and I looked at one another, then turned and in silence began to walk back toward the hotel.

When we were about halfway to the building, he turned to me and took my hand. "Dee, you know I'm still crazy about you." Then he kissed me. Tenderly.

I pulled away slowly and took a breath. "We better get back." I said and walked toward the hotel.

The band was just beginning to play, and we found seats toward the back room. As the music surrounded us, my thoughts swirled around Evan's kiss. Thoughts of the passion we'd shared years before rushed back. The heartbreak I'd felt when we'd decided to end our relationship. I felt Evan's hand find mine and give a gentle loving squeeze.

As I drove away from the hotel, I watched the beautiful gardens fade into background in the rear-view mirror. A few leaves still dangled on the autumn trees, but most had already fallen to the ground. The gray sky mimicked my mood as I headed for home. Should I tell Barry about Evan? What if someone told Barry they'd seen us together? How would he take it?

Slowly the car rolled along. No longer as anxious to get home, my foot eased up on the gas petal. I needed time to think. Time to digest everything, put it in order in my mind. I pushed the guilt aside to consider that someone had died.

Could the dead body be someone from our church? It couldn't be Candi, but aside from her, I hadn't seen anyone else I knew. I hadn't seen Evan either. Of course, it was probably someone I didn't know. Afterall there were a lot of people at the conference. But what if... I pushed it aside. I needed to figure out what to tell Barry...how much to tell... My mind kept returning to The Vestige Seven band.

The music resonated throughout the room, the audience tapping their feet and bobbing their heads to the beat. Sueann had been right, and even though I normally didn't listen to Christian music, the band played well. Evan and I, at the back of the room, smiled at one another and savored the sound. For several minutes I delighted in the uplifting music, intoxicated by the mood.

But before the band stopped playing, Karly's words flashed through my head. That's how I lost my life. I had an affair and that's how I lost everything. I glanced over at Evan. He smiled and squeezed my hand again.

What was I doing? I loved Barry. He was my world. I pulled my hand from Evan's. I didn't look at him, but I felt his eyes on me.

Applause filled the room when the band finished, and we stood to leave. Evan pulled me toward the door to the garden, anxious to escape the crowd and pick up where we'd left off.

"Evan, I can't. I'm sorry if I gave you the wrong impression. I love my husband. I can't do this to him."

Pain and confusion crossed Evan's face, as if he'd been hit head on with the most tragic of news. "I'm not interested in just an affair Dee. If that's what you're afraid of? I'm interested in you. In a relationship."

I shook my head. "No Evan. I'm sorry."

At dinner, I sat with Sueann, a man I didn't know, Liz, Darren, Owen, and Candi, with an empty chair next to me.

Evan sat at a table across the room, next to his sister. He appeared quiet, saying little to the others at his table. Had I hurt him? I'd enjoyed the attention he'd showered on me. The romance. I loved Evan at one time. I enjoyed reliving the old feelings for a while. Had I led him on? Allowed him to believe there was a chance to rekindle the passion I'd once felt for him?

I felt sick with guilt. Evan had recently suffered the loss of his wife. How could I be so cruel as to let him think we could be together again? I would never leave Barry.

Our table was boisterous. Darren made a joke, his obvious attempt to flirt with Candi. He flashed her a wide grin, and let his eyes linger on her. Candi seemed embarrassed; however, Darren didn't notice. Perhaps he thought she enjoyed it.

Sueann looked appalled, turned her body toward her gentleman friend and whispered something.

Liz, using a phony sexy voice, turned to Owen and asked a stupid question. Owen smiled politely but unamused, turned his head so his gaze landed elsewhere in the crowded room. Liz tried again, but Owen ignored her attempts to get his attention. I could tell he wanted nothing to do with her, didn't find her sense of humor appealing. Didn't want to play along.

"He's not paying attention to me." Liz pouted out loud.

The lively roaring 20's wait staff once again, brought beautiful platters of food, embellished with flowers, and set them down in front of us. I marveled at the artistic arrangements and decided to try something similar for Barry. I wasn't at all sure any of the others appreciated the effort put into the creations. Yet everyone piled the food on their plates.

"We should hit up the hotel bar after dinner," Darren's invitation pointed at Owen and Candi more than anyone else.

"Their margaritas are excellent!" Liz said. "I love the strawberry."

Owen looked at Candi. "I don't know—what do you think?" He raised his eyebrows.

"Um, I'd rather walk in the garden." Candi threw a sideways glance at Owen, suggestive and barely subtle.

A waiter presented a tray of assorted desserts in front of us. I selected a plate with two petit fours, one chocolate and one vanilla. They were beautifully decorated, and I wished Barry were here to share them with me.

Liz selected a large piece of chocolate cake. Darren watched as she shoveled in a third bite before commenting.

"Wow, look at her pound that cake!" He laughed. "I see where it's heading. Straight down to the hips!"

Liz stopped eating for a moment and glared at her husband.

Darren laughed again. "Or more likely the ass."

Liz set her fork down. A look that said, "shut up, or I'll throw it at you."

But Darren was enjoying himself. "What? I'm just telling the truth." He glanced at Candi.

It was a stupid move. No woman likes hearing another woman put down publicly. I couldn't believe Candi would find it funny either. Embarrassed for Liz, I turned my attention back to Evan.

He stood up and spoke with some of the people at his table, then glanced over at me. I looked away quickly, not wanting to encourage him.

My eyes landed on Karly, who sat at a nearby table. We exchanged smiles.

I glanced back at Evan's table, but his chair sat empty. He would get over me, I decided. He'd find someone else who could give him the love he deserved.

Owen leaned over the empty chair between us and whispered to me. "Can you meet me tonight? There's something I'd like to share with you. Later, in the bar?"

"Can it wait until tomorrow?" I didn't feel like talking. I couldn't imagine what he wanted to discuss, a donation to the church maybe? Or did he want to ask me not to mention his indiscretions to his wife? It didn't matter. I needed time to think. Should I tell Barry about Evan? Should I continue to see Evan, as a friend? I needed alone time.

"Sure." Owen nodded, then returned his attention to Candi.

Karly walked over to our table. "Mind if I join you?" She sat down in the empty chair next to me.

Liz pushed her cake further out in front of her. The hurt look still drawn out on her face.

Candi grabbed Owen's hand. "Let's go to the garden!"

Owen allowed her to pull him up. “Sorry.” He said, not sounding sorry at all. They headed toward a door to the garden.

Sueann and her gentleman also stood up to leave. Moments later Liz got up, said goodbye to us and left. Darren jumped up. “I guess we’re leaving.” And followed his wife.

Karly and I were alone at the table. “I guess it’s just us two again.” She grinned at me.

“I’m not really feeling up to doing anything tonight, Karly. I thought I’d just go back to my room and read.” I wanted to be alone. Sueann and her friend would be out, as would Candi. I could have the room all to myself, and right now that sounded comforting. “I’m sorry.”

“Ok.” She looked and sounded disheartened.

“Thanks for the offer, Karly. Maybe we can meet for breakfast in the morning.” Tonight, I wanted only to sit with my kindle. The kindle Barry had given me for my birthday.

Barry, all smiles, pulled my luggage from the trunk and carried it inside when I arrived home. “So, was it fun?” He asked.

Boris, our terrier, and Jewel our cat, ran to greet me when I stepped inside the door. I hugged Boris and petted Jewel on the head. It felt good to be home.

“Well, it was interesting.” What could I say? What should I say?

“Is the hotel nice? What’s it like?” Barry pulled me to him and gave me a kiss and a hug.

“It is beautiful. But… something happened.” I hesitated. “Someone died. I don’t know who or how. Jim and a lot of other police officers were there investigating.”

Barry stepped back slightly, hit by the shock. “That’s terrible.”

Except for glossing over the time spent with Evan, I told Barry about the conference. How he had been correct, several people had paired off and I had the big room to myself almost the entire time. The girls stopped back only to change clothes or pick up something. Neither had spent a night in our room.

The food had been incredible, the hotel stunning, and the news of someone dying a shock. "Jim said we'd probably hear more on the news tonight." And I told him about meeting up with Evan. Not that Evan had tried to revive our old relationship, but I did say he'd lost his wife recently.

After dinner we assumed our usual places in the living room. I fidgeted in my comfortable swivel chair; my Kindle cradled in my hands and opened it to a new book. My eyes skimmed the words, but nothing registered. I read the words again. After the third time, I doubted if I'd retain any of the story.

At 11pm, Barry and I were ready and waiting to learn more. We weren't disappointed. A "breaking news" alert popped up on the screen. "Man's body found in The Marseille Resort this morning."

A man's body. So, it had been a man. Not Evan! Dear lord, not Evan! I said a silent prayer.

Barry, ready with the remote in his hand, turned up the volume. I leaned in a little closer to the television.

Anchorman Kevin Mathews sat behind a table speaking with co -anchor Marla Douglass, who was on a large screen beside him. The camera zoomed in on Marla who stood in front of the Hotel, wind blowing her hair around her face while she spoke. "So, tell us Marla, what do we know about the death that took place at the Marseille?"

"Well Kevin, we know that the victim was a 50-year-old man."

The screen flashed back to the anchorman, "and do we know his identity, are the police releasing that information yet?"

"Kevin, the police tell me his name was Owen Chapman, and he was here at a Christian Retreat." The anchorwoman replied.

Owen? Owen? My heart began to beat even faster as I strained to hear more.

"Do we know anything more about him?" The screen flashed back to Kevin and then back to Marla, the anchorwoman.

"Kevin, we know that Mr. Chapman was married to a professor at the University, and he was the sales manager for a local security company."

"And do the police believe this was foul play?"

"Kevin, so far, the police have not ruled out foul play and they are talking with conference goers and asking a lot of questions right now. I guess it was a large conference, about 150 in attendance from many of our local churches." The camera stayed on the anchorwoman. "There was one other interesting piece to this puzzle Kevin. The police said there were little red marks left on the man's body."

"Little red marks? That is strange. Ok, thank you Marla." Kevin faced the camera. "We'll keep you updated as more news of this case becomes available."

I wiped a tear from my eye. "I had dinner with him last night. We sat at the same table." My voice choked up. "Who would want to murder him?" I recalled Candi and Owen laughing together at dinner, then heading toward the garden after Liz and Darren's bizarre behavior. And I thought about Candi's strange performance before we left the hotel. Making sure I knew she was with Roy and not Owen.

It was hard to believe that the carefree, happy-go-lucky, Owen was gone. Barry came over and took me in his arms and held me.

The morning sun brought light, but my feelings were still drab from the night before. Had Owen been murdered? Although the police had not officially confirmed, but had only said they suspected foul play, I felt pretty sure they thought so. I finished cleaning up the breakfast dishes and felt Jewel rub against my leg. I gave her a little pet and fixed her breakfast. Boris immediately marched over for his own meal and attention.

If Owen had been murdered, was it someone I knew? Or had it been some random act? My mind could not stop going over all the events of the past few days. What reason would someone have for killing Owen?

Boris, anxious for a walk, tottered to the door, then looked back at me. I took the hint, but before we set off for Lily Park, I called my friend and asked her to meet us there.

The bright yellow sweater and yellow plaid pants could only belong to one person. "Hi Mitzi!" I waved, and unleashed Boris so he could run around the park with her little red poodle. Mitzi wore yellow shoes and a yellow visor to match her outfit. The poodle wore a yellow bandana. "Don't you look all matchy-matchy!"

Mitzi laughed. "Thank you, Delila. It wasn't easy finding all the same color yellow you know."

Eager for the news, Mitzi glued her attention to me. "It's awful about Owen. Do you think someone killed him? What happened at that conference? Please, tell me everything you know!"

We sat down at a picnic table, and I carefully laid out the story, trying to give only facts. Mitzi listened intently, then remarked. "You know Roy is very jealous. I once saw him get in a fight with a man because he said he didn't like the way the guy looked at Candi."

After a moment of thoughtful silence, Mitzi went on. "Of course, I can't imagine Owen's wife Ellie would have been happy either. Last year, he had an affair with Sueann."

"What?" I stared at her. "I didn't know that!"

"Oh yeah. She was crazy about him. I think Ellie put an end to it though." Mitzi paused to recall the details. "I'm guessing it started at the same conference last year. I'm surprised Ellie let him go again this year."

I nodded.

My phone vibrated in my pocket. I took it out and read the text message. Jim needed to ask me a few questions. We agreed to meet at my house in 30 minutes.

"Sorry Mitzi, I've got to go. I'm meeting with Officer Higgins." As I stood, Boris noticed me and immediately came over to get reconnected to his leash.

Mitzi was aware of our friendship with Jim. She gave me a sideways glance. "Is he investigating Owen's death? Or possibly murder?"

"Yep. And if I can help him, I will."

"I'll keep my eyes and ears open too. If I hear anything, I'll let you know." She gave me a big friendly smile.

"Thanks Mitzi!" I gave her a hug, then Boris and I headed for home.

Jim arrived a short time later. We sat at the kitchen table, and I walked him through the events of the conference.

Then Jim pulled out his phone and showed me a picture. "Have you ever seen these earrings?"

I looked at his face and nodded. I remembered seeing them in our room that first day. "Yes, they belong to Candi Barnes. Why?" But I guessed even before he told me.

"They were found in the room on the table beside the bed where Mr. Chapman's body was found."

We sat silently for a few moments. Finally, I said, "Jim, Candi's husband Roy was at the hotel."

Jim looked at me with interest. I told him what Candi had told me. Jim nodded but didn't appear too concerned.

"Do you think he killed Owen?" I asked cautiously.

"Don't know. What we do know is that when we reviewed the hotel's hallway cameras, we saw someone going into the room wearing a black hoodie and carrying a bag." He paused. "This is just between us for now Delila."

"Of course."

"Because of the hoodie, we can't see the face to tell who entered the room. In fact, it's difficult to say for sure if it was a woman or a man. The video isn't good. And it wasn't a very good angle, so it wasn't as helpful as it should have been. We also found little red marks on him. We can't trace them, but we are doing DNA testing now." Jim took a breath and finally asked, "Do you think Candi could have killed him?"

Jim had facts, but now he was fishing for something more. He wanted to know who was capable and who had a motive. And for that, he would need to get to know the people involved in the case a little better.

"I don't think she has a bad temper if that's what you're asking." I pushed a plate of cookies toward him, but he shook his head. "What floor was his room on?"

"The second floor."

"So, could someone climb up the balcony? Could they have gotten in that way?" I tried to picture the wall outside the hotel.

Jim raised his eyebrows. "We've been considering that possibility. What about his wife? Do you know her?"

"Ellie? She's very smart. A professor. But she wasn't at the conference." I thought for a moment. Had I seen Ellie? Or was it someone who looked like her? I couldn't be sure.

After mulling it over for a moment, I confessed what I'd seen or not seen. "And Jim, I heard...this is gossip of course, but I heard that last year Owen had an affair with Sueann. Please don't tell anyone I told you."

After Jim left, I mulled things over in my mind. Roy might have had a reason to kill Owen, but what motive would Candi have? Had she slept with him and left her earrings behind? A definite possibility.

Had Roy climbed up to the balcony? There was no trellis or other ladder like apparatus to climb. Could he have thrown a rope and climbed a rope to get up? I tried to picture it. Roy wasn't especially athletic. I doubted if he would or could do that. Anyway, he was more likely to bang on the door, make a big scene. And he wouldn't have known to bring a rope strong enough to climb. No, that wouldn't make sense.

But Candi? I just couldn't believe it. What about Ellie? Had she showed up unexpectedly and found him with Candi? Had she finally snapped?

My phone rang, yanking me from my musing. Karly. Reluctantly I answered.

"Hi Delila. I just wondered if you want to meet for coffee?"

No, I didn't want to meet her. However, instead of saying 'no', which seemed rude and unkind, I blurted out "Sure. When?"

An hour later, I sat across a table from Karly in our local coffee shop, La Cafetière. It wasn't crowded, so we took a table next to the window.

The room was warm and filled with the smell of fresh coffee. I sipped my chocolate latte and noticed that Karly had ordered a regular coffee, I assumed even that was an extravagance for her. I felt a little guilty for not offering to pay for it.

"Isn't it awful about Owen?" Karly asked. "He was with Candi that night, wasn't he?"

It occurred to me that Karly's intent for asking me to meet her, included gossip drilling. Not sure how I felt about it. After all, I didn't know her all that well. She wasn't a part of my 'tell-all comfort zone'.

"They were together at dinner." I admitted. But Karly knew that, after all she was there too.

"Well, did she come back to the room that night?" Karly demanded.

Apparently, no one had ever versed Karly in the finer points of gossip. One needed to pose a question carefully. Selectively. Not quite so bluntly. And one needed to be prepared to offer something up in return.

I shook my head.

Karly took a sip of her coffee. She looked thoughtful, then her eyes turned to meet mine. "I saw them that night you know."

I didn't know. I waited for her to continue.

"Later, after dinner I went to the bar. I saw them there at a corner table. I don't think they saw me." She took another sip of coffee. "Then your friends Darren and Liz came in."

Why call them 'my friends' I wondered. "Well, I don't really know them all that well."

"He's kind of a jerk. He just kept negging. Said...let's see what was it? Oh yeah, he said, 'you are pretty honey, it's just that I like to look at skinny girls. Pretty girls. What's wrong with that?'" Karly's lip tightened. "Why do guys do that?"

"I don't know, but I hate it too." I agreed. "It really bothered me that night, the way Darren treated her at dinner."

"Anyway, then Sueann came in. She went over and sat with Candi and Owen."

"Was she alone? What about that guy she was talking to at dinner?" I asked.

"I don't know what happened to him, but she was alone. They talked for a while and then..." Karly took a deep breath, raised her eyebrows, and said with some satisfaction, "Sueann and Candi got in an argument. Then Sueann dumped her drink on Candi." Karly smiled as she recalled the drama.

My face must have given her the reaction she was looking for, so she continued. "Yeah, they were both pissed. Candi stormed out."

"She didn't come back to our room." I interjected.

"Probably afraid of Sueann coming back for her."

"Yeah, they were probably both afraid of seeing each other. So, what happened after that?" My latte cooled; I took a large drink. Anxious to hear the rest of her story.

"Sueann and Owen talked for a while. Then your friend came over and sat down with them."

At first, I wasn't sure who she was referring to. Then a light bulb went off. "Oh, you mean Evan?"

"Yeah. Owen introduced him to Sueann. I heard him say something about knowing each other from high school." She stopped and thought for a moment. "Strange thing. Owen pulled a note out of his pocket and handed it to your friend. Your friend didn't stay long though. He took the note and left a little after that."

I digested her story silently. "So, did Owen and Sueann leave together?"

"No. She left first, then he got up and sorta staggered out. He looked kinda drunk to me." Karly looked at her watch. "Ooh, I gotta go. My shift starts in a few minutes." She swallowed the last of her coffee. "See you later Delila."

My coffee cup cradled in my hands; I stared out the window of the café. Candi did not leave with Owen. Did she go to his room later? Could she be the mystery person in the hotel video wearing the hoodie? She hadn't come back to our room to change. Had she told the truth about Roy? None of it made sense.

And why would Owen give Evan a note? Evan and I knew Owen from high school, but we didn't hang out with him back then. My memory was foggy, but I thought Evan and Owen didn't really get along. I tried to remember why. It was so long ago.

The smell of lasagna drifted throughout the house. I pulled the dish from the oven and decorated it with sprigs of fresh basil on top. The salad already on the table had been carefully arranged with each item equally placed around the plate. My first attempt to make food look beautiful, like I'd seen at the Marseille.

Barry entered the kitchen, walked over, wrapped his arms around my waist and gave me a kiss. "Oh, this looks and smells delicious Delila!"

I laughed. "What's this about?"

"I really missed you! You know, if I didn't have you, I believe I'd starve."

"Ha, ha. I'm sure you'd survive just fine without me! How did work go?"

At that moment the doorbell rang. "Oops, that's probably Jim. I asked him to dinner, since Aleena's out of town. You don't mind, do you?"

Jim's girlfriend Aleena, had flown to Florida to visit her parents, leaving Jim to fend for himself.

"No, of course not." Barry said and headed to the front door.

We sat down for dinner. "So, anything interesting happen today?" Jim grinned at Barry, eager as always to hear a 'Barry Story'.

"As a matter of fact..."

Jim and I focused our attention on Barry.

"One of our patients showed up early," Barry began. He put a helping of lasagna on his plate, then continued. "The staff could tell he'd been drinking already." Barry poured himself a glass of water. "The guy showed up just before 1pm but his appointment wasn't until 1:30pm. So, he said he'd come back. Someone had dropped him off, so he was on foot. Well, apparently, his walk took him to the pub down the block. When he finally showed up, he was completely sozzled." Barry rolled his eyes. "I couldn't work on him. Had to reschedule." He shot us a grin. "What can I say? It's an interesting profession!"

Jim and I both laughed along with Barry.

After dinner we moved to the living room. Barry listened intently as I told Jim what Karly had shared with me.

Jim jotted down a few notes. "So, she thought Owen was drunk when he left the bar? Did she say what time that was?"

"No. And I didn't think to ask."

"It's ok. I'll check with the bartender and wait staff. They might know. Thank you, Delila!" Jim left with the new leads, and Barry and I settled into our evening routine.

The 11 o'clock news showed the video of the person in a hoodie entering Owen's room and asked for help identifying the person. I could easily see why the police couldn't get an id from it, or even tell if the person were a man or woman. Whoever it was must have realized there was a camera there. They came from the stairwell next to his room, with their back to the camera. Jim had told us they couldn't even see the person's hand, something that could have given them a clue, they would have known then if it was a man or woman.

That night, I couldn't fall asleep. I tossed and turned. Thoughts of Owen played over and over. Owen flirting with Candi. Owen ignoring Liz's advances. Owen asking me to meet with him. What had he wanted to tell me? Did it have anything to do with his death? Would he still be alive if I'd met with him?

I rolled over again, gently so as not to waken Barry, and so I wasn't facing him. Evan knew Owen. We had all gone to school together. And Evan talked to Owen that night. Maybe he had an idea what Owen wanted to tell me.

Evan's kiss replayed on my lips. His scent. His arms around me. No! I pushed the memory away. We were just friends, nothing more.

Had Owen said anything to Evan that night at the bar that might give a clue to what had happened? Karly said Owen passed Evan a note. What was that all about? Should I speak with Evan? How else could I find out? I closed my eyes and tried to force sleep to come.

The next morning, Barry's breakfast consisted of an omelet with all the fixings, hash browns, and orange juice. He commented about being treated like a king and how lucky he was to have me, how much he appreciated me, then kissed me and rushed out the door for work.

After feeding Boris and Jewel, I quickly got dressed, cleaned up the kitchen, then ran out the door for work. I'd made up my mind to call Evan later and see if we could meet. I needed to find out what the note said.

People were usually in and out of the church office all day long. This morning, to my delight, no one had come in and I found myself alone for the first hour and a half. I managed to get caught up on paying bills and reconciling accounts.

Filing is not my favorite task, but it is necessary. Fortunately, there wasn't much to file. As I placed the last document in its assigned folder, the door opened, and Sueann entered. She looked haggard, as if she hadn't slept in some time.

The previously sweet and bubbly Sueann now slumped down into the chair next to my desk. "Hi Delila." Her eyes looked hollow, distant.

"Hi Sueann." I sat quietly and waited for her to unload.

"I wonder when they will have the visitation for Owen. I guess the police haven't released the body yet."

"Well, I assume it takes a few days for the autopsy."

Sueann pulled her cellphone from her purse and scrolled through the photos. I glanced over and watched as she stopped scrolling here and there to look at a picture. There must have been dozens of pictures of Owen. Some selfies of her and Owen, some of just him.

"Are all those pictures of Owen?"

Startled, as if she'd completely forgotten about me, she scrolled to her pictures of the conference. "These are the pictures from dinner that night."

She showed me pictures of the hotel and dinner both nights, yet most were of Owen.

"Sueann, were you in love with Owen? You must have been to have that many pictures of him!" I swallowed the idea hard. "Aren't you afraid Milo will see all these pictures?"

"Milo is never around. He's married to his work." She hung her head. "I'm so lonely. I get depressed. I'm home alone all day, and weekends. Owen paid attention to me. He cared about me. Milo's so busy working all the time he barely knows I exist. He doesn't care about me. He only cares about his work."

The diamond on her left ring finger sparkled and seemed to say otherwise. I wasn't going to be part of her pity-party. I'd seen them at church. Seen the loving looks Milo cast her way. Yet, Sueann didn't seem to notice. Wrapped up in her own insecurities and sense of self, I thought she'd missed the fact that her husband treated her like a queen.

She wanted to blame Milo for her unhappiness. I guessed her loneliness more likely stemmed from boredom. Only she could remedy that malady. And she'd chosen adultery.

"But you're not afraid he'll find out?"

"I don't care if he does!" She looked at me in defiance. "Don't judge me, Delila!" Anger flashed across her face. "Look, I don't want to talk about it anymore."

Neither of us spoke for a few minutes. I wondered why she had come. If she just needed someone to talk to or if there was another reason. What did she know that I didn't? I knew from what Karly told me, that she'd spent time with Owen at the bar that night. Maybe he told her something. Something she might not realize was significant. Or perhaps she did? I waited for her to cool down.

"Sueann?" I checked her mood temperature before I went further. "That night at dinner. Owen said he needed to 'share' something with me. We planned to meet the next day. But I have no idea what it was about. Do you?"

She thought about it for a minute before answering. "I'm not sure, but I wonder if it had anything to do with your friend."

"Who Evan?"

Sueann nodded.

"Why? Why do you think it had something to do with Evan?"

"I don't know. I was at the bar that night with Owen, and Evan came up to our table. Owen introduced him to me; said they knew each other from school. I don't know, I just had a strange vibe."

"What type of strange vibe?"

"I don't know. Tense. It just felt kind of awkward between them. I don't know."

She seemed to want to dismiss the topic, suddenly growing antsy. I didn't want to push her away too soon. There were still questions she might be able to answer.

After a moment I asked, "What do you think happened to Owen?"

Sueann pondered the thought for a minute before answering. "I don't know. The police had Candi in for questioning this morning. I think they might suspect her of killing him." She raised her eyebrows and looked up at me to see if I thought so too.

"Candi told me she and Roy got a room together. So, I think Candi has an alibi, she was with Roy."

She looked at me as if I were the most gullible person she'd ever met. "Candi wasn't with Roy."

"How do you know?"

"Because they got in a big fight that night. We were out in the garden when Roy showed up and said he'd gotten a room. He'd seen her with Owen. And he was super pissed. He called her a whore and all kinds of names. Then she slapped him. No, she wasn't with Roy that night."

"Oh." So, Candi had lied to me. Intentionally misled me. But what about Sueann? She fought with Candi at least twice while we were at the hotel. What was that about?

"So, what's Candi's game?" I wanted to put her at ease. "I saw you and Candi arguing."

Sueann sighed. "I told her to stay away from Owen. She was leading him on. Flirting. Bouncing around him showing off her body. She knew how much I liked him and wanted to be with him. I called her out on it." She squirmed in her chair and looked down at her watch. "Oh, I gotta go."

She left a trail of questions in my mind as she raced out the door. Alone once again, in the solitude of my office, I considered everything Sueann had told me, and some of the things she hadn't said. If Owen had been killed, it now appeared that neither Candi nor Roy had an alibi. And Sueann hadn't provided one for herself either. Roy certainly had motive. And perhaps Sueann did too, if Owen had turned her down. But I couldn't come up with a reason Candi might want to kill him. And what about Evan? How did he play into all of this?

I pulled my phone out and started to send a text. I needed to meet with Evan. Find out how he fit into the puzzle and what he might know. But where should I meet him? I knew he would be in town for another week, wrapping things up with his business accounts. I hoped he could meet for lunch. But what about Barry? If I were meeting a girlfriend, it would not be a problem. But an old boyfriend? Would he understand?

It took me a few minutes to fire off two text messages. Then I returned my focus on the spreadsheet in front of me, until Candi flung the door open and marched in. She plopped down in the same chair Sueann had occupied only a short time before.

She wore super short shorts and a sweater. I wondered who she wanted to impress here at church, or if she just liked to be prepared. Afterall, you never know who you might meet.

"Oh, you won't believe what a day I've had." Candi began. "Can you believe the police made me come in?" She looked at me to make sure she had my full attention before continuing. "Yeaah. They found my earrings in Owen's room." She paused for my reaction. "I swear I don't know how they got there Delila! I told 'em that too. I wasn't even wearing those earrings." She crossed one thin leg carefully over the other and sat straight in the chair. I was reminded of my youth when we practiced walking with a book on our head to keep our backs straight. Candi carried herself as if she still wore that book.

Her hair and make-up were perfect as usual, and she appeared to be as composed as normal too. But maybe this was her nervous. I think I wear my fear for everyone to see. If it were me, I'd be totally rattled. Yet Candi simply looked like a little girl pouting. And I believed her.

"So how could they have gotten there? Had you left them there earlier? Like the day before or something?"

"No." She shrugged. "The police said they were left on the table next to the bed." She looked directly at me. "I didn't sleep with him Delila."

She hadn't slept in our room either. "So where did you sleep?" I felt bold now, asking the question everyone wanted the answer to. But would she tell me the truth?

"I told you. I was with Roy, in the room he got." The question on her face said why don't you believe me?

If I were going to get to the truth, I'd have to explain why her previous alibi was in trouble. "Sueann said you and Roy got in a big fight in the garden."

"We did. But we made up after that. You can ask him!" Her voice grew louder.

"Oh." I shook my head and hoped to calm her. She had a way of quickly getting excited and causing a scene. I didn't want a tantrum in the church. "Ok." I let it go, gave her a moment to readjust herself. "Candi...Owen was going to tell me something. That night at dinner he asked to meet with me. Do you know what he wanted to say to me?"

But she wasn't in the mood. "No. I don't know anything."

I could tell she hadn't even considered my question. Her emotions ran so strong they blocked any rational thought.

Candi stood up, edged her jaw slightly higher in the air. "I have to go. I'll see you later." When she reached the door, she turned back. "Oh, and you need to tell your friend, Officer Higgins that I'm innocent."

Now I'd upset both Sueann and Candi. Yet, I had to get to the truth. We were all wrapped up in this horrible situation. Any one of them could be guilty of something terrible. If Owen had been killed, it could have been an outsider. Someone we didn't even know. I clung to the idea. Deep down, however, I couldn't be sure. Little red spots of doubt were showing up all over.

The clock on my computer read noon. I printed out the P&L's (profit and loss statements), and the balance sheet for the new treasurer to look over, placed them in a manilla envelope and wrote her name on it, then turned my computer off and gathered my things. I dropped the envelope in our internal mailbox on my way out the door.

Outside the fresh air woke my senses. The wind had picked up. Excited and nervous, I hurried to my car.

Evan had suggested The Prominade restaurant, located downtown. We'd eaten dinner there the night of our high school senior prom. Evan sat at the table in the back of the room. His eyes transfixed on some invisible thought. His body poised, distinguished.

Did he think I had changed my mind? That I wanted to get together with him after all? Why hadn't I thought about that before firing off a text message asking him to lunch? In my haste to find out all he knew; I had failed to consider that he might get the wrong idea.

"Hi Evan." I slid into the seat across from him.

"Dee, so nice to see you." He looked at me, as if we'd just met. A blind date. A tricky encounter where you didn't know what to expect.

My heart rate increased as I tried to ease into a conversation. "Remember when we had dinner here for prom?" The room seemed warm, stuffy.

"Yeah," He nodded and grinned. Evan looked around the restaurant, inspecting it, mentally noting the recent changes. "Looks different." His gaze went around the room then returned to me. "Better."

My mind flipped back to prom night. My dress, light blue, sleeveless, that shimmered and showed my shape well, had taken me forever to find. And a month to save up the money to pay for it, on my part-time salary.

Evan picked me up at 6pm in his father's BMW. I tried to recall what I had for dinner that night, but it had escaped my memory. From there we'd headed to prom where we met up with some of our friends.

Owen was there with a girl I didn't know. For some reason, Evan had been angry with him. I couldn't remember why, but it seemed like it had something to do with the girl. About halfway through the night, an argument hatched between them, that resulted in Evan and I leaving the dance.

Did I know what they'd fought about? I searched my memory.

"Can I get you something to drink?" The waitress smiled at Evan.

"Just water. Thank you." He returned her smile.

She looked at me, somewhat impatient, and raised her eyebrows.

"Iced tea, please." I watched her leave, then turned my attention to Evan. "It's terrible about Owen, I still can't believe it happened."

He nodded. "I know."

"I sat at the same dinner table with him that night." I hoped Evan would tell me about his conversation at the bar with Owen. I wanted him to tell me what he knew. And about the note.

Evan picked up his menu and looked it over. "Looks like the menu has changed a bit too." He joked. "I never came here for lunch, only dinner. They used to have an excellent shish kabob." Apparently, he didn't want to discuss Owen's death.

I looked at my menu. "Oh yeah, I do remember you used to love it. That's probably what you ordered senior prom night."

"Doesn't look like they have it any longer." He continued to study his options. Finally, he closed his menu and laid it on the table.

I did the same. The waitress brought our drinks and took our orders. Evan went for the soup and sandwich. I ordered a salad.

After the waitress left, we had a moment of silence. I knew he wondered why I'd asked him to lunch. But I wasn't sure if I should throw my cards on the table yet. I wanted to lead up to it. I wanted him to share what he knew with me naturally.

"Evan, I want to be friends. I know things were getting warm at the conference, and if I were single, believe me it would have been very different."

He shot me a brief smile. "Of course. I understand Dee. I'm glad you have a good marriage."

"Thank you." I looked around the room. My eyes fell on a table near the window. "I think that's where we sat that night."

He wrinkled his brow. "What night? Oh. Senior prom night."

"I remember we didn't stay at the dance very long. You and Owen got into it, but I don't remember why."

"I don't know. It was a long time ago, Dee."

"I think it had something to do with that girl he was with." I prompted. I wasn't going to let it go. I needed to know.

He knew me too well. He rubbed his thumb up and down on the glass, then took a drink. "He was supposed to take my sister to prom. He'd asked her out a couple weeks before that. She'd spent a lot of money on a dress, told all her friends. She was so excited. Then he stood her up. He came with someone else. He didn't even tell her. When I saw him there with that girl, I was so mad, I wanted to punch him. He really hurt my sister."

I could see the pain still lingered as he relived that night. Owen had been a jerk.

"Did he ever apologize to her?"

He shook his head and took another drink. The waitress came and put our food down in front of us. Evan quickly changed the subject. "Let's talk about you Delila. Tell me about your hopes and dreams. How about your aspirations?"

Taken by surprise I had to think about it. I liked my work at the church. Number crunching seemed to suit me, but I hadn't really thought much about my future and what I wanted it to look like. Right now, I just wanted to find out who killed Owen and why. But I couldn't exactly tell Evan that, could I?

"Well, I like my job." I began. "And I suppose I expect to retire one day and have grandchildren." It sounded boring, even to my own ears. Was that really all I wanted?

After we'd finished eating, I tried to steer the conversation back to Owen. "I keep thinking about Owen. What do you think happened that night?"

He said he didn't know, yet his answer felt vague. He must have had some thoughts about it. How could he not? Then he looked at his watch and said he had to go. Had an appointment. We parted the restaurant, neither of us with the outcome we'd hoped for. Me wanting to know what was in the note, him wanting to advance our relationship.

That afternoon I cleaned for a short time, then plopped down on the floor, my back against the sofa. Jewel silently strolled up and rubbed against me, then rolled on her back, exposing her belly. She eyed me to see if I'd take the bait.

"I'm not going to pet your belly and let you bite me." I told her. She wriggled around back and forth on her back and side. She clearly wanted to play, but I wasn't in the mood. Boris lay on the other side of me, content just to have me next to him.

Evan would only be in town for a few more days. I might never find out what was in the note Owen gave him, or what Owen wanted to tell me that night. I replayed the events of the conference over in my mind.

I thought about Sueann and Candi fighting, apparently over Owen. Sueann still in love with Owen; Candi flirting with him. Roy seeing Candi with Owen. Darren, clearly infatuated with Candi. Liz obviously jealous of that point. Karly. Evan. Had I seen Owen's wife Ellie? The memories swirled around in my brain. How could a church conference go so wrong?

The following afternoon when I returned home from work, Boris acted especially anxious. It had been a couple of days since I'd taken him to the park, and I knew that I owed him a walk. So, I called Mitzi and asked her to meet us in half an hour. I ate my lunch, cleaned up, and then Boris and I set out for Lily Park, aka, the Gossip Garden.

Her yellow-orange tie-die shirt and bright orange pants reminded me of a sunrise over Lake Huron. She loved her colors, and they looked fabulous on her. Boris immediately ran to greet the little red poodle with tangerine-colored ribbons.

"I need to make an appointment with Barry," she said, and moved her tongue around in her mouth. "I think I have a cavity."

"Oh, he'll take care of you," I grinned.

"I'm going to ask him to whiten my teeth too." She smiled big enough for me to see her already white teeth. "Does he do that zoom whitening?"

"Yes, they do that and the bleach trays too." I smiled, showing off my own white teeth.

Boris and the poodle were sniffing the small garden near the pavilion. "They look happy. Mia has missed her friend Boris."

"He missed her too!" I agreed. Although the two dogs seemed to be more interested in the smells around the garden than each other.

"Are you going to Owen's visitation tonight?" I asked.

"I'll stop in for a bit, yes." She looked thoughtful for a moment. "I heard something interesting from a friend of mine." Mitzi gave me a side glance, a check to make sure she had my full attention. She did.

"Go on."

"Well, my friend's daughter, is good friends with Ellie and Owen's daughter. They go to school together."

Boris had started to wander. "Boris!" I interrupted momentarily. He turned and headed back toward us. "Sorry."

"Anyway, the kid told my friend's daughter, that they were going to be rich. That her father had a huge life insurance policy."

I didn't even try to hide my surprise at the revelation.

The funeral home was filled with the smell of flowers, mostly lilies, I thought. The beautiful arrangements lined either side of the closed casket, and soft music played in the background. I'd debated with myself for some time what I would wear and had finally decided on a nice pair of black slacks and a light-colored blouse. As I looked around the room, I saw some people in jeans with holes and all types of extremely casual attire. Apparently, people no longer dressed up to pay their respects.

Barry and I added our names to the book on the podium next to the door, then joined the line up to the casket, stopping to look at each of the beautiful bouquets and read the cards. Some of the arrangements carried banners that read 'uncle', 'brother', 'nephew'. The spray that covered the casket was done in white roses and peace lilies, with blue ribbon entwined throughout. It was gorgeous. I wondered what would happen to this beautiful spray after the funeral.

Numerous floral baskets, dish gardens, and bouquets had been placed on tables around the room. Many were from businesses. Many were quite large. Barry and I looked for the one we'd sent. Although expensive, its size seemed dwarfed in comparison to some of the others. Then we looked for the arrangement from the church.

Chairs lined the walls of the room, where some people sat, but many stood talking with one another. I spotted Ellie surrounded by friends and family, nodding solemnly from time to time. I recognized their two teenage children from church, talking with other kids their age. Friends or cousins, I presumed. I looked around the room for other faces I recognized.

Milo and Sueann sat together along the side of the room. He was a good-looking man, and even his thick shock of pure white hair didn't give away the fifteen-year age difference between them. And although he held her hand, Milo wasn't looking at his wife. Instead, he stared blankly into space. Sueann looked tired, her face ruddy, probably from crying, I suspected.

Candi stood talking to Liz and Darren. Her short black skirt complimented by a cream-colored blouse made me wonder if she was heading to a dinner party later in the evening. Her high heels elevated her to the same height as Liz. Darren, obviously impressed with the skirt and heels, smiled cheerfully. Liz smiled too, but to me it looked forged. Barry and I approached them, said hello, and made small talk for several minutes.

I felt a tap on my shoulder and turned to see Karly. I included her in our group as the chitchat continued. From time to time, I saw Ellie send little daggers our way and assumed they were meant for Candi.

The discussion had turned to the new 'clothing for the homeless' fundraiser the church planned for the following week.

"You wouldn't believe the crap people donate." Liz told us. "I mean, stuff from the 70's, pants with holes and blouses all stained. We throw half of it away."

Liz had a habit of exaggerating, in this case, however, I thought there might be some truth in her story. "And filthy." Liz continued. "I mean nasty."

We all cringed and made faces, but I guessed that for our sake, the story had been embellished.

It was at that moment that I heard Ellie's raised voice, deep and angry. "Don't talk to me! I don't even know why you came!"

We all turned and looked at Ellie. Sueann and Milo were standing near her. Her glare told us all we needed to know.

"I'm sorr..." I heard Sueann's meek voice against the silence of the room.

"I bet you are." Ellie cut her off.

Milo pulled Sueann's arm and led her from the room.

For several moments, no one said a word. Eventually people started talking again, as if the emotional outbreak had never happened. No one wanted to draw attention to the uncomfortable encounter.

A few minutes later, Candi, her usual sparkling smile now a polite line on her face, said her good-byes to us. She avoided Ellie as she made her quick exit. Darren's eyes followed her legs all the way out the door.

Barry and I stayed for another twenty minutes. It didn't escape me that Evan had not shown up, but that wasn't surprising. He never claimed to be friends with Owen. Roy also hadn't been there. But given he had gone into a jealous fit after finding his wife and Owen together, that too was understandable. I was silent as we drove home, thinking about Ellie, and wondering how many of Owen's affairs she knew about.

The next morning a formal funeral took place at the church. People seemed to be on their best behavior and there were no further incidents like the one at the visitation. I didn't go with them to the cemetery, but instead went with several other women to the church kitchen to prepare food for the luncheon. The new reverend had performed a dutiful eulogy, filled with beautiful sentiment and praise for a virtuous life, a life well lived, that sounded to me as if he didn't know Owen very well.

The funeral luncheon, also void of any confrontations, lasted for about three hours. By the time we had cleaned up after everyone left, I arrived back home exhausted, around 5:30pm, ordered pizza and waited for Barry.

When we finally retired to the living room around 9pm, Barry turned on a World War II movie. All the shooting and army scenes bored me. I tried to read, but couldn't get into the story, so I picked up my phone and scrolled through some news articles for a while. My eyes landed on the icon for my photos, and I remembered the pictures I'd taken of the conference.

The reverend had asked me to take photos for our church bulletin, and the community events board. With all the turbulence surrounding Owen's death, I'd completely forgotten them.

Barry, now fully engrossed in the movie, barely noticed my departure. In my office, I switched on my computer and downloaded the pictures. It was much easier to view details in the photos on the larger screen.

I began clicking through them. I'd snapped pics of the garden from the window in our room, and from inside the garden. There were pictures of the lobby, our church members in the reception room, and from both dinners. I'd gotten several of the band and some from the lectures.

After having looked over all of them, I went back and looked more carefully at the pictures that captured Owen. Candi stood or sat next to him in most of them. Candi loved having pictures taken and managed to get in more of them than anyone else.

Could there be a clue here, hiding somewhere in one of these photos? I looked at them repeatedly, until finally Barry called me. "News time." I turned off the computer and sat down with him for our nightly routine of watching the local news.

The new development in the case was highlighted by the news reporters. A preliminary autopsy report showed Owen had been drugged before being suffocated, most likely smothered by a pillow. Other than that, the newscaster reported that police had spoken with 'a person of interest', but that no arrests had been made.

At around 4am I woke up and couldn't go back to sleep. I tossed and turned for a while but kept thinking about Owen's murder. Candi was the police department's main suspect, largely because her earrings had been found at the murder scene. But I couldn't see her drugging Owen and then smothering him with a pillow. Candi just wouldn't do that. Besides, what motive would she have?

I rolled over and began to think about Sueann. Where had she slept those two nights of the conference? She'd been with someone I didn't know at dinner. Could she have been with him both nights? I tried to remember. I'd been so wrapped up in my own situation with Evan, I hadn't paid much attention. Clearly, Sueann was in love with Owen. Had she been trying to make him jealous?

Quietly, I slipped from the bed and padded back to my office. I searched through the pictures again. My eyes fell on a photo of Evan that I especially liked. Looking at his smile made me smile. It was sad to think that he'd be leaving soon. After our lunch, he'd sent me a text saying he'd accepted a position in New York and would be leaving. But it might be for the best, I decided.

There were plenty of pictures of our group. I enlarged several to see details that I might have otherwise missed. I kept the photos in chronological order and paid special attention to who sat where and everyone's expressions, clothing, and interactions with one another.

I'd also taken some videos and studied them as well. I found the still photos allowed me to zoom in on things, whereas the video let me see actions. For at least an hour I examined the videos and the photos, until finally my eyes fell upon two curious details. And they had to do with Candi and Sueann. I thought about it for a long time, jotted down some notes, then shuffled back down the hallway to bed.

The aroma of fresh coffee brewing lifted me from my slumber the following morning. I'd overslept, but fortunately Barry had not. A mini breakfast-bar of fruit, scrambled eggs, hashbrowns and toast were laid out on the counter. He set a cup of coffee down in front of me and handed me a plate.

As soon as Barry left, I quickly cleaned up the kitchen and got ready for work. It wasn't until later in the morning, once the accounts had been reconciled, and I had some free time, that I began to think about the photos again.

What I'd noticed could be significant, yet I wasn't sure it was enough on its own to report to Jim. Just an idea in the raw for now. I wanted something tangible to give him.

The photos had shown Sueann with an unknown gentleman friend at dinner on the first night, and the second night, yet Karly said she'd shown up alone at the bar. She hadn't come back to the room either night. She might have been with that guy the first night, but what about the night Owen was killed? Where had she slept that night?

I'd zoomed in on the photos of Candi and noticed something odd. She had not been wearing the earrings they found on the nightstand in Owen's room either night. Yet, they did belong to her, and I had seen her with them before.

Caught in a fog of daydreams, my thoughts soon drifted to Evan. He'd be leaving in a few days, and I still didn't know what was in that note. He might leave town before I ever found out. Could it help shed any light on the investigation?

I pondered calling him and just asking. I could tell him that someone, whose name I'd prefer not to say, told me they saw Owen give him the note. Then I realized that sounded rather bold, rude. After all, it wasn't my job to solve this crime. It wasn't really any of my business.

Soon my mind wandered to Sueann. Should I ask her where she had been that night? We were friends, but maybe not that good of friends. I wondered if Jim had asked her.

My cell phone rang. Karly. I debated picking up the call. For some reason I just didn't care about talking to her. I let it go to voicemail. Then I wondered if she might have any more information that would be helpful to the case.

In her message she asked if I wanted to meet for lunch. I texted her back and we agreed to meet for a late lunch at a little restaurant between the church and the tavern where she worked.

The door to my office opened and Mitzi popped her head in. "Hi Delila, gotta minute?"

"Sure!"

Today she wore bright green leggings, high heels, a purple-gray top, and a large orange handbag. Solid colors, a bit plain by Mitzi's standards, but quite attractive.

"Hey, I just wanted to let you know that our HOA is having a mid-year election for secretary of our board. I'm thinking about running." The excitement in her voice made the pitch higher than normal.

"That's great Mitzi! You'd be perfect." I motioned for her to sit down in the chair next to my desk.

"Yeah, I'm excited. I've been so bored since you started working!" She looked at my desk and computer, seemed thoughtful for a moment and then said, "I wish you could be on the board too. I think when the next regular election comes around, you should run for office. With your experience in accounting, you'd make a great treasurer!"

I wrinkled my nose and shrugged. I hadn't any desire for getting myself into something like that.

"Promise me you'll think about it." Mitzi teased. She looked over at the office manager's empty desk and asked, "Where's Anie?"

"Still on vacation. I've had the place all to myself for a week, and I love it."

Mitzi tossed a devious grin, got up and closed the door. She sat back down, leaned toward me, and with her deep quiet voice said, "Ellie's daughter says her parents had been talking divorce before he died." She waited for that to sink in.

She had me where she wanted me, all ears. "Really?" Yet, as I thought about it, it made sense. I certainly wouldn't want to stay with someone who constantly strayed.

Mitzi nodded. "Apparently, Ellie's parents died and left her a lot of money." Her eyes gleamed with delight in relaying the confidential information. "She was worried that if they divorced, she'd have to split her inheritance with Owen." An expert in storytelling, she paused for effect before moving on.

"She was worried he'd remarry, and his new wife would get all her money." Mitzi took a quick breath. "Not that I blame her. It would bother me too."

The little restaurant where Karly and I planned to meet was only a few blocks from the church. I decided the walk would do me good.

Karly sat in a booth near the back, her lanky body bent over the menu. Had she lost weight, or hadn't I noticed before how thin she looked? I decided to buy her lunch.

"Hi Karly," I pulled my jacket off and scooted in across from her. "Whew, it's warm out today. Nice and cool in here though."

The waitress hurried over to take our drink orders, having few other customers, she seemed anxious to wait on us. I ordered iced tea. Karly ordered water.

"My treat today, Karly." I smiled brightly.

"Oh, you don't have to—."

"I want to. Make it two iced teas." I picked up the menu and scanned the specials.

"Thanks, Delila, but you really don't have to." Karly shot me a grateful smile.

We placed our orders and made small talk for a while. The waitress brought our drinks and took our food order, then Karly offered up some details previously omitted from her story of the night Owen died.

"I thought of something else from that night." She took a drink of her tea and looked up at me.

Once I'd given her the 'I'm interested' look, she continued. "Ok, let me see." She thought for a moment, "after dinner, you went back to your room. Owen and Candi went out into the garden. I'm not sure where Sueann went, but I wanted to go out in the garden too. It was a nice night and I thought I'd get a few steps in before it got super dark out." She pointed to her fitness watch. "I like to get at least 5,000 to 10,000 steps a day."

I nodded and shifted in my seat. "Yeah, I do too."

Karly seemed to sense my impatience. "Anyway, as I was walking around, I heard Roy and Owen and Candi arguing. I guess Roy saw Candi with Owen and he was mad. He accused them of sleeping together and started yelling at Owen that he should kill him for trying to steal his wife."

I imagined the scene as she relayed the incident. It must have been a shock to Roy, or maybe not. He'd probably been through it before. Candi liked the attention of men. Had he really meant to say he should kill Owen?

"I was hidden by bushes so they didn't see me, but I could see the three of them." Karly continued. "Candi grabbed Roy's arm, and kept saying 'oh, nothing happened' but he pulled away. Owen kept trying to calm him too, and he said something like, nothing happened, that they were just taking a walk in the garden, and stuff like that. Trying to get Roy to settle down."

"Wow." I said, to show my interest so she would continue. I knew much of this from Sueann, yet I wondered why Karly hadn't mentioned it before.

As if she'd read my mind, Karly blurted out, "I didn't tell you before because I worried you would think I was spying on them or something. I mean, I guess I was in a way, but I wasn't going to say anything in the middle of their fight."

"Of course." I assured her.

She held her glass in both hands, and seemed to think something over for a few moments, then took a sip and looked up at me. "Your friend was there too."

"Evan?"

"Un hun," She nodded, "I mean he was sitting on a bench nearby. I'm sure he heard the whole thing too."

The waitress brought our food and hovered for a moment, waiting to make sure we had everything. After she left, Karly asked, “Have you heard anything from your friend, the detective? Has he said if they have any suspects?”

“No.” I said and shook my head. “He can’t tell me anything anyway. Not allowed to, I guess.” I didn’t want her to keep pumping me for information. She wanted me to spill the beans on whatever I’d heard, but that wasn’t going to happen. In the end, I changed the subject, and we finished our lunch without further discussion about the murder.

Since Aleena was still in Florida visiting her parents, I decided to invite Jim to dinner once more before her return. I could fill him in on the fine points I’d discovered, and while they might not mean much, each crumb of a detail took us one step further to solving the crime.

Jim likes fish, so I decided to make him flounder with crab stuffing. I had the day off and spent the better part of the morning studying the fine art of making garnishes to go along with the meal.

Mitzi called around 11am and wondered if I wanted to meet up at the park. So, Boris and I headed to the park to see our friends. Clouds covered the sky, and I could feel the dampness in the air. Boris too sensed the possibility of rain and walked a little faster than normal.

The little red poodle wore a pink rain jacket that matched Mitzi’s. “Where did you find matching raincoats?” I asked. “I mean, is there a store that sells them?”

“Oh, I actually had these made special for us.” Mitzi grinned. “I have a friend who is a seamstress. She’s amazing!”

“I want her number! Maybe I’ll have her make Barry and Boris matching clothes!” I laughed at the thought.

“Are you enjoying your day off?” Mitzi asked.

"Yes! I'm learning all about food art, and how to make beautiful garnishes."

"Well, you missed some interesting stuff at the church this morning." Mitzi said.

"What happened?" My eyes popped wide, my curiosity on full alert.

"You know how Ellie pledged to donate all that money for the new wing?"

I nodded.

"Well, this morning she gave the reverend a list of names and asked that they be expelled from the church." She glanced over at the poodle then back to me, "said she didn't think these were the type of people our church should be known for. That they are not really Christians." A satisfied grin crossed her face. "But I think they were all women that had been with Owen. Anyway, she told him that if he didn't renounce them, she wasn't giving the church another dime!"

My eyes didn't blink but stared firmly at Mitzi. "Did you hear her say that?" I asked.

"No. But I heard it from a very reliable source."

Her wily smirk made me laugh. She certainly was connected and often heard the gossip first. "Who?"

"The reverend's wife."

I finally blinked. Ellie had been a good supporter of the church. Had always given large donations in the past. The poor reverend. What a terrible spot to be in. He'd already committed to building the new wing, based on her promise. "Wow. So, what's the reverend going to do? Is he going to kick them out of the church? How many are we talking about?"

"I guess he told Ellie he couldn't do that, but now he's not sure what to do." Mitzi turned her head toward the poodle who had wandered to the edge of the park. "Mia,

Get back here!" The little poodle ignored her. "Mia!" Finally, the dog turned and ran back toward us, and Mitzi turned her attention back to our conversation. "I wish I could see that list!"

My little lemon rose garnishes didn't turn out as charming as I'd hoped, but they looked ok. I set one at each end of our plates. Leaving plenty of room for the fish, I placed tomato roses on the opposite side. I'd watched several youtube videos which proved to be very helpful in teaching me to make food art. I added celery leaves to each flower for even more color.

Barry and Jim discussed sports while I cooked. When we all sat down to eat, both men were impressed with our dinner, and complimented me several times throughout the meal. We didn't discuss the case until I brought out desert.

As I handed Jim a plate with a slice of cherry pie on it, I began to tell him all the new developments I'd learned about Owen's death, with hopes he might share whatever he'd found too, however unlikely that might be.

I told him about Ellie, her inheritance and plans to divorce Owen, and the life insurance policy. I also shared the newest information I'd learned from Mitzi regarding the 'list' Ellie had given the reverend.

"Jim, there's something else I discovered. I noticed something when I was going through my pictures from the conference."

He raised his eyebrows with piqued interest.

"I noticed that Candi wasn't wearing those earrings in any of the photos. Not the first night, nor the night Owen was killed. But I know she had them at the conference. I think she wore them the day we checked in, then changed before the welcome reception."

"You're sure you saw them?" Barry asked.

I nodded.

"Humm, it is interesting. Maybe she changed them again before going to his room." Jim scratched his head.

"Maybe. Is there any video of her going into his room that weekend?" I asked.

"We aren't sure. She could be the person we saw in the hoodie the night he was killed."

I reached for a large manilla envelope I had sitting on the table and handed it to him. "Here are some pictures I took from the conference. I don't know if they'll help but... I can send you the digital copies too if you want them." I handed him the envelope.

"Jim," I hesitated, torn between betraying Sueann, and helping the police solve Owen's murder, "have you asked Sueann where she was the night Owen died? She...She didn't come back to our room that night."

He was silent for a minute then said, "Thank you Delila, for the photos, and for telling me what you know. I'm sorry, I can't share details of the case, even though I appreciate all you bring to me." He smiled up at me, "And, thank you for the best dinner I've had in weeks!"

The next morning at work, I sat staring at my computer, unable to focus on the numbers before me. Jim hadn't told me where Sueann was the night of Owen's murder, but if he suspected her, I assumed she would be brought in again for questioning.

Anie, my co-worker and the Church office secretary, back from vacation, wiggled in her chair. "Everything ok Delila?" She asked.

Irritated by the jolt from my meditative thoughts about the case, I smiled and replied, "I'm fine. Just thinking." Secretly, I wished Anie was still on vacation.

"Anything I can help with?"

"No, thanks." My tone sounded rude even to me. I wanted quiet time for my thoughts, not chitter chatter.

Anie and I weren't exactly friends, nor were we enemies. I found her annoying at times. She was nosey and she liked to suck up to the reverend. The phony flattery and overly eager desire to please him grated on my nerves.

Yet, she did seem to know things. I wasn't sure if the reverend shared these things with her, or if she learned them from her snooping. I guessed the latter.

"Anie," I softened my voice. "Do you know if Ellie is still planning to give the church a big donation? The one the reverend wants to use for remodeling?"

"Well, she was going to. But I'm not sure now. Why?" Anie had radar that seemed to sense I was headed into confidential territory.

I pretended to look at the accounts. "I just wondered. I'm thinking about some of the plans the reverend has in mind for future projects."

"She was going to give us a half million dollars." Anie looked at me sharply.

"Oh yes, now I remember. Was going to? So, she might not?" I tried to sound naive, as if I didn't know.

"Apparently, her donation comes with strings. She wants the reverend to kick some of the members out of the church." Anie said in a matter-of-fact voice. "But he doesn't know if that's the right thing to do." She looked at the door to make sure no one could hear then whispered, "you know, the women Owen slept with."

If I wanted to learn more from her, I'd need to continue my act of innocence. "What?"

"Yes, she gave him a list of names, and asked him to force them to leave the church."

"A whole list? Have you seen it?" I wondered how many names could be on that list.

Anie nodded. "But I can't tell you Delila."

I stewed over the thought of Ellie trying to have people removed from our church by throwing her money around. Would the reverend go for it? I couldn't believe he would. How could he? Can people even be thrown out of a house of worship? Yet, the church had already hired the contractor to begin work on the new wing. The wing that Ellie had promised to pay for. Not a good spot for the reverend to be in. How would he pay for it if she pulled out now?

I was certain the list contained at least the names of Sueann and Candi. And, while I knew they weren't angels, it didn't seem right. I placed some receipts in a file folder then closed the drawer a little harder than I had intended.

"I don't know how she can ask the reverend to kick people out of the church! None of us are perfect, and we come here to learn how to become better people, right?" My voice sounded loud and angry and seemed to startle Anie. "What's the reverend supposed to do now? He's already started the addition and Ellie knows it! This is blackmail and it's not fair to the reverend or the church!"

Ellie walked in the room just as I finished my rant. I knew she'd heard me, but I was unable to stop myself.

Anie looked embarrassed. She opened her desk drawer and pulled out her purse.

"Mind your own business, Delila." Ellie's eyes were packed with contempt. She turned and looked at Anie, as if she'd just been betrayed by her friend. Then the two women walked out the door together. Apparently for lunch.

Feeling guilty for having been caught talking about Ellie behind her back, I began to file some papers. I didn't even notice Candi come in until she plopped down in the chair next to my desk.

"I'm exhausted!" Candi said. "I haven't been able to sleep ever since Owen's murder."

I suspected her of fishing for sympathy, but I had none to give. My mood had turned sour, and I had no desire to appease her need for pity. After all, as Mitzi liked to say, she had been breadcrumbing Owen throughout the conference. She may or may not have intended to sleep with him, but she had surely given him and everyone else the impression she would.

"I think the police suspect Roy." Candi continued. "They called him in for questioning and kept him all morning. I wonder if they are going to arrest him?" Her eyes were wide and questioning.

I shrugged.

"I thought you might know since you are such good friends with that cop." Suddenly she sounded concerned. "What am I going to do if they arrest him? I can't afford to pay the rent all by myself. Plus, he'll have to get a lawyer. That will cost a lot of money!"

"Do you think he did it?" I asked.

"No, why would he?"

"Well, I'm sure he was jealous of you and Owen. He saw you guys together."

"Nothing happened between me and Owen. We were just friends."

"Candi I was there. I saw you flirting with him and I'm guessing Roy did too."

Her voice grew loud and angry. "You don't know anything Delila! You don't know what I've been through." She sat up straight in the chair. "Besides, how do they know it wasn't your boyfriend!" She spat it out with some satisfaction.

"What do you mean 'my boyfriend'?" The words tumbled from my mouth at the same time I realized she was talking about Evan.

"Yeah, I saw you with him. So did Owen. He told me that guy hated him too. Said that guy had threatened him."

"Back in high school Candi. Evan and I dated in high school, and Owen and Evan had a falling out back then. But that was years ago."

"Oh, he still hated him alright. He found us in the garden. He was super angry and told Owen that his sister was dying of cancer. He said it looked like Owen hadn't changed at all and that Owen was the one who deserved to die." Candi stood, tilted her chin up and growled, "Tell your friend the police officer to lay off Roy." She walked out the door without looking back.

Dumbfounded, I sat for several moments attempting to reign in my thoughts. Had Candi seen the 'kiss'? Did she think Evan and I were having an affair? It sounded like she wanted to blackmail me. Was it a threat? She'd tell Jim about Evan and me unless I could get Jim to leave Roy alone? She gave me more credit than I deserved. Did she think Evan might have killed Owen?

Evan wasn't like that. He would never hurt anyone. At least not the Evan I knew. But why hadn't he told me about his sister's cancer?

He planned on leaving in just a couple of days. I needed to meet with him. Find out if what Candi told me was true.

I sat back in my chair and thought about all the people who might have killed Owen. Sueann had no alibi that I knew of for that night. She was in love with him, and he seemed to have tossed her aside for Candi. She'd been with him at the bar just before that. She could have slipped something in his drink and then gone to his room later.

Jim said a woman could have smothered him. If Owen hadn't been drugged, he would have been strong enough to fend off the assassin. But, in his drugged state, he wouldn't have put up much of a struggle. Therefore, a woman killer couldn't be ruled out.

The video camera had showed someone come up from the stairway and go into Owen's room. Since the room was right next to the stairway and from the angle of the camera, the police were unable to tell the height of the hooded person or even see a hand on the doorknob. So, no way of knowing if the suspect was a man or a woman.

I still suspected Roy too. Catching his wife with Owen had to be devastating for him. He must have suspected something might happen at the conference, otherwise why show up at all? Then to see them together. His jealousy could easily have taken over.

What about Candi? Her earrings were evidence that she'd been in his room. But why would she do it? To prove to Roy that she didn't care about Owen? That seemed farfetched, even to me.

Ellie had motive. A cheating husband who embarrassed her, who she had planned on divorcing. Yes Ellie, who had worried about splitting her money with him in the divorce, then became the recipient of a big life insurance payout.

And now even Evan had become a suspect. He'd threatened Owen that night. Although, it wasn't really a threat-threat. More like a 'you're a jerk and deserve any karma that comes your way' threat. It wasn't like he'd said "I'm going to kill you" or something like that.

Still Evan couldn't be ruled out. And Candi would surely tell the police what she'd heard if it meant saving Roy. I pulled out my cellphone and sent Evan a text.

Normally I like to clean when I get home from work, at least for an hour or two. But that afternoon, I found I had no ambition to do anything. What if Candi told Jim about the kiss, and he told Barry? It might change my whole marriage. I loved Barry and even though I still cared for Evan, it was Barry I wanted to be with. Should I tell him or just wait and see how the chips fell?

The phone rang and Mitzi wondered if Boris and I wanted to meet her and the little red dog, Mia, at the park. Boris perked up as if he knew what the conversation was about, and we agreed to meet them. "I think I may have more news for you," she'd promised.

Boris, happy to get me out of the house and out of my funk, pulled me down the street and toward the park. The wind was blowing, and the air had a definite chill to it. As Mitzi and I stood facing one another, I wrapped my arms around myself, to keep warm.

"You're going to love this," Mitzi began.

I forced a smile and gave her my *spill-it* look.

"My friend said that Ellie's daughter stayed over at their house the night Owen was murdered. And the son stayed at his friend's house. So, Ellie has no alibi for that night. She may not have been at home grading papers like she said she was."

"Wow, if that's true, the police need to know."

Mitzi nodded.

We watched the dogs in silence for a moment while they sniffed the same ground they always sniffed.

I contemplated this new information. Ellie had the best motive as far as I could tell. Her behavior after Owen's death also made her seem guilty. My thoughts drifted back to the list. How many people could be on that list? For some reason it felt important to know who Ellie wanted to oust. How could I get a hold of that list?

Finally, I said, "I sure wish I could get my hands on that list Ellie gave the reverend."

"How do you think that would help?" Mitzi asked.

"I don't know." I admitted.

Mitzi looked over at me and smiled. "Don't worry Delila, I got this!"

When I got back home, my phone buzzed. Evan's text said he could meet at the coffee shop in an hour. Then I sent Jim a text to let him know Ellie no longer had an alibi.

Evan was waiting at a table near the back of the coffee shop. He still looked like the man I'd dated in high school. I smiled thinking about the first time he asked me out. I was sixteen and thrilled to be going on a date. It was also my first concert.

As the music played, Evan's hand had found mine. He held it through the whole first set. About two weeks later he told me he was 'wild' about me. I smiled. We were so young. So innocent.

I slid into the chair across from Evan. "How are you?"

We made small talk for a few minutes, then went to the counter and ordered our drinks. Evan insisted on paying for my hot chocolate, complete with a swirl of whipped cream. He had plain black coffee.

As we sipped our drinks, I came to the point. "Evan, I heard your sister is very ill."

Evan looked at his coffee and nodded.

"I'm so sorry. Why didn't you tell me?"

"Look, it's hard to talk about it, Dee. You know how close we are. With my parents gone, she's all I've got left." His voice began to crack. He took a deep breath.

"So why take the job in New York?"

"No choice. My company gave me two options and New York is closer. I can't afford to quit my job."

We were silent for a few moments. Finally, I spoke. "Evan, Candi says you threatened Owen. That you said Owen should be the one to die." I watched for his reaction.

Evan's face had turned pale, but he met my eyes. "I was angry."

"I think she might tell the police." I told him. He needed to know.

"I didn't do anything, Dee. I didn't kill him if that's what you're worried about."

"No, I know." But the police didn't know. And Candi would spin it to make Evan look suspicious.

Barry arrived home in his usual good mood and kissed me on the cheek as I pulled the chicken satay in peanut sauce from the oven. "What have we here? Looks delicious!"

I set the plate of satay garnished with Italian parsley, along with a bowl of coconut ginger rice and cooked vegetables on the table. Barry's grin indicated he was more than pleased. He guessed correctly. I'd gotten my inspiration from the Marseille.

"So, how was your day, honey?" Barry asked.

Barry hadn't had any updates on the case, so I shared with him the new information I'd learned. I decided to include most of the stuff about Evan. Leaving it out would make me feel guilty, as if I were hiding an affair from him.

He listened carefully and when I'd finished, he commented, "you've told Jim all of this? I'm sure he will find Owen's killer. I think you should be careful Delila. Someone who has killed once, might not be afraid to do it again. Especially if they think you pose a danger to them."

"But I don't even know who did it. I can't be much of a threat if I don't know." I countered.

"Maybe you know more than you think. All I'm saying is, this is police work and you have helped, but you need to be careful. I don't want anything happening to you." He shot me an affectionate smile.

He knew of course that I wouldn't stop. "Did I tell you that Owen wanted to talk to me that night? He had something he wanted to tell me?" Barry shook his head. "I asked him to wait until the next day. Barry, I should have let him tell me. I don't know if it had anything to do with his murder, and now I might never know."

At work the next day, I felt a little off. Perhaps it was all the excitement and emotional turmoil of the past week and a half. I paid the bills on autopilot, not really thinking about what I was doing.

My cell phone rang, and even though I don't like talking within Anie's earshot, I answered anyway. It was Mitzi.

"Delila, you're not going to believe this. You know my friend, the one whose kids are friends with Ellie's? This morning, she told me about something that happened about two weeks ago. Ellie was bitching about Owen. Called him a two-timing male whore, and wished he was dead."

"Ellie actually said that-- she said she wished Owen was dead?" I'd meant to whisper, yet my voice had been louder than intended.

"Yes. Oh, and by the way, I've got a copy of the list. Want to meet for lunch?"

"How did you—" I noticed Anie watching me and turned away from her. "You can tell me at lunch." We made plans to meet at The China House restaurant on Main Street, at one o'clock.

Anie acted as if she hadn't been listening, but I suspected she had. I watched as she opened the mail, sorting out what went to me. The phone rang, and Anie picked it up. "Delila, the reverend wants to see you."

"Did he say why?" *Why didn't he ever call me directly?*

"Nope. Just asked if you'd come down to his office."

I closed out of the open documents and folders on my computer, then began a slow journey down the hall to the reverend's office. Was I in some sort of trouble? Had I done something wrong? Worse yet, was I on Ellie's list now? I couldn't imagine why I was being called into the office.

The reverend sat at his desk looking seriously at some paperwork. He glanced up at me, then back at his paperwork and said, "Sit down Delila."

With the large mahogany desk between us, I felt like a child in the principal's office. After a moment he said, "I've been going over the costs for the new wing, and how much we have in our accounts right now."

A sigh of relief surged through my body. He only wanted to talk about the church's finances.

"I'm thinking we may need to take out a loan to complete the new wing. I'd like your opinion. Is this something we can afford to do? The loan, I mean. Or do you have any other ideas of ways to bring in the money?"

I decided not to mention Ellie's decision to recant her donation. "Well, we might try a gofundme page or do another fundraiser. I can also look over our monthly expenses and see if we can cut anything and see how much of a loan we can afford."

As if I'd offered to pay for the wing myself, the reverend smiled and said, "Oh, thank you Delila!"

I returned to my office in much better spirits than when I'd left and quickly got to work looking for places to cut costs. With my face buried in numbers, I didn't notice Ellie enter the room. She'd probably stood glaring at me for several moments.

When I looked up, I saw her, arms crossed and the look of an angry bug about to spit venom. "So, you like to gossip about me?"

Violent confrontation was not my strong suit. I cowered behind my computer. "Ellie, I'm sorry—"

"Sorry my butt. You're not sorry. You're just a petty little gossip!"

I looked at my computer, couldn't meet her eyes. Perhaps she was right.

"You call yourself a Christian Delila? I just lost my husband and all you can do is gossip about me?"

I sat and waited for another slap.

"My children will grow up without a father now. What do you think of that? And your friends, all wanting to get in his pants! Owen didn't stand a chance, with them pushing themselves on him like that."

As is often the case when someone dies, they move into sainthood. All their sins are forgotten, and people remember a great person. Did she really expect me to believe she thought Owen played no role in his infidelity? Or was this all part of an act she was putting on?

I tried to reason with her. "Look Ellie, what they did is unforgiveable. And I get that you are hurting—"

"Shut up Delila! You don't know anything."

I took a deep breath and sighed. There was nothing I could say that would pacify her. She wanted to release a lot of rage, and currently I was the target. My best bet was to keep my mouth shut.

When I didn't respond, Ellie turned to Anie. "Come on. Let's get out of here."

Feeling a little sorry for myself, I continued to stare at the door for a while after they left. Seemed like everyone I knew was mad at me. Everyone except Mitzi. And Barry. And Jim. With Ellie's threat running through my thoughts, I felt almost certain she had killed Owen. She had the most motive of anyone. And I'd seen her at the conference. Motive and opportunity. But how was I going to prove it?

The smell of the Chinese food cooking perked up my spirits and seeing Mitzi dressed in jeans, a white shirt with a bright pink sweater and turquoise scarf, lifted me even more. The morning had been so stressful, I needed the welcome break of a peaceful setting and a good friend.

I sat down in the booth across from her and grinned. The waitress had left a pot of tea and empty cup for me, so I poured the warm liquid and held it between both hands. "Ah," I said closing my eyes and lifting my head to the heavens. "Just what I needed!"

Mitzi laughed, "hard day?"

"You could say that." I relayed the recent scene between Ellie and me.

"She'll get over it." Mitzi set her menu down and the waitress hurried over to our table.

"You ready to order?" The young woman asked.

I didn't need to look at the menu as I had it memorized. "I'll have a number 40."

"Me too." Mitzi grinned.

It was our favorite and we always ordered the same thing. At least when we were together.

"Mitzi, I've been trying to figure out why Candi was all over Owen anyway. I mean what was she hoping to gain?"

She smiled her know all smile and said, "I'm sure she was impressed with the fact that he owns his own business and lives in a big house. There are girls who are looking for a free ride you know. And Owen had more to offer financially than Roy ever would."

I nodded. "You really think she thought he'd leave Ellie for her?"

"Candi loves the attention. She loves to think that every man she meets wants her. That she's the hottest thing going. Oh yeah, I think she saw opportunity."

My cell phone buzzed, and I looked down to see I had a text. Annoyed, I gave the phone a little push. Mitzi raised her eyebrows.

"It's Karly."

"Oh."

I pulled the phone back and read the message. "She wants to get together again tomorrow." I felt bad for her, and a little guilty for wanting to avoid her. After a moment, I agreed to meet her for lunch the next day.

"You're too nice, Delila. You should just tell her no." Mitzi smiled in a way that said you're so gullible! Then she opened her purse, pulled out a folded piece of paper and pushed it across the table to me.

I unfolded it and scanned the contents.

"No wonder she wanted to do away with him, right? You look surprised."

I nodded. "Yeah." Slowly I refolded the list. "Can I keep it?"

"Oh sure, it's a copy."

"Do you think Owen slept with all of these women?" I could tell by her smile that she did think so. "How'd you get this copy anyway?"

"Well, you're gonna owe me for this one." Mitzi said, with mischief in her eyes. "I had to promise the reverend's wife I'd be in her Warmth for All group. You know they make quilts for the homeless and little blankets for shelter animals."

"It's a great program Mitzi, I'm proud of you!"

"Delila, have you ever seen my sewing? They'll probably end up with triangle shaped quilts!"

I had to laugh at the thought of Mitzi trying to quilt.

The waitress set our food down in front of us and Mitzi picked up her chopsticks. I was amazed at how skilled she was. I picked up my fork.

"Ellie killed Owen, but I sure wish I knew how to prove it. I mean she certainly has more motive than anyone else. And she threatened to kill him. She had opportunity because Karly and I saw her at the conference."

Mitzi stopped me. "I thought you said you thought you saw her?"

"I'm sure it was her. It looked just like her."

We ate in silence for a moment. Finally, Mitzi said, "I guess we'll just have to let the police prove the rest."

The waitress returned full of smiles. "Everything taste good? You need anything else?" We smiled and shook our heads no. "Ok, thank you ladies." She set the checks down on the table between us.

I picked up both bills, "I got this." I gave Mitzi my best thank-you girlfriend grin.

When I returned home after lunch, I immediately contacted Jim. I told him about the witness who heard Ellie say she wished Owen were dead, and I reminded him that I'd seen Ellie in the garden at the conference. I figured he'd check the cameras at the hotel again, this time for proof that Ellie had been there.

Boris and Jewel followed me around, rubbing against my legs and looking at me with big hopeful eyes. The look that pets get when they want attention. It's difficult to ignore. I gave them each a couple of treats and they seemed appeased, at least for the moment.

As I sat down at my desk, I pulled out the list and read each name again, shaking my head in disbelief.

I opened my computer and pulled up my pictures from the conference. I studied each photo carefully, checking all the people around Owen and then took a closer look at the people in the background.

It's amazing what you see when people don't know they are being watched. Most of the time people put on their best behavior and disguise their innermost feelings. But when they think no one is watching, you can catch them in their true form. That's where you might find a clue as to who they really are. Pictures come in handy because they can capture those moments, and sometimes, even shadowy figures that blend into the background.

My mind replayed the events of each night of the conference, filling in the blanks between photos. I enlarged a few to get a better look and tried to recall as many details of the night as possible. Logic told me that anyone of these people in the pictures could have killed Owen that night. Many of them had a motive and opportunity. But only one was the killer.

I'd taken a class in creative thinking in high school, which included a lesson on brainstorming. The teacher had said, just let every thought come to you and write it down. Don't try and evaluate it or you will stop the free flow of ideas. After you've done that for some time, you can go back through and assess each point. I decided to use that method now. I spent about an hour typing each thought that popped into my head.

When I'd finished, I sat back and looked over what I'd typed. I was surprised by some of the things. I moved the thoughts around and placed them in groups. After meditating on each group, I concluded that one person had some serious explaining to do.

The police had spoken with the staff at the hotel; however, Jim couldn't share any of that information with me. I'd have to do my own investigation. I had the following day off work and decided to return to the hotel in the morning.

Later, while Barry watched another WWII movie, I hid in my study and made a call to the Hotel Lounge. I spoke with the bartender named Aspen and asked if he'd worked that night. He had. Not sure if he'd share any information with me, I let him believe I was working with the police on the case. It wasn't entirely accurate, but it wasn't a total lie either. Afterall, hadn't I been feeding them all kinds of information?

Aspen went over what he'd probably already told the police about that night. He'd been busy, so he hadn't really paid much attention to them. He'd seen the guy sitting at the corner table, and he'd noticed the two ladies having some sort of 'disagreement'. That was about it. He thought Daisy, who waited on that table, would be a better source. Aspen said Daisy would be in at 11am the next day.

I printed off a few of the pictures and prepared my strategy. I'd need a trip to the hotel to confirm a couple things, Then I softly padded down the hallway and sat down in front of the television.

In the morning, after Barry left for work, I grabbed the pictures and headed for the Marseille. With any luck, some of my questions would be answered, and my suspicions confirmed.

As I entered the grand hotel, I remembered that first day of the conference. Once more I stopped to marvel at the lobby's ornate décor, and the monumental domed ceiling with intricate design trimmed in gold. My eyes moved down to the enormous bouquet of color on the table in the center of the vast open space.

A porter stood speaking with the concierge, and the two front desk employees also appeared to be taking a break. Only a couple hotel guests wandered about, so I gathered there was no conference going on.

The gift shop, located on the right side of the room, wore a closed sign. The lettering on the door indicated it would open at 10 am. I looked at my watch. 9:54 am. I peeked in the windows at an array of fine clothing as well as a wide selection of souvenir items.

When the salesclerk opened the door, another customer entered the shop. I looked around for a minute while the other customer asked the clerk some questions about jewelry and made her purchase. Once she'd finished, I approached the young clerk with my own questions. I noted the name on her nametag.

"Good morning, Jasmine." I smiled warmly, as I thought about how to approach my questions. "I'm trying to track down some information for the police on the murder that took place here a couple of weeks ago."

The girl, unsure what to do, waited for me to continue.

"Were you working that weekend by any chance?" I tried to sound official, as if I really worked for the police.

"Not the night the guy was killed." She answered quickly, as if afraid I'd consider her a suspect. "Anyway, we close at 7 pm on weekends."

I smiled again, hoping to put her at ease. "Yes, of course. But were you working that day or at any time during that conference?"

She nodded.

I pulled out my pictures and showed them to her. "Do you remember if any of these people came in and bought anything?"

She shuffled through the photos and paused at one. "This one. I'm pretty sure." She nodded her head and tapped the photo. "Bought one of those black hoodies." She pointed to a rack of sweatshirts. "We don't sell many of them."

I put the photos back in the envelope, thanked her, and left. As I walked down the hall, I passed the large ballroom that held the reception that first night. I peeked in and found it empty. I turned the handle. Locked. Flashbacks of the conference darted in and out of my mind.

Back at the elevator, I rode to the second floor and walked down the hall toward Owen's room. I looked up at the camera in the hallway. Another could be seen at the other end of the hall, too far away to catch anything. The door to the stairway was right beside the room.

As I walked down the cement steps, I looked around but found no security cameras. The stairway ended in the basement, where I assumed the killer had hidden the hoodie. It would be easy to put it on unnoticed before going to Owen's room, then return later to remove it.

I walked back up to the first-floor landing and found a door leading to the garden. After wandering about for a little bit, I found the bench where Evan and I spent that first night catching up. It had been an enchanting moment. I'd enjoyed the romance, that fairytale feeling. I loved Evan. But not like I loved Barry. Barry was my rock. My reality.

Suddenly a gusty wind shook me, and I retreated inside the hotel. It was close to 11 am so I sat down on a bench outside the lounge and placed a call to Jim, asking him to meet me here.

Where had Owen been drugged? In the bar? Or later in his room? Why hadn't the killer given him a lethal dose? Why wait and smother him later?

A young woman unlocked the doors and propped them open, then flipped the sign on the door. I smiled and looked at her nametag. Daisy. She told me to take a seat anywhere and she'd be with me in a moment.

I looked around for the table where Owen sat that night. Karly said she'd been sitting at the bar. There were two seats at the bar with an unobstructed view of the table. I sat down in one of them. Karly said Darren and Liz had been sitting at a table between them. I imagined her watching as the night unfolded.

Daisy came to take my order. I ordered a coffee with cream, then asked, "How is it that everyone here has a flower name?"

She smiled. "Everyone chooses either a flower or a tree name when they start working here. Management says it's for our safety."

"That's a great idea."

About 15 minutes later, Jim entered the lounge, and I waved him over. I laid the photos out on the bar, and when Daisy returned to take Jim's order, I asked her questions about the night of the murder. Jim sat quietly as she pointed to a photo and confirmed my suspicions.

Helen's Kitchen served only breakfast and lunch, with Helen herself overseeing the little sandwich shop and rarely taking a day off. The diner was known for its homemade soups and deli style sandwiches. My watch confirmed that I was early for my lunch with Karly. I wondered what news she planned to feed me today.

When she finally arrived, I greeted her with what I hoped was a warm smile. "Hi Karly."

"Hi Delila." She unzipped her windbreaker and scooted into the seat across the booth from me. "Ooh, it's so foggy out today. I wonder what their soup of the day is?"

"Shrimp bisque and Vegetable." I replied.

Helen set a glass of water down in front of each of us. "What can I get ya, ladies?"

We both ordered the bisque with me selecting a tuna sandwich, and Karly the roast beef.

As soon as Helen left us, Karly seemed to look me over as if to gauge my mood before speaking. "I see Ellie put her house up for sale."

"She did?" I hadn't heard.

"Yeah, I think she's planning on moving out of state." She took the wrapper off her straw and placed it in the water, then took a long sip.

I followed her lead with the straw and took a drink. "Where's she going, do you know?"

She shook her head. "I don't know. Maybe Colorado."

Had she really heard this or was she just making it up? I couldn't be sure. "Is she applying at other universities? She has tenure here. It seems silly to give that up."

Karly took another drink and nodded. "Yeah, I don't know why she'd move."

Neither of us said anything for a minute, then we made a little small talk before the young waitress who worked with Helen brought our food. After we finished eating, and the waitress took our dishes away, I made my move. "Karly, why didn't you tell me you had an affair with Owen?"

She looked up with surprise. "I..." She didn't say anything more.

"You took Candi's earrings from our room that first night too. It took me a long time to figure that out. You must have swiped them when I wasn't looking. Then you left them in Owen's room to frame Candi."

"That's a bunch of crap Delila. What are you trying to say, that I killed Owen?" She looked angry.

"That's exactly what I'm saying." I didn't back down. "I asked the girl in the gift shop, and she told me you bought a black hoodie, just like the person caught on camera going into his room that night."

"So? I'm sure lots of people have bought hoodies from that gift shop." Karly hissed.

"Not really. Black hoodies aren't a popular item it seems." I let it sink in for a minute. "Besides, I spoke with the server who waited on Owen that night. She backed up everything you told me. But then she also remembered you going over to Owen's table after everyone else had left. I'm guessing that's when you drugged his drink. Did you offer to come up to his room too?"

Karly didn't say anything.

"Were you in love with him?" I asked.

She seemed to consider my question then finally spoke. "I did love him at one time. I thought he loved me too. But he didn't. He took advantage of me. He ruined my life."

"So, you killed him?"

"He killed me, Delila." Tears began to roll down her face. "Because of him, I lost my family, my home, my life. Look at me. I went from having a good life to having nothing. He still had everything. He just used me!"

We were quiet for a moment. I felt bad for her. She'd made a terrible mistake, but rather than starting over, she'd decided to end it all. Destroying the person she felt ruined her life. "Karly. Tell me what happened." I softened my voice.

At first, she didn't say anything. She looked around the room. Both Helen and the waitress had disappeared into the kitchen. The other two customers appeared deep in their own conversation. Slowly Karly leaned in closer to me and in a low quiet voice she said, "I brought the drugs intending to kill myself that night." She leaned back. "But after both Candi and Sueann had ditched him, I thought I still had a chance. I offered to come to his room. At first, he said he didn't want me. I'm sure he still thought he could get together with Candi that night, so I told him I'd seen her with Roy. I guess that's when he decided he might as well take me. You know, last resort." She cradled her glass in her hands and looked up at me for understanding.

I saw the pain in her eyes and waited for her to continue.

"He went to the bathroom, and I sat there thinking about what a loser I was. Then I thought what a jerk he was. I slipped the drugs in his drink. We talked for a while, and I said I'd come up to his room later. I changed into the hoodie down in the basement of the stairwell where I knew no one would see me, then snuck up to his room." She shook her head and sighed as she replayed the evening in her mind.

"I could see the drugs starting to take effect. I told him to get in bed, which he did. I waited for him to fall asleep. I wasn't sure if the drugs were enough to really kill him, so I took the pillow and covered his face."

We sat silently as I absorbed her story. Then I said, "Karly, you need to tell the police. You need to confess."

"No way! He deserved what he got. And think of all the other women I saved."

"But Karly—"

"No Delila. You can't tell anyone. You're the only person who's even nice to me. Everyone else hates me. Swear to me you won't tell." Tears rolled down her face.

"I can't Karly. I know what he did to you was terrible, but you could still have made something with your life. Murder is permanent. You not only punished him, but you also punished his children. Now they have no father."

"They're better off without him." Her tears had stopped. Karly suddenly looked alert. She checked the room to see if anyone else was watching us or listening.

The two other customers appeared not to have heard anything. "Give me a head start Delila. I'll go away and no one here will ever see me again. I promise."

I watched her walk away. Outside, with a light rain falling, I could see a police officer take Karly by the arm. Jim opened the door of the diner, came in and sat down with me.

"Thank you, Delila. We got it all. The recording was nice and clear."

I began taking off the wire from behind my ear, when one of the men pretending to be a customer, came over and took it from me.

"I feel sorry for her." My eyes met Jim's.

"She's a killer." Jim obviously didn't share my sympathy for Karly.

"I know."

Evan sat smiling at me as he sipped his latte. He'd asked me to meet him at La Cafetière for a quick cup of coffee before his late morning flight. A line had formed at the counter, with the smell of the fresh brewed coffee and sounds of newly awakened people flowing throughout the room.

"So, you're excited about New York now?" I asked. "I mean you feel ok leaving?"

"Well, I feel better than I did. My sister is going to be part of a new trial that has had promising results."

"That's great news! I'll pop over and see her. Maybe I can help her from time to time too. Pick up groceries, take her to appointments or something." I imagined making dinners and taking them over for her and her family.

"She'd like that, Dee."

Our eyes met and I knew I'd always have special feelings for Evan. I'd been so fortunate. I'd had an incredible boyfriend and then I'd married a wonderful man. I thought about Ellie, and Sueann, and Karly.

I took a drink of coffee and braced myself for what I'd been afraid to ask before. "Karly told me that Owen passed you a note that night he died." I paused a moment. "Do you mind if I ask what it said?"

He grinned and wrapped his hand around the paper cup, then cocked his head and said, "it was a note for my sister. He apologized for having been an ass at prom. Said he'd felt bad about it ever since." He shook his head. "I was surprised. It was a good note."

"How did she take it?" I asked.

"She laughed. Said she'd decided years ago how lucky she was that he'd stood her up. She might have married him and that would have been a much greater tragedy!"

We shared a look and feeling between us that said we'd always be there for each other. Then Evan looked at his watch, finished his coffee and said, "I better get going. Don't want to miss my plane."

Our guests began to arrive around 6:45 pm for our little dinner party. Aleena was back in town, and I'd invited her and Jim along with Mitzi and her husband, Ned, to dinner. I'd spent all afternoon preparing the meal as well as decorating the table with fresh flowers. I'd become increasingly aware of how presentation plays a role in the meal.

I set each chicken breast carefully in my new serving dishes and placed the little flowers I made from carrots and sprigs of rosemary along the sides of the dish. The mashed potatoes looked fancy too, with shredded cheese and tiny specks of chives sprinkled on top. I pulled the salad from the fridge, a beautiful plate of colors and textures, and set it on the table, then stood back and watched my delighted guests fill their plates.

I reflected on all we'd been through and how fortunate we were to be here together. I thought about relationships, and how each was made up of decisions. How we communicate. How we meet one another's needs. How we show affection for each other. And I thought about how our relationships shape our lives. Naturally, my thoughts turned to Karly.

The trial hadn't taken place yet. I pictured Karly sitting in her jail cell. She'd thought her life was over when she lost her family and old lifestyle. Now she faced life in prison with time to consider all the mistakes she'd made. All the other options she hadn't considered. She may even someday realize her own role in creating the situation.

After dinner we shifted to the living room, where Aleena told us about her trip to Florida and showed us pictures on her phone. We ogled the photos of her parents' new home and pool. Then the conversation turned to Owen's murder.

Mitzi dressed in white shirt, blue jeans, bright blue boots with matching scarf, purse, and jewelry, and looking elegant and stylish as usual, was the first to broach the topic. She turned to Jim and said, "Now that Karly has been caught, I expect Ellie will be able to get the insurance money."

"They'll probably release it after the conviction." Jim said.

I turned to Jim, "I'm curious. When you reviewed the cameras from the garden, was Ellie there?" I'd been thinking about this for a long time. Had I seen Ellie? Or had I thought that based on Karly's suggestion?

"We couldn't confirm one way or the other. There was a woman who looked like her, but the video was a little fuzzy and too far away to tell for sure." Jim shook his head. "If we'd been able to confirm it was her, we probably would have arrested her."

"Won't Karly's lawyer try to use that as part of her defense?" Barry asked.

"He will if they go to trial. But there is so much evidence against her, they'll probably settle out of court. Especially her confession in the restaurant. We have it on tape, and the two police officers we had stationed in the restaurant overheard some of that confession too. We owe Delila for that." He smiled at me. "Of course, they will probably try and have it thrown out."

"Then there might not be enough evidence to convict her?" The idea of Karly not going to jail worried me. Would she come after me? Afterall, I had betrayed her.

"We still have the little red marks." Jim smiled. "The DNA from those marks matched her DNA. And the camera caught only one person entering his room that night."

"Why did she leave those marks anyway?" Mitzi wondered, "Didn't she realize they could be traced back to her?"

"Apparently when she had the affair with Owen, he always left little marks on her. It's what caused her husband to become suspicious in the first place." A little piece of information Karly had slipped me when she confessed in the restaurant.

After a few minutes Barry took Jim and Ned to see the rec room. He couldn't wait to show off his newly remodeled room.

Once they'd left the room, Aleena looked thoughtful, then asked, "Did Ellie ever donate the money to the church?"

"Nope. She's moving. We're having a fundraiser next weekend to try and raise more money for the new wing." Mitzi said. "I hope you guys will come." Then she turned to me. "And remember Delila, we have an HOA board meeting next week."

How could I forget? Mitzi had nominated and gotten me elected treasurer of our homeowner's association as well as getting herself re-elected as secretary. I wondered if we'd gotten ourselves involved in a new adventure or a crazy fiasco.

After our guests had gone and we'd finished cleaning up, Barry and I took our normal places in the living room. Barry in his bark-a-lounger reading a novel, Jewel in his lap, and me on the sofa. The television murmured in the background, while Boris lay asleep at my feet. My Kindle rested in my hands, but my eyes no longer focused on the words. The story was good, but I couldn't seem to get into it. I kept thinking about Owen.

I remembered that last night at dinner. Owen reaching out to me, wanting to tell me something. I'd never really know what he'd wanted to say. I wondered if it had something to do with Evan.

Evan was settled into his new life in New York now. I'd visited his sister and learned he had started dating again. I hoped he'd find someone wonderful. He deserved it.

I looked over at Barry. He must have felt my gaze because he turned and smiled at me. Our eyes met and I felt the love and friendship of a thousand years. I set the Kindle aside, walked over and wrapped my arms around him. For the first time in a long time, I embraced contentment.

Termite Turmoil

The stranger-danger alert and excessive yapping came from our dog, Boris, as he raced across the living room to look outside. I followed him to the window and peered out to see what had riled him.

It was Saturday morning and the President of our Homeowners Association, Helda, a burly woman with hair cropped close to her head, walked past our house, and stopped in front of my elderly next door neighbor's home. She bent down and stuck a ruler in the grass. Then she pulled her cell phone out and snapped a photo to prove the grass was over three inches long.

"Oh brother!" I shook my head in disbelief and watched her scour the lawn for weeds or bare spots. Boris snarled.

Erle, my 89-year-old neighbor, did most of his own yard work. He hired someone to mow the grass but applied the fertilizer and weed killer himself. I'd also seen him out fixing his sprinkler system and planting grass. Even while he cared for his dying wife, he made sure he kept up his yard. Now alone, one of Erle's daily pass times included pulling weeds from his flower beds.

In early June, Erle's daughter had given him a couple of tiny tomato plants and he'd nurtured them over the summer. They'd grown into big, beautiful crops with plenty of luscious fruit. He'd proudly shown them off to me, explaining how he used eggshells and banana peels for fertilizer. In the past week, four of the larger tomatoes had turned orange and were ready to be picked.

Helda looked up having completed her evaluation of the grass and surveyed the rest of the yard. I watched as she marched up toward Erle's house and headed straight for the tomato plants.

I knew our Homeowners Association didn't permit us to have fruit bearing trees, nor could we have a vegetable garden. To get around those rules, I planted my pepper plants and some herbs in pots in my back yard. But Erle planted his two small plants in the front flower bed, where the soil was rich, and he could easily tend to them.

Boris gave an excited squeal, as he watched Helda snap a photo of the plants. Poor Erle! Clearly, she planned on slapping him with a large fine. I wished there were something I could do, but we had to abide by the rules, even if we didn't agree with them. I supposed he could try and dig the plants up and put them in pots like I did. I would suggest it to him later.

Our monthly board meeting was scheduled for two p.m. that afternoon, and I expected it would be brought up then. My good friend, Mitzi, had nominated me for treasurer in our yearly election, after she'd taken over as secretary a few months before. Since no one else had run against me, it was an easy win.

Today was to be my first meeting and I already felt a tad nervous about it. I wondered if I dare mention going easy on Erle to Helda and the rest of the board. Confrontation was not my strong suit. I wanted to get along with everyone.

I pulled the curtain back a little more to get a better view. Helda hovered over the tomato plant for a minute, then tucked her phone into her back pocket, and with both hands, reached down and grabbed the plant by the stem.

She yanked it with so much force I thought she might fall over. She didn't. Instead, Erle's prize tomato plant sprang up, its roots spraying dirt through the air. She tossed the carcass to the ground, its limp body still clinging to the precious fruit.

"Aah!" I covered my mouth to muffle my scream. Erle would be horrified when he saw his cherished tomatoes mutilated and left to die. How could she do such a thing? And to someone as nice as Erle?

Then Helda stepped over to the second plant and did it again.

I stood there motionless, not sure what to do. I saw Helda turn and look in my direction. Did she see me in the window? I stepped back and out of view; afraid I'd been caught watching her in the act. Would she say anything at the meeting? Reprimand me or try to embarrass me in front of everyone? Or would she view my witnessing this cruel act as some sort of indoctrination for me as a new board member?

"That infuriating woman!" I wailed. As soon as I saw her leave, I hurried to my garage to look for a couple of pots. I hoped the tomato plants would live.

As I thought about the cruel act, I knew I had to change the HOA. To somehow make it nicer. An organization that respected members. Helpful instead of hurtful.

That afternoon, Mitzi sat in her car in the driveway and honked the horn. I'd been ready and waiting for more than ten minutes, I hated to be late. Especially to my first board meeting. But Mitzi rarely made it anywhere on time. I slid into the seat next to her.

As we drove toward the library where we would meet with the other board members, I told Mitzi about Helda and the demise of Erle's tomato plants. "Should I say something at the meeting?"

"Should you? Yes. Will you? Probably not, knowing you." Mitzi threw an affectionate grin my way.

Mitzi, always a fashionable dresser, wore tight pink capris leggings, a turquoise jacket, and white blouse. I looked down at my own plain outfit and sighed. Then I noticed her hair. Shoulder length and a reddish-brown color, it seemed to sparkle. Really *sparkle*. I looked more carefully.

"Are those gold strands of hair?"

Mitzi smiled and nodded. "Do you like it?"

"I love it! It's beautiful! But how did you get gold strands?"

"Fairy strands. Also known as hair tinsel. There's a woman in town who does it," she said, and turned the car into the library's parking lot.

The library meeting room had a large rectangular table with chairs on each side, and a chair at the end of the table that faced the door. Helda, at the 'head' of the table, glared at us as we entered. Mitzi and I took the two empty seats next to each other and closest to the door.

Being new to the HOA meetings, and not knowing most of the people, I was grateful for the placards that sat in front of each person, displaying our names and titles. Mitzi and I took our placards and put them in front of us, then opened our laptops.

"So glad you could make it, ladies." Helda said in a low, sarcastic guttural voice. "I'll call the meeting to order at 2:05pm." She was still wearing the same khaki shorts and navy tee shirt she'd worn earlier.

Several papers sat in a stack on the table in front of us. I picked up my pile and leafed through them; an agenda, minutes from the previous meeting, and the treasurers' report I'd submitted the day before.

Helda looked around the meeting table, her eyes darting around at each of us, then finally turned to Sheldon, who sat to her right. "And it looks like we are all here, so we have a quorum."

Sheldon, our LCAM, or *Licensed Community Association Manager*, took care of all the management aspects of the association. He sent out the invoices, violation letters, collected dues, paid bills, and handled complaints. A big job with few accolades.

I'd only spoken with him on the phone before, although I'd heard about him from Mitzi, who frequently raved about him. He looked to be in his mid-thirties, trim and professional.

Sheldon also had a laptop open in front of him. He gave Helda a quick smile and nod.

"Ok, has everyone read over the minutes?" Helda asked.

I started to read through the papers in front of me.

"You should have read them over before you came." Helda looked directly at me without smiling. "Can we get approval for the minutes from our last meeting? I know I found at least one mistake. Shelly Catapuck is spelled wrong. Should be C-a-t-a-p-u-c-k. With a 'k' not an 'h'."

Mitzi, with an indignant look on her face, made a note on her paper.

"Does anyone else have any changes?" Helda looked up, but no one said anything. "Ok, can someone make a motion to accept the minutes with the change."

"I motion to accept the minutes." Darla said. Vice president of the association, Darla sat on the left side of Helda. She pushed her glasses up further on her long heavy face. Her stringy shoulder length hair hung down the sides of her head and looked in need of a professional cut.

"Do we have a second for the motion?" Helda looked at me as if expecting me to say something. After a moment she seemed to remember that I hadn't been on the board the previous month, and therefore wasn't at the last meeting.

"Can I second it?" A gray-haired man named Marv, with no title shown on his placard, said and raised his hand. Later I learned from Mitzi that Marv headed up our arc (architectural review form) committee. He, along with three others, assessed all arc submissions and determined whether they met the requirements. Things like roofs, paint colors, sheds, and any changes to the outside of our homes and yards required approval from the HOA. A form had to be submitted and approved before any work could be done.

"No, Marv, you can't. I'll second it." Helda said. "Ok, let's look at the treasurer's report. As you all remember, Delila Clarke was elected treasurer last month at our annual meeting. Welcome Delila." Helda shot me a non-committal smile. As if she hadn't yet decided, if she approved of me as the new treasurer.

I looked at the report and wondered if I should say anything. I wasn't sure how things worked, so I waited for someone to prompt me. I didn't have to wait long.

"Ok, so we spent nine thousand on legal fees." She looked at the attorney, seated on the other side of Sheldon. "I assume that was for—" She waited for him to explain.

"Yes," The attorney, Morton, an older, heavy-set man with a thick mustache pulled a file from his briefcase, then spent a few minutes fumbling through the paperwork.

I wondered if we were paying him by the hour to be here today, and guessed we were. Finally, he said, "We put liens on four houses, logged twelve hours consulting time, and of course, the foreclosure."

There was silence in the room then. Foreclosure? I leaned over and whispered to Mitzi. "What foreclosure?"

Mitzi glanced up at Helda, then whispered back. "I'll tell you later."

Helda continued down the list of expenses to the association. Among them were the sealcoating costs, lawncare, and mailing fees. "Oh, and I ordered mums for the flower garden in Lily Park. They should be here next month." She then called for approval of the treasurer's report.

"Ok, I'm going to ask that everyone who is not a board member leave the room for a short time while we consult with the attorney." Helda said and looked around the table.

Marv, the two subdivision leaders, and two interested neighbors all left the room. Sheldon started to stand as well, but Helda put her hand on his arm. "You can stay Sheldon."

Helda looked at Darla and then Sheldon and said, "Ok, so we are moving forward with the foreclosure." She turned to Morton. "What's the next step?"

Morton pulled additional papers from his briefcase and pushed them toward Helda. "You and Darla will need to sign this paperwork, then we'll submit it to the court. Once approved by the court, the property will need to be sold to pay off the debt." He did not smile as he said it but kept his expression neutral.

I tried to take in the meaning of the situation. I felt as though I'd walked into the middle of a conversation and had no idea what they were talking about. Whatever they were doing must be legal, because the lawyer had drawn up the paperwork. I felt an anxious sensation deep in my stomach. Something didn't feel right.

Helda, pen already in hand, quickly signed the papers and shoved them toward Darla. Darla glanced at the papers then signed as well.

"When will they get the notice to move, and how long will they have to get out?" Helda asked.

"It depends on how busy the court system is. Could take a couple of weeks to process the paperwork and once the notice goes up on their door, they'll have exactly one month to vacate. I'd say no more than two months total."

I looked around the room. Sheldon appeared to be looking intently at something on his laptop. Darla scratched her head and looked at the papers. Mitzi had her head down as well, holding her pen to her notepad. Everyone looked uncomfortable with the situation, except for Helda, who said, "Ok. Mitzi, we don't need these details in the minutes."

"I wanted to mention one more thing." Morton's heavy voice cut through the silence. "I get the impression you all think that you can use fines as revenue for the association. That is not correct. Fines can be used to encourage people to keep their properties in good condition, but they should never be considered a source of income." He looked directly at Helda. "And you need to keep them consistent. You can't fine one person one amount, and someone else a different amount for the same offence."

Helda, lifted her chin higher and said in her low voice, "Note taken."

The others were brought back into the room and the new discussion centered on a pothole that had appeared in one of the streets. We listened to the ARC report and then Helda brought up violations.

She threw some pictures down in the center of the table. "I've taken pictures of several yards where the grass is either too long or they have brown spots or excessive weeds in the lawn. Sheldon, I'll give you the addresses later."

"Did you get Trey's yard?" Brock Morris spoke for the first time. He was a large man, stocky with reddish hair and a military style haircut. "You need to fine him for excessive noise too. That kid is always partying."

Helda smiled. "Yes, we've written up another complaint against him too. But, since he's a young millionaire, and has his own lawyer, it's a little harder to fight him." She looked at Sheldon over the top of her glasses. "Sheldon had a bit of a problem recently over the letters that were sent out last month. Would you please share what happened with the rest of the board?"

Sheldon nodded his head but took a moment to look over some notes before speaking. "Last month the board agreed that everyone should use the same Exterior Satin Superpaint #7570, Egret White on the mailboxes. I sent out the letters about the change of the color to all association members."

No one spoke. Instead, we waited patiently for Sheldon to explain.

"I had a lot of complaints about the cost of the paint and people wanting to use a slightly different shade or different paint. Anyway, one guy became irate when I told him he couldn't use anything else. We kinda got into a shouting match, and he threatened me. I had to call the police."

"Who was it?" Brock asked.

"Ziggy Geis."

"The old hippie?" Brock gave a quick laugh.

Sheldon nodded.

"Well, since you contacted the police, it seems like you've taken care of it." Helda said.

I thought Sheldon wanted to add something, but Helda didn't give him a chance. "What about the cats? Have you found anyone to remove them?"

"I've found one rescue, but they couldn't do anything for about three months. There's animal control, but they have so many cats now, they said they'd probably have to euthanize them."

I jotted down a note on a piece of paper and shoved it to Mitzi. She wrote something and shoved the paper back. 'Yes, the feral cats.' The feral cats that had been living in the neighborhood since before Barry and I moved in. We sometimes joked about them being the neighborhood security guards. Most of the time we didn't even see them, but occasionally we'd spot one sunning itself or racing across the back yard.

Helda twisted her lips to one side as if considering an unpleasant thought. "But they could do it sooner?"

Sheldon nodded.

"Ok, let's chew on that for a while. I also noticed lot 127 had tomato plants growing in his flower garden." Helda continued, she lifted her head and stared directly at me.

Was she daring me? Should I say something? This was my opportunity. I knew I needed to speak up. It was now or never. I took a deep breath, then said, "Erle is an elderly man, he's eighty-nine years old and I think we should give him a—"

"I don't want to get into this argument now. He violated the rules. End of discussion."

"His wife died recently, and—"

"I said end of discussion." Helda clenched her teeth tightly and looked at me as if she would bite if I said anything further.

I didn't. Instead, I sat there seething for the rest of the meeting.

I waited until we'd gotten in the car before unleashing my anger. "She's horrid!"

Mitzi, much calmer than I, started the motor, gave me a sly grin, and pulled out of the library parking lot. "Yes, she is."

"Someone should do something about her!" I looked at my friend as if she might hold some magical answer. "I mean, I can't believe she would hurt Erle like that. He's never done anything mean to anyone."

"That's why..." Mitzi pulled into the left lane, then turned to look at me, and continued. "That's why there is a recall for her position."

"A recall?"

"Yup. I'm not sure who started it, but there is a petition going around to recall her. Lots of people are unhappy with her."

"You've seen it?" I asked.

"I signed it." Mitzi appeared amused by the idea.

"Where can I find it? I've got to sign it too!"

"I'll see if I can figure out who has it now. Trey brought it to me."

"Who's Trey? I get the impression Brock doesn't like him."

"Trey? Oh, he's a character!" Mitzi laughed. "He's a young guy, mid-twenties. A rich kid whose grandfather died and left him lots of money. He bought a house on Rose Ave. next to Brock. Trey likes to throw wild parties. I think he does it intentionally to tick off Brock."

Brock Morris, resident complainer, had lived in the neighborhood for at least thirty years, and who, I guessed, was responsible for many of the fifty-nine pages of the HOA rules.

"What about this foreclosure? What's that all about?" I realized I needed to be filled in on what had been happening.

"Oh, that." Mitzi's cheerful smile had morphed into a more concerned look. "Pierce Andrews. Do you know him?"

"No. I don't think so."

"Umm." Mitzi shifted her attention to the traffic for a moment before continuing. "Two years ago, he had a heart attack. Pretty serious one. Apparently, while he was in the hospital his wife forgot to pay the association dues. She must have been busy taking care of him, their kids, plus, I think she works." Mitzi stopped for a red light and turned to look at me. "Anyway, they totally forgot about the dues. So Helda had the lawyer put a lien on their property. Then, I guess because of the medical bills they couldn't pay the dues for a while. Anyway, Helda had that lawyer Morton foreclose on their house."

"What? The HOA can do that? They can take our house away if we don't pay our dues?"

"I guess they can." The light changed to green, and Mitzi's attention returned to the road. "Anyway, Pierce tried to stop them. He offered to pay it off, but Helda told him he was too late, nothing he could do. Morton says we'll auction the house off for what he owes the association plus legal fees." She gave me a look that said it's not right!

Mitzi pulled into my driveway, but I didn't get out of the car right away. Still reeling from the shocking news that my HOA was cruel and merciless, and that I was now a part of that bully power, I needed time to process it all.

We sat in silence for a moment. "I don't know if I can do this Mitzi." I thought about Erle's reaction when I'd showed up at his doorstep with two pots, a shovel and half a bag of potting soil. He hadn't seen Helda try to destroy his tomato plants. He didn't yell or cry when he saw them dying on the ground. Instead, he simply gave me a sad, grateful look, like a dog who has been rescued after years of abuse.

"You can't quit." Mitzi said, her voice firm. "If you were to leave, we'd probably end up with another Helda on the board. We need new people. People who care about others and not just about their own power."

"You know I'm not good at speaking up. If I try to say something she doesn't like, she'll eat me alive." My voice sounded whiny, even to me.

"It doesn't matter. We can't let another Helda get on the board." Mitzi, the normally fun, happy-go-lucky one, sounded serious. "I mean it Delila. You can't quit."

I sat silently contemplating the situation, and the piles of problems with our HOA. A rap on the car window startled me, and I turned my head to see a serious-looking seventy-three-year-old standing beside the car. I opened the door and stepped out.

Ziggy stood about six inches taller than me. His faded tie-dyed tee shirt and holey blue jeans had seen better days. He pulled a few of his long grayish blonde strands of hair behind his ear. "You on the board now?" He forced a half smile.

"Err, yes." I immediately sensed the tension.

His expression grew more serious. "You guys gotta lay off! There's nothing wrong with my bushes! I want 'em to look natural, not like some plastic Disneyland shit!"

I backed up a bit. "I, I'm sorry Ziggy. I don't know anything about it. I've only been on the board for a couple of weeks."

"I'm sick of all these BS rules!" He shook his fist at me. "Mailbox colors, measuring my grass, and now you want my bushes to look like I'm in some theme park? No thank you! And that Sheldon guy... You need to get ridda that guy! He's got nerve tellin' me what I can and can't do in my own yard. I pay my dues. That s----," he stopped to collect his words, "that guy called the cops on me!"

"I'm sorry Zigg—"

"Yeah, sure." Ziggy looked around me, then stooped down to see Mitzi. "What about her? She on the board too?"

Mitzi put the car in park. I hadn't closed the door all the way, and she called out to him. "Yep. We are hoping to make changes. You know, we want to hear from members, find out what's important to them." She gave him a sweet smile and wink.

His face relaxed, and I decided Mitzi must be a natural born politician.

Mitzi watched as Ziggy walked back home. "What's his name again? Zippy or..."

"Ziggy." I said, "He told Barry he gave himself that name back in the 60's when he was living in a commune. I've never seen him angry like that."

Mitzi gave me a quick grin, then peered around me toward the sidewalk. "Sorry, gotta get going, Ned is waiting." She barely waited for me to close the car door before she backed out of the driveway.

I turned to see Muriel, my neighbor who'd earned the nickname 'crazy cat lady', waving to me. Too late to escape her, I waited patiently, my computer bag feeling heavier than ever. I forced a smile.

"Ah, I'm so glad I caught you." She stopped to catch her breath.

"Hi Muriel."

"You're on the board now, is that right?" When I nodded, her demeanor transformed from friendly neighbor to angry ailurophile maniac. "What is all this about removing and destroying the cats? Don't tell me you're a part of this?"

"What? No. I wouldn't--"

"Nobody better touch those cats! You know they've lived around here longer than most of these people. They help keep the mice and snakes away too, we need them." She'd gotten herself really worked up by the time she finished her rant. Beads of sweat showed on her forehead and her cheeks turned a dark pink.

I'd always thought Muriel was an attractive woman, with well-defined facial features and long silky dark brown hair. But the anger on her face and in her voice changed her into someone I didn't recognize. Someone I didn't want to be around.

"I'll see what—"

"Is Sheldon behind this? Or Helda? I know it's either one or the other." She continued.

My nerves began to give out. I considered running in the house and locking the door. "I'm sorry Muriel, I don't have—"

She shook her finger at me and shouted. "I'm getting an injunction… or whatever to prevent you guys from taking these cats. You let the rest of the board know that. There is no way I'll let anyone take them! You get that?"

"Muriel," my arm was aching from the weight of my laptop. "I have to go." I headed for the front door.

"Wait a minute!" Muriel yelled, then followed me up the sidewalk. "I want you to look at this letter. Someone sent me this letter and I want something done about it." She pulled a letter out of her pocket and handed it to me.

I took the handwritten letter from her and read:

> *If you care about these creatures, I suggest you make a giant kitty litter box in your backyard. I'm sick of them crapping in the park. I tried to catch them but couldn't. My next step is to poison them. Either you do something about them or I will!*

The letter was unsigned. I couldn't imagine who wrote it. Or who would want to kill the cats in this manner. "Can I keep this?" I asked.

Zombies staggered toward me, through the post-apocalyptic streets. I could hear the thunder against the heavy metal music and watched as bullets whizzed by the undead. One by one their tattered bodies fell to the ground as the projectiles hit them.

I heard Barry cuss under his breath as he shook the game controller, pressing hard on the buttons. His favorite headphones gripped his head, the small microphone sticking out of the side. “Ahh! Ha!” He yelled out, his voice excited, “yeah! Ok next level.”

Barry, and his friend Jim often played these games remotely. I didn’t share their love of video games, even though I had played with Barry a few times. It was fun, but not something I cared about doing often, not like Barry and Jim, who could play for days without getting bored.

For a minute or two I stood watching. Barry hadn’t noticed me come in. I walked down the hall to my office and set my laptop and the letter down on my desk, my arm baring the indentation from holding it for so long.

Frustration surged throughout my body, until I finally took a deep breath. I didn’t want this job. I thought I was going to do the bookkeeping for the association. That I would be the numbers lady. Collect the dues and pay the bills. I didn’t expect to be the recipient of my neighbor’s pent-up anger.

I could quit. Afterall, no one was forcing me to do this. And if I did quit, who would replace me? Mitzi was right, it could be another Helda. Or Brock. I thought about Erle and the defeat after seeing his tomatoes uprooted and left to die. And Pierce losing his home.

As I stood there thinking, Jewel, my cat, rubbed against my leg. I thought about the cats and Ziggy. The association had so many problems, how was I going to change things? I picked up Jewel and carried her to the kitchen to make us dinner.

Barry must have smelled the chili I'd made, because he finally turned off the video game and came searching for something to eat. He stood next to the pot sniffing, with a large when-do-we-eat grin on his face. "How was the meeting?"

As I dished out the chili, I began the day's narrative, starting with Erle's tomatoes. I hadn't meant to let all of it out, but once I started, like a water faucet that finally got going, I couldn't stop. Barry had stopped me at various points to ask questions. He was especially concerned about the foreclosure.

"I'm thinking about quitting." I told him. "I don't think I'm cut out for this."

Did I want him to talk me out of it? I liked the idea of being on the board, of having an important role. Being respected. Being noticed. Feeling like I mattered.

Barry looked at me blankly for a moment. "It's your choice. There's no need to decide this minute. Wait until morning, see how you feel then."

Later that evening, we sat next to one another on the couch, a blanket draped over us, watching a movie, and eating popcorn. We laughed and I teased him about his skill at killing zombies. How I wouldn't have to worry, he could protect me.

The phone call must have come around nine-thirty, about halfway through the movie. I picked up my cell. Sheldon. Why was he calling so late on a Saturday night?

"***I*** apologize for calling this late," Sheldon said, "I was going over our financials. Some things just haven't been adding up for me. I came into the office to look over some of this paperwork again. I don't know, it's just... it seems like the balance statement isn't right. I wondered if I could have you look at a couple of things...again, I'm sorry to call you so late. I hope I haven't interrupted anything."

"It's fine." I said and grinned at Barry. "What can I help with?"

"I can't find..." I heard him shuffle through some papers, "just a minute..."

I thought he might have set the phone down. Sheldon's voice grew distant. "Is someone there? Who's there?" I heard him say. I heard talking in the background, but apparently, he'd moved away from the phone because it was difficult to make out any words. Then came what sounded like gunshots.

"Sheldon! Sheldon!" I shouted into the phone, but no answer.

Barry had heard the entire conversation and now looked at me with alarm. When Sheldon didn't respond after a few minutes, he sprang to his feet, grabbed his own phone. He called 911, and then his friend Jim, a detective on the police force. Moments later we were on our way to Sheldon's office.

The police arrived before us. The police car headlights offered little visibility, and we weren't allowed to get close to the crime scene, so we waited in the darkness, dreading the possible outcome. About thirty minutes after we arrived, we watched a stretcher brought out and put it in an ambulance, that left without turning on its siren or flashing lights.

"Sheldon." I whispered.

I texted Mitzi. I thought she should know. She immediately called me back and listened as I told her what had happened. Barry saw Jim and went over to speak with him.

Still on the phone with Mitzi, I paced in a small circle. I couldn't stop thinking about my conversation with Sheldon. The sound of gunshots. The fear when he didn't answer me.

"Are you still there?" Mitzi asked.

"Yes, I'm still here."

Barry came back and put his arm around me. He squeezed me toward him. "It was Sheldon. He's gone. I'm sorry honey."

I couldn't believe someone had killed Sheldon. And that person had killed him while he was on the phone with me. I was a witness to his murder!

Neither Mitzi nor I knew what to say. We were silent for a few moments. Finally, we agreed to meet at Lily Park, the following afternoon.

Barry and I stood in the darkness, numb. I leaned in closer to him for comfort. There was nothing either of us could do.

Sleep didn't come easily that night. I obsessed over the events of the day. The board meeting, my irate neighbors and Sheldon. Once I fell asleep, zombies invaded my dreams. Zombies with the faces of my neighbors being shot at by Helda. Then my face appeared on one of the zombies, and I awoke frightened.

Normally on Sunday mornings, Barry and I have a cup of coffee and something to nibble on, then go to the early church service. Afterwards, we enjoy brunch and lollygag around the house. Then we escort Boris on a walk in the late afternoon.

We decided to skip the service, since neither of us had slept well. I couldn't stop thinking about Sheldon. I rushed through breakfast with Barry, anxious to take another look at the association's books before meeting

Mitzi. Maybe I could discover some details that had been previously missed. Maybe find what Sheldon had been calling me about late on a Saturday night. It may not have anything to do with his murder, but then again, it might.

I'd learned that over the years, where there's money, there's someone trying to take it. Whenever there is a problem, look for the trail of money dust.

Our association income came from dues, lien payoffs and fines. I looked to see which neighbors were victims of the heavy and often unfair punishments, but there were too many to consider. Now I understood what the lawyer, Morton had meant. As much revenue came from fines as dues. Did we need all that income? If so, why not just raise the dues?

The Brookstone subdivision consisted of 342 homes, and each paid dues of $620 per year. The park accounted for a large portion of our expenses, as did the roads and painting the walls in front of our subdivision. The signs also required maintenance. Those were the actual costs for our subdivision. But the major portion of our budget went for attorney and management company fees.

Two thirds of our annual dues went toward these two items. It felt like an enormous amount. Only one third went toward our subdivision. My brain stuck on the attorney and management expenses. Clearly, our administrative fees were the greatest money eaters, consuming most of the funds and leaving traces of powder in their wake.

Perhaps if we didn't have so many rules, liens, and fines, we could reduce our lawyer and management fees, since they wouldn't need to spend as much time chasing down would-be HOA lawbreakers. And turning normally nice people into suburban monsters.

Could all these rules have gotten Sheldon killed? Ziggy had been angry enough for Sheldon to call the police on him. Had he gone back last night and shot Sheldon? He'd been upset when he approached me. Something to ask Mitzi about I decided, as I grabbed Boris's leash.

The humid air made the summer temperature feel even warmer than usual, as Boris and I hurried down the street toward Lily Park. I felt the hot sun on top of my head and regretted not bringing a hat.

Lily Park, aka The Gossip Garden, had long been our favorite meeting place. We could spend a little time together catching up, while our dogs enjoyed a play date.

Mitzi and her little red poodle, Mia, were already waiting for us. Mitzi wore a new blouse. Mia's leash matched the blouse. Mitzi sat at a picnic table in the shade of the pavilion. Her face still held the shock of someone processing the fresh news of a death. "Oh Delila, I still can't believe it!"

I sat down across from Mitzi. The heat seemed to fade away as we eased into our conversation. I searched my brain for comforting words. I hadn't really known Sheldon. Had only talked to him once or twice when we were in violation of some rule or another. He'd been professional, yet unyielding.

But Mitzi had been on the association board with him for several months. Had come to know him, and perhaps come to rely on him. She'd confided in me that he often checked over her minutes to make sure she hadn't missed anything and to correct her mistakes. Mitzi had never been cut out to be a secretary.

"I was the last one to talk to him before he died." My voice began to crack.

"Except for the killer," she pointed out. "Did you hear anything else?"

I thought for a moment. "I heard him talking to someone. But I have no idea who it was or what he said. It was muffled." My thoughts wandered about in my head for a few minutes. Finally, I asked, "do you think it had anything to do with our association? I mean it seems like a lot of our neighbors were upset with him and our board."

"I don't know." Mitzi admitted. "People get so angry anymore. And we've added so many liens and fines. Poor Sheldon though. He's only the messenger. Was, I meant to say. He was."

I nodded agreement. "I wonder if most of our members realize that?"

We sat silently contemplating the situation. Finally, I broached the topic I'd been thinking about all morning. "Mitzi, Sheldon wanted me to check on something. He didn't think the financials were correct."

Mitzi looked puzzled. "I heard him talking to Helda about the financials when we were leaving the meeting. He asked about some invoices, and she said she'd given them to you."

I nodded. "She did."

When I arrived back home, Jim and Barry were sitting at the kitchen table waiting for me. Jim had some questions. I told him all I knew. Unfortunately, Jim was unable to reveal any information the police had learned.

"I'm going to look over the books some more this afternoon." I told him. "There might be something there that can help."

"Or it might not have anything to do with your association." Jim countered. "Sheldon's company worked with a couple of other associations too, although, I believe yours was his main account." He looked at Barry, then back at me. "Delila, I know you want to help, and you've helped me in the past, but I really think you need to leave this up to us."

Barry looked at me and agreed. "Honey, Jim's right. You need to leave it to the police."

"Of course." I said, "But sometimes I learn things through the grapevine. Things people would never tell the police."

"Sure. And please tell me when you do." Jim said. "Just don't go putting yourself in danger."

Obviously, Jim and Barry had been discussing the issue before I arrived. I smiled at them. "Aww, you guys are so sweet and caring. Of course, I'll be careful."

"That's not what we said Delila. We don't want you snooping around." Barry had a serious look on his face. He knew me too well to believe I wouldn't continue to try and find out as much as I could to help solve Sheldon's murder.

I shook my head as if in agreement. Thirty minutes later I sat at my computer, combing through the accounts looking for inconsistencies.

Barry came and stood beside me. "Looking for clues?"

"Yes. I wish I knew what to look for though." I turned and looked up at him. "Did Jim say if there were any other witnesses? I mean did anyone see a car in the vicinity or a person?"

"No. All the businesses in the area were closed. There was no one around. They are checking the cameras at Sheldon's office and all the other nearby buildings. Hopefully they'll get something there, but it may take some time." He put his arm on my shoulder and kissed the top of my head.

Thefollowing day Helda sent each board member a text requesting an emergency board meeting. I say requesting, but it seemed more like an order. Later that Monday afternoon, we all assembled in the conference room at the library once again.

Our group was smaller than Saturday's group; just the four actual board members and Brock. I wondered why Brock was invited. He wasn't a board member. As far as I could tell, he was just a guy who liked to stir up trouble.

"So," Helda began, "As I'm sure we all know, Sheldon is dead. It could take a long time, but we need to find another management company. I've started to look around and found two that might work. I'll be talking to them in the next couple of days."

Mitzi and I exchanged a look that said, unbelievable! And yet, we both knew she was all about task. Getting the job done, regardless of the effect it had on others. Hadn't she proven that when she went ahead with the foreclosure?

Brock and Darla bobbed their heads in agreement, and Helda continued. "I also plan on going to his office and trying to retrieve our files and all of our association's information, if the police will allow me to." Helda looked down at the notes she'd prepared.

Mitzi seemed more reserved than normal. She hadn't said anything and the solemn look on her face told me something was seriously bothering her. I knew she was thinking of Sheldon. She looked from one board member to another, studying them. And like me, questioning whether they had anything to do with his death. If not directly, then indirectly.

"I also want to discuss the feral cat situation. We need to do something about them. I know a lot of people want them gone but there are a few hold outs that are quite vocal. Muriel Gibbs for one." Helda's eyes swept around the table.

"The crazy cat lady? Who cares what she wants? She's nuts." Brock readjusted himself in his chair, his voice slightly raised.

"Well," Helda tilted her head slightly, "it's not just her. She's got a few others riled too."

"They're a nuisance!" Brock's voice boomed.

It seemed like most of the neighbors didn't mind the cats, at least none of the people I spoke to. Yet, it was a hot topic. As a board member, it was my duty to represent the other members. Someone should play devil's advocate so that we could consider both sides. "They do help keep the mouse population down." The words spilled out of me before I had time to prepare for a fight.

"So does rat poison." Brock overruled with a look that said you don't count.

"Let's not get into that," Helda went on. "Darla, why don't you call the shelters and see if you can get one to come pick up the cats."

Helda looked back down at her notes and missed the irritated glance thrown her way by Darla.

"What are you doing about Trey?" Brock asked. "He had another party Saturday night. Drinking and making all kinds of noise. And I found trash in my yard the next day. Something needs to be done about him."

"The city has an ordinance about loud music or noise after 11pm. You can call the police if it goes on after that." Helda said.

"He also shot out my security camera. Wrecked it." Brock's face flushed with anger.

"Did you report it to the police?" Helda looked at him directly.

"Not yet. But I think the association should be able to do something about it. I mean, are we allowed to shoot up other people's things? Don't we have a rule about that?"

"That's a law, you need to take it up with the police." Helda said.

"Can't we kick him out?" Brock asked. "I mean he's dangerous."

"We can make a motion about shooting off guns in the neighborhood and add it at our next regular board meeting. In the meantime, I'll contact Morton and ask him to write Trey a letter." Helda said, dismissing the conversation. "Right now, my concern is getting our information back from Sheldon's office. I've written a letter requesting the police release our files to us, and had Morton look it over. I want each of us to sign it. Then Morton will turn it over to the judge." She looked up at us and then added, "Brock you don't need to sign."

Helda passed a sheet of paper around, and we all signed it. Once she had the signed copy back in her possession, Helda looked up and said, "Ok, that's all. We can adjourn."

As we prepared to leave, Brock said, "Sad about Sheldon. I mean that's wild stuff. I heard the police said someone was talking to him on the phone when it happened."

"Yeah, me," I said, then quickly regretted it after seeing the horrified look on Mitzi's face.

As soon as we were in the car, I asked her about it. "Shouldn't I have told them I was the one talking to Sheldon when he died?"

"I'm not sure. It's just that I wouldn't give out too much information right now. Someone just murdered Sheldon and if they think you know something, well it could be dangerous for you."

She was right of course. I would need to be more careful in the future.

"Why did Helda invite Brock? He's not a board member." I wanted to change the subject, move on from my blunder.

Mitzi looked over at me and rolled her eyes. "Helda always invites Brock. I don't know why. They have a thing between them. I don't think it's a physical relationship, but something."

"I can't believe that Trey kid shot Brock's camera."

Mitzi had been rather somber up until I mentioned the camera. Then a broad smile emerged across her face. "Don't you wonder why Brock didn't call the police?" She held my gaze for a second then looked back at the road. "

"Yes, actually I did wonder about that."

"Maybe it was because he had the camera aimed at Trey's swimming pool in his back yard."

"What? Is that legal?" I began to think about my own yard and privacy. Did any of my neighbors have a camera aimed at my house?

"I don't know if it's legal, but I'd bet that's why he didn't go to the police."

I shook my head. It hadn't occurred to me that someone's next door neighbor might be spying on them. I was silent for a moment as I contemplated the thought. "Mitzi, how do you know these things?"

"Trey told me." Mitzi stopped at a red light and looked over at me. "Helda seems pretty intent on getting those files back right away. I wonder what she's up to."

"What do you mean?" I asked.

"I don't know, but I don't trust her. I guess it's because of what happened with Nolan."

"Who's Nolan?"

"Nolan Baker? He was the treasurer before you, silly. Don't you remember?"

I should have remembered, but I hadn't really paid much attention to the board and what went on before I was elected. I'd attended a few of the annual meetings when we first moved into the neighborhood. But after a while I grew busy with other things and lost interest. I'd read the minutes, but unless it affected me personally, I didn't worry about what was going on in my community's political arena. Or with the players.

Mitzi flashed me a look that said you're pathetic, but I like you anyway. "There was an issue between him and Helda. I don't know exactly what happened, but Nolan quit the board. Sold his house and moved across town. That's how you got in." She smiled at me. "He'd been treasurer for eight years."

"Maybe he would know what might have been worrying Sheldon the night he was killed." As treasurer I had access to all the financials. I'd poured over the numbers a few times. A lot of numbers. It would certainly help to have his insight. "Do you think he'd talk to us?"

"I'll see if I can find his contact info."

Nolan Baker agreed to meet with Mitzi and me at La Cafetière for coffee the following Thursday. I brought my laptop with the HOA's financials just in case we needed to look at them.

We waited at a table in the back room and Mitzi ordered a lavender white chocolate mocha. I'd planned on getting a regular coffee, then changed my mind after hearing her order. "I'll have the same."

Nolan showed up about five minutes after our coffee came. Well dressed in a polo shirt and khakis, he looked to be in his mid-forties. Mitzi had filled me in on some of his background on our way to the coffee shop. Nolan worked as an accountant, drove a sports car, had a wife and two children. Aside from that, she knew little about him. He placed his order at the counter then came and sat down across the table from us.

Mitzi made the introduction. Nolan had a pleasant smile, but clearly a businessman, he quickly got to the point. "So, ladies, what can I do for you?"

"Well," Mitzi flashed him a warm smile, "Delila had a couple of questions about the association's books, and we thought you might be able to help."

"It's really more about the process," I began. "Did you get invoices from Helda or Sheldon? I mean, does someone have to approve them? Can anyone just give me an invoice?"

"I can't believe they didn't go over this with you." The waitress set his coffee down in front of him. He thanked her and took a sip. "Usually, Sheldon gave me the invoices after he had Helda approve them."

"That's how I thought it was supposed to work too. But after the meeting Saturday, Helda handed me some invoices. She asked me to just print out the checks and give them to her."

At the time, I didn't think anything of it. I was new to the process and assumed that was how things worked. But now I wondered. Sheldon had also given me some invoices.

"The invoices should all go through Sheldon. That way a copy is kept on file."

Mitzi looked at me then gently said, "Sheldon was murdered Saturday night."

Was it shock or fear that I saw cross Nolan's face? I wasn't sure, but he was visibly upset.

"How did it happen? Who killed him?"

"He was shot in his office. We don't know who killed him." I wanted to tell Nolan I was on the phone with

Sheldon at the time, then I remembered Mitzi's warning. "Do you know of any issues with our financials?"

Nolan studied his coffee for a minute as if trying to decide how much he wanted to share with us. Finally, he said, "I had questions about the financials when I was on the board. Things didn't seem to add up. We were spending far more money than I thought we should be. I showed Sheldon. The next thing I knew, I was being accused of embezzlement." He took a deep breath. "That was just before you came on the board, Mitzi.

The situation had clearly had a big impact on him. He seemed to be re-living the experience. "Poor Sheldon. I never thought he had anything to do with it. I don't think he really thought I was guilty. But others were making a big deal about it. So, I kept my suspicions to myself. I couldn't prove anything. If they made a big thing of it, spread it around that they thought I was embezzling, it could get me fired from my job. Ruin my reputation. I couldn't risk it."

"That's terrible!" Mitzi whispered. "No wonder you left!"

"My advice to you ladies, watch your back! Don't trust anyone." Nolan finished his coffee and set some money on the table. "Sorry ladies, I've got to get back to work." He left before I could ask him anything more.

My work schedule at the church had been reduced to three days a week, four hours a day, to do the bookkeeping and pay the bills. I'd managed my workload efficiently and it didn't take as long to complete everything. Both my Tuesdays and Thursdays were free, along with my weekends.

The Tuesday after Sheldon's funeral, Mitzi and I decided to meet up in the park again in the late afternoon. I waited at the picnic table staring into the bright blue space above the grass. I barely noticed the chattering squirrels darting in and out of the trees that bordered Lily Park, or the shimmering sunlight that trickled through their branches.

Yet, even with all the beauty surrounding me, my thoughts were dark, and traveled about aimlessly, in search of answers. What had Sheldon wanted me to look for? Who had come to his office and killed him?

I tried to recall our exact conversation. He'd been looking for some papers. That's right! I'd forgotten that. He couldn't find some paperwork.

"Can I ask you a favor?" Mitzi's voice woke me from my reflective state. "Would you look over the minutes for me?"

I knew that Sheldon had done this for her in the past. I guessed she worried about Helda embarrassing her in front of everyone. "Sure!" I smiled at her and looked for Boris. He had sniffed his way to the edge of the park but came running when he saw his playmate, Mia.

"I'll email them to you. If you could just fix any mistakes and add anything I missed."

I gave her a reassuring smile, then looked around the park. "Mitzi, I've been going back over all the expenses for the association. Have you noticed a lot of improvements to the park these past couple years?"

"Well, we've added a few things. Some new flowers. We had the pavilion and picnic tables worked on. We planted a couple new trees and put up a new sign."

"Yeah." I thought about the cost of the improvements. "Ok. What about the roads?"

"Well, we did have to patch a few potholes. And we put up new speed limit signs. Why?"

"I'm just trying to figure out why Sheldon questioned the financials. What part of them did he have issues with?

And Nolan too. I wish I had thought to ask him specifically where he felt there was a problem. What he suspected."

"You could call him." Mitzi offered. "I'll send you his phone number when I send the minutes." She looked over to where the dogs had discovered some interesting smells.

"I wonder who hires the contract work? I mean who calls the guys to come out and trim the trees for example."

Mitzi thought for a moment. "Well, I remember at one of my first board meetings, there was a fight between Sheldon and Helda. Sheldon said he should hire the sign maker and contact all the contractors. But Helda said the association didn't want to pay him to do that, when she could do it."

We sat quietly for a couple of minutes, both of us caught up in our own thoughts. Neither of us had ever been a board member before. Did they all operate the same? Was there a right way and wrong way?

I had attended one of the church board meetings, but that was the extent of my knowledge. And it was a special situation. I still had no idea of the inner workings of a homeowner's association board. My thoughts continued in this way, trying to ease my feelings of inadequacy because of my inexperience.

Mitzi pulled me from my world of insecurity. "Did you get a call from Pierce?"

"No." I shook my head.

"You will." Mitzi said. "He called me last night begging me to stop the foreclosure. I told him I couldn't do anything about it. He wanted your name and number. I'm sorry, I had to give it to him. He is still a member." She offered me an apologetic look.

"There's nothing I can do, is there?" I felt a tremor of panic. What could I say to him? How could I tell him he would lose his home and there was nothing he could do about it? Nothing I could do about it either. "I had nothing to do with this. I wasn't even on the board when the decision was made."

"Oh, I know! I was there, but I couldn't do anything either. He needs to talk to Helda or Morton. We can't do anything." Mitzi had the same sound of anxiety in her voice. "Sheldon didn't either, but I think Pierce blamed him."

"Why would he blame Sheldon?"

"Sheldon got blamed for a lot of things he had nothing to do with." Mitzi shook her head. "He was the face of the association. All the mean letters came from him. His name was on all the paperwork. Even though it was Helda or the board behind it."

I remembered when Barry and I had first moved into the association. We too, had been upset with the Community Manager. We'd received threatening letters about weeds in our lawn. At the time, I blamed him for harassing us. I didn't realize it wasn't him calling the shots.

Now I knew it was the board behind the bully tactics. And now, *I* was on the board.

"I'm sorry, I'm going to have to get going." Mitzi sighed and stood up. "Mia!" The little red poodle came running and Mitzi attached her leash.

I watched them walk down the street, then looked at Boris. He was still sniffing the same ground as before. "Boris... Boris!" I called. He didn't lift his head, but I thought I saw his eyes look my way. Then I walked over to him and hooked up his leash. "I guess your hearing isn't very good anymore." I laughed and patted his head.

On Wednesday, two and a half weeks after Sheldon's murder, I drove past my neighbor's house on my way home from work. I waved to Ziggy who had been raking leaves, but he didn't smile or wave back as he normally did.

Safely inside my home, I listened to my voice mail. I had three messages from Muriel, demanding I leave the cats alone. Each message sounded more aggressive. How many times had I told her it was not up to me? Why had I agreed to be on this board?

I peeked out my window at Erle's house. It occurred to me that I hadn't seen Helda walking the streets measuring grass and looking for violators since our last board meeting. One good thing for me to appreciate.

My phone rang and I expected to see Muriel's name show up. Instead, it was a number I didn't recognize. "Hello." I answered with my usual caution these days.

"Delila Clarke?" Came a voice I didn't recognize.

"Yes."

"This is Pierce Andrews. Mitzi gave me your number. She said you are the new treasurer, for the Brookstone Homeowners Association."

My heart rate sped up a bit. "Yes." I'd been waiting for his call. Expecting it. Yet, I still didn't know what I could say. How could I explain that I had no part in this act of cruelty? Nothing I could say would ease his hardship.

"I need you to stop this foreclosure from going through. I know Sheldon wasn't willing to budge on it, but I think we should be able to work something out." He took a breath. "I've got most of the money to pay off what I owe the association."

"I'm sorry. This all came about before I became treasurer. Have you spoken with Morton, our attorney? Or Helda?" I tried to keep his hostilities from coming in my direction. They were the ones in control here, not me. It was Helda who made the decision to move forward with the foreclosure. She should be the one chewed out by the wrath of the desperate homeowner.

"I can't talk to them. I tried. They just say there's nothing they can do. Well, there is something someone can do. I have the money and I want to give it to you. Then you can release the lien and the foreclosure."

"Mr. Andrews...I don't have the power to do that. I just do the bookkeeping."

"I worked my whole life to pay for this house. We finally paid it off two years ago. Can you imagine what that's like? To spend a month in the hospital, then your association manager tells you they are foreclosing on your house because you didn't pay a $620 bill?" He paused. "I didn't think so!" His voice echoed a mix of anger and terror. And desperation.

I didn't say anything. It sounded as if he was nearly crying as he continued. "What am I supposed to do? We have nowhere to go."

"Mr. Andrews, believe me, if there were anything I could do, I would."

After we hung up, the conversation stayed with me. As I usually do when upset, I began to clean my house. In my head, I explained it to Pierce repeatedly, as I swept, vacuumed, and dusted. There was nothing I could do to stop the foreclosure.

When Barry arrived home from work, I still hadn't started dinner. I began to share all my troubles with him. "Get your coat honey, I'm taking you out to dinner."

His calm demeanor usually helped me settle down and I felt much better as I slipped into my jacket.

Barry backed the car out of the garage and was nearly out of the driveway when Muriel stopped us. She stuck her face in the car window, and I rolled it down part way.

"Did you get my messages?" she demanded.

"I'm sorry Muriel, we are just heading out. I've been working all day and was planning to call you back later tonight."

"I saw a truck from the shelter here earlier today. What are they going to do with the cats?"

"I...I don't know anything about it, Muriel."

"You people on the board need to call them and tell them to stop. Since Sheldon is no longer with us, they don't need to come around here anymore."

"What does Sheldon have to do with it?" I asked.

"He's the one who called them. He kept saying he was going to, and I assume he did it before he died."

"Sheldon didn't call them." I looked her squarely in the eyes. "You thought he did this?"

"Of course. Who else would have? I think he wrote that horrible letter too!" Her face looked angry with resentment.

"Muriel," Barry said, in a tone that didn't allow for objections. "I'm sorry but we have a reservation. We need to get going now."

At that, Muriel backed away from the car and Barry was able to pull out of the driveway. As soon as she was out of sight, I thanked him.

"She's out of control." He said, "She doesn't need to harass you like that."

"I'm so lucky to have you!" I said and meant it.

Another week went by and there had been no news of Sheldon's murder. If the police had any new information, it hadn't been released to the public. I'd gone back over the books several times and found nothing.

Muriel called me again, and I'd finally agreed to speak with Darla about the cats. Find out if she'd hired the shelter to come and trap them.

Darla lived a few blocks from my house in one of the newer homes in the subdivision. Her house looked larger than mine, with a lush green and perfectly manicured lawn. Once inside, I noticed her extra-large posh furniture. We sat across from one another, me on her overstuffed sofa, her in a matching chair. I sunk down into an uncomfortable position.

We talked about the association, and I learned that Darla had been on the board for three years. She'd moved into our neighborhood around five years ago with her husband, however they'd divorced two years later. Darla didn't seem at all shy about sharing her history with me. In fact, I thought she might be trying to become friends.

"How long has Helda been on the board?" I asked. "I should know this, but honestly, I never really paid much attention to the association before."

Darla motioned to a plate of cookies on the coffee table. "Have one." She picked up a cookie. "Let's see now. She's been on the board at least as long as I've been here."

I wasn't sure how Darla felt about Helda. They could be friends. If so, I'd need to tread carefully. "Helda seems to be very..." I grasped for a good word, "hard-working." It wasn't the first word that popped into my mind, but it felt like a safe word.

"Hump." Darla made a funny face. "I'm the one who usually does the work. But she is good at taking credit. She likes ordering people around. That's why she and Sheldon were always fighting." She took another bite of the cookie. "Sometimes I think she sees me as her personal assistant."

It surprised me to hear her speak so frankly about Helda. Apparently, they weren't as chummy as I'd thought.

"Oh, you mean like having you deal with the cats?" I asked, excited for an opportunity to bring up the topic.

Darla's glasses had a habit of sliding down her face and she pushed them up as she considered the question. "Yes. Like the cats." She rolled her eyes.

I looked around the room, trying not to seem too interested, too obvious. "Muriel said she saw the shelter's van in our neighborhood. Did you call them already?"

"Yeah. I called them. They said they set live traps, but I don't know how many they've caught."

"What will they do with them?" I asked, not sure I really wanted to know the answer.

"I don't know. Probably look for homes for them." Darla looked at her watch. "Say, I'd love to sit and chat, but I have an appointment."

"Oh, of course. Thank you so much for having me. You have a lovely home, Darla."

"Yeah, thanks to my ex.," she said as she walked me to the door.

I walked back toward my house thinking about Darla and Helda and the board. I passed Ziggy's house and saw him outside painting his mailbox. We hadn't spoken since the day he'd confronted me in my driveway. I decided to stop and have a chat with him. Maybe if he had talked to Sheldon again, he'd let something slip.

"Hi Ziggy," I gave him a friendly smile as I approached. "How've you been?"

"What do you want? Are you here to check the color of paint? It's the right one. HOA Exterior Satin Superpaint #7570, Egret White."

"No, I just wanted to...well I wanted to apologize for how you've been harassed Ziggy. I mean sometimes the HOA gets carried away. I've been hassled by them myself, so I know what it's like. I'm hoping we can change things." I wanted to set his mind at ease, help him trust me.

"Yeah, sure." He continued to paint, not stopping to look at me.

"Well, things are rather turned upside down right now, what with Sheldon's death and all." I thought I might draw something out by bringing up the murder.

"Yeah, I bet." He stopped painting for a moment and looked at me. "You might want to watch your back too, missy. Whoever killed Sheldon could come for you."

I shivered at his statement. Was this a threat or a warning? Did Ziggy know something?

The morning of my second board meeting started off as expected. Barry worked on his crossword puzzle at the kitchen table while I cleaned up after breakfast.

"I heard you talking to Jim last night." I'd been thinking about it ever since.

"Yes, we're playing golf tomorrow afternoon." Barry continued working his puzzle without looking up.

"Did he happen to say if they have any news on Sheldon's murder?" I'd been hoping he would tell me. I couldn't wait any longer. I had to know.

"He did say they have a couple of leads. But he can't really talk about it you know." He looked up at me. "Don't worry, they'll catch the killer."

Yet, I was worried. It had been nearly a month, and I grew impatient for closure. Restless. Anxious. A killer might be lurking in my own neighborhood, and I didn't know who. Didn't know if or when they might strike again.

My cell phone rang and suddenly, all that changed. After hanging up, I immediately rang Mitzi.

"I have news. Meet me at the park in ten minutes, ok?"

"Is it juicy?" She laughed.

"I don't know about juicy, but you'll want to hear it!"

I called Boris and hooked up his leash. Jewel, my kitten, nearly full grown now, followed us to the door. I picked her up and gave her a little hug. "You're one lucky kitten." I gave her a little kiss on the forehead and set her back down.

A light summer mist had begun to fall. Excited with my news, I pulled a light jacket over my head, pulled up the hood, and Boris and I set off at a brisk pace.

When we arrived at the park, I unleashed Boris, and he rushed to his playmate, Mia. Mitzi wore her bright pink and white striped rain jacket, while Mia was in plain pink rain gear. They didn't match perfectly, but almost. We both stood under the protection of the pavilion roof, and even with the outrageous humidity, Mitzi's hair looked good. She gave me a cheery grin that begged me for the big news.

"So, let's have it!"

"They took Helda in for questioning this morning. I don't know if she is a suspect in Sheldon's murder or what, but they kept her for several hours. She's totally freaked out."

"Helda? Who told you?" Mitzi eyes opened wide with curiosity. "I mean how did you find out?"

"Darla called." I waited for her to process the information. "Helda told her. The police said Helda's cellphone was in the vicinity of Sheldon's office the night and time of the murder."

"And Darla told you all this?" Mitzi sounded surprised. Normally she heard gossip before me.

"Yes." I felt thrilled to be the one to have the news first. "I went to visit Darla the other day about the cats. Now we're friends." I grinned. Then I saw the pained look on Mitzi's face and quickly added, "Besides, she couldn't get a hold of you."

At two o'clock, Mitzi and I took our seats in the library conference room for my second board meeting. Darla sat in Helda's spot at the head of the table. The rest of the group chatted with one another throwing curious glances toward Darla.

Eventually the noise grew quieter. Darla readjusted herself in her seat and displayed a rather joyful look, then began the meeting. "Ok, are we ready? Darla will be leading the meeting today. Helda can't be here, due to...well something came up and she won't be able to make it." She looked around the room. "Ok, it looks like we have a quorum."

Why did she refer to herself in third person? It seemed strange to me.

"Helda has been searching for a new management company, however the two she was looking at may have too many accounts to take us. They are both more expensive as well. Anyway, she can give us an update next month." Darla took a breath.

"Do you know the names of the two companies she's looking at?" Brock asked.

"No, but I'll try and find out." Darla looked at the paper in front of her. "Darla contacted the animal shelter on the west side of town, and they came out and set live traps. I think they have caught about three cats so far." She smiled, obviously pleased with herself.

I thought of Muriel and wondered if she knew, and how upset she must be. My thoughts were on the cats when Mitzi handed me some invoices. I took them and smiled. I hadn't heard what Darla said, but realized it had to do with the statements. I glanced at them. More bills.

As we listened to the ARC or architecture report, I looked around at the various members. Darla seemed especially happy today in the lead role. She pulled her hair behind her ear and pushed her glasses up her face. She'd dressed better today too, nicer clothing, and her hair looked as if she'd put more effort into it.

I smiled to myself and wondered if she had a date tonight. Then I glanced at Brock. His smug look caught me off guard. Had he really aimed a camera at Trey's swimming pool? He cleared his throat and Darla called on him.

"Madam Vice President," He began, "Helda wanted me to make a motion for an amendment to our bylaws that prohibits shooting a gun in the neighborhood."

Darla nodded. "Do you have a written proposal you can submit to the board members?"

Brock had lost some of the smugness. "No." He looked around the room. "Let's just do it now." He looked across at Mitzi. "The secretary can write it down and we can vote on it today." His voice had grown excited. He tilted his head, and in an even louder voice, as if he might force everyone to agree with him, said, "It's a big waste of time."

"Morton?" Darla called on the attorney for a response.

Morton lifted his thick head and said, "In order to amend the bylaws, a written proposal must first be submitted to each board member for review. Once that is done, members can have a discussion on it and decide if they wish to proceed with the amendment." He looked at Darla and continued. "I should warn you; it is a rather costly endeavor as you will need to have me look things over and write up the legal documentation." He looked back at Darla as if tossing her the baton.

Darla looked around the room and said, "As acting president, Darla says we need to follow the rules." She looked at Brock. "If you still wish to proceed, please email us your proposal. We need at least one month to read it over and consider it. Then we can put it on the agenda."

I was impressed with Darla's handling of the meeting. As vice president, she'd seemed like an onlooker. A puppet to the president. But she'd really stepped up to the plate with Helda gone.

After the meeting was adjourned, and Mitzi had gone to get the car, I packed up my computer and got ready to leave. Darla came over and stood next to me. We made small talk for a few minutes until the others had left.

"You wanna meet for lunch Monday?" She asked me, her professional persona peeling away, as she slumped into her more comfortable twang.

We had nothing in common, other than both being on the HOA board and living in the same neighborhood. Darla was single and younger than I. She didn't like cards or reading or cooking. And I wasn't interested in video games and chat rooms. What would we talk about?

"Sure." I stammered. "I don't get off work until one. Is that too late?"

On Monday, Darla and I met at Helen's Kitchen. I liked the light and breezy atmosphere of the little diner, with its old-fashioned curtains, simple tables, and booths. A refrigerated cabinet by the cash register held fresh pies, and I'd decided I'd bring one home for Barry.

Darla waited at a booth for me, and I slid in across from her. I wondered why she'd asked me to meet with her. Maybe she needed friends, or maybe she wanted to pump me for information. I couldn't be sure.

"I love their soups and sandwiches here." Darla said smiling over her menu.

"Me too."

We placed our orders and I waited for Darla to lead the conversation. After the waitress left, she jumped into the topic of Helda. "I can't believe the police are questioning Helda. I mean, it's crazy right?"

I smiled in agreement, and she continued.

"I know Sheldon and Helda used to argue a lot and she was super frustrated with him. But I can't believe she'd kill him." The waitress returned with our drinks and Darla paused for a moment. "She called me Saturday after the meeting to see how things went."

I listened intently wondering if I might learn something new.

"Apparently she lost her phone and it somehow ended up near Sheldon's office at the time he was killed." She took a drink of her diet cola, looked up at me, then continued. "But I already told you that."

"Yes, it is strange!" I tried to consider how Helda's phone ended up near Sheldon's office.

"We had been at his office after the meeting that day. She thinks she might have dropped it then or something."

It seemed plausible. After all people forgot their phones all the time.

"Anyway, the police aren't so sure. She thinks she might need to get a lawyer." She looked at me over the top of her glasses. "And she couldn't get our paperwork or files or anything from his office either." Darla chewed on her straw, then took a long drink.

"Can we still get another management company without the paperwork?" I felt naïve, asking what was most likely, a stupid question.

"Oh sure." She eyed me as if to determine if she wanted to share more with me. "You know," she spoke slowly and deliberately, "yesterday, I stopped over to see Helda, see how she was doing. She'd told the police that she lost her phone, but when I was at her house, I saw it there, on the counter."

The waitress came and set our food down in front of us. I must have had a surprised look on my face, but I waited until after the waitress had gone before saying anything. "Really? Do you think she just didn't realize it was there?"

"I don't know." Darla took a bite of her sandwich. "I just thought it was strange." She said and took another bite.

As we ate, the topic changed to Darla's love life. I listened as she told me about her upcoming date and how she liked some dating apps better than others. I suspected Darla was desperate for friends. Especially of the male gender.

We finished our meals and conversation and walked up to the register to pay. I selected a blueberry pie from the display case and paid the waitress at the cash register. Darla paid for her lunch, and we walked out together. Darla hesitated for a moment, and I thought she wanted to tell me something more, but she seemed to change her mind.

"See you later." She said as she turned and walked in the opposite direction.

After my lunch with Darla, I worked on the association's bills. I printed out the checks and put them in envelopes. Helda had suggested they come to her, and she'd pass them along to the contractors.

Boris needed a walk, so we headed over to Helda's house to hand deliver the checks. The late summer breeze felt nice as it brushed against my cheeks. Boris pulled hard on the leash. He was a bit confused when we didn't turn to go to the park, but quickly adjusted to the change and walked along beside me, uncertain of where we were going.

A police car pulled up in front of Helda's house and parked behind another police car. Boris and I stopped and watched as the officers went in and out of the house. One officer carried a box out to his vehicle. Obviously not a good time. Boris and I turned and walked toward Lily Park.

Had they arrested Helda? Which came first, an arrest or a search? I decided to ask Barry to call Jim when I got home and find out.

Upon seeing Mia, Boris tugged hard at the leash, pulling me down the sidewalk to the pavilion. I too was happy to find Mitzi and the little red dog in the park. I filled Mitzi in on what I'd seen at Helda's house, and what Darla had told me at lunch.

"But why would Helda kill Sheldon?" Mitzi wondered.

"He must have known something she didn't want him to tell."

"Yeah," Mitzi's voice carried doubt.

I finally whispered the thought that occupied both of us. "I wonder if she might have been embezzling and he caught her." We chewed over the idea for a moment.

The sound of a car honking startled us. We turned to see Brock wave and hop out. "Good afternoon, ladies!"

Mitzi and I flashed him our less-than-welcoming smiles, curious as to why he would stop to talk. He'd never shown us any interest in the past, and clearly had something on his mind.

He didn't hesitate to let us know his intention. No beating around the bush or small talk. Instead, he blurted out his rather controversial pronouncement.

"I'm not sure if you ladies were aware, but I am the resident agent for our association. That means when one of the board members is unable to fulfil their obligation, I fill in. Now Saturday, Darla, as vice president filled in for Helda. But, as resident agent, I think it should be my job."

As I grappled with the idea, Mitzi said, "I don't recall hearing about a resident agent, is that a position we voted on?"

"It's an appointed position. Helda appointed me." Brock must have been expecting a little push back as he didn't seem even slightly put off by her bluntness. "Anyway, I've had experience as president, I'm really a better candidate for the job."

I'd nearly forgotten that Brock had been president. Overlooked memories, or memories intentionally suppressed, began to resurface.

When Barry and I moved into the neighborhood, we were thrilled with our new home. Swimming pool, two and a half car garage and a generous yard. Everything about the house was perfect. Or so we thought when we signed the closing documents. The realtor handed us the keys, a copy of the bylaws and what looked like a book that contained fifty-nine pages of the association's rules.

Three days after we moved in, and before most of our furnishings had been put in place, we received a letter from the association that our grass was too long. It should be no more than three inches. A week later a new letter came; too many weeds, followed by a letter regarding the bushes and a tree branch that needed to be removed. It felt like every time we turned around, there was another letter of intimidation.

We began to feel anxious every time we saw a weed or brown spot in our yard. We'd scold one another for leaving the garage door open too long or forgetting to put the rake or shovel away, terrified of receiving a fine. The HOA became a warden, forcing us to comply with an endless cycle of trimming bushes, edging the sidewalk and driveway, spraying grass and flowerbeds with chemicals and fertilizers.

Suffocated by overly restrictive policies, Barry and I made it a point to attend the annual meeting.

Brock, commander and chief, sounded like a general going to war. He didn't ask for volunteers, but instead assigned people to tasks. He made new rules and put them to the vote. For some reason, no one ever spoke up or disagreed with him. No one voted against his proposals. He ran a tight regime. It was pointless to try and go against the grain.

Memories flooded back into my thoughts. We didn't bother to go to the meetings after that. What was the point? Democracy did not exist in this monarchial style neighborhood government. Instead, power was maintained through surveillance and financial punishment. For the most part authority went unchallenged. There appeared to be no recourse, other than to comply with the rules that were thrust upon us.

Brock's brash voice pulled me from my reflection. "Besides," he said, "we all know Darla isn't really cut out for the job. She just doesn't have what it takes. She's too...I don't know, ineffectual?"

He hadn't said it, but I suspected he meant because she was a woman.

"We really need at least one man on the board anyway." He continued. "Someone who can get things done."

Mitzi wore a tight lipped, well-guarded half smile as we watched him get into his car. As soon as he pulled away from the parking lot, she groaned, "oh man, are we in for trouble now!"

"Exactly. We can't let him take over!"

The paid invoices sat on the counter waiting to be taken to Helda. The police might still be searching her home, or even have arrested her. In that case, who should get them? Darla? Brock? No, certainly not Brock. My phone vibrated and showed the arrival of a new text message.

Darla: Hey, do you have a minute?
Me: Sure, what's up?
Darla: Can I stop over and pick up those checks?

Hesitant to agree to hand them over, I thought for a few moments before answering. Did it really matter? The checks were made out to the various businesses anyway. It shouldn't really matter who distributed them. For that matter, it seemed silly that I didn't just mail them. After a short discussion with myself, I texted Darla back and invited her over.

"Why don't we just mail the checks?" I asked, as Darla stepped inside the house.

"Oh, I know." She shook her head and rolled her eyes. "Helda likes to do it this way."

She seemed happy in the role of president, it only seemed fair to let her know about Brock's plans. Was it possible to break it to her gently? Probably not, but the only way to prevent him from taking over, would be to prepare Darla.

"I saw Brock today." I waited for her to look at me. "He said Helda appointed him as resident agent of the association." I paused for a moment, "that his job is to fill in whenever someone is unable to fulfil his or her duties. He said he should take over as president."

At first her face showed surprise. Then she smiled and shook her head. "He's not going to. I'm the vice president. The whole reason to have a VP is to take over for the president. Nope, he's not going to pull anything over on me." She gave a triumphant nod of the head.

Her phone rang and she pulled it out and looked at the name on the screen. An animated smile flickered across her face as she peered down at the undisclosed caller, then turned her back as she answered.

"Hellooo." She spoke in a low, guttural voice. "Yesss. It's meee." She whispered something I couldn't hear. "Ok, I'll be waiting for you. Bye Bae." She turned back, still wearing an inescapable expression of excitement.

It must have been obvious from the look on my face that I was curious about the call.

"I have a date." Dressed in her happiness, she almost looked pretty. "He's soooo good looking too." She scrolled through her phone's photos and found a picture to show me.

My jaw dropped as my curiosity turned to surprise and a touch of embarrassment.

Darla laughed. A full-length photo of a man filled the screen of her phone. He was completely naked. Not even socks. Posing to show it all.

Dumbfounded I let out a little "oh." Not sure what had shocked me more, that he'd sent her the photo or that she'd shown it to me.

She enlarged the picture focusing on the face. "Here, is this better?"

The man looked to be about ten years younger than her, and yes, attractive. Where had she met him? I felt ashamed to think such a thing, but why was he interested in her?

"Isn't he gorgeous?" She said, still looking at the photo. "He's my sugar-tot. Dude candy." Her grin reminded me of a lovesick animal. "He found me online a couple of months ago. We've only met in person once, but we talk and text all the time. I'm in love!"

What do you say to someone who is clearly doing something you know is stupid and dangerous? And you know there is nothing you can say to change their mind? You don't say anything. You just paste a dumb smile on your face and say, "oh, wow."

"He's coming over tonight." The dreamy look on her face said, don't even try to talk me out of this.

With no personal experience in this new dating scene, it was difficult to understand how she'd been sucked in. Or more likely, how she'd plunged headfirst into a relationship with someone she'd just met online. What did she know about this guy? It seemed to me that she was being taken for a ride. But where?

Darla looked up at me. "Can I get those checks? I need to get going. Gotta get ready for tonight!" She stuffed the envelopes in her purse, then left with a look of eagerness toward her evening ahead.

It had only been about ten minutes after Darla left, when I heard another knock at my door. To my surprise, Brock stood facing me, a smile on his face and looking like a numbat eyeing his prey.

"Hi Delila. I need to get a check from you." He hesitated, cleared his throat, then said. "Or, I should say, from the HOA."

Without saying a word, I let the question mark in my wrinkled brows tell him I needed more information.

"I ordered a new sign for the park and it's ready to be picked up." He lifted his chin and dropped the smile. "You can make it out to me. It's $500."

What was he thinking? Did he really believe I would just hand over a check made out to him? "I'm sorry Brock, I can't just issue a check without an invoice and without prior approval from Helda or the board."

"Helda and I discussed this before you showed up. You can just call and ask her. She'll tell you."

Maybe this is how they'd done things in the past, but in my mind, it didn't seem like a good operating procedure. There needed to be a paper trail showing approval for an expenditure. Checks and balances. And above all, there was no way I would issue the check with his name on it.

"I still need an invoice or statement and I'll need written approval from Helda." I had to protect my own derriere and the association.

"That's not how we operate." He dropped his chin and threw a strong look my way.

It's rare for me to stand up to people, but in that instance, irritation caused the words to escape. "That's how ***I*** operate." It felt good to hold my ground to him.

He seemed to back down and think about it for a minute. "Sheldon knew about it. He probably had the paperwork."

My instincts told me not to trust him. "The sign maker should give you an invoice."

"Fine." Brock turned to leave.

"And please have Helda sign off on it too."

He turned back to glare at me. Chills shot up my spine. Had I just made a dangerous enemy?

Friday morning dragged on at work, as there was little to do. Excited about our dinner plans with Jim and Aleena for Saturday night, I felt anxious for noon and the end of my workweek. Three invoices and a few donations still needed attention. I entered the data into the computer, filled out a deposit slip and put it in the bag with the contributions to take to the bank.

I wrote checks for a plumber, a painter and for tree trimming services. In late summer the shrubs were cut back, and in the spring, they would grow nicely shaped, and more beautiful than ever. For some reason, my eyes lingered on this invoice.

Our association had also hired someone to trim back shrubs. The ones that grew next to the entrance signs and in Lily Park. The association didn't have as many shrubs as the church had. Yet, the association paid almost double this amount. I wrote down the name of the company the church used. Maybe the association could save some money if we switched contractors.

My phone rang. Darla.

"Hey, are you going to the fundraiser tomorrow?"

One of our neighbors, a woman I didn't know, had been in a car accident. Some of the neighbors and her friends were holding a luncheon and silent auction to raise money for her. Darla had sent an email invitation to everyone in our association.

I hesitated. I hadn't planned on going. I'd asked Mitzi, but she said she and Ned were going to be in Chicago for the weekend, to attend her niece's wedding.

"No. I mean... I don't really know her."

"So? You should come anyway. As board members, we need to show support for our community. Brock's not going. Mitzi's not going. Helda's not going. Some of us board members should be there."

That seemed true enough. But I didn't want to go alone. "I...are you going?"

"Yeah, I'm going. You want to go with me?"

We agreed to attend the fundraiser together. Darla said she'd pick me up at 11am the following morning. I looked at the clock and saw it was nearly time to leave work.

The afternoon drive home was calming, and I enjoyed seeing a few trees that had begun to turn red, nestled amongst their green colleagues and cobalt sky. Soon they would be a barrage of colors, but for now we still had a bit of summer. I switched the radio station to soft background music so I could soak in the effects.

I turned my car into the subdivision and saw that the shrubs next to the entrance had been carefully trimmed. I passed Pierce Andrews' house and noticed the family packing their belongings into a U-Haul truck. My heart sank. The children's faces were sad and their father, Pierce, looked defeated.

Had he seen me? Did he blame me as well as the rest of the board? I wasn't there when they made the decision to foreclose on his house. Yet, I was as much a part of the tyrannical HOA as the others now.

I turned my head and kept it on the road ahead of me. I didn't want them to know I'd seen them packing up to leave. I didn't want them to think about me at all.

Lily Park was right around the corner from the Andrews' home. I checked to see if the bushes there had also been trimmed. The small flower garden next to the pavilion held the only shrubs in Lily Park.

Much to my surprise, Helda was bent over the ground in the little round garden planting some yellow mums. I'd forgotten she'd ordered them. And I hadn't seen her since the police had taken all those boxes from her house.

Had she been arrested and posted bail? Or had they decided she wasn't guilty? She looked up in time to see me pull into the parking lot next to the pavilion.

She finished pushing the mulch around the plants then grabbed a small shovel and quickly stood up as I stepped out of my car.

"Hello Helda," I said, as I shut my car door.

"Oh." She stared at me for a moment with a blank look, as if she didn't know me. "Hello," She shoved the small shovel she'd held in her left hand under her arm and rubbed her hands together, clearing the dirt and mulch from them. "I forgot my gloves." She shook her head.

I smiled and tried to put her at ease. "I wanted to let you know that Darla picked up the checks for those invoices."

"What invoices? Oh. She did?" She still had a blank look, then seemed to remember me. "Oh. Ok."

"And" I paused. "I'm not sure what you think about this, but my church uses a company called," I looked at the paper in my hand. "Yancy's Lawncare. I think we could save a lot of money if we switched companies."

"Oh. Ok. Well maybe next year." Helda seemed distracted. "Nice seeing you. I have to get going."

Before I could turn back to my car, Muriel drove by. When she saw us, she slammed on her brakes and backed up to where we were standing. Her car still running, she hopped out and began yelling. "It has to stop! I'm telling you; it has to STOP!"

Speechless, both Helda and I waited for Muriel's rant.

"All this hatred! People trying to kill little animals. Creatures that aren't doing anyone harm! Why?" Muriel was crying. "Look!" She opened her passenger side door and with great care, pulled out a box.

Muriel carried it over to us and we peered inside. There lay a bandaged and heavily sedated, chewed up looking tabby cat. Through tears and a choked voice, she said, "Someone tried to kill it! Shot it in the back! It's a miracle that it lived!"

She stood looking down at the pitiful animal. "And that's not all." She took the box back to the car and picked up something else, and brought it back with her.

"Look," she said and pushed a zip lock baggy in front of us.

The plastic bag contained three bullets. "There's more!" She stared at her evidence. "I found these in the back woods in a blanket I put out there for them." She produced a second bag. "And this is the one they took out of the cat."

"No one should be shooting that close to our houses." Helda said.

"And you haven't done anything to protect them! We have an infestation of murderous neighbors here and you haven't done a thing about it. Well, I'm going to!" She stomped back toward her car. "I'm going to the police and whoever did this is going to pay!"

Muriel slammed her car door shut and drove away. I turned to say something to Helda, but she had begun walking back across the park toward her house. The air felt dead as I stood, alone in the park, with more questions than ever, running through my mind.

The next morning after breakfast, Barry kissed me good-bye and left for the office. He didn't usually work on Saturdays, but today he had an emergency patient. Darla planned on picking me up just before 11am for the fundraising event. I hurried to finish cleaning. Through my living room window, I could see her pull into the driveway. I hurried to put on my jacket, grabbed my purse and patted Boris on the head. "We'll go for a walk later." I promised.

The fundraiser was being held at a large Presbyterian church several miles from our subdivision. Darla chattered happily as she drove, clearly in a good mood.

"How was your date?" I asked.

"Great. I just hope he pays me back the money he borrowed." She chuckled in a way that made me think she didn't truly find it funny.

"He borrowed money?" It didn't sound good to me. It sounded like someone had taken advantage of her.

"Yeah, I lent him $10,000 last month. I thought he was going to pay me back the other night. But he didn't." She confessed.

I tried not to let her see the shock I felt. $10,000? I knew there were predators who looked for vulnerable women on dating apps. "Are you worried he might not pay you back?"

"Oh no. He'll pay me back."

A car honked its horn and pulled around us as Darla turned into the Church parking lot. I guessed they were upset she hadn't used her turn signal. She just ignored them and kept going, completely oblivious of the other drivers.

Large arrows directed us to park in a lot near one of the wings off the main building. The church was larger than mine, and well-marked with more signboards directing us where to go. We walked toward the door. Darla, who stood about four or five inches taller than I, had puffed up like a soldier who'd been promoted to queen.

Skirted tables lined the perimeter of the room. Colorful balloons and posters decorated the various tabletops, each vying for our attention. A basket of goodies and miscellaneous individual items, along with a bid sheet attached to a clipboard for each, were evenly placed for onlookers. A table at the far side of the room held a spread of coffee and snacks. In the center of the room were several round tables for supporters to sit at.

The room was noisy with the sounds of people deep in conversation; however, it wasn't as crowded as I had expected.

There was no charge for attending the event, just a donation box, set up next to the door. Darla walked right past it, obviously not planning to contribute. I stopped and pulled out some money. Slightly annoyed, I hoped it was enough to cover both of us.

We walked along the room looking over the items, oohing and ahhing and admiring the beautiful quilts and crocheted hats and scarves. We lingered over some of the baskets, and I put my name on several of them. I went back to the quilt and added my name and what I felt was a high bid for it. I also put my name on some of the items no one else had bid on.

When we got to the food and coffee table, we both took a plate of cookies and a coffee, then found a seat at one of the round tables. Several ladies, many of whom I didn't know, stopped by and said hello to us. It felt like we were celebrities in a way. I could only attribute it to being a board member.

I didn't win the quilt, but I did leave with several items and a basket. Darla won a bottle of wine that she said was worth at least $30 and she paid only $15 for it. She was happy about that.

On the way home, Darla was still in a good mood over her winnings. I tried to bring up my concern over her new boyfriend, but she brushed it off, then changed the subject. "I see Brock's been going over to Helda's house a lot lately."

"You think he's trying to get her to help him take over? The Resident Agent thing?" I asked.

"Oh, probably. But I think." She stopped short. "I probably shouldn't say anything."

"What?"

"Well. It's just something Sheldon said."

I couldn't take my eyes off her face as she drove through the entrance of the neighborhood. "You have to tell me now! You can't leave me hanging."

"Sheldon said he thought they were having an affair. I think he saw them coming from a motel room."

"Really?"

"Yep. Sheldon said he'd had a talk with Helda about it. How it didn't look good and might be upsetting to members if they found out." She turned to look at me and smiled. "Anyway, he told her she might need to step down as president if she were going to keep seeing Brock."

"Because he's married?"

"Yep. And his wife has a lot of money."

Still gnawing on what Darla had told me as Boris and I headed for the park, I wondered how it would all play out. Had Helda given Brock the ability to take over the association? He was a tyrant. I shuddered at the thought.

As soon as we reached Lily Park, I unleashed Boris and let him run. It wouldn't be as much fun without his playmate, the little red poodle, Mia. It wouldn't be as much fun for me either without Mitzi to help me sort out this new information.

Boris ran around for a bit then sprinted over to the flower garden. I watched him sniff at the new mums and laughed. "Do they smell good?"

My thoughts roamed through all the things that had happened since I joined the board. The hierarchy of respect for members. I felt Mitzi and I were on the bottom tier. How did one get to the top? Apparently, Brock had done so by hooking up with Helda. How could Mitzi and I move up the ladder?

Darla had played along as mandibulate soldier and then secondary queen, hoping to move up to the top of the colony. And if she weren't replaced by Brock looking to be crowned king himself, she just might get there.

Why didn't they recognize the contributions Mitzi and I added? After all, we were the workers. Without us, they couldn't devour that sweet pulpy juice of power.

Boris began digging in the flowers. "Boris! Boris!" I yelled at him. "Stop digging." He stopped for a moment and turned to look at me. Then he began to bark at the flowers and dig some more. "Stop it! Boris!" I called. Finally, I walked over to see what all the fuss was about.

He gave a little yip and pawed at a spot next to one of the mums. "What did you find? Oh!"

Boris watched as I leaned down to get a closer look at the object he'd uncovered, then started toward it again. "Get back Boris!" I reached down and brushed away some of the mulch and dirt.

Nestled in the debris lay a slate-black handgun. I stepped back as if it were toxic and stared. Who would bury a gun here? In our park? In the flower garden? My heart raced. I could barely breathe. Or think.

It wasn't until Boris began to whimper that I finally decided what to do. I pulled my cell phone out and dialed Jim.

"Wait there for me. Don't touch anything. Don't let anyone else touch anything. And Delila, don't tell anyone. If this gun has been used in a crime, we need to preserve the evidence and not alert anyone to the fact that it's been found."

Fifteen minutes later Jim arrived. He no longer drove a marked police car. Ever since he made detective, he'd been driving an unmarked SUV. I watched him in silence and pointed to where the gun was stashed.

After taking several pictures, Jim pulled out a pen and used it to carefully pick up the gun by the trigger guard, and then place it in a plastic evidence bag. He sealed the bag and put it in his car.

I told him about Muriel and the cats and the bullets in baggies. Had Muriel brought the bullets in to the station yet? I told him about Trey and his gun collection. About Trey shooting at Brock's camera. Had Brock reported it to the police? Jim promised to check into these things before our dinner with him and Aleena that night.

Barry and I arrived at Aleena's house at seven o'clock as promised. The spicy savory smell of Thai noodles and chicken found us the moment we entered. We were ushered to the dining room, where Aleena had set out candles and her prettiest dishes. Then Jim brought out a bottle of champaign.

"Wow." Barry said. "Champaign?"

Jim stood next to Aleena. "Yes. We have some news we'd like to share with you. Since you introduced us, we wanted you to be the first to hear." He put his arm around Aleena. "I proposed to Aleena, and she's accepted."

Aleena held out her hand to showcase the new diamond ring.

"Congratulations!" Barry said, a split second before I did.

Jim popped the cork and poured us each a glass of the bubbly liquid. Barry made a toast, and we all drank. Then Aleena went to the kitchen and returned with the food.

I waited several minutes before pumping Jim with my questions. "Did Muriel bring in those bullets?"

"Yes, she did."

"Did Brock report that his camera had been shot out?"

"No, we never received a call about that."

Finally, I asked the most important question on my mind. "Do you think that gun was the one that killed Sheldon?"

"It's possible. We'll be looking for fingerprints and at ballistics. And if it is the weapon that was used to kill him, we'll be able to tell."

The food tasted delicious, and we all raved about it, then Barry began one of his tales from the dentist chair.

"A guy shows up this morning, super hyper." Barry began. "He's anxious, almost paranoid. Says he thinks he has a wisdom tooth coming in and it's all infected." Barry stopped for a moment to take a drink.

We waited. All eyes on him, begging him to continue.

"Well, I look inside his mouth and sure enough, it's all puffed up. Infected. He asked if I could see the tooth sticking up. I saw something pointed." Barry chuckled. "I poked around a little more. Turned out, it was a rather thick marijuana stick lodged in there. He's been growing his own and making brownies. Said he doesn't like to waste any, so he includes the stems. Well, I got it out of there. Then I suggested that he grind the stuff up a little better from now on." Everyone laughed.

The night had been lovely. Just what I needed, however, on our way home, my thoughts raced back to the gun. If it turned out to be the gun that killed Sheldon it must mean that someone from our neighborhood had murdered him. But who?

After church the next day, I went directly to my computer and pulled up the association accounts. Then I saw my note with our previous treasurer, Nolan Barker's name and phone number.

He'd said he had concerns about the financials. It had nearly cost him his job. Why had they accused him of embezzlement? What had he done that upset the board so much? I searched through the various vendors, making a note of companies unfamiliar to me.

Could one of these companies be providing kickbacks to a board member? Something was going on, but what? Sheldon had a question about the books when he was killed. I must be missing something.

I looked for additional trails of money dust. I found the payments for lawncare services to mow the grass at Lily Park and around the entrances. I added them up. More than $15,000. That was a lot of lawn mowing for one summer. More than $1,000 per month. And new shrubs that cost $10,000. Had we replaced all the shrubs? I didn't think so.

Filed under collections expense, additional payments were made to a certain JPI Firm. Another $6,000. What was that for? Sheldon sent out the letters and collected the fines.

There was no back up for me to look at. No paper trail, since all that had been stored in Sheldon's office. Helda had not gotten any of it back from the police. Could this have something to do with Sheldon's murder?

My phone rang. Darla again. This time asking if I could meet at her house for an emergency meeting at three o'clock this afternoon. It was already one o'clock, that gave me only two hours.

Barry shook his head. "You're spending a lot of time on the association."

I couldn't tell if he was worried, or unhappy that I wasn't spending as much time with him. "Aren't you and Jim playing your video games this afternoon anyway?" I hadn't told him I was going over the books, but he probably had guessed. He knew me too well. "Don't worry, I'll be home in time to cook dinner."

"I'll cook tonight." He gave me a silly grin. That meant one of three options: burgers, breakfast, or takeout.

I'd only been in her living room before, but this time Darla led me into her family room. The room was sparse but comfortable, with a sofa, coffee table and small round end table between two cream-colored barrel chairs. No pictures hung on the walls, but one wall had a shelf pushed up against it with a few nick-nacks.

None of the other board members had arrived and I looked around wondering who else she had called.

"Oh, it's just you and me. None of the others can make it. Helda is, well, she's not coming. And Mitzi is in Chicago. Brock isn't really a true board member, and truthfully, I didn't want him here." She smiled. "Can I get you anything? Something to drink?"

I shook my head. The books were still on my mind as I sat down in one of the chairs. I said, "I've been going over the books." I checked Darla's expression before going on. "Do you know what the JPI Firm is or what they did for us? We paid them $6,000 this summer."

Darla drew a blank look. "Humm. No, doesn't ring a bell for me."

"I've also noticed we've been spending way too much money on lawncare. Over $1000 a month."

"Wow, really?" Darla shook her head. "That's ridiculous." She stood up and headed toward the kitchen. "Are you sure you don't want anything to drink? I have soda or tea or coffee."

She returned a moment later with a can of coke in her hand. Darla took the reins of the conversation once more. "That's not good. But we have other issues right now. We don't have a quorum, so we can't make a decision on anything, but I really needed to talk to someone else on the board about this." She took another long drink from her can. "We're being sued."

"What?"

"Yeah, the association is being sued. And what's worse, each of us board members are being sued individually too." The look of shock on my face must have compelled her to go on. "Yes, every one of us. Morton, our lawyer just called me a couple hours ago."

"But...why? And who?" My mind went automatically to Pierce Andrews. Afterall, if anyone deserved to sue us, it would be him. I thought of the look on his children's faces. The family packing everything they owned in that U-Haul trailer.

Of course, it could be Muriel. I remembered her holding the battered cat in the box and pelting us with her anger. Or Ziggy. He had after all made a sort of threat toward me. Could this be what he meant?

Darla set her can down on the end table between us. "Trey. Trey Samuels. He says we have been harassing him since he moved in. Said we have put surveillance cameras on him and everything."

"But that was Brock, not us! And we send letters to everyone, not just him."

Darla nodded. "I know. The jerk! I think Trey's one of those guys who sues everyone to get money."

"Do we need to get our own attorneys?"

"I'm not sure. Morton warned me that we would probably be served paperwork tomorrow. I'll have to send the others an email."

We chatted for a while longer, then Darla stood up, and I took it as my cue to leave.

Still flush with anger about the news Darla had thrust upon me, I barely noticed the cool breeze on my face as I headed for home. How was I going to tell Barry about the lawsuit? Ever since Sheldon's murder, I'd sensed he wanted me to quit the board. Now this.

Should I resign? Leave now, in the middle of all this mess? Would my name be removed from the lawsuit if I did? Maybe not.

Our association spent far more than it should. And some of those expenses needed an explanation. If I left, would the new treasurer check into it? Maybe I didn't want to leave yet. Not if I wanted to fix these problems in our association.

How could I get to the files to figure out where this money was going? I could ask Helda or see if Jim would allow me to look through the records in Sheldon's office.

It wasn't only the money. Lots of things weren't right. Members being harassed. Not just Trey. I thought about Erle's tomato plants. Fines over grass that was an inch too long, mailboxes that required an exact paint color, and bushes that needed trimming.

I couldn't change the rules. I couldn't persuade the board to stop badgering members. To stop foreclosing on homes or levying fines for having a weed in their yard. I stood at my front door for a moment, took a deep breath before I went inside.

Mitzi was livid. "How dare he? That little twerp!" She was wearing blue jeans and a new jacket, boots, and scarf she'd likely acquired while in Chicago.

Ned and Mitzi had flown in Sunday night. She'd called me immediately after reading Darla's message. That's when we decided to meet at the park after I got off work on Monday.

Boris followed Mia on a sprint around the park. She stopped to sniff, and he waited patiently until she had finished before he sniffed.

"Now what? What do we do?" Mitzi adjusted her scarf tighter around her neck.

"I don't know. Barry put a call into our lawyer, but we haven't talked to him yet. There are more new developments too." I caught her up on Muriel and the wounded cat, and about Brock demanding money for the sign. Then filled her in on the story about Brock and Helda's affair.

We sat down at a picnic table.

"Wow, looks like I've missed a lot! Anything else?" Mitzi looked at the garden. "I see we have new mums. They look pretty, who planted them?"

"Helda." I thought about the gun. I'd made a promise to Jim not to tell anyone. But Mitzi wasn't just anyone. Aside from Barry, she was my best friend. Still, it might be better to hold off telling her for now.

"Oh yes. I remember her saying she had ordered some." Mitzi adjusted her scarf again. "You mentioned something about expenses, were you talking about the mums?"

"No. I've been doing some digging. We've been overpaying for a lot of things. I think that's why Nolan was concerned. Have you heard of a company called The JPI Firm? We paid them $6000 this summer."

"What? Heck no. I've never heard of them." Mitzi's face held a funny confused look. "If we paid them that much, I should have known about it. The board would have had to approve it." She thought for a moment. "And it would have had to go in the minutes. I can look back through them and see if I can find anything."

Back home, I headed straight for the computer and back to the accounts. This time I scrutinized the check register. I noted several checks made out to cash. Why? And people seemed to use the debit card way more than I expected.

The bank had granted me access to online banking for our account. I opened it and went over the three months before I'd taken over. Several different signatures appeared on backs of the checks made out to 'cash'. I printed them off.

Our statements didn't show who had used the debit card, but it appeared that it had been used freely. This would need to change. But first, I needed to get the paperwork from Sheldon's office. Reluctantly, I called Jim for another favor.

Friday morning at work, my phone rang. Not wanting my officemate to overhear our conversation, I kept my voice low. "We've finished looking through and dusting the paperwork that was in Sheldon's office. I've got approval to return it to the association," Jim said. "I'll stop by after work and drop it off."

True to his word, Jim was at my door by 4 pm. He carried in two large boxes. "Where do you want them?"

"You can just set them down here." I offered. They looked heavy.

"There are nine more in the car."

"Oh. Let's put them in the office." We began to carry the boxes inside. "Is this it?" I joked.

"There are more old files stored in a warehouse somewhere I believe." He grinned.

"Do you know what these files are?" I looked at the huge stack of work. Was the information I needed even in this pile?

"Looks like there is a separate file for each house in the subdivision. They have violation letters sent from the HOA, and complaints from the household members sent to the association. Pictures, that sort of thing. We've been through most of them." He stopped for a moment and looked at me. "And Delila, no one else knows you have them. I think it would be better if you don't tell anyone else either. Just in case."

When we'd finished stacking everything against a wall in my office, I offered Jim something to drink.

"No thanks. I'm heading over to Aleena's."

"Jim, is there any news on the gun I found?"

He was quiet for a moment, thinking. "Yes." He looked serious. "The ballistics test came back today. You have to promise you won't say a word to anyone." I nodded. "It was the gun used to kill Sheldon. Listen Delila, you need to be very careful. There is a killer out there, and it might be someone in this neighborhood. Someone who might have a quarrel with your board."

The weekend went by without incident. I'd managed to get through two of the boxes of paperwork. Nine more remained stacked up against the wall waiting for me. By Tuesday morning, I was anxious to get back to my house cleaning. After finishing up laundry and mopping the kitchen floor, I sat down for a short break. That's when Darla called.

"Hey, can you do lunch today?" She sounded eager, needy.

My day had been planned. House cleaning and back to the boxes of paperwork. This wasn't in my plan. In fact, it would set me back. But there was something almost desperate in her voice. "Ok."

"Great. I'll pick you up around 11:30?"

"Let's make it noon."

Instead of waiting for me in the car, Darla came to the door. I let her inside while I slid into my jacket. She looked around nervously for a moment. "Thanks for going with me today. I've been a little down lately."

On our way to a local Coney Island, Darla unleashed her dilemma. "We spent the most incredible night together last week. Now he won't return my calls. He won't answer my texts. And I think he's blocked me from social media too." Tears pooled up in her eyes and rolled down her face. Darla wiped them away with her hand. "Why would he do that to me?"

How easily she had been tricked by this man. Fallen prey to a small amount of attention, and given him not only her heart, but her money too! Her loneliness made her vulnerable. She must have been an easy mark.

It wasn't a surprise to me though. She'd just met him on a dating site, then almost immediately agreed to lend him $10,000. He was a con artist. He clearly had no intention of paying the money back.

We slid into a booth at the Coney Island. They were busy and noisy as usual at lunch time, but the waitress moved in swiftly to take our orders. Darla wanted soup and a sandwich; I ordered a Greek salad.

"Do you know where he lives?" I asked after the waitress had left.

"The dating app says he lives in South Carolina."

"Oh." Not good. It would be much harder to find someone who lived far away. "You should go to the police Darla. Really."

"Yeah, I thought about it. But I don't think there's much they can do. Besides, I might still hear from him."

I admired her faith in the man, but I didn't hold out the same hope.

Darla then turned the conversation to the association, our common denominator. "Helda called me this morning. She'll probably call you later today. Says we need to give Brock the money for the sign."

"As soon as I get an invoice, I will." I said as the waitress set my salad down in front of me. As always, I was amazed at how quick the service was at this Coney.

"Sometimes we just get a check for cash so we can speed up the process." Darla said as she picked up her sandwich. "We get an invoice later. At least that's what we do a lot of times. It's easier." She took a large bite.

"Not a good idea. I think we could get in trouble for that." I took a drink of water, then added. "If we were audited."

"Why would we be audited?" She asked.

It was a great question, and one I mulled over the rest of the afternoon as I finished my house cleaning. Who would order an audit? Did anyone require it of us? The state? The federal government? Did anyone check the financials? It seemed dangerous to me, all our money could be eaten up, with no accountability.

When Barry arrived home, he found me still grinding my way through more of the files. Having lost track of the time, I ran to the kitchen and pulled the casserole from the oven.

Barry said it was still edible as he scraped the too crusty part to the side. He was more interested in what I'd found. I told him about Darla's date that went bad.

"I'm thinking of inviting her for Thanksgiving." I informed him. "I mean, I don't think she has anyone. She's lonely."

"Sure." He agreed. "If you want."

"Barry, do you think an HOA ever gets an audit? I mean are we ever required by the government to get one?"

"That's a good question. I don't know. Maybe you can ask the lawyer when you talk to him tomorrow."

Around nine o'clock that night, still digging through the files, I found the invoice for the JPI Firm. There was no information on it, no indication of what we were being charged $6,000 for, other than 'services rendered'. But there was a phone number. My 'to do list' grew a little larger.

My appointment with our attorney was scheduled for 1pm, plenty of time to get home from work and prepare for him. He rang right on time.

After hearing my explanation about the lawsuit, he assured me everything would be ok. The claimant would most likely be unsuccessful in his suit against me, or at least I should be covered by our HOA insurance or our association's governing laws. The HOA on the other hand may see a different outcome, may be held accountable.

When asked about an audit, he told me that in our state, and based on our income, we wouldn't be required to have an audit. I expressed my surprise. How would anyone ever be caught embezzling?

"It's up to the members to request an audit. If your members feel there is a problem, they should insist on a certified audit."

Relieved to be off the hook for the lawsuit, but still troubled over the audit, I leaned back in my chair and thought for a few minutes. Why didn't the state require some sort of review? After all, when money is involved, there is always opportunity for fraud.

Members could request an audit, but how many had to agree on it? Could one member request it or did it need to be voted on by the entire association? A certified audit was expensive. I didn't want to be the one to order it. I didn't want to be the bad guy. The accuser.

I looked over at the eight boxes still waiting to be dissected. I decided to get back to work while I still had the energy.

The invoice for The JPI Firm still sat on my desk next to my computer. They'd be open now. I placed the call.

Boris announced with excessive barking that someone was at the door. Then the bell rang. I pushed a box of files aside and went to find out who.

Helda and Brock stood at my front door. Neighborhood royalty ready to meet their challenger. I'd never noticed before, but queen Helda stood at least three or four inches taller than Brock. The hair on Boris's back stood upright ready to defend me against adversaries. I held on tight to his collar and cracked the door open.

"Hello Delila," Helda forced a half smile. She looked down at Boris, who tried to push through the door, and said, "Brock needs to get a check so he can pay the sign company."

"Were you able to get an invoice?" I tried to sound cordial, friendly, still holding tight to Boris, and keeping the storm door cracked just a little.

"We'll get it later. You can just give him a check made out to cash. He'll pay them and bring the invoice later." Helda looked down at Boris again, then fixed her gaze on me.

My heart pounded hard against my chest. How would they react if I refused? Would they threaten to vilify me as they had Nolan? It had worked with him. Or might they have something else in mind?

"It's not a good idea to write checks out for cash. If we are ever audited, we could be in trouble. The best way to do this is to get the invoice and I'll write out a check to the sign maker." It was a bold move. Yet if I gave in, I'd put myself in even more jeopardy. I'd potentially be aiding in careless or fraudulent bookkeeping that could lead to criminal charges.

Boris had calmed down some and I let go of his collar but held the door so he couldn't get out. He kept a watchful eye on them and kept his nose at the door.

"We aren't going to get audited." Brock zipped his jacket a little higher, then put his hands in his pockets. "Look, we've been doing it this way for years and it's never been a problem."

Seeing Helda's tense, red face, I wasn't going to offer to let them come inside. I looked from Helda to Brock. They no longer wore their nice guy masks, instead anger had taken over.

Helda lowered her eyebrows and took a step closer to the door. "You have a duty to the association to pay the bills."

Had Sheldon refused to back down? Is that what had gotten him killed?

"I know. I've been paying the bills." My voice had begun to crack. Boris gave a low growl. "Bring me the bill and I'll get it paid right away. But I can't do sloppy bookkeeping. I --we owe it to the members of the association to do things the right way. Afterall, it's their money, not ours."

They stood there for a moment and looked at one another in silent communication. Then they threw a quick look of disgust toward me, turned, and walked away. I shut the door, and as quietly as possible, turned the lock. I felt the target on my back had just gotten larger.

I returned to the piles of paperwork, discovering even more zombie spending. In other words, out-of-control purchases with no oversite. With saw-toothed determination, I bit off small fragments of the files, one page at a time, and whittled my stack down to five boxes.

The doorbell announced another caller, and once again Boris backed up the alarm with his barking. I peered through the bedroom curtain. Darkness had covered the world outside. Standing under the glow of the porch light, my friend stood waiting at the front door.

Mitzi and I had planned to have dinner together, since Barry worked late on Wednesdays, and Ned was away at a conference. A perfect chance to get together and 'catch up'.

She watched me re-lock the front door after she came in, giving me the "what's that all about?" look. Instead of answering, I led her down the hall to the office. Files and papers were in neat stacks on the floor, next to the boxes. Mitzi surveyed the association's paper frass for a moment, then asked, "What is all this?"

I plopped down on the soft carpet and motioned for her to sit down next to me. Then I selected a pile of papers and handed it to her. "These are invoices made by companies that I can't seem to find anywhere on the internet. None of them have an address or phone number. And, they are all paid by checks that were made out to 'cash'."

One by one, Mitzi studied the invoices and matching checks.

"You can see that the checks are signed with different names, and none of the signatures are very legible. Do you recognize any of these companies?"

Mitzi shook her head. "No, I don't." She looked up at me and I saw a flicker of alarm in her eyes. The same feeling I'd had when I'd made the discovery. It could only mean one thing.

I told her about my visit from Helda and Brock. About Brock demanding a check for cash and Helda supporting his demands.

The normally bubbly, carefree Mitzi sat looking serious and thoughtful. "Do you think they killed Sheldon?" She whispered, as if afraid someone might overhear her.

"I don't know." I'd promised Jim I wouldn't tell anyone about the gun discovery. I'd also promised not to say anything about the files. But Mitzi was in danger too. She needed to know. So, before we headed out for dinner, I gave her a full update.

We settled into a booth at the Chinese restaurant. The smell of quick fried oil, oyster sauce, and several fragrant spices including Sichuan pepper, permeated the air. My stomach let me know I was ready to eat. As frequent patrons, it didn't take long to decide what we wanted.

As soon as we placed our orders, I shared one more piece of information with my friend. "I found out what the JPI Firm is."

Mitzi had been solemn since my confession, so very unlike her. But a slow mischievous grin surfaced as she leaned in closer. "What?"

"It's a private investigation firm. Apparently, the association hired them to spy on some of the people in our neighborhood."

"Like Trey?"

"Yes. They didn't tell me everyone they were hired to spy on. But I think we were also on that list."

"You mean you and me?" Mitzi grew excited. "What were they looking for?"

"They wouldn't tell me. Said I should ask Helda. I think they are going to charge us for the damaged camera that Trey shot, too. I haven't gotten that invoice yet."

Mitzi shook her head. "Wow. I wonder how much that lawsuit is going to cost the association."

Our food came just as I was about to tell her the association members would likely blame us too, since we were board members. But I decided it would be better not to say anything.

On the way home, I made Mitzi promise not to tell anyone about my discoveries. I hoped she'd be better than me at keeping a secret. We pulled into the subdivision, and I checked my watch. 8:40pm. Barry would be home by now.

Most of the houses in the neighborhood showed light pouring from their windows as we passed. Aleena had changed the landscaping around her front door, adding new bushes and flowers. Even though dark out, I could tell how nice it looked. I expected to see Jim's car parked in the driveway but saw only Aleena's little red Camry.

"Jim must be working late. His SUV isn't there."

"Maybe they're out to dinner." Mitzi said and turned onto my road.

I gazed out the car window to admire the familiar McMansions on my street. Then my thoughts drifted back to the boxes of paperwork awaiting me. The car edged closer to home.

"What time is Ned getting in?"

"Around 10pm. His flight gets in at nine and I expect he'll —"

Flashing red and blue lights flooded the space ahead of us. We saw the two police cars parked in the street in front of my house, and Jim's SUV in the driveway.

My heart hammered hard against my chest. What had happened? My mind went swiftly to Barry. Was he ok? Suddenly I found it hard to breathe.

Mitzi pulled the car up in front of Erle's house and parked it. I jumped from the car and raced up the sidewalk to my home, Mitzi trailing close behind.

The policeman at the door stopped me. "I live here!" I shouted and attempted to push my way past him.

"It's ok, let them in." Jim's voice called out to the officer.

Jim stood in the dining room, where he could see us in the doorway. Two other policemen stood talking to one another in the hall. Jim began to walk toward me.

"What's happened?" My voice started to crack. "Where's Barry?" My eyes searched the room for my husband.

My head swirled around a variety of irrational scenarios. Something must have happened to Barry. Had someone attacked him? Had he fallen and hurt himself? Logic left me as absurd theories popped, one-by-one, into my mind.

Jim put his hand on my arm. "It's ok, Delila." He said to calm me.

I hadn't realized I'd been hyperventilating.

A moment later Barry came around the corner from the kitchen and put his arms around me. "It's ok, Honey. Everything's going to be fine. Someone broke into the house, that's all."

I squeezed him tightly. "Thank God you're ok!" Finally, I pulled away and looked at him. I'm not sure why, but I felt guilty. As if I'd somehow put us in jeopardy. "I locked the door. Didn't I Mitzi?" I turned to my friend.

Mitzi nodded.

My heartbeat slowed and I took a deep breath. "Did you get an alert on the camera or check the recording?" I asked Barry. We had installed a new camera on the front porch a couple months before. An expensive one, with all the bells and whistles. One that recorded everything.

"They broke in through the back door." Barry tried to soothe me. "The police dusted for fingerprints." He added.

We'd ordered new cameras for the back; however, we hadn't installed them yet. I cringed. "What about Boris?" I looked around for my protector, my bestie. Where was he? I pulled away from Barry to search for him. "Boris, Boris!" I yelled.

"Delila, it's ok. Boris is fine. He's shut in our bedroom for now, along with Jewel." Barry grabbed my arm and led me to the dining room table. "Jim's got some questions he needs to ask you." He motioned for Mitzi to follow us.

We all took a seat at the table. Jim had his notepad out ready to document my statements. It appeared the burglar had mostly been interested in what was in my office. No valuables were missing, at least as far as Barry could tell. And I would need to look at the paperwork to determine what might be missing there. Jim asked what time Mitzi and I had left for dinner.

"They must have been waiting for you to leave." Jim noted.

"How did they know I would leave? And I don't understand how they got past Boris." I looked at Jim as if he might hold the answer.

"We found a piece of raw steak near the back door. We believe it may be poisoned. The police sent it to the lab." Barry said.

"Oh," I gave a little chuckle. "Boris doesn't like beef, especially raw. He probably backed down and didn't try to bite, since he was offered a treat." I tried to imagine Boris and the intruder. "Or maybe he did bite them." I added hopefully.

"Delila," Jim began, "Can you think of anyone who might be after those papers? Someone who knew you had them here?"

I took a deep breath then described the afternoon encounter with Helda and Brock. Their demand for a check made out to cash. I shared what I'd discovered in the books and my concern regarding embezzlement.

Jim listened carefully and jotted down several things in his notebook. "Did they know you had these files?"

"I don't think so. I didn't tell them. Jim, there's more. I should have told you before I guess." It was time to let him know about Helda and the gun. When I'd called him that day, I omitted the part about Helda planting flowers where the gun had been found. I skipped over the detail that she had behaved strangely when I spoke with her, and I remembered the look of guilt etched in her face.

Barry seemed more upset than Jim that I hadn't said anything sooner. I knew if I'd told him, he'd have made me say something right away. Yet, I needed to be sure before I could say anything. I didn't want to accuse someone without a good reason.

"Ok, we still need to find out what's missing from your office." Jim said and led us down the hallway.

I'd left the files and papers in neat little stacks on the floor. I gasped. Those papers now covered most of the floor. My neat stacks no longer existed. Instead trampled on documents littered the room, with little regard for their value.

"Ah!" I heard Mitzi's groan behind me.

"It may be difficult, but can you kind of look around and tell me what you think might be missing? Any documents you can remember that aren't here now?"

I glanced around trying to recall where I'd left things.

Two police officers walked up to Jim and whispered to him. I looked at him, anxious for any new information.

"They've finished fingerprinting and photographing everything." Jim said as if he hoped to reassure me.

Mitzi had been walking around and carefully scanning the mess. "Looks like they got to everything. The only thing they didn't touch is that pile there." She pointed to a pile next to one of the boxes.

"Ok, can you tell if there is anything missing?" Jim looked at Mitzi then me.

I began picking through the debris. I frantically searched for the invoices I'd flagged as possible problems. They had vanished, along with some of the copies of cashed checks.

How would I prove someone had been embezzling from the association now? The bank would have copies of the cashed checks, but without the statements...I dug through more of the papers. This time my eyes fell on something familiar. One of the invoices! Then another. Excited, I continued to dig through the excrement, finding five of the questionable documents. The potential evidence.

Around five o'clock the following morning I slipped out of bed and made myself a pot of coffee. I hadn't slept and I didn't think Barry had either. Every little sound had me on edge wondering if there was someone in the house. If the burglar had returned. I'd even gotten up twice to check that all the doors were locked and had placed a large chair in front of the back door, thinking if someone did enter, I'd at least hear them.

The warm coffee felt good against the cool morning, yet a sadness hung in the air. And although nothing of any real value had been taken, our home no longer felt safe. Someone had eaten through the walls of our refuge, leaving us weakened and vulnerable.

Boris lay on the floor next to me. Thankfully he didn't like steak. If he had, he might not be here now. I reached down and petted the top of his head, then hugged him tightly. "Oh Boris. What would I do without you? I'm so sorry!" Tears welled up in my eyes and slowly ran down my face.

It was my fault. I wanted to help, to make a difference in the way the association did things. Instead, all I'd done was jeopardize those I loved. If Barry had been home at the time, would the intruder have killed him?

Boris put his paw on my arm, as he tried to tell me he'd had enough hugging. Anger replaced melancholy. I had to make things right. "I'll find out who did this Boris, I promise!"

Unable to face my office yet, I made Barry a nice breakfast and tried to push thoughts of the break-in from my mind. Once Barry left for work, I finished my coffee, and allowed thoughts of the night before to run through my mind at rapid speed. Who knew about the paperwork? Only the police and Mitzi and me. How could anyone else have possibly known? I had to find whoever was responsible for defiling my home and endangering those I loved. One by one my plans for the day evolved.

Finally, I grabbed my courage and walked back down the hall and into my office, cell phone in hand and Boris at my heels. I had found five of the invoices, but some were still missing. Copies of the cashed checks were also gone. Maybe the five statements would be enough. I called the bank and requested copies of the checks that went with them.

As I began to put my office back in order, I found an older credit card statement. In all my excitement and digging into the invoices, I realized I hadn't really scrutinized the previous credit card bills very well.

Since I had taken over, the card hadn't been used much. A few things here and there, nothing big and nothing suspicious.

The statement showed several purchases that couldn't be explained including lunches and dinners, gasoline, paint, and some tools. I wondered what the paint and tools were for. The meals and gas were clearly a misuse of association funds, however, there was only one card, and everyone used it. It would be difficult to prove who had made the fraudulent charges. I'd put a stop to that right away, but at this point, I didn't even know who had the card.

An email from the bank provided another copy of the checks that I immediately printed out. I'm not a handwriting expert, but after half an hour of comparing them, it looked to me as if there were two different people who'd signed. More digging through my files, I found handwritten notes from association members and compared these to the signatures on the checks. Then I called Jim. He promised to pick them up on his way to work.

"Thank you, Delila, we'll have these analyzed right away." Jim said.

Excited, I asked, "Do you think that's why Sheldon was murdered?"

"This may prove someone was embezzling from the association; however, we don't have anything to connect it to the murder." Jim said.

"But if they were embezzling and Sheldon found out, they might have killed him to keep him from telling."

"It's possible, but we have no proof. Don't worry Delila, we do have some leads in the case. Let's just wait and see what the experts determine, ok?"

By late morning, I'd begun to think of excuses to leave. I needed to go grocery shopping, I wanted to get a new rug for the bathroom, along with a whole slew of things to take me out of the house and away from thoughts of the break-in. But the fear of leaving Boris and Jewel alone in the house prevented me from going anywhere. I couldn't take a chance that the intruder would return. That this time they might kill Boris.

The doors were all locked, yet I checked them once more to make sure. I needed to pull myself together. There were answers in that office. Answers in that paperwork somewhere. Why else would someone break in only to steal a few documents?

Mitzi called and offered to take me to lunch, but I turned down her invitation, citing my desire to keep investigating, rather than admitting my fear of leaving the house. When the phone rang again right after that, I assumed Mitzi had come up with a new plan to get me out of the house.

Instead, Darla's eager voice caught me off guard. She'd heard about the break-in. "Are you ok?" She asked. I assured her we were all fine. "Oh, thank God. Do they know who it was?"

"No, they tested for fingerprints, but I haven't heard anything yet."

"Do you want me to come over and help with anything?" she offered.

"Thanks, but I think I'm fine." As I spoke the words, I heard the doorbell and Boris.

"Are you sure? I don't want you to be alone right now."

I pulled the curtain back and saw Mitzi at the door. "Oh, Mitzi's here. Looks like she brought lunch." I said, "Thanks for the offer but I'm fine. I'll talk to you later."

Mitzi dropped off lunch but couldn't stay. "I'm picking up a few things for Ned, then I have a doctor appointment I can't miss, otherwise I'd join you." She flashed an uplifting smile, and then she was gone.

She'd brought my favorite soup and sandwich from the little bakery café we sometimes visited. I sighed as I realized how lucky I was to have Mitzi as a friend. After eating I went back to my office and began looking through the documents once more. Boris jumped up. He gave a bark and headed for the front door. I heard the door open and the sound of footsteps in the hall.

I'd forgotten to lock the door after Mitzi left, my heart went from zero to 60 in a second. Paralyzed, I remained on the floor covered in files and fear.

"Hello! I'm here to help." Darla's voice sounded upbeat as she bounced into the room, Boris following close behind her.

"Oh." I stood up allowing the files to fall from my lap. "You really didn't have to come." I reached down and picked up the papers, stacking them in a pile.

"I know. I just wanted to make sure everything was ok. I thought I should help." She looked around the room. Her eyes fell on the stacks of boxes then she looked up at me with questioning eyes. "Were any of our association documents taken?"

It hadn't occurred to me that I should share information with the other board members. Maybe she should know. After all Darla held the title of acting president and would likely hold the official title soon.

"Just a couple of papers, I think."

"I'm wondering when the police are going to turn over the documents from Sheldon's office. I've asked a few times, and so did Helda."

Guilt took over. "These are the records. The police brought them over. I asked them so that I could check our accounts."

"Why would they give them to you?" Darla frowned.

"I," I stammered. I needed a quick explanation for not having told her before. "I guess I asked at the right time. Since there are a lot of accounting documents, they probably thought the treasurer would want them." A lousy excuse, but I had never been good at coming up with a quick response when put on the spot.

"I need them. In case I want to hire a contractor that we used before." Darla stiffened. A serious expression took over her face. "Why did you ask for them?"

Caught off guard, I blurted out, "I think Helda was embezzling from the association."

"What? Are you sure?" Her irritation turned to surprise. "Why do you think that?"

I led her back down the hall to the kitchen, and we sat down at the table. As acting president of the association, Darla had a right to know what was going on. She was in charge now, after all. She should be the one to decide how to handle things. Suddenly I realized I should have informed her sooner. That I had barged ahead of her, without thinking of the effect on my friend and fellow board member.

She listened as I explained about the invoices and checks made out to cash. I pulled a bowl of candy from the counter and sat it in front of her on the table. "Can I get you something to drink? Tea, soda?"

Darla shook her head and waited for me to continue with my revelation. Careful to leave out anything to do with the gun or murder, I filled her in on the methods of embezzlement I'd discovered. "I guess if we prove that Helda and Brock did steal from our HOA, we need to get the police involved."

She seemed to think about it for a minute. "Wow, so where are these invoices? Show me."

I walked toward the bedroom, with Darla close on my heels. The invoices in question sat on the desk. I picked them up and handed them to her. I felt some assurance knowing I'd already given copies to Jim. I still wasn't sure how close Darla and Helda were. She might feel like protecting Helda.

She glanced at the invoices for a moment, then asked, "Are these the files from Sheldon's office?" And pointed to the boxes.

I nodded.

"I'm going to take the rest of these documents home. If Helda is guilty, it means I become President. I'll need to give the files to the new management company. By the way, I found a company I want to switch to." She set the invoices she'd been holding on top of a box and started to pick it up.

I reached out and grabbed her arm. "I'm not quite finished with them." I said, feeling surprised by my own defiance.

"I'm the President now. I'm in charge. You're just the treasurer." Darla's voice had become loud and demanding. She began to lift the box.

If I allowed Darla to take the boxes, I wouldn't have a chance to find any additional information. There could be evidence of Sheldon's killer or the person or persons responsible for breaking into my house. Once they left my office, that evidence could be lost forever.

Applying additional force on her arm, I said, "Darla, I'll be happy to turn them over to you when I'm finished. I can give them to the new company when I have gone through everything." My determination had taken over. She would just have to wait.

With a huff, Darla stepped back and folded her arms. "Why? You said you'd already found what you needed to prove Helda and Brock embezzled. If I'm the president, I should give the files to the new company."

So that was it! She wanted to show the new management company that she had control now. She needed to flex her imperial muscles. I took a new approach.

"I'll turn them over to you, but I need more time to look through them. There could be additional evidence in there." I spoke in a slightly softer tone, hoping to mollify the situation. "After all, the police gave them to me." I added as reinforcement for my stance.

At that, Darla's demeanor changed. She lifted her chin and said, "Fine. I'll pick them up tomorrow." She turned and walked down the hall.

I followed her, making sure she left. Then, I locked the front door.

Pressured to find any other evidence that may be hidden in the files before giving them to Darla, I spent the next couple hours chomping through the files nonstop. Exhausted and frustrated, I sat down and thought about the stolen invoices.

It occurred to me that I'd been following what was left behind by the thief. Instead, maybe I should look for what had been taken. I looked through the check register and located the missing check numbers. Then I requested a copy of those checks from the bank. Once the bank got back with me, I would compare the signatures to the ones I'd sent to Jim.

The floor felt hard after sitting for so long reading through files. Some of the boxes remained untouched yet, so I turned to those. They were files of correspondence with homeowners. I began looking at the addresses with the thickest files.

Pierce Andrew's file stood out. There were several legal papers threatening foreclosure, as well as letters to the various lien holders on his house. Then I read the numerous letters from Pierce begging the HOA not to take his home and leave his family homeless. How he'd been sick and unable to pay the fees at the time. He went on to say that they had lived in this house for fifteen years. He'd put his heart and soul into making it beautiful, remodeling the kitchen and bathrooms. They'd added new flooring throughout. He'd spent most of his savings to make it nice.

He said his children were inconsolable, crying, and lashing out. Afraid of changing schools and losing their friends. Now they had nowhere to go. Tears welled up in my eyes and I wondered how the board members had read these letters and not felt sympathy for the man.

Another thick file stood out and I recognized it as Ziggy's. He'd received a variety of letters throughout the years. Fines for several complaints that he had ignored or objected to. He'd responded with letters that were less than polite. He'd called them names and said they should be locked up for their "evil" and "cruel" behavior, and a few other choice words.

I figured he must have spent at least $6,000 in fines over the past several years. I could understand why he felt angry and fed-up with the association. Many of the complaints seemed petty and as he'd pointed out in several letters, these fines were only levied on him and not on other homeowners with the same conditions. He had good reason to be furious with the association.

Deep into my research, I heard my cell phone ring. Still holding a letter from Ziggy to Sheldon, I reached over and picked it up.

"Hi, just wanted to check in and see what you're up to." Mitzi's voice sounded cheery.

"I've been reading through some of these letters from homeowners. I didn't realize how many fines we've imposed on people and how upset they are with the HOA."

"Yeah. Unfortunately, there's nothing we can do." Mitzi said, probably to ease my concerns, or maybe her own.

Nothing we could do. I'd become a board member to help, and because Mitzi asked me to. I hadn't expected to be involved in a murder. Or have my home invaded. I didn't realize how messed up our HOA really was. But, as Mitzi had suggested, what could I do?

Then I remembered I had only a short time to finish going through the files. I told Mitzi how Darla had come over and demanded I turn the files over to her. "I'd planned on inviting her to Thanksgiving dinner, I felt sorry for her." I said, "but I've changed my mind."

"You felt sorry for her?" Mitzi asked.

"Yes. After her boyfriend took her for $10,000."

Mitzi didn't say anything for a minute, then she sighed. "I wouldn't feel too bad for her. She... well she's weird when it comes to men."

"Weird?"

"Um, you know she was hot for Brock at one time. Kept calling him, chasing after him." Mitzi waited a moment, then continued. "I'm not sure what happened, but it didn't last long."

"Really?"

"Yeah. Darla's always trying to pick up a man. Pathetic." Mitzi had little sympathy for people she deemed weak or trivial. "Have you found anything in the files?"

"I've been looking for a reason someone might want to kill Sheldon, or what they wanted in my office. You know, a lot of people had reason to be mad at the HOA and the management company. Anyway, I still have more files to look through."

"I wish I could help you, but tonight is date night. Ned's taking me to dinner and a movie."

After we hung up, I thought about the Andrews family. I'd heard they'd moved in with Pierce's parents. A tiny two-bedroom house. I tried to imagine Pierce, his wife and two children all sleeping in one room.

And poor Ziggy. For as long as I'd known him, he'd worked hard to improve his house. Yet the HOA still fined him for little nit-picky things. Over the years he'd changed from a happy-go-lucky retiree to an angry old man who hated everyone.

Jewel rubbed against my leg, and I reached down to pet her. My mind turned to Muriel and the cats. They'd been shot at and trapped, the poor little creatures. And she'd poured her heart and soul into protecting them, not to mention a lot of money.

And although upset with Darla, I still felt a little sorry for her. Even though, as Mitzi pointed out, she brought it on herself. Finally, I shook off these thoughts and looked back at the files.

I don't know how long I'd been in there, but at some point, Barry popped his head in and asked if I wanted dinner. I apologized for not having anything ready.

"That's ok, I made us sandwiches. Take a break."

I took a short pause to eat. Normally at dinner, Barry and I tell each other about our day. But today, I dominated the conversation with what I'd discovered in the files. Then he insisted he'd clean up and sent me back to my office.

Having made some progress, I needed to see the light through the tunnel of paperwork. I'd dissected the records of homeowners I knew had complained the loudest about being fined. I even read my own file. There were still a few boxes to go through. Without looking I reached in to grab another file. My hand dug down between two hanging file folders and caught on something at the bottom of the box.

Lodged underneath the other hanging files, I discovered a large manilla envelope. Had it been intentionally hidden? The envelope had no markings, nothing to indicate what was inside. All the other files had been carefully cataloged, yet this envelope gave no indication of its contents. I pulled it out and began looking through the collection of documents.

The first, a letter from Helda to Sheldon read:

> Sheldon,
> We need to shoot out at least thirty to thirty-five violation letters per month. That should give us around 10-12 fines at an average of $200 each, that's about $2000-$2400 a month in additional income. We could even increase the number of violations if we want more revenue. These folks can afford it, and if they can't we don't want them here.
> -Helda

Another letter from Helda.

> Sheldon,

I'm sick of Muriel and those damn cats! I just shot down every reason she gave for not getting rid of them and she still won't back down. She's threatened to hire a lawyer and says the cats are 'grandfathered in'. A bunch of bull of course, but we'll have to be careful what we say. Our legal retainer doesn't cover court costs.
-Helda

There were several other letters too. Some were lists of violations she wanted Sheldon to address, along with his handwritten notes.

Sheldon,
Please add this list to the one I fired off yesterday. - Helda

3417 Marigold Dr. – Grass is a dull green color. Should be greener. *Cannont fine: There is no rule on how green grass has to be.*

1214 Rose Ave. – Sign in front yard. *This is a small garden welcome sign, acceptable per rules.*

2563 Iris Dr. – Dog poop in yard. *Owner says he doesn't have a dog. Doesn't belong to him.*

4290 Magnolia Court – Basketball net above garage door. *Need to check with ARC committee.*

It seemed Helda's game involved slaying zombie-homeowners by depriving them of their hard-earned cash and peace of mind. A power trip and a money grab. I skimmed several more of her letters. They all sounded similar.

Finally, I moved on to the other documents in Sheldon's secret file. That's when things became even more interesting...

In addition to the correspondence with Helda, I discovered a restraining order Sheldon had filled out. Apparently, he hadn't given it to the police. Why? Then I found a background check on one of our members. It showed a felony conviction for threatening someone with a gun at a nightclub.

At around midnight, I emailed Jim. Then I tip toed down the hall and slipped into bed, next to my sleeping husband.

That night I dreamt someone chased me through Lily Park and shot at me as I ran for my life. I woke up in a sweat. In the distance, I heard the rat-tat-tat of gunshots. I pulled the covers up over my head. It sounded like an assault rifle. Again? Who the heck was target-practicing in the middle of the night?

*I*n the morning, after Barry left for the office, I called into work and asked for the day off. Stress made it difficult for me to focus and my mind flitted around like a butterfly from one thought to another.

The HOA had shown evidence of structural weakness for a long time. We'd noticed small cracks for several years. What began as a way of holding people accountable for keeping their homes nice and property values up, had been seized by a colony of autocratic parasites.

Yes, cracks. Murder. Embezzlement. Burglary. Cats were being shot at, elderly people harassed, families displaced, and careers threatened. Had our peaceful community turned into a zombie necropolis?

Had we allowed this to happen because we were too busy, too tired, or too lazy to pay attention? Or were we afraid? Afraid of what others thought. Afraid of what the HOA might do to us? The truth was, we'd been complacent for too long.

Power hungry board members had eaten away at any advantages and benefits the association initially created. Those predatorial board officials saw our members as easy prey. Did my neighbors and I ever have a chance against these predators? Or would they always reign?

What was I? I'd never thought of myself as tough or powerful. But did that mean others saw me as weak, as prey? Now that I was a board member, would I be seen as a predator? Could prey become predators? Could predators become prey? Could there be a middle ground somewhere? I didn't want to be either.

Boris nudged my leg, and I reached down to pet him. Boris, my best friend. My baby. If he had eaten the poisoned steak, he might have died. Next time he might not be so lucky...I took his furry head in my hands and looked into his big, brown, loving eyes.

There couldn't be a next time. It had to stop. Someone had to stop the destruction. Time for a change. Time to expose a killer. No more worrying about how to fit in. No more hiding behind fear.

Evidence pointed me in the direction of the murderer. Yet, I'd need proof. There were many loose ends I needed to straighten out. I hoped I'd have enough time. I went to my office and picked up one of the letters to Sheldon, then I called the previous treasurer.

It was pure luck that Nolan Parker could meet with me right away. As I prepared to leave, I gave Boris one final hug and kissed him on the head.

La Cafetière was surprisingly busy for a weekday morning. Even so, I managed to secure a small table in the corner with a bit of privacy. I flagged Nolan down as he entered the coffee shop.

Once we'd ordered our coffee, I unzipped my portfolio and pulled out the letter. I pushed it across the table. Nolan gently picked it up and read it. When he finished, he set it back down and looked up at me.

"I hoped Sheldon would be able to do something about it." Nolan added some cream to his coffee and stirred. "I'd seen the lawn care workers go to some of the board member's houses right after mowing the HOA's grass. I suspected they must be charging the association to mow their lawns too, that's why the bill was so high. I also questioned some of the invoices for other services, since there was literally no information on the companies they claimed to be using." Nolan fixed his eyes on me as he explained.

"So, the association had paid for lawn care services on their personal houses. And they embezzled money from the HOA by making up dummy invoices, then cashing the checks?" I glanced around the room in case anyone was listening to us. "Then they threatened to blame it on you." I understood. He'd been afraid. He couldn't have known it would go this far.

"Like I said before, I couldn't prove anything. I have a family. A wife, two small kids. I'm a CPA. The board's accusations could ruin my reputation. Then how would I support my family? But after we moved out of that neighborhood and settled into our new home, I kept thinking about it. That's why I finally wrote the letter to Sheldon, explaining what was happening. I thought, maybe he could stop it."

I put the letter back in my portfolio. "Would you be willing to testify?"

He nodded. "I've also kept copies of what I found, just in case I ever needed them."

As we walked out of the café, Nolan turned to me, with a troubled look on his face. "Do you think that's what got Sheldon murdered?"

The drive back to my house allowed me time to process what I'd just learned. Nolan gave me more to go on, yet it wasn't enough. As I eased through the neighborhood, I saw Ziggy trimming his front bushes. I slowed down and waved. He motioned to me, and I pulled my car up to the side of the street in front of his house.

Ziggy walked up to the car, and I rolled the window down. He stuck his weathered face in and sputtered, "You gonna do something about those damn gunshots? I'm sicka being woke up in the middle of the night. Happens three, four times a week now. This ain't no shooting range!" He threw his anger at me with full force. "What do we need an HOA for anyway if you don't do nothing about people shootin' up the place? Naw, you'd rather pick on people like me."

I too had been upset hearing the gunshots in the night. I had asked Jim about it, and he said he'd check into it. He'd said it violated a noise ordinance, and he could give whoever a ticket for it. And although I agreed with what Ziggy was saying I felt defensive. "Look Ziggy, I don't know what I can do..."

"Course not. You spend all your time thinking of how to extort money from honest homeowners like me."

He had a point. After reading the letters Helda wrote to Sheldon, it appeared as if the association levied fines on homeowners to generate income. But was I responsible for everything the board did? And, as for people shooting guns in the middle of the night, that should be a police matter. "Did you call the police? I wish I could do something, but I don't even know who's doing the shooting."

"It's that numskull kid lives next to Brock." He stared at me as if everyone knew this piece of information and there must be something wrong with me.

"You mean Trey? How do you know it's him?"

"He sells guns. Everybody knows that. Hell, even I've bought some from him."

Some? I wondered how many guns Ziggy owned. How many people in my neighborhood kept an arsenal in their homes?

"Ah..." Ziggy shook his head as if in disgust, turned around and walked back to his shrubs.

Back home, I sat in my car, thinking. Darla would be coming to pick up the files this afternoon. Of course, I'd already found as much as I could in them. She could have them now.

My mind swirled around the murder and the embezzlement and finding Helda burying the gun that murdered Sheldon in Lily Park.

The gun. Jim said the gun's serial number was scratched off, so no way to trace it. And whoever had planted it there had wiped it clean. Too many guns. Too many people with guns and a grudge. My neighborhood had become a battleground.

But could I prove who killed Sheldon? Maybe. I'd guessed and second guessed myself too many times already. I would try. Someone in my neighborhood had answers, and

I had a hunch who that might be. I put the car in reverse and backed out of the driveway.

At four o'clock the doorbell rang. I unlocked the door and let Darla in. We didn't say much, nor did we smile. I led her down the hallway to my office. Once inside I pulled a paper from my desk and handed it to her.

"What's this?" Darla took the paper and read it over. She eyed me with a mix of suspicion and irritation.

"Why did Sheldon want to take out a restraining order on you?" I edged my way back toward the doorway.

She folded the paper up and put it in her pocket. "Sheldon and I dated for a while, but we broke up. He was mad and told me to stay away from him. He threatened to take out a restraining order, but I said I didn't want anything to do with him, so he dropped it." She brushed it off. "It was nothing."

For a long moment I just stared at her. I knew she was lying. I needed her to admit what she'd done. I tried another angle. "You were all embezzling from the association. I know the HOA paid to take care of your lawns and that you created invoices for make-believe companies. I have proof."

"You mean Helda and Brock were embezzling."

"No. I mean you too." I tried to sound calm. But I felt my heart race, and hoped she couldn't see it.

"You don't have anything on me." Darla crossed her arms and gave me a smug look.

"I know you broke into my house to steal those documents. The bank sent me more copies of the cashed checks and your handwriting is on the back." I waited to see what she would do. She studied me for a moment but said nothing. "That's not all." I continued. "Nolan Parker made copies of those invoices before he left." I watched as a little confidence drained from her face. "Sheldon knew, didn't he?"

Darla shook her head and walked over to the boxes. I had to think of something fast. "I know you killed Sheldon. But why? To protect yourself from embezzlement charges? Or to protect your pride because he wasn't interested in you?"

Darla shook her head slightly. "You can't prove anything." The smug look returned.

"I can prove enough. I went to see Trey today. He's willing to testify that he sold you the gun that murdered Sheldon."

She thought for a second, "I gave that gun to Helda. She said she wanted it for protection."

"I don't think so. You set her up. You buried the gun in the garden at Lily Park, knowing she planned on planting those flowers. You counted on her getting caught with the gun."

My mind reverted back to when I watched Helda spreading mulch over the gun. She must have found the gun and then I showed up. She must have been terrified at that point. I took a breath. "Why did you do it? I thought you two were friends."

"Friends? Friends?" She laughed, but kept her eyes fixed on me. "I did all the work, and she took all the credit. I was supposed to become president of the association. As vice president, I was next in line. But she wanted Brock to take over." Darla shook her head, "No, we were far from friends. Helda said I wasn't capable. I'm ten times smarter than she is!" She tipped her head back with a small snort. "She deserved to get the blame."

I knew if I could keep her talking a little longer, she'd tell me what I wanted to know. What I couldn't figure out was how Helda's phone ended up near Sheldon when he was killed. "If you weren't friends, why did Helda help you?" I saw the confused look on Darla's face. "Her phone..."

"See, you think you're so smart. Just like her. But she's not smart. That's why all the evidence points to her. It was easy. I just grabbed her phone when she wasn't looking and took it with me. I made sure the GPS tracking was on, that way it looked like she was at the scene. I returned it without her seeing me. Then I told you I saw it on her table."

Had she really confessed to me? Darla, who I'd thought of for so long as prey, was in fact a predator. But now, in a way, she'd become my prey. I'd gathered evidence on her and trapped her into confessing to her crime.

Maybe she saw something in my expression. It's true, I don't have a good poker face. I looked up at the camera mounted in corner of the room. Darla followed my eyes. Then her eyes were on me, studying me, like a cornered animal looking for an escape.

Things happened very quickly after that. I'd been standing in front of the door when Darla rushed me. She pushed me aside and nearly knocked me to the ground, before running down the hall.

Jim stepped in front of her and blocked the front door. Two other police officers prevented her from getting out through the back. They handcuffed her and led her down my driveway to the police car.

Lily Park had changed into her autumn wardrobe, the trees, now clad in brilliant reds, oranges, and yellows, felt warm and welcoming. Our neighborhood had changed too.

Brock and Helda had both put their homes up for sale and were waiting for the judge's decision in their embezzlement cases. We all hoped the association would receive restitution for what they'd stolen.

Trey would spend at least five years in prison for violating his probation and illegal sale of weapons. In exchange for testifying against Darla, they were dropping the charge of discharging a firearm within less than four hundred yards of a house.

Darla herself was in jail awaiting her trial. A victim. Seen as prey by her boyfriend, who'd stolen $10,000 from her. And prey, to Helda and Brock too, who brought her into their scheme and made her a part of it, only to use her to do their dirty deeds for them. They'd seen her as a natural mark.

Yet all along, she'd been as cunning a predator as any other. Stalking her victims, ready to kill, in what she saw as an eat or be eaten world. As if becoming a predator herself would prevent her from further victimization.

It could be at least a year before she went to trial, and I dreaded the thought of having to testify. The proof against her was mostly circumstantial. Yet, she'd confessed to me, and it had all been recorded on my security cameras. Later, she'd confided in a cell mate that she'd killed Sheldon because he not only dumped her but threatened to have her thrown in jail for embezzlement. Jim thought there was enough evidence to put her away for a long time.

Mitzi and I stood under the pavilion watching the dogs. They chased each other around for several minutes then stopped to sniff. Mitzi turned to me. "What do you think of Marv as the new president? Think he'll do a good job?"

"He did an excellent job as head of the Arc committee. I think he'll do great." I smiled and we sat down at a picnic table. We were quiet for a few moments, each of us in our own head.

Finally, I said, "you know I used to hate the association. All the rules and bullying. I thought we'd be better off without one. But yesterday I noticed how nice our neighborhood looks. I think everyone here works hard to keep their homes and yards nice. Maybe there are benefits to being part of an association. At least now that the board and members work together."

Mitzi nodded in agreement. It was comforting to just sit and take in the peace. After a while Mitzi said, "by the way, I was wondering. Did anyone ever find out who wrote that note and who shot the cat?"

"Jim said it was Trey. Apparently, he has a bad temper. One of the documents in Sheldon's file was a background check on him. About two years ago, the police arrested him for threatening to shoot someone at a nightclub. The person bumped into him, and it made him mad. So, he pulled a gun on the guy. He's not supposed to be in possession of firearms, let alone sell them. The police found about thirty-four guns in his house. And they found he'd been target-practicing in his back yard."

"How did you get him to tell you about the gun that killed Sheldon?" Mitzi asked.

"I just told him I wanted to buy one, and that Darla told me she got one from him. I showed him a picture of the gun I'd taken when Boris uncovered it at the park. He didn't realize it, but my phone was recording us. I think he'll get his sentence reduced, that is, if he testifies against her."

"Darla should get at least twenty years to life." Mitzi said. "It's a good thing you had those cameras in your office and caught everything on video." She turned and smiled at me. "You've become quite the sleuth!"

We called the dogs, leashed them back up and began walking home. The autumn wind had picked up. Mitzi tugged at the zipper on her jacket. "I like the changes you proposed at the last meeting." She looked thoughtful. "You know, I'm proud of you Delila. You've made a real difference in our association. I don't just mean the GoFundMe you started for Pierce and his family. People seem friendlier, happier." She smiled at me. "By the way, I'm not really a cat person, but I am sponsoring one of the feral cats. That was a brilliant idea. I donated to spay one of the female cats and I'm going to name her Kittzy. She's a calico."

I laughed. "I sponsored one too. I picked a black and white male and named him JoJo."

Mitzi gave me a sideways glance. "I don't think I'm going to run for secretary next time."

It surprised me to hear her say it. I'd thought Mitzi enjoyed being part of the board. "Why not?"

"I heard the local animal shelter is really in need of volunteers and I think I'd like to help out there." She flashed a playful grin at me. "What do you say? Wanna join me?"

Recognition & Appreciation

So much goes into the creation of a book. Writing, rewriting, research; super early mornings, super late nights. Most of the time we do this alone. Yet, it's really our support team that deserves the credit. If not for them, we might not finish our stories. Some of my greatest pleasures come from discussing ideas with my writing group and my friends. They move me along; encouraging me and letting me know when I might want to change direction, words, punctuation, or cut something altogether. It's these most valuable people who I'd like to credit, for all they've done to make this book possible.

To my writing group: Heather, Judy B., Sharon, Judy W., Kathy, and Deby, thank you for your endless hours of support. For reading and critiquing and rereading it again. For gently noticing where little changes can improve the story. For the fun times we spend exchanging ideas and knowledge. You are the best team a writer could ask for!

To my husband Scott: for all your support, and whose patience and understanding made it all possible.

To my family: Scott, Dereck, Dustan, Sommer, Cheryl, and my parents, for encouraging me, and putting up with my sometimes overly passionate talk of my stories, and for the love and inspiration you've given me.

Devising plausible scenarios can be especially fun and exciting. I want to thank some special people who've put in time and energy to help plot and strategize with me, and who made the journey much more enjoyable. Thank you, Paul, Scott, Judy and Cheryl, for all the hours you put up with discussions about these stories, and for all your exceptionally valuable input.

Eventually stories require a credibility check. There are some very important people I'd like to thank, as without them… well let's just say they made an enormous difference!
My heart and thanks go out to my Beta Readers: Ann, Cheryl, Judy, Paul, and Dianne and to C.S. Lakin for your expertise and incredibly helpful suggestions.

Discussion Questions

1. In ***Killer Bees***, Delila wanted to fit in with the clique. How do you think her feelings about being part of the in-crowd changed?

2. In ***Mosquito Bites***, Delila went behind Barry's back, investing her 401k. In what way was she justified, in what way was she wrong?

3. In ***Praying Mantis***, deception and theft take place within the church by one for selfish reasons, by another to help others. Do you think they were equally in the wrong?

4. In ***Bed Bugs***, Delila comes close to having an affair with an old boyfriend. Do you think she should confess everything to Barry?

5. In ***Termite Turmoil***, Delila joins the HOA board and finds herself in the hot seat with her neighbors. How might things have turned out differently had she quit after the first day?

6. In ***The Gossip Garden Mysteries***, what symbolism did you notice throughout the various stories and in what way do you think it added to the narrative?

Made in United States
Cleveland, OH
26 July 2025

18778509R00236